Roam

Revenge of the Grey Angel

By Jon Cole

Contents

*

*

Preface

The Reverend Thomas Ellis, Vicar of the parish of Malbury. March 2010.

I wish people would not bring their bug-infested children into my church. Though I should be safe here in the Vestry, a damp and stony chamber well-suited to my mood, I hear them outside, beyond the door, children, scrabbling around the pews. These toxic dribbling midgets, seething with disease, are the children of my parish and I christened most of them. Stinky devils with their viruses, measles, God knows what. They catch these bugs at school deliberately to infect their parents, and then me. I am susceptible to colds, and it takes only one blast from some bug-laden infant's jaws to lay me out for a week. Then my wife catches it, and she is as miserable as Hell. Then the damn bug mutates and I catch it again. So it goes all winter long, an infernal yo-yo of disease for which children are to blame.

As the Vicar of this parish, I should be more charitable. Darling children, hope for the future, et cetera. Damn the lot of them. They make me sneeze. I am allergic to children, and every Sunday I make sure that there stands between me and that army of little buggers some person such as the church warden, who is robustly healthy and very large.

For one child I make an exception. Her name is Lily, bless her. I have to be careful here, because gentlemen of my age who enthuse about twelve-year-old girls might be hauled before the courts. What I must say, though, is this: it is for Lily that I have an overwhelming need to write these words now on the parish typewriter. If I and my wife had been blessed with a child then perhaps I would have a feeling like this, but we will never know. Dread Necessity, as Aeschylus said. If the children of this parish had the vaguest tinge of anything Lily-like in their being, then I would call them all my children with a contented and fatherly heart. If they had one-

1

hundredth of her courage and her sweet nature - I think you get the point. But sadly they are disgusting and no better than trolls.

Meanwhile the viruses must not get in the way. Before I forget, I must write it all down in the old-fashioned way, on paper. Paper survives. Do not expect literature, for I am a writer only of sermons and articles for the parish magazine. I will write as well as I can, before I am swept away by the meningitis which at this moment is creeping under my door. On the way, I must use what is left of my imagination. I will try to be accurate, from what I know.

Be prepared for a strange tale. It is about people who call our Universe a 'sea'. It is about the never-ending struggle between light and dark, and it has religious overtones which I - as a vicar - find unsettling. It is about war. It is about a place which I have visited but am unsure how I got there. Most of all, it is about a child, Lily Moss. I see her in my mind's eye now. I shall try to do justice to her, and to her family.

It is a story which my wife says was a dream. I agree with her that many of these extraordinary events occurred while I was in a dream-like state, under the influence of a poisonous gas. I still feel the after-effects. Every time I pass the old Hall where that happened I shudder. But it was no dream. I have evidence - a photograph and two boxes of hand-written papers. I have not shown them to my wife, who is of a nervous disposition.

Now it is March. I must write quickly, for I do not know how much time I - or any of us - have left. When my text is written I will not know what to do with it. Perhaps I will give it to the sexton to bury in a box.

So now to the beginning, to the arrival in this world of that devil Chatham, who brought only pain to the child I hold in the highest regard, the gifted and adorable Lily Moss.

2

1 - A Thousand Islands

The St Lawrence River, Canada, 1998

After a quiet day of reading, and then sitting on a rock and dipping his toes into the waters of the St Lawrence, Henry Chatham was stuck.

Of the thousand islands dotted around the seaway he had chosen one of the smallest, a few feet above water with only a scattering of rocks under one spindly tree. Though he could glimpse the Canadian shore this was a remote, un-visited spot which was perfect at the beginning of the day; but now at its end, with the sun falling fast through an orange sky, he knew that something had gone horribly wrong. As he peered into the tattered shrouds of mist rising from the water, he heard only the lapping of waves and a seagull overhead.

No boat had come. He had booked it for five o'clock, and it was now seven.

This was supposed to be a holiday, to relax and to improve his colloquial French. It was stressful enough to hike out of Kingston with all his worldly goods in the backpack which lay on the rock behind him. To be stuck in the middle of a watery nowhere in twilight, as the mist rose and the mosquitoes with it, tightened the grip of stress around his heart.

The evening was no longer warm, and he reached into his backpack for a sweater. As he did so, he saw a light on an island to the west, a fireball which vanished as quickly as it came. That other island was barely bigger than his own, but more densely wooded. Do trees spontaneously combust? More likely, a tourist had left a cigarette burning, perhaps by a canister of camping gas which had flared up with that alarming red light. Perilous though his position was, Chatham would rather be here than there.

From that other island, though, came the sound of a boat's motor. Chatham's gloom began to lift, and he dropped the sweater into his backpack. Through the mist came a spectral white boat barely making waves, at its bow a single yellow lamp which threw a sickly light on a man hunched over a suitcase. At its rear stood the boatman, his hand on the tiller of an outboard motor. This was not the boat that Chatham had ordered, and no bigger than a rowing boat, its paintwork worn and scratched, but it was a boat at last, and he waved his arms to catch the attention of the boatman.

Along the rocks of the tiny island the boat puttered and the boatman raised his head. Under a woollen hat his face was grey, and his raincoat flowed over boots of black leather. "Ho!" he cried, as the boat stopped under Chatham's rock, and he threw up a rope which Chatham held.

"Thank God!" Chatham cried. "I thought I was here for the night. Could you get me to the shore?"

"What shore is that?" the boatman called back.

"North. Canada. Somewhere near Rockport would be ideal."

"Rockport? Shoals all along. Needs skill to get to Rockport."

"I'll pay. What do you want?"

"Two dollars."

Surprised at the modesty of the fee, Chatham said, "May I get in?"

"Sure. But first," said the boatman, "my two dollars. Run the rope around that tree-stump, and I'll come up."

Chatham wrapped the rope around the stump and tied it with what he hoped was a nautical knot. He fumbled in a pocket for his change, as the boatman stepped from the boat and trod cautiously over the rocks. "You got yourself marooned," the boatman said. He was around Chatham's own height, with a thin and pale face, and dark eyes which glistened in the failing light. "Bad luck. Can't trust a soul around here."

4

Chatham put out a hand, two dollars on his open palm. "That will do very well," said the boatman, extending a grey arm and fingers that closed over Chatham's own.

In a single motion, the boatman grabbed Chatham by the arm and pulled him forward till their faces were an inch apart. "Bad luck, sir," the boatman hissed, as his other arm scythed upward into Chatham's ribs.

The knife plunged up into Chatham's heart, pushed further, twisted, and as the light in Chatham's eyes died the boatman let his body fall onto the rocks. The boatman leaned over him, took the contents of his pockets, then stepped back a few paces and opened his arms wide.

From each claw-like hand a bolt of fire flashed onto Chatham's body, melting it, incinerating it but without smoke, in seconds leaving no trace, no flesh, no bone, only scars on the rock and an oily residue that would be mistaken for the remains of a camp fire.

The boatman reached down for Chatham's backpack, and slung it over his shoulder. He untied the rope and carefully stepped down to join his partner.

Without a backward glance the boatman swung the boat around and steered towards the Canadian shore.

2 - Arrow and Chain

London, England, 1999

South of the Thames by Battersea Bridge, high-up in the dismally beige office-block of the Soulbury Centre, a man peered out across a grey city, rain coursing over the window as if melting its glass. He could be anywhere in the world, but today he saw only the towers of other offices huddled around a square of dying grass, and a reflection of himself. The day was wet and grey, but hardly as grey as Henry Cornelius Chatham, known to his staff as The Gargoyle.

Chatham smiled at himself. Grey was his brand. His bony face had a grey pallor, his suit always dark grey. Does it matter if a man is less than beautiful? Does it matter if there is no hair on his head, if his skin is pock-marked, his cheeks hollow, and his ears stick out like butterfly wings? If his style of walk was shambling, that was because he had been created as a bag of bones which fitted at unusual angles. If his manner was arrogant, that was natural for one born to command.

They called him the Gargoyle, whispering in their corners, but that was typical of these creatures - always ready with some silly word to normalise what they fail to understand, what they fear. Perhaps deep down they sensed that he was a fraud, not the Henry Chatham he killed in Canada, not the Henry Chatham whose identity he stole, but a Chatham who came from somewhere they would never go, who had seen what they would never see, a Chatham to whom they were as insignificant as drops of rain on a window.

The Soulbury building lay on the wrong side of the Thames. He could barely make out Battersea Bridge through the rain. Over there, across the water lay Government and its mansions of imperial splendour. As his smile turned to a scowl, Chatham turned from the window. His office was so small he could stretch out his arms and nearly touch both sides of it. It was his eyrie, a converted kitchen, sparsely furnished - two chairs on a pine-plank floor, a laptop on a rustic table, a lamp in the centre of the ceiling with four bulbs, one of which had never worked, and a Modigliani print of a long-jawed woman with a brown hat, covering a gash in the plaster where pipes had been ripped out. From scruffy red curtains came an odour of fried bacon.

Only one item in this office was uniquely his. It hung on a wall by the window, a penny-in-the-slot machine, a pinewood box with metal castings at its corners and the image of a grinning clown. The idea was to flick a silver ball up and around the spiral of its track to land in the mouth of the clown. This was a machine which Chatham could trust. He had adjusted the spiral so that it was impossible to lose.

Trust was good but control is better. His employees were all very clever, all conscripts from the globe's finest universities, younger and more beautiful, and they were free-thinkers, which made them good at their job but a devil to control. Chatham called them 'squirrels', because they collected tasty scraps of information and hid them away for later. His predecessors had engaged them and trained them up, to give the impression of just another set of staff in just another company, but like so many in this city they suffered from the vice of ambition - too emotional, too human. Not one had the slavish obedience which Chatham demanded.

Quietly along the corridors his squirrels in their offices were putting the day's business to bed. There was business for Chatham too - a tedious email from Personnel. He sat at his table. From a drawer he fished out a tub of black powder, into which he dipped his forefinger then sucked on it. A supplement of minerals, was his story, with a black herb which he found in India, expensive and not for everyone, all in a powder tasting of the sea with an undertow of plastic. It was invigorating, and now he was ready to tackle the last of the day's business.

Personnel. The level of sickness in this office. Very high. His staff called it the 'Gargoyle disease'. As if he were radioactive, those closest to him caught it first and worst. Symptoms were flu-like, but then skin became dry and grey, nausea was permanent, with an overpowering lethargy. Why? He replied that the entire building was sick, built over a wartime arms dump. No-one knew what was buried down there, between the sewers and the Tube's Northern Line. He suggested more modern, healthier premises, perhaps closer to Government, Whitehall?

Lightning flashed across his office and Chatham blinked. Lightning brought on memories of defeat, of effort wasted. He counted the seconds till thunder rumbled from the south. It was humid, but Chatham did not sweat.

An email flashed onto his screen. It came from the Master of a Cambridge College, one of Chatham's usually less welcome contacts, but this was a message which made him smile. It read, 'Your servant waits'.

Chatham rose from his chair and for a few moments played with the penny-in-the-slot machine. Around the spiral clattered the silver ball, and into the clown's mouth it dropped. Success. Still standing, Chatham replied to the message with - 'Bring on the day'.

*

He was about to meet the most senior commander of the army in which he served. To say that Twine was fearful as he approached the Soulbury Centre towards which his legs were dragging him, that he had waited for so long in this globe that he thought the call would never come, would be to underplay the terror which the man he was about to meet inspired in those whose life he touched. This was a man whom he had first seen on a field of battle when Twine was on the losing side. This was a man under the direct command of the Lord God Himself. This was a man who could turn him to dust with a flick of his fingers.

His life had been a preparation for this moment. As he walked on, Twine asked himself whether he was ready.

In all things he had obeyed God's Will. He had taken on the role prepared for him. His aspect was of a man who would neither take nor give offence, small and thin, with spectacles which threatened permanently to topple from his nose. Every week he visited a barber in the Strand to tame the mop of blonde hair which made him look younger than he was. He always dressed to suit the occasion and did not stand out in a crowd. He was a spy - a very good spy, he thought, who had woven himself into the fabric of MI5 as if born to it.

For one year he had been a servant of the secret State, hidden away in a malodorous office high-up over Victoria Street. In that short time, with help and an imaginatively forged back-story, he had risen high and fast. He was well regarded, even trusted - gets his hands dirty, finger on the pulse, useful product. How many electricians do we own in the Czech embassy? Twine knew. That Yardie in Bayswater, where does he get his guns? Twine knew. Much of his product was mundane, tittle-tattle spiced with a few gems from other departments of the Service, the Police and GCHQ. Sometimes, though, it required a more physical set of operations, even force. Who can handle this delicate matter, wet work, high risk? Twine knew, for it was Twine.

He had much to offer. What he offered, was unquestioning service. It was his purpose, though he did not want to appear too eager. A butler is not eager. A Permanent Secretary of the Civil Service is not eager. To Twine, the correct demeanour of a servant is one of calm efficiency, not of eagerness. Service was what passed for blood in this body of his, and it was still the highlight of his week to drive a van down the A3 to Chertsey with the files for Archives, for that was menial, a servant's task.

For that one year he had waited to be summoned by the Lord Commander, when all would become clear. It had become Twine's custom to sit at his computer, put on his headphones, and pretend to do the paperwork but stare out of his window, listening to the monumental sweetness of Wagner or to bebop for its manic life, and to wait, for a day that did not come. Every evening he would scuttle back along the river to his bachelor apartment with a heavy heart, wondering why he had been put on this globe only to be forgotten.

But then, the call came.

Twine's apartment was a one-bed flat in Wapping High Street, three floors up with a view of the river, a pizza parlour nearby and all manner of entertainments for a young man who could afford them. In the words of the estate agent it had been 'knocked out' - a warehouse of brown brick converted to apartments with magnolia walls, picture windows, kitchen equipment which gleamed, and furniture of the same, functional Swedish design. Even the pictures were of Swedish landscapes, trees, ponds and mist. It was a hotel by another name. There were penthouses on the top floor, and muzak in the lobby.

One night, Twine had waited in that apartment as usual, sitting at his desk by the picture window. The river shimmered under its lights. His laptop whispered. A pizza box and a half-empty bottle of Bulgarian merlot stood at his elbow. He waited. He poured himself another glass. The laptop pinged. He looked back at the screen and saw something new, from inside the Government Secure Intranet; a 'Promotional offer' from a sender whose name was a simple substitution cipher, of the name of the man who had secured his appointment to MI5 in the first place.

'Soulbury Centre, Battersea. Friday 3pm. Chatham. Ready?'

With his eyes wide and with a deep breath, Twine replied, 'Yes sir'.

*

Other office blocks, their windows shuttered, rose beside the Soulbury building in towers of concrete around a square of bare grass strewn with bottles and children's toys. In his best blue suit and black shoes polished for the occasion, Twine meandered up from the main road with what he hoped was an authoritative swagger which would not betray his nervousness. Two uniformed police eyed him as he pushed through the revolving door into a lobby, where a plump woman was more interested in her television than Twine. She flapped her hand towards the elevator, which with a clanking of chains raised him to the top floor.

When the doors of the elevator opened, Chatham stood before him. "Twine," he said. "Welcome." It was a high voice, clipped and with a flattening of vowels which renamed Twine as 'Twain', as if he were a stable-hand addressed by an Earl. Twine had expected fear, but in his chest something sizzled, an unexpected admiration. The man's ugliness was monstrous, but something Twine had heard stirred his heart. His employees had given Chatham a nickname - the Gargoyle. That was cruel, but it was hard to think of him as anything else.

"Thank you, sir," he mumbled.

Chatham led Twine along a carpeted corridor and into his office. There was an aroma of cologne which was pleasant, and of fried bacon, which was not. They sat, Chatham with his back to the window. Chatham smiled. It was a winning smile, and the grey light gave his bald head a lighter halo. Twine admired the stillness in his face, the hoods of eyelids over dark eyes, a nose as pronounced as the beak of a predatory bird, the mouth thin and cruel, teeth sharp but with a smile that lit the room, shoulders broad and a boxer's neck. Yes, his ears were prominent, his lips black, and his skin was grey, but that could be explained by a medical condition or over-work.

"Understand, young Twine," Chatham said. "Here, we are safe. This is a cage within a cage. Here we can be ourselves."

"We understand, my Lord."

"Good." Chatham tilted his head to one side and narrowed his eyes. "So, Twine. You should regard this as an interview," he said. "I am concerned that my people are in their correct positions. First, credentials. Remind me who you are."

From inside his jacket Twine produced a small arrow, a crossbow dart, and placed it on the table. Its shaft was of a golden metal, with black feathers and a silver tip. "From the third sea, my Lord," he said. "Bowman."

Chatham poked a grey hand at the dart. Twine saw on the middle finger of that hand a ring, gold with a bright ruby-red stone. "Your

11

arrows," Chatham said. "So small, but the sky was full of them. In turn, this is my credential."

From the drawer of his table Chatham pulled out a chain of silver links. From it hung a small mirror in a setting of silver, wrought with curious leaves and the heads of insects. It was antique, shiny on its surfaces but black in the pits of the decoration. "Hold it," he said, pushing the chain over the table. "It took me a few favours to get that back from Istanbul. My chain of office."

The chain sparkled in what was left of the afternoon's light. As Twine held it, reflections twinkled over the table's surface as a sheet of drifting, scintillating fireflies. In the chain's mirror he saw Chatham with a glow around him, for it was concave, the polished inside of an egg, and when he looked at himself in it he felt light, as if he could fly. But something was working away at the front of his head, behind his eyes. From his finger-tips he felt the heat growing. His hands were warm, and he clenched the chain in his fist. His arm was strong. He had only to extend it and thousands would die.

"An ancient thing," Chatham said. "Dangerous in the wrong hands."

Twine nodded, but lifted his head in alarm. His heart raced. His eyes closed. Only fear and obedience counted in war. There were no lovers in the conquered seas. They were all selfish, useful beasts, only dust. God help me, came to Twine's mind as his eyes blinked open, I am drifting and these are not my thoughts.

"You recognise the chain?"

Twine coughed modestly and replied, "Yes. Yes we do, my Lord."

"Then tell me who I am."

"You are Lord Commander of the First Wing. To you God speaks. All other commanders are subordinate to you."

"Correct. Now let the chain go. On the table, before it burns you."

Twine let the chain slip through his fingers. Chatham put out a hand and dragged the chain back into the drawer. He sat back and said,

"When last I was in this globe, Twine, some called me a monster, a destroying angel. The thousands I slaughtered might agree. Isn't that fun? In the east, to this day I am more myth than history."

Chatham smiled, and on the table he flattened his right hand and spread his claw-like fingers, massaging the table-top. "Such nonsense. Here I am now, and you see me. I am no angel, Twine. I am merely a commander of our God's army. Agree with me. There is only one angel, our Lord God."

Twine was taken aback, as if anything to the contrary would be blasphemous. "Yes, yes my Lord," he said. "We have heard that our enemy calls him the Grey Angel. As if there were other angels in many colours. My poor soul thinks that shows no respect."

"Grey is the colour of God's armour, and I have adopted that colour as my own. It pleased our God that I did so." Chatham pursed his lips and frowned. "But you speak in the manner of the third sea. I hope you do not speak to the globers as you do to me."

"No, my Lord. In your presence our true self is revealed."

"Very well." Chatham tapped on the table-top. "I hear good things about you, Twine," he said. "You have become a master of information. Tell me, who does your security Service say I am?"

"You are Henry Cornelius Chatham, my Lord. Chairman of the G-Range company, based in India. You were educated at the University of Oxford, but we have no birth certificate, no details of family. There is such mystery about you that the Service has decided that you are American. We will not investigate further in case we tread on the toes of our American cousins."

"Ha!" Chatham grinned. "I detect your hand in that piece of theatre."

Twine modestly lowered his head but kept his eyes fixed on Chatham.

"No doubt you remember our landfall in Canada," Chatham went on. "I have had a fondness for boats ever since." From a drawer of his table he pulled a tub of black powder, wetted a forefinger, dipped it into the tub, sucked on his finger and blinked. His eyes had a new shine. "Let us move on. I am satisfied with your credential."

"We thank you, my Lord."

Chatham leaned forward. "By God's command we went our separate ways," he said, "and by that same command we are drawn together. I have decided what to do with you. I offer you a position at my right hand. And I suggest you take it."

Twine's eagerness began to show, in the widening of his eyes and the constriction of his throat, but he calmed himself with a deep breath, clasped a hand over his heart, and said, "My poor soul and I are not worthy. But we accept, my Lord."

Chatham leaned back and smiled. "Good," he said. "We are entering an executive phase, Twine, and I will need your support. I cannot be everywhere at once. It is executive, because we shall execute as many Roamers as we can find. We have found them here, Roamers, the enemy. Their contagion stinks across this globe."

"Roamers, my Lord? Here?"

"They infect this globe, but not for long. Use or destroy. That is our mission. We shall seek them out, you and I and my little band of warriors. Between us we have the secrets of Government and the powers which I can bring to bear. Together, we can look forward to a magnificent adventure."

"Yes my Lord."

"But first, I have a task for you. Are you ready?"

For the first time, Twine thought himself on the verge of discovering why he was here - when he would earn respect, and to be respected by the Lord Commander would be precious above all. "My Lord, what is to be done?"

Chatham looked away towards the lights on the river. "You are going to meet your first Roamers," he said. "A woman and her daughter. The woman is Russian. We want the daughter. I have high hopes for her, eventually. The Russians want the mother."

He rapped his fingers on the table-top and turned to face Twine squarely in the face. "So split them up," he went on. "Use the resources of your security Service to remove the mother. You can tell your people that you caught a Russian spy. So amusing."

Twine made a rapid calculation. Any operation to do with Mother Russia meant calling in favours. The mandarins had bound him with manacles of steel, threatened him with tongues of flame and told him not to touch Russia. Yes, we put wires into every building they buy, but they are bringing a mountain of cash into the country and we have to tread as carefully as if every little stone in our path was an explosive device. But no-one questions the will of the Lord Commander. "We shall see to it, my Lord," he said.

"And…" Chatham said with a smile, "you will catch your Russian spy with the full blessing of the Russians themselves. Isn't that fun?"

3 - Entering without Breaking

They came at three in the morning, night-workers. The first two, a man and a woman dressed for an evening in the City, sauntered down from the South Circular into a quieter back-street of Wandsworth's East Hill. Half-way down, by a modest Victorian terraced house, they stopped while the man courteously re-arranged the lady's scarf. When they reached the bottom of the hill and paused under a street-light, the woman raised a hand to her mouth and in a plume of frosty breath appeared to cough. They rounded the corner and disappeared into a lamp-lit mist.

At the rear of that house, three men and a woman clad in black balaclavas and overalls waited on the square of concrete which passed for a back garden. One removed his ear-piece and stuffed it into a pocket. He opened the back door with the keys he had copied the day before when the lady of the house let him in to fix the boiler. He had also reconfigured the security alarm and disabled the detector in the kitchen. He reached for the alarm pad under the overhead cupboard and input the code to turn it off, then let in his colleagues, who stepped slowly through the kitchen and into the hall.

This was a typical London two-up two-down, sitting rooms off the hall, and upstairs the main bedroom was at the front, with a smaller room at the side where the child was, and a bathroom under a sloping ceiling at the back. In the moonlight the intruders could make out the floral pattern on anaglypta paper which lined the dado of the hall and staircase. They paused. The leader nodded to his companions. One stepped forward to unlock the front door, and opened it a few inches.

Outside, a grey Transit van had been parked across the road since pub closing-time. In that van another black-clad figure tapped the operation director on the elbow. The operation director was Twine. Together they climbed out of the van, and stepped quietly across the road. The door opened and they entered the hall. The first intruder

16

demonstrated the safe way to get upstairs, feet planted on the far edges of each stair. Even these few resources so close could be noisy, but Twine heard nothing, no creaks, all breathing by mouth. It was a pleasure to work with professionals.

One by one they ascended, and backed off into the bathroom, Twine at the rear. The front man looked back. Twine nodded. Green light.

In the main bedroom, the first two targets were isolated as planned within twenty seconds.

The man struggled briefly but pressure on his carotid sinus allowed two of the group to gag him, then cuff and hood him. He was left on the bed. Simultaneously the woman offered no resistance to the same procedure, nor to the injection which followed. She was carried downstairs. There was a report to the Service later that an elderly man across the road, caught short in the middle of the night, had seen a suspiciously large black bag of rubbish carried into a Transit van. This was explained to him by Police as the collection of building material from works by the Council to improve drainage.

The child could have been difficult. Children at the age of two are not known for their compliance, and their pattern of sleep could be irregular. But though the cry of a child at night could have carried along the street, it was not likely to raise the local plod. As it turned out, the child was awake, sitting up in her bed, and took an interest in what was going on. "Auntie?" she said to the female officer who unzipped her overalls to reveal day-wear of jeans and t-shirt. "Yes darling," the officer replied. "I've come to give you a treat. Mummy's taking us all for a drive. She's downstairs. Shall we go?"

The result, as Twine explained with great satisfaction to Chatham later that morning, was that the woman, the mother, was now in the process of exchange with a British agent of equal value. The father - Riley Moss by name - was in custody. As Chatham had instructed, the child was in safe hands, and would undergo a top-to-toe MRI scan at a local clinic on the following morning. The results of that scan would be available in three days.

No-one enquired whether Twine's hands were safe, nor did his MI5 superiors know - in an operation to remove a threat to the security of the State - it was the child who mattered.

*

"Mister Moss."

"Twine. What day is it?"

"Tuesday. We're nearly done."

Riley Moss could not believe there was more to do. There had been three days of questions and his answers were always the same. No, I had no idea my wife was a Russian national. I never met her parents, because Anna said they had 'passed over', for God's sake, which meant they were dead. And she had a Polish passport. No, I did not discuss with her any matter of national security. My work in Defence Intelligence was permanently off limits. Then how come the SVR hold a log of your pillow talk, in which you refer to members of this Service and other agencies by name? Forged. Are you telling me that you could live with a woman for three years and not know she was a fake, an officer of the Russian SVR? At no time did I suspect that my wife, Anna, was anything other than a research assistant from Cracow, Poland, working for a Member of Parliament, and if you've quite finished I insist on talking to your superior, because this is an infringement of my human rights and I object in the strongest possible terms.

In the room which had become his cell Riley Moss sat wearing a white t-shirt and Government-issue pants. They were small and he was large, but this place was not designed for his comfort. He knew where he was. It was a red-brick house just the other side of Wandsworth Common. He could walk to it from home. He had borrowed it himself a few times, as a quid pro quo for letting MI5 use the garage where Defence Intelligence left their bicycles. What a mistake that was - the sheer arrogance of these people, who call themselves a security Service, and what sort of service is it that steals into your home, attacks you, takes your wife and child and then makes out it was all your fault?

Riley Moss knew that he smelled. The rumpled sheets of his bed were evidence of that. He was also aware that the smell of Twine was different, sweet, from an expensive bottle. Maybe ten years younger than Moss himself, he had a studious air which was only cover for his nervousness, with something of the pomposity of smaller men. All that could be said of him favourably was that he had a pretty face, good blonde hair, and his suit was always immaculate, and very blue. He had come into this cell - a white-washed cubicle with no window, one bed, one chair riddled with woodworm whose patterns Moss had traced in case they held a clue to what was going on, one sink and a bucket, one yellow unshaded bulb permanently lit - with a smile he might have thought gracious but which was without doubt sinister.

"What have you done with Anna?" said Riley Moss.

Twine sniffed. "As I said before, Mister Moss," he replied, "I am not at liberty to tell you that. But I can assure you that your daughter is well and currently looked-after by highly capable staff."

"This can't go on," said Moss. "I've told you everything I can."

"You may well be right," Twine said. Moss saw in his eyes the detachment of a man-machine, a job to do, get on with it. "And today," Twine went on, "we are letting you go. It was just an error of judgement on your part."

Riley Moss smothered the urge to swear. "Remember, Twine," he said, "Anna was vetted by MI5, your Service. Polish, from Cracow. Research assistant. If I happened to fall for a Russian agent there's more than my error of judgement going on here."

"I am not at liberty to discuss decisions made by my predecessors," Twine said as if reading from a card. "Tidy yourself up, and go home. Your daughter will be there."

In a cubicle along the corridor Riley Moss was allowed to shave. The stubble made him look rough, a middle-aged man, stocky he would say, broad-faced, with a tangle of dark hair which was thinning and needed a comb. He put on the clothes which the MI5 house-breakers had brought with them, and allowed Twine to take him by the arm downstairs and out through the front door. "Don't want you breaking a leg, dear chap," Twine said. "But you look steady enough. No need for a cab, is there? You can walk home from here."

Riley Moss felt that Twine was looking for something by way of thanks. He remembered that the victim of a public-school flogging was obliged to say Thank You to the flogger, a prefect or similar sadist. Twine was probably public school and a sadist, but he got no thanks, only a glare and a snort as Moss turned his back and stalked off towards St John's Hill.

*

That night, according to Chatham's instruction, Twine made his report in a public house east of Greenwich, the Griefer's Head. This was a brown-brick and brassy pub in the middle of a wide area under demolition, broken buildings on every side. As Twine approached, the sign of a severed head and guillotine creaked in the wind off the river above a placard - If you don't like Beer, Get out of Here.

He was to report to whomever was behind the bar. Tonight it was a woman and her name was Max. Behind a bar of polished mahogany she stood in dim light cleaning a glass, her hair tied back behind her ears in a bun, exposing a forehead that glistened. Tonight she was a Goth, panda eyes and a black mouth. A purple turtle-neck sweater led down to baggy black trousers which billowed over her boots. Her chest, unrestrained, wobbled with a sideways motion as if two footballs were competing for space.

Twine perched himself on a stool, in front of him a jam-jar with a layer of algae through which the head of a goldfish poked.

Max pouted. "So you got it?" she said.

"Got what?" Twine replied. In his opinion, reporting to anyone but his Lord Commander was quite wrong, even dangerous to them both.

"The scan," Max went on. "You did that, yes?"

It was nonsense. The child was a nasty wrinkle in the business and in Twine's view it would be better to stick a plastic bag over its head for a minute or two than to bother with a physical scan. What use was a two-year-old girl?

"We took her to the clinic," Twine replied. "The results are in our pocket. What's it to you?"

"Whoah, tiger," said Max. "Tell me about the girl."

"Two years old, small. Name of Lily."

Max began to sway as if the river's wind was sweeping around her. "Is she pretty?"

"Blonde hair. Thin-faced, blue eyes. Mother Russian. It shows."

"That's nice," Max said, and put the glass down on the bar's top. "Now you'd better let me have what's in your pocket, love. I need to check one little thing."

Slowly and half-closing his eyes Twine drew from the inside pocket of his jacket a brown envelope, which he prodded over the bar's top. Max picked it up and, looking at him with an expression of pity, ripped it open and pulled out one white page. She studied it for a moment. "The anomaly."

"What anomaly?"

"The Roamer mark, dear. Something funny in her head. All I do is confirm the diagnosis. This little girl's a Roamer. Use or destroy. Think you can kill a little kiddy?" Max raised an eyebrow. "It might take years to see how she turns out, but that's the rule," she said, propping her chest on the bar. "So macho. But don't you worry, dear. The Boss will sort it out. How's the money situation? Shall we bung a few grand in your account?"

"That would be helpful."

"Consider it done. Well, you better bugger off and do what you have to do then, dear," said Max.

As Twine left the pub he looked back through a cracked window into the dim light of the bar. It had been a long day. He was tired, and unsure whether he had done what the Lord Commander expected of him. Surely, if the child was a Roamer he should have disposed of her, neatly.

When he saw the figure of Max blur and around her gather the bulkier frame of another human form he knew that he was over-tired, hallucinating. The Lord Commander, Chatham, divine in a dark-grey suit, stood behind the bar cleaning a glass. Twine blinked, and there stood Max again. Twine drew a deep breath and blew it out, then wiped a hand across his forehead and set off back to his bachelor apartment in the City.

It would be ten years before Twine saw that child again.

4 - The Child

Sussex, February 2009

Lily Moss was in two places at once. She was in the LRA classroom on a winter's day, looking across the playing field from her window. Her arms, in the maroon-and-gold of her school uniform, stretched out on the desk in front of her. By the blackboard, Miss Schwarz was burbling about Pythagoras. At the same time Lily was looking through a window of the hotel in Roamers Cross, from a room where she had lived for a week but had no money to pay for it, so there might be trouble. The brown leather of a bomber jacket was on her arms.

Far away, against a blue sky the Great Tower rose from its grassy hill. No, that was the mill at Halnaker beyond the playing field. No, it was the Tower, and she saw it over the red-tiled roofs of the town. Now she stood on the spire of the Tower and she looked down into the forest, but she was called by her mother and flew to a rocky hill where others flapped around her as she looked down at a scene so fearful it brought on a buzzing in her head, acid in her throat, and the weakness in her arms which meant that she was passing out.

The conflict was too much, and as her head slipped down into the cradle of her arms she knew that she had been spared whatever danger the others were facing.

*

"Dad, are you there?"

"Yes, Lily, I'm here."

"I can't see."

"Try to open your eyes, my love."

"Oh. They're sticky."

"You've been through the wars, my darling. Better now."

In a room off the children's ward of Chichester Hospital, Riley Moss sat holding his daughter's hand. It was a private room, and at twenty-five pounds a night he could ill afford it, but he would pay anything to give Lily a better rest. They were lucky to get it. A cruise ship from the Caribbean had returned awash with elderly patients struck down by a norovirus, and they had taken over most of the private rooms along England's south coast. This room, though, was a work in progress, with tins of paint stacked in one corner, yellow on the walls against the lilac of the curtains in so ghastly a clash that patients might leave sicker than when they came in. A tubular hospital bed and bedside cabinet, one minimalist plastic chair which was challenging to the man's backside, a drip, and a bank of monitors were all that it offered. Fresh paint at least overpowered the odours of antiseptic and other hospital life which had greeted them in the corridors.

Riley Moss had grown bear-like in his fifty-five years, his broad face weather-beaten, his black hair tangled, and his jacket, shirt and ex-Army trousers failed to hide the belly which had expanded in recent months of idleness.

Lily was now a few weeks from her twelfth birthday. Small, slight, blonde and at this moment very pale, wearing a lightweight hospital gown she lay flat on a bed by an open window. An antibiotic drip was fixed into her right arm and an ECG monitor over her chest. The room was cold, to bring down her temperature which earlier that day had soared.

"Rapid-onset infection, like croup," was the emergency ward's diagnosis, but her father knew better. It was another of Lily's 'turns', giddy spells which he put down to her time of life and to over-work. Lily was a swot, everyone agreed. To the rural communities of Sussex, having your nose always in a book will lead to all manner of ailments curable only by fresh air and sport. Lily was not sporty. She was too small, and she had the common sense to stand aside when big girls pushed their way past. Besides, her 'turns' made her special, and interesting to some (Berthold in her class was infatuated) and to others a sign that she was a witch.

"I've seen him, Dad," said Lily Moss, breathing hard.

"Who's that, darling?" Riley Moss replied. He had been assured that Lily was out of danger, and soon she would be fit to go home.

"Death," she said.

"No," said Moss. "No, don't say that. You're going to be fine, Lily. I promise." He squeezed her hand.

"But I saw him," she insisted. "He was grey. Like stone. And he had a bull's head with great white horns. And he had wings folded round his back. I saw him. He was standing on a hill and the sky was dark and down the hill he had an army of dead things. Monsters and insects with the faces of people." Lily's violet-blue eyes were wide open now, her cheeks flushed a dark pink, and she propped herself up. "Don't let me die, Dad. I don't want to be in the army of dead things. Please don't let me die."

"Lily," Riley Moss had to swallow hard, "you are not going to die. I promise. You've just had one of your turns. You'll be fine now, and I'll look after you. You know I always do, and I always will."

"Yes Dad."

"You need to rest. I'll be here. They're bringing in a little bed for me."

"But he's coming. I saw his eyes. They were big and red. He looked at me. He's coming. I'll tell you when I see him."

"You do that, Lily. But we're safe here. Just rest."

"Yes Dad. I need to dream." With that, Lily Moss sank back on the bed, and her father knew that she was asleep.

25

Lily dreamed of her mother.

This was a dream which recurred but varied every time, for all that Lily knew of her mother she had learned only from photographs and from the little her Dad had to say. "She was a Polish woman," he said, only once. "We met in London. Yes I loved her of course. But we lost her, Lily, when you were two. Now that's a closed book. Please don't ask me any more about it. We have to move on, my darling." This brought to her father's face an anger which was hard to bear, but for a child with any curiosity that could not be enough.

By her bed at home she had her mother's photograph in a silver frame, and every night she kissed it as if it were a holy icon. Every night, she asked the same questions. How did you die? Where, and why? Her mother was not old in the photograph, a slim, thin-faced blonde woman always smiling, with eyes of violet blue. Sometimes, a picture popped into Lily's mind, the image of a grave somewhere, Poland perhaps, a heap of earth under whispering trees and at its head a stone that sparkled like the granite work-top in the kitchen, a gravestone, on it her mother's name. On the other side of the grave, three men stood motionless, a vicar, her Dad, and in the background a man in a black suit. It was a horrible image and whenever it surfaced she willed it away and tried to think of something else.

When Lily entered secondary school, her father bought her a laptop computer. Most children in her class had one, but hers was small, plain black, slow and - even worse - second-hand. She could work at home, and send in her efforts to the school by email, but no games, at least not the games the boys played and talked about every day. Instead it was just a tiny window on a new world, not all pleasant or useful, but to a small child with an enquiring mind it was an oracle of information. Why did Berthold think he had a spell from Hermes Trismegistus which would make any girl in the world fall in love with him? Who was Hermes Trismegistus? She found out, and that was worrying, but the spell was a failure. She still thought Berthold was creepy, following her around all the time and muttering. Have aliens arrived from Space? This entertained her for days, and she decided they had not. Who was Anna Moss?

Her mother's name was Anna. Lily scoured the Web for an Anna Moss who was Polish, but the results were useless, with one exception. It was an article in The Times from 1999 about an Anna Moss, a research assistant, and it questioned whether foreign nationals should be working for Members of Parliament, especially MPs involved in the defence of the realm. Lily seized on this, convinced that there could be only one Anna Moss, Polish, but there was no more about her. Amongst the all-pervasive reports that in 'Year 2000' the world was coming to an end there was no Anna Moss.

Other children had mothers. It was so unfair. They would drop their children at the bus stop in the morning, and pick them up from school in the afternoon. Their children had snacks in special boxes, and they would complain about their Mum and Dad, and tell tales behind their backs, but they were the lucky ones. Lily had to queue for the school bus in the morning and in the afternoon and there was no-one to hold her hand, no-one to smile and wish her Good Luck, only her Dad - and he had to work in his shop, all day. Her mother, was only a dream.

Dutifully, Lily wrote down what she recalled of her dreams in school exercise books of red and green which she hid under sheets of newspaper in a bedside drawer of her tiny bedroom. Everything else in that room would be usual for a girl near to teenage years - posters, an Indian wall-hanging her father found in a Portsmouth junk-shop, stuffed toys which she threw around the room when she got cross, which was often. But her dream books were secret.

She dreamed of a place where her mother was alive.

Even when she was small she knew its name. Roamers Cross. It was a town in a landscape of green hills and valleys, which she knew must be unreal but the persistence of it night after night, year after year, made it familiar. Her mother lived there, and so did others.

In her early years she had a special friend, a little black-haired boy who wore a black-and-white school uniform. In her dream she would land in a forest clearing, raising the dust, and there he would be, sitting under a tree. He would speak, but in music. He had only to open his mouth for melodies to pour out, and around him were his animals, the rabbit, and the donkey in a dunce's cap which pawed the ground and spouted out bubbles. With a wave of his hand the black-haired boy would let Lily play with them in the shade of the forest trees. But as she grew older, she landed ever closer to the town, until the boy and his animals became just another memory.

The town was a hard, grown-up place where people bustled about, grunting and rushing. Its buildings were old and crumbly for the most part, like the Tudor reconstructions in the local country park, but one was modern and glassy, huge and menacing, and the music of the town was harsh and mechanical. In the town, she could never tell where she would land. It could be in a hotel, where she had lived in a room for a week and had no money to pay for it. It could be in the shadowy old house, which belonged to someone whom she heard only through a wall, and she knew she had no right to be there. It could be in the office of the Grand Council, a whitewashed hive of closed doors where there was a hum of someone else's business and she could sit for hours ignored.

These were no more than dreams, but their impact would wake her. At dead of night she would fumble in the drawer, fetch out an exercise book and scribble by the light of a bedside lamp. Every so often she would pull out a book and try to make sense of it all.

Through this her mother was a constant thread. Their meetings could be short and uneventful. They could be long, especially when they walked hand-in-hand through the streets of Roamers Cross and Lily felt that her mother was showing her off, a trophy. To the questions which bothered Lily most - 'How did you die? Where are we now? What am I doing here?' - her mother would only raise a hand and tell her to "Shhh."

Weeks might pass between one such dream and another, but Lily knew that the dream of her mother would come at any time of crisis, when she was under stress or - as now - when she was ill.

"Mum?"

"Yes, Lily?"

"I'm here."

"I know. Come and sit with me, baby."

Lily's mother sat on a wooden bench with her back against a pine tree. She wore a blue uniform dress and her short blonde hair curled around a face which was delicate and pale, her eyes shining from some interior light. She smiled as Lily emerged from the undergrowth and smoothed down her school skirt. "What have you done to your hair?" she said.

"They are called bunches, Mum," Lily replied, sitting at her mother's side.

"They look like floppy dog ears. You're a spaniel."

"Woof woof."

"Cheeky girl."

Mother's Hill was always the same, dusty, with straggly pine trees and a view from the cliffs over a wide boiling blue sea. Now there was an evening light and a gentle breeze which rippled the grasses of the undergrowth. Dark clouds gathered in the distance, trailing curtains of rain through a bank of mist. Seagulls whirled, too far away to hear their cries.

Lily frowned. "You scared me last time, Mum," she said.

"I'm sorry, baby," her mother replied. "It was a nightmare, I know. I'm sorry."

"What were those creatures? I was so scared."

Lily's mother took her hand and their eyes met. "You need to know about these things, darling," she said. "You are growing up. Your father has cared for you, but we are getting older, and one day you will have to care for yourself."

"You're scaring me again, Mum."

"I don't want to do that, my darling. You have to be brave."

"I will try. But…"

"Those creatures." Lily's mother let go of her hand and gazed out over the sea towards a sun sinking behind the clouds. "They came suddenly, from behind the Tower. The Council sent us to investigate. It was an emergency, and I forgot you were with me. I'm so sorry."

"But what are they?"

"We can only guess, baby."

Lily Moss breathed deeply. "They belong somewhere else."

"I'm sure they do. But someone is coming," said her mother. "You have to go now, Lily. Be a good girl for your father. We will meet again soon."

"But Mum…"

*

In a pale green room which had chairs with sufficient padding, Riley Moss sat with a consultant neurologist. His name was Reynolds, and though Moss had the notion that medical high-ups should be called Mister, this one had said "Josh, please. I was named after the painter," with a beguiling smile. He was around Moss's age, but with luxuriant brown hair and no unnecessary fat. His sharp black suit put Moss's own dishevelled look to shame and the aroma of aftershave reminded Moss that he needed a bath. The room lay between the Hospital and the outside world. From beyond a wall of fish-eye glass blocks came the pacing of visitors and nurses. Through the window the sun shone on the distant South Downs.

Moss was on edge. It had appeared that Lily was on the mend. Her temperature was coming down, and the Hospital would release her when it had been normal for two days. To be called in for a 'chat' with a specialist, one who dealt with the mysteries of the brain, was an unwelcome surprise.

"The first thing I want to say, Mister Moss," said Reynolds, "is that I don't want you to worry."

Moss had already decided that this languid individual was expert in giving bad news, and was ready to believe the opposite of anything he might hear. "I wasn't worried," he said. "But I am now."

"Your daughter, Lily, has a DVA. It's quite common. Around one in fifty of the population have one. I believe you have been told about that."

"I have, yes. You took her for a MRI scan. Why exactly?"

"Oh, a long history of episodes, 'turns' I believe you call them. Symptoms very approximate to narcolepsy. It was only a precaution. And I have to admit," said Reynolds with a smile, "the machine was free. Wonderful thing, nine tons of pure magic. We do like to see it used."

"So what did this magic machine tell you, about Lily?"

Reynolds shifted in his chair and peered at Moss as if he were a laboratory specimen. "A DVA, Mister Moss, a developmental venous anomaly," he said, "showed up on her scan as a malformation of a blood vessel in her brain. This is congenital, genetic. We call it a benign lesion, because usually it is nothing to worry about."

"That doesn't sound benign."

"There can be side-effects. It depends on whether and where in the brain the DVA exerts pressure, and if there is any chance of a haemorrhage." Reynolds raised an eyebrow. "In Lily's case," he went on, "we see no evidence of that. It is only a slight malformation of a vein in her brain. You know that - when one of her so-called 'turns' is imminent - she says something like 'I need to dream' or 'I need to sleep'. That is her DVA playing up. This is not

31

epilepsy, though it may appear so. Sleep for a few moments should restore her to full working condition. A cat-nap. A power snooze. Did wonders for Churchill in the War."

"And there's nothing you can do about it?"

"Anything we might do could make matters worse. We might offer her a drug to help with the giddiness, but the best medicine is to make you, and her, aware of her condition. And I would like to see her again in six months."

Eleven years old, nearly twelve. As Riley Moss trudged through the Hospital's corridors back to Lily's room, he remembered the elation he felt when she was born. That was in South London, when love at first sight hit him in the chest with an electric jolt that turned on a light in his head. She was so small, wrapped-up in her hospital blanket, snub-nosed and perfect, a cheeky little cap framing her wrinkled face. Then, as he went back to his car, he felt as if he were floating ten feet above the asphalt of the car park, to become a father in his forties, to have that little scrap dependent on him and her mother. The Christmases that would follow, he planned them already.

But now, as he wandered through the paraphernalia of medical wards, the sponsored art, patients on trollies, the vending machines, desks, telephones, nurses smiling through the stress, it was all in the past. Her mother, gone. His career, over. His health, up and mainly down. And now Lily, all he had of those three years with her mother, his perfect Lily was altered and strange. Now he wanted to hold her even closer, not easy as she entered her teenage years. At times like this he could feel the pressure rising in his chest. Especially at times like this, Riley Moss needed the wife he had lost.

*

Lily woke up. She was cold, and the hospital gown was sticking to her. She propped herself up on her left elbow, for inside her right elbow she felt the pricking of a drip whose tube led up to a plastic bag shrunken on its stand. In the shadows of this paint-smelling cell she made out a screen and her Dad's clothes slung over it. From behind the screen came a gentle snoring which she recognized.

It was the middle of the night. She was better. She had no reason to be here. Outside, the February wind slammed into trees along the perimeter fence and rocked the yellow street-lights. The window was open and the wind was brushing over her, ice-cold.

She needed to get home. She needed to write down her dream in the red book which was the only one with empty pages. Where were her clothes? Probably in the bedside cabinet, folded-up. But she could not leave her Dad just like that, and she had this thing stuck in her arm which kept her tethered to the bed. With a sigh of frustration she dropped back on the pillow. Much more of this, and she would freeze to death. She propped herself up again and reached across the bedside cabinet towards the window.

Here was something odd. A bunch of flowers, not in water, just lying there in a wrapper of newspaper, daisies and carnations. That was very nice of someone, perhaps her Dad, but probably not, for it was not the sort of thing that he would think of. She hoped it was not Berthold. That would be totally embarrassing. A white card was attached, with a message in wriggly writing -

For the Child

5 - The Elite

Swivelhurst, Sussex

The greatest fear of Berthold Minimus was that he would stumble upon The Elite without warning. They were savages, he had heard, witches. So, on a cloudy afternoon with wood-smoke in the air, when he had run across the playing field of Swivelhurst School and rounded the corner of the bike-sheds, only to find all three of The Elite at netball practice, his jaw dropped, his cheeks reddened, and his legs tried but failed to get into reverse.

"Bertie!" cried Nathalie, the worst of them. "Come here this minute you scum."

"How can we help, Bertie?" said his target, Lily Moss. With a smile that would make angels weep at the beauty of it, she was his ideal, and untouchable. His obsession with her was doubly romantic because he knew she was vulnerable, often not well, subject to strange fits of fainting, from which he always had the urge to pick her up.

"Sit!" commanded Nathalie. "On the ground, vermin."

Berthold sat on the ground, which was damp. All eyes were on him - the dark eyes of Nathalie, exotic, dangerous, and rumour had it she was the love-child of an Indian film star; the piercing grey eyes of Swan, thin-faced, destined to be a teacher; and Lily Moss, the most dangerous of all, probably a witch. It was marvellous how these girls could make their netball outfits so special, with bits and bobs of ornament not allowed in the school buildings. And their shapes, oh Lord. Berthold's eyes widened as he tried to control the magical power they had over him.

Nathalie sniffed. "What do you want, worm?"

Berthold squirmed. On the one hand The Elite could turn him into a frog and make a decent starter out of him. On the other hand, he had a job to do. "I got a message for Lily," he said.

"Out with it, Bertie, then bugger off," said Nathalie.

Berthold said to Lily, "Visitor, Miss Chesterton's office," then buggered off, with relief.

*

No-one went to the office of the Headmistress unless they were in trouble, and Lily approached the door of Fate with a feeling of doom. It was just another panelled door, polished like others in the corridor, but what made it special was the gold-script label which identified the woman beyond, the Head, Hitler's favourite daughter.

Lily consulted her conscience. What had she done? Her homework was up to date. She hadn't had a detention in weeks. Who was the visitor? Could it be Mister Ormerod complaining of her obsession with his son? But that was love, Eternal Love, Love Divine all loves excelling, and who could complain about that? Oh my God, could it be the Police? Her Dad had been crushed under a car; he had fallen off the roof of the shop while mending the gutter; he had poisoned her mother ten years ago and the body had just been found; he had fallen off the roof and been crushed by a car, as God's vengeance for poisoning her mother ten years ago?

She took a deep breath, smoothed down her school skirt, and she knocked. She was called. She entered.

The Headmistress, Miss Chesterton, smiled. Standing, she looked oddly casual, but Lily never saw the Head after mid-day, when Miss Chesterton put aside her academic gown and slipped into her jeans and t-shirt for the afternoon's tasks of administration. Long auburn hair, even lipstick - purple which did not suit her colouring at all - the Headmistress looked close to human, even young. But that was by comparison with her guest, an old lady.

35

"Lily," said Miss Chesterton. "Thanks for making the effort. I hope you haven't missed the bus home."

"No Miss Chesterton. I was just... ah..."

"I'm sure you were. Say hello to Lady Meizel."

The old lady turned her head.

There were times when what was around Lily became a part of her. The white blinds on a window overlooking the green of the playing field, the yellow walls, the shelves of books, box files, the noticeboard and post-it notes, a desk of grey wood and a carpet of brown so as not to show the dirt, a telephone, a computer screen that was black and where is the box bit of it? And chairs, not worth much. Some moments stuck in her memory as if fixed to a wall.

In a plain wooden chair sat the old lady, knees properly together, hands on lap, black shiny shoes, a beige twin-set, black leather handbag, and a double string of white pearls, oh my God are they real? This was an intelligent woman. She was sharp. Her hair was grey and tied-back into an elaborate bun, her eyes twinkled, violet-blue. Lily had no grandmothers, no family other than her Dad, but she knew grandmothers and this one was familiar, merry but sharp. At some time, somewhere, Lily had seen her from the corner of her eye, but she could not remember when.

A Lady? "Very pleased to meet you, my Lady," she said. Something about this woman spoke of Great Houses, and servants. No-one had taught Lily to curtsey so she managed only a down-and-up bob which she hoped was not ridiculous.

"Lily," said the old lady. "So formal. I've heard so much about you."

"Lady Meizel is the Chair of Governors of a school not far from here," Miss Chesterton said, glancing at the old lady, "She has something quite interesting to say to you. I would say take a seat but sadly there is none. Funding."

The old lady smiled. "Any excuse for a dig, Frances," she said, as the Headmistress resumed her seat. "Lily. I hear you are an outstanding student. What is your favourite subject?"

"English, my Lady. And Computer Science."

"Not Religious Education? I hear you are one of only three pupils studying Religious Education in the whole school? Is that correct?"

"Yes my Lady."

"And what do you think of the subject?"

Lily did not like to lie. Religious studies were an excuse to have a quiet hour after lunch on a Friday, when one of the teachers normally an atheist would work through texts from across the world which were so tedious that at least one of the pupils, and even the teacher herself, would end up asleep. "I hope you will not take this the wrong way, my Lady," said Lily, "but I would prefer more about philosophy and politics, about how people think."

"Dear me," said Lady Meizel. "How old are you? Twelve?"

"Yes my Lady. Just."

"You look younger. You sound older. That's very promising."

"Thank you, my Lady."

Miss Chesterton stood. "I'll leave you to it," she said. "Staff meeting till six. Don't forget the bus, Lily."

"No I won't, Miss," Lily replied. "Thank you." Miss Chesterton picked up a file of papers and with a backward glance and a smile, opened her door and stepped out into the corridor.

The old lady lifted her chin and said, "Take the Head's chair, Lily. It will suit you very well." Lily hesitated but took this as an order, so she walked around the desk and perched herself in the chair of the Headmistress, nervous at this terrible breach of protocol, but as she sat she realised that the old lady was right. It did suit her, to be in charge. Something in her woke up.

"There," said Lady Meizel. "Now. Let me see. You are an only child, and your father has a shop in the village. Is that right?"

"Yes my Lady."

"And you find your lessons dull, they don't stretch you. For every book you are told to read, you read two more on the same subject. Why is that?"

Lily shrugged and said, "I want to know."

"You want to know. Well, there is something, Lily Moss, I want you to know. You, are a pain. P-A-I-N. A pain."

Lily gulped. She had not gulped before so the experience was new and interesting.

"Your class-mates must think so," Lady Meizel went on. "Cute as a button, and smart as a whip. Such a pain. You may be somewhere on the spectrum of autism. What do you think?"

"I don't think so, my Lady."

"Well said. You do not flinch. Perhaps a modest constriction of the throat. Too polite, though. You need to work on that."

The old lady spoke so quickly that it was difficult for Lily to follow, but she was left with the feeling that she had been insulted in some way, but that the insult was a test, of nerve. "If you say so, my Lady."

"And you can cut the 'my Lady'. Call me Meizel. People do."

"Yes... Meizel."

"Good. Now. Let me introduce myself. I am the Head of an Academy, not far from here. My Academy is exclusive, so exclusive that sometimes I don't let myself in." The old lady chortled, and fetched from her handbag a tissue, with which she wiped her lips. "It so happens," she said, "that every so often we give bursaries to outstanding students, which pay for their studies. Only today, a place has become available at my Academy, a place which - due to an ancient grant of funds - is intended for Religious Education. But I wouldn't worry about that. Once you're in, you're in, and you can study what you like. If the Academy were to offer you a bursary, would you be interested?"

To Lily this sounded like Money, and money is what her Dad needed. Even if that money had to be spent on education, if this place was exclusive then there was a good chance there would be people with money in it, people who had grand houses full of valuable objects, and even rich people die, so she would be in a good place to hear of that and maybe leave a business card by this Academy's front door. "Could you tell me more about it?" she said.

The old lady needed no prompting. She launched into a vivid description of what she called The Lodge, becoming so animated that she dropped her tissue under the chair and had to fumble for it.

From her account it appeared that The Lodge was a private school. Lily could just hear her friend Swan making a mockery of that, but not only was it private it was independent, independent of all other schools on God's earth, independent even of other independent schools. "Don't look for it on the Web," the old lady said. "It isn't there." Its facilities, as she described them, were modest, only a few classrooms, because the number of pupils was low. "Never more than twenty. We can't offer you residential accommodation, and can offer only one day of study per week. But that one day - which would be every Friday, for two years - would be fully paid-for, and our bus can pick you up from your home. Whichever courses you choose will be a challenge, but I am told you have the ability to rise to the task. It will prepare you for Higher Education, university perhaps. What are your thoughts?"

Lily thought that this was very odd. From nowhere came a grand Lady who talked about University, and Money, and a bus that would pick her up from home so she would not have to traipse up Swivelhurst Road to queue in the rain. "Please can you tell me… Meizel," she said, "what are the courses, at the Lodge?"

"A good question," the old lady replied. "Science, Mathematics, Information Technology, History, Comparative Religion, Public Administration. Navigation."

"Navigation?"

"We all need to know where we're going. But it will be your choice, when you have met our staff, and they will tell you more."

"Is there some sort of information, so I can show my father?"

"I will email you some factsheets. But you will be able to read them only once, then they delete themselves. Can't have them broadcast. Exclusive, as I said." The old lady ran a hand over her grey hair and looked Lily squarely in the eye. "Just remember, Lily," she said. "This is an opportunity. There's a whole new world out there. We don't want you ignorant of it, do we?"

"No, my Lady," Lily replied, and at Meizel's use of that word she shuddered.

6 - People like himself

As the years passed, Twine stood between two worlds in parallel. In one, he was a spook in a land of shadows, and few questioned his behaviour for he had perfected his act, and he needed only to play the game for as long as that was useful.

In his second world, Twine's role became clear. He was the servant of the Lord Commander, his secretary and confidant. Information which passed through Twine's hands passed also through Chatham's. Operations he undertook were as much for the benefit of Chatham as of the State. And Twine changed, in small but significant ways. He ditched his spectacles for contact lenses which made the pupils of his eyes grey. Now, even his suits were dark grey. Something had created an aura around him, which he could almost see. Even on the Tube, however crowded, punters would make way and he would stand alone in a bubble of contemplation, always thinking of how best he could serve the Lord Commander.

Between those two worlds were bridges, bridges of people, people he knew, from the media, from the politics of Westminster, from the City, people he had once believed to be natives of this place but now he saw to be inhabitants of his other world. People like himself.

He lived for the nights. There were gatherings, in apartments or hotels where entire floors would be roped-off for what masqueraded as a party, but which for Twine and the people who now courted him was an excuse for gossip. Does the Lord Commander think this or that? Is there news from the Crossway? These were people of influence, sober grey-haired men from the City and ladies of the highest society twittering like perfumed parrots.

At one of these events, in a London hotel, Twine became the focus of attention. The evening was ceremonial. One by one the members of the audience ascended from the dance floor and presented themselves to the Lord Commander, who for the occasion wore a simple grey robe and his chain of office. An oafish, blonde-haired man in a tuxedo came forward. Twine recognised him - a senior politician. He bowed to Chatham, he knelt, and Chatham laid his hands on the man's head. "My Lord," the man breathed. "Bring on the day." Chatham nodded. The man rose and returned, hands clasped.

One by one they came forward, words were exchanged, and they returned, eyes glistening. Finally, Chatham turned to Twine. "Come forward," he said. Twine was about to kneel, but Chatham grasped him by the arm.

"No, Twine," Chatham said. "I shall introduce you." Turning to his audience he said, "This is Twine. Come to him, and you come to me. Come to me, and you come to Twine. I have chosen him above all others. Give him your obedience."

People Twine recognised and people he did not know bowed their heads. Some stood, opened their arms wide and with heads uplifted uttered cries and guttural shouts. "Now Twine," Chatham said, "we will share." He raised a hand. Above him a red light grew from the ceiling and edged downward in a plume. It spread around Chatham's body, along his arm and then over Twine, an aura of red that twinkled so brightly that Twine lowered his head. He saw through his flesh. The bones of his legs and feet stood out as if in an x-ray. In a whirl of the red aura, flesh began to close over them. He was to be re-made, rebuilt from below. As the whirl ascended to his head, Twine heard Chatham speak, "My heart is your heart. My mind is your mind. The memory you have, is what I give you."

Twine's head jerked up. As thunder rumbled through the walls, into his mind came pictures - a tent, flapping in the wind; tornadoes of dust which curled downhill across the plain of the Crossway to the trees of a forest, and in the distance a white tower on a green hill. The town of the Roamers lay beyond the tower unseen, well defended, our losses are great and we must out-flank them, through the sea itself. The spikers are in, and the shellflies, but still the cursed tower stands. Twine cleared his throat and said, "We see it, my Lord. Bring on the day."

The red light dispersed into a thousand glittering fragments, and Twine was met by a thunder of stamping and applause. It was all so simple. Here were his people and they were pleased with him. He was empty but ready to be filled. He smiled, and in a daze of joy he resumed his seat.

In the months that followed, among the exotic Twine was exotic above all, and they flattered him, they flirted, and some gave him photographs. The first time one of his new friends gave him a photograph, Twine had no idea what to do with it. It was black-and-white, an amateur photo of an ancient bridge, with a man's elbow protruding into it. It was given to him by a black-haired woman in a purple sari, who called herself Saida. She took it from her purse, handed it over, said "For the Lord Commander", nodded, and then vanished back into the crowd. The next day, when Twine handed the photograph to his master, Chatham smiled, and dropped it into a drawer of his table, where it lay on top of others. "From Saida. Images of Henry Chatham," was his explanation.

Twine needed no explanation. Mysteries surrounded him but he was untroubled. His comfort lay in the wisdom of his master, and in the joy of his service, for Twine had no will of his own.

*

It was after this ceremony that Chatham's executive phase began. Twine executed. He killed. He killed Roamers, one by one as his master directed. Chatham sent him out into the world on a divine mission, but Twine's preparation for that mission took time.

For some days there was no call from the Lord Commander. Twine settled back into his rhythm of office work, returning every evening to his apartment, gloomy and forsaken.

One night, Twine expected not to sleep. At best he rested for only a few hours every night. He sat at his desk by a picture window, waiting. In his reflection he noticed strands of blonde hair which had come adrift, and he ran a hand over his head to restore their order. The river shimmered under its lights. A full bottle of Bulgarian merlot stood at his elbow. His laptop whispered. He studied its screen, and comforted himself with pages of inconsequential news.

The laptop pinged with an incoming email, from inside the Government Secure Intranet. The message was only - 'Watch your back'.

"Good evening, Twine."

Twine shivered. It was Chatham's voice. Twine turned in his chair. Chatham stood in the half-light by the door wearing a grey raincoat, a finger delicately massaging his lower lip. He raised an eyebrow and said, "Aren't you going to say Hello, take a seat, have a cup of tea?"

"How...?"

"How did I get in? I see you have a triple lock here, and a mortice. It's a mad world out there. But no door can keep me out." Chatham stepped forward to the middle of the carpet, lit by the reflected glow of an uplighter.

Twine jumped to his feet. "Of course, our master," he said. "Welcome. But..."

"Thank you," Chatham said, looking around. "Interesting apartment you have. Not yet put your personal stamp on it perhaps."

"No, our master. Excuse us, but it was a surprise to... see you there."

"No doubt," said Chatham with a smile. "But a simple matter of projection." He took a further step forward and rubbed an ear. "So far, Twine, you have done well, settled in, showed your face. You deserve a reward. I shall allow you to project. You will need to, for what I have in mind. You will need to control your image, Twine."

Chatham settled himself into an armchair. He steepled his hands on his chest and gazed at Twine with a smile. "Like you," he said, "I am an image. Physically present, and vulnerable only to some sudden shock. Like you, my body lies in our Vault, safely out of the way. But, unlike you, I have control of that image. I am familiar with the instrument." Chatham patted his heart. "Look outside," he said.

Instantly Chatham's chair was empty. Twine turned his head to the window. Outside, in the shadows of the warehouses which led to the river, stood a man in a grey raincoat. He stepped forward into the light of a street-lamp, then returned to the shadows. It was Chatham. The next moment, he appeared as he had before, sitting in his chair.

Chatham tapped his heart as if to bring it back to life, his tongue flicking between his lips. "Projection," he said. "The gift of our Lord God to me. I am able to project my image from the Vault to any location in this globe. Unfortunately we do not have the energy, nor the will, to allow this for every one of our officers. We may do so when we control the Crossway. That control is our key objective."

Twine nodded. "Yes our master. Bring on the day."

"Has it been frustrating for you, Twine, that you have no control of your image?"

"No, our master. We are happy to serve as we are, in whatever role the Lord Commander thinks appropriate. We were projected to this globe, but expected no more."

"Expect it now, young Twine," Chatham said. "I have re-made you. You have the ability, but do not know how to use it. You might find it difficult at first, but practise, practise."

"Yes, our master."

"You will sleep tonight, Twine. I have arranged that with the Vault. But from now you will be able to project. I allow you to practise tonight, but hereafter you project only at my command. Do you understand?"

"We do, our master."

"Very well. Now how about that cup of tea? Black, if you don't mind."

"Yes our master." Twine stepped into his kitchen. He put a hand to his forehead. He was sweating. Suddenly his eyes itched and he rubbed them. Shaking his head, he filled the kettle, put teabags in two cups and stepped back. The only sound from his living space was the low hum of his laptop, until the kettle boiled and he made the tea.

Twine returned. The armchair was empty. Chatham had gone.

*

Twine rested on his single bed under the small square window in the cubby-hole which passed for a bedroom in his apartment. He closed his eyes, but he was too excited and sleep did not come. Every noise from outside, every squeal of brakes, every sigh of the river wind, kept him alert. He patted his heart as if to calm it. Even the beat of hoverfly wings at his window was more of a rattle than the soothing murmur he remembered from the third sea.

But there are no hoverflies here.

He lay in a coffin with a glass lid. He saw through it to the dusty ceiling of a dimly-lit cavern. Hoverflies circled above, newly born, sweeping with a mighty flap of their insect wings from side to side then swirling out of his view.

On the inside of the lid, at the level of his chest, four dials were engraved in white, to the right and the left, one forward, one back. Further down, two more dials, one up, one down, and below them - buttons, grey, black, red. He was re-made, and recognised the instrument. There was space inside the coffin to raise his arm, and he did, planting a finger on the dial to the left, moving its arrow fractionally. He pressed the grey button.

Twine lay on the carpet of his bedroom, a few feet from the bed. There was a tightness in his chest. He patted it, as if bringing his heart back to life. He closed his eyes, drew a deep breath and exhaled.

In the coffin, he restored the setting of the left-hand dial, moved the dial of the right-hand dial fractionally to the right, and the arrow of the downward dial some degrees to the left. He pressed the grey button.

Twine lay in the street, his head on the pavement. He felt the cold, and heard footsteps. A drunk passed. Twine closed his eyes, patted his heart, drew a deep breath and exhaled. In the coffin he pressed the black button.

He lay on his bed. Outside the river wind sighed and somewhere in the building a toilet flushed. Practise, practise. He practised. He tried the red button in combination with the left-hand dial, pre-programmed. Anyone who at dead of night had been walking up that hill in a Wiltshire village would have seen Twine lying under a hedge, but luckily the street was empty. He moved the arrow of the left-hand dial, and found himself lying on a street by the side of a yellow taxi in daylight. That demanded an immediate return. He tried another setting and found himself in the light of morning lying on a rock looking up at a rain-swept cliff through clouds of spray.

In the coffin he pressed the black button, and returned to his bed, where he lay gasping, too excited to sleep.

7 - The Roamer Mark

On the morning of a Friday, in his Victoria Street office, Twine received a call from the on-duty secretary of the tenth floor. We have received an invitation from a Mister Chatham of G-Range, she said, for Mister Twine to visit his company's headquarters to discuss a matter of strategic importance. Thank you.

Chatham was in a relaxed mood. "Are you comfortable with projection?" he said.

"We are, our master."

"Good. Then we shall begin. There are many Roamers in this city, Twine, in this country and in the globe. You will dispose of Roamers in this region, as many as we can find. Understood?"

"Dispose, our master?"

"Terminate them. That is a phrase your Service uses, does it not?"

"We understand, our master. But where do we find them?"

Chatham paused, but suddenly urgent he stood, pulled back his chair and stepped over to the penny-in-the-slot machine hanging on the wall by the window. He laid an index finger on the metal casting at its top corner. The glass case swung open. Chatham pushed his finger into the mouth of the grinning clown, pressed, and withdrew it. The entire board revolved, to reveal a black screen. "Stanley," he said.

On the screen appeared the head and shoulders of a young and fair-haired, bearded man in a blue t-shirt. He was sitting at a desk against the background of a white wall. "Lord Commander," he said.

"I hear New York is under several feet of snow."

"It is, Lord Commander," Stanley replied. "The whole place is at a standstill."

"How distressing. But, to business. No doubt you have heard that I have selected as my servant an officer of the security Service, Twine. You know him?"

"I do, Lord Commander. I know the name."

"Good," Chatham said. "I need you to update him. A report. The Roamers. Make it short but add a little about the Andreyevs. And I need contact details, United Kingdom only. Where do we stand on numbers, globe-wide?"

"Over a hundred thousand, Lord Commander. The report is ready."

"Send it to him, by whatever encrypted channel your Services use."

Stanley leaned forward. "Done," he said.

"Thank you Stanley. That will be all." Stanley nodded as Chatham reversed the screen to restore the image of the grinning clown, then turned and resumed his seat. "No-one knows more about these vermin than Stanley. Read the file that he has sent you. But not at your office. Then I expect action, immediate action." His hooded eyelids all-but closed, as if Chatham were on the verge of sleep. "That is all. For now."

"This poor soul shall read it, my Lord. And act. As you command."

*

That night, Twine sat by the picture window of his apartment, a pizza-box and a glass of merlot at his elbow, and read the report sent by Stanley. It was an unusual text file. After a few seconds its lines moved on of their own accord.

The Denver Anomaly

This is the Roamer Mark. This is the unique malformation of a human brain which we identified at the Crossway. We have found it in every Roamer corpse, and in every Roamer brain we have dismantled live. Now we have found it here, in this globe, a perfect match. Roamers are here.

A doctor by the name of Elizabeth P. Dennison was the first to identify it, in Denver. She worked in a prison hospital. Though on the outside her criminal patients looked normal, it was her idea that on the inside they shared a marker, a genetic flaw, which identified someone 'born criminal'. This was an old idea, rubbished on all sides, but Dennison was a Calvinist, and something in her makeup made her look for a mark of Original Sin.

What Dennison had - and her predecessors did not have - was access to imaging technology, CT and MRI scanning. She peered inside people's heads, traced the pathways in their brains, the pulsing of veins and arteries, the flash as a memory surfaces.

After a year's work, she found something. It was a trivial mutation, a kink in the wiring of the brain, one tiny misfiring vein. Easily overlooked in the human head, this vein was an oddity. It had a valve. The vein would swell, then in a burst discharge its contents. Simultaneously, the patient would show intense excitement, and speak of visionary episodes, messages from dead relatives or victims, hallucinations. By itself, that was a useful footnote in medical history, but what excited Dennison was how common this anomaly was among the population of her prison.

Was this the mark of someone 'born criminal'?

To test her theory, Dennison went looking for the anomaly in communities, regular folk. Hospitals, clinics, morgues, wherever there was information about what is in people's heads she went through the records. She hoped to find nothing, because then her findings at the prison would statistically be significant. But, she found it again and again. She estimated that around one in forty thousand people have the anomaly, and they were not all criminals.

Or were they? Dennison began to predict. If a person has this genetic anomaly, what is the chance of their developing criminal behaviour in future? After five years she declared that the chance was Very High. But she did not declare that in public, because by then her register - the Dennison List, which we use to this day - had fallen into the hands of the FBI and then the CIA.

The Roamers

Since then, the Dennison List has grown seriously long. Agencies across the globe have been looking out for anyone with that anomaly. Some of the religious among them call it the Mark of the Beast. Why? Because the people who have this anomaly are a threat. Something in them lies dormant, but flares up and all Hell breaks loose. Anti-State, violent, these creatures are scum, genetically warped, and they have to be watched. And in all their mischief, they think they are on the side of Right, because they have a kink in their brains which tells them so.

Now, we know that these freaks have a name for themselves. Roamers. Not Romans. Not R-O-M-A, not gypsies. Roamers. As soon as I heard that, I knew that we had God's enemy in this globe, and there are many thousands of them.

One of Dennison's patients was an elderly black from one of the poorer districts of the state, banged up for violence at a political demonstration. David was his name, a family man, no previous, and Dennison made a particular study of him. She removed him to a psychiatric hospital with proper beds and clean air, and he was grateful. Everyone learned a lot from David.

For a start - Roamer. That was what he called himself. According to David, Roamers are a community of like minds. A light goes on in their brains and suddenly they know what they have to do - like get violent at political demonstrations. But he was only a foot-soldier. Others were on their way, 'seniors'. According to our David, there is some intelligence behind them, some beastly structure on its way, some uniform purpose. That exercised the minds of US agencies no end.

51

So what are they, David and the other Roamers of this globe? They are only human, no doubt, but warped genetically to respond to some stimulus from outside. Some of them say it is the voice of God. But we know better. It is the voice of the Roamer hierarchy, from the Crossway.

Some time ago I compared the anomaly in David's scan with what we know from the Crossway. Identical. The anomaly is the mark of a Roamer.

This could be a bad sign, or good. It is bad that we have found an army of new Roamers in this globe. It is bad because it means that they know we are here. But it is good, because it shows that the Roamers are under pressure at the Crossway, pressure from us, and for reinforcements they have had to create new Roamers, in a globe which previously they had allowed to go its own way.

Wherever they are, we know the Roamers for what they are, God's enemy. It is they who are holding our Lord God back, standing in the way of His Will, preventing Him from entering this sea. It is our duty, across this globe, to seek them out and use them for God's purpose or destroy them like rats in a bucket. That is our rule, the rule of the Lord Commander and through him the rule of God Himself. Use or destroy. If a Roamer cannot be turned, cannot be made useful, then he or she shall be destroyed.

The Andreyevs

The anomaly can run in families. The most-quoted case comes from Russia, the Andreyevs. One branch of that clan produced an inordinately high number of Roamers. They were a pest, noisy and rebellious, but the Russians came up with an elegant solution. All members of that Andreyev clan were invited to a family celebration. The Russians got Chechens to bomb the place. Bang. Goodbye Andreyevs, those that were there. One of those Andreyevs, though, was not in the country. She was in England, where she had a child by a father who does not interest us.

I heard some time ago that the mother and child have been separated. The mother has been returned to Russia thanks to excellent work by the servant of the Lord Commander. There, we expect she has died. The child remains in England. That child, a girl, is one we have to watch.

God is with us. Bring on the day.'

Twine rubbed his head. Not once in his time in the security Service had he heard of this Dennison List, the catalogue of Roamers. And in the attachments to Stanley's report came a list, a sub-set of the Dennison List, UK only. They were everywhere. He was surrounded by enemies. But his work had been 'excellent'. A mixture of pride and fear rumbled inside him.

At the top of the list was the name Usher. To Twine he sounded like a drunk - hit his head in a pub, taken to hospital, scanned. Lo and behold, the Roamer mark, the anomaly, picked up by Stanley from the hospital's records. His contact details, though, included a warning - 'NB safe house UKSS'. Usher lived in a safe house operated by Twine's own Service, MI5.

Twine marked him as his first target.

Sean Abel Usher. The name rang no bells. Twine pummelled at his laptop, and built a dossier on this man Usher from the files of his Service. It appeared that he was a casualty of the Irish drama. Nearly seventy years old, formerly an agent of the RUC, connections with the INLA, involved in the Airey Neave affair 1979, lifted from Belfast 1982 and dropped in a safe house on the south coast. On a stipend of hardly anything, medical problems due to alcohol. Usher was a spy, a plant inside the INLA, with a good many Irish after his blood.

This was awkward. Twine's two worlds were in danger of collision. But the plan he concocted by daybreak made him smile. He would get the Irish to do his job for him.

*

53

Late in the afternoon of a grey February day, Twine set off in a hired Volkswagen to the south side of the Thames east of Greenwich and the pub, the Griefer's Head, which was his master's out-of-City rendezvous. He made his way into the main bar, where Max the barmaid stood alone idly polishing glasses. With a twist of her head she pointed him towards a back room where a cold breeze whistled through cracks in window-panes but failed to dispel the odour of the toilets. Under a window, on the other side of a pock-marked wooden table, his contact sat facing him.

In the car, Twine had thought himself into the role he had to play, and he sat in the opposite chair and smiled. "Mister Jolly? Lovely weather it is not," he said.

"Correct. It will be better tomorrow. And you're Mister Jason," the man replied. He was a small, dark and thin-faced Irishman in a black overcoat. He was old, he had a purple scar at one side of his throat, and every time after he spoke he flared his nostrils.

"Correct," said Twine. "Are we ready?"

"Give me the fecking gun, man," said the man who called himself Jolly. "I'm not going to drop this fellow putting a finger to his head and saying Bang."

"It's in the car," Twine replied. His role was that of the Disgruntled Employee, selling the secrets of his Service for cash, selling a man called Usher to those in Belfast eager to pay for their revenge.

"Well the fecking money's in my pocket," the Irishman said, "and that's where the gun will be in one minute or I'm back on the train."

"Then we had better get on with it," said Twine.

Not only had this cheap-jack assassin insisted on Twine supplying the weapon, he also demanded transport, to and from. Twine had no idea which sect of the IRA Jolly represented, or if he was IRA at all. There had been a queue in Belfast of those wanting to dispose of Usher, and Jolly bargained his way to the front of it. Twine was also concerned about the fumes of whisky that flowed around this monkey.

Outside in the car, Twine took from the glove compartment a wrap of black leather and passed it to his passenger, who said only "Go on then," and waited till they were clear of the derelict buildings which surrounded the pub before unwrapping his prize. "What the feck is this?" said Jolly, brandishing the pistol as they cruised down a crowded High Street.

"A Welrod," Twine replied. "And it might be a good idea if you kept it out of sight."

"A what? It's fecking long."

"Built-in silencer," said Twine. "Nine millimetre. Bolt-action. No markings. Quiet, very reliable. Not used one before? Thought you guys got your hands on all our stuff. Ammunition's in the box."

"Less of your fecking lip. Take me somewhere I can have a go."

This meant a detour, but Twine knew the fields around Chertsey so headed for one. What he had not expected was the number of stops Jolly wanted on the way. Two at a pub - 'Need a leak, pull over' - and one at an off licence - 'Got to make a phone call'.

When they got to the wooded track where Twine used to have his lunch, it was nearly dark and the Irishman was wobbling. In the trees he could barely stand. His shot towards a particularly wide poplar zinged off into bushes, but he declared himself satisfied. "Top hole, old bean," he said. "We must do this more often, don't you know."

Gradually as Twine drove south, the Irishman fell apart. Past Horsham, he plugged in a CD of Irish ballads and started singing. At Steyning he was asleep, with the pistol on his lap, and Twine turned off the CD with relief. When Twine parked the Volkswagen off the A27 at the end of Jenkins Road, the Irishman was flat out and snoring. "For God's sake," said Twine, poking him in the ribs and getting only a grunt in reply. "Wake up you stupid, stupid bastard." Nothing, dead to the world. Twine was on his own, on a cold night, in a car which was not his, in a side road which stretched ahead into a vale of shadows, with an assassin who was too drunk to hit an elephant with a tennis racket.

He would have to do it himself. He owed it to the Lord Commander, for his trust. He owed it to himself, and as he forced open the back door of the target's cottage - an old brass lock that gave way with barely a touch from his screwdriver - he fingered the pistol in his pocket as if it were a part of his master, directed by his divine will.

Moonlight fell onto the boards of the floor. He removed the bulb from the brass light-fitting by the front door. Apart from a glow from the embers in the fireplace there was no other light. In an alcove he parked himself behind the door, took the glove off his right hand and stuffed it in his pocket, pulled the pistol from the inside pocket of his coat, clicked off the safety and held the gun up, its barrel poking out from just under his chin.

He went into a holding pattern but did not wait long.

8 - The Black-haired Boy

It was typical of God's humour that Sean Abel Usher, gentleman of Ireland, had no talent for the job in which he had been a success. He drank too much. He talked too much, and he was conspicuous. He had few of the qualities of a spy.

There were many in Belfast who would call Usher a traitor to the Irish nation: a Catholic, but a British stooge, what was he thinking of? Those he betrayed were astonished to find Usher pointing the finger at them. *"Usher? But he's a drummer in a showband, a Belfast corner-boy. Are the British so desperate they employ drummers?"* His victims - those who lost their liberty or their loved ones - could not care less about the murder of his friends, or the poverty from which he dragged himself by taking cash for information. If they heard that he lived in England under the protection of Her Majesty's Government, they might consider a trip across the water to make their protest privately, and with a hand-gun.

His victims, though, might be comforted to know that Usher lived in a haze of whiskey and nicotine which day by day was wearing him down. Regret was his constant companion, just as now, on a bitter night in February, he stepped out of the Hotspur public house in the melancholic mood of the continually drunk.

A dark stick of a man, wrapped in a close-fitting overcoat and with his scarf tight around his neck, he confronted a scene of mist and shadows with the stare of one who should not have had that last whiskey, poor stuff though it was and no better than a glass of Oxo with a few herbs thrown in. But, snapping himself upright he remembered that it was only his two legs that would get him home so he had better be sure where they were.

He set off. Between the puddles of the car park his stride was unsteady, arms flapping as he hopped across the mud of a grassy verge onto the pavement. The road puzzled him for a moment, but he let himself go downhill until he came to a corner where he paused, shook his head, and took in a deep and calming breath. A truck with lights of fire came over the ridge heading south towards the coast. As it clattered past he gave out a defiant "Ha!" at its rear end, which dimmed and vanished into what was fast becoming a fog, nothing as sweet as the fogs of his native Donegal but a harsh salt-tasting murk lit by the glow of streetlights under an ailing moon.

This was a bad night to be outside. It was a bad night to be alone. Usher stooped as tall men do, but his overcoat was thin and threadbare, his sneakers lightweight, and he felt the cold seeping into him, pinching his nose and stealing his breath. For a man of seventy he could still put on a show for the ladies, but decades in the bars of Belfast had left him with a bladder unreliable in the cold. Caught short, he unzipped and relieved himself in a bush.

How contradictory it all was, and how worthy of a drink. As he zipped himself up he reflected on the steaming bush whose shape in the shadows was the head of the Queen. That deserved a salute, which he cut short as he heard other revellers leaving the pub. He coughed and shivered as they passed and pretended to admire the moon. Hunched-up, he drew from his overcoat pocket a brass tin, fetching out a book of matches and the dog-end of a cigarette which he lit, and exhaled a plume of smoke which drifted over the road whiter than the mist and then just as grey as the match expired and fizzed into the gutter. He turned, crunching over leaves blown from the woods, down into a wet asphalted lane, a tube of shadows which went by the name of Jenkins Road.

Whoever Jenkins was, he must have been a penny-pinching sod to have given his name to this gloomy lane with no discernible end. Call it the wearing-off of whiskey, but Usher was overcome by foreboding as he let his feet carry him down into the tunnel made by silhouettes of trees. He had not seen it by day. You never knew who might be passing, someone who came from the old days to make a bloody example of Usher the grass, the traitor who stood up in a British court and pointed a finger at his friends, declared them criminals and went off with the Queen's money in his pocket and a safe house to live in.

Not once had he felt safe. One moment he had been your man for a grenade or a rifle, a quartermaster of the INLA, passing through the shadows of Belfast as softly as the breeze over a Connemara bog. But say nothing of the IRA for then, whiskey or not, there might be blows and repercussions, and maybe a cause to call the undertaker. Next time you see Usher, the Judas, he's pointing the finger and you're away to prison, the Maze. Of the men and women Usher sold to the British some still lived, and still had the rifles he gave them. One could be pointing at him right now.

I was stopped by a soldier he said "you are a swine"

He hit me with his rifle and he kicked me in the groin

I bowed and I scraped, sure my manners were polite

Ah, but all the time I was thinking of me little Armalite.

Ahead, the narrow lane was lit only by moonlight. Bushes were banks of shadow, above them the dark arms of trees casting off leaves that flittered around his feet. As Usher walked, he tried to remember a favourable tune but they were all laments, the shadows every so often merging into deep pools of inky black. He puffed on the roll-up for comfort so that its sparks gave him the illusion of sight, but there was twilight only in the drifting mist, and sound only in his footsteps and in the rumble of a car engine.

He stopped and turned. Up by the road a car had parked, on the curve half-hidden by trees. Through the mist he saw only one of its headlights, which flicked off. In Derry he'd call a cab if he was going to a funeral. The rumbling stopped. Now it was only his footsteps, as he quickened his pace downhill, with the familiar and ridiculous feeling of being followed. But something in his past surfaced, that when you are followed, when you are driven, it is what is in front of you that you have to fear.

Usher was breathing hard and it was noisy. He switched from nose to mouth but it was worse, sounding like panic, with still a quarter-mile of wet road to go. It was the usual paranoia. He stopped and looked around. He waited. He listened. He waited. No-one. He flicked the cigarette into a bush and set off again.

In South Armagh there was a man who had a long ranged gun

He said "I'll show them army boys there's nowhere they can run"

He was the South Armagh sniper

He'd pick a spot and wait the whole day through

Until a Brit patrol came into view

The Armagh sniper he never missed his mark

He was lethal in the daytime and deadly in the dark

From his left came a crash in the woods, a branch falling. Usher paused and turned his head. For some minutes he stood still and calmed his breathing, listening and trying to control his heart. Then out from the undergrowth an animal darted across the road, a flash of moonlight on wet fur, a fox or a ginger cat. In this darkness he could not be sure. He shoved his hands into his overcoat pockets, took a deep breath and walked on.

At the bottom of the hill he came to a dusty track leading into the woods. All was still, and quiet. Even at this time of night there should be birds, there should be rustling in the undergrowth, but there was none, as if every sound had fallen into some vortex and been sucked away. Usher walked on a few yards, conscious of his footsteps even in dust, and unlatched a metal gate that swung back creaking on its hinges. He fastened it behind him and set off on a dirt path that led to the silhouette of a low building, his cottage, hidden in the trees.

The woods were full of eyes. Whether they were gaps between branches, droplets of the day's rain, or the watery eyes of assassins or Satan himself, they were too many and no time to count. He fumbled for the key. A light over the door would be good, to see the lock so he wouldn't scratch around, wasting seconds on the doorstep. A light over the door would be bad, for he would make a better target. There was no light over the door.

The rustle of footsteps in dust. A key in the lock.

60

The key turned, he opened the door and walked in.

The door opens. Tall man.

Usher flicked the light switch. Nothing. Light came only from moonlight onto bare boards through the front-room window and from the embers of the coal fire in a far corner. No power, again. He would have to fire up the generator, again. This was home, with its familiar aromas of coffee and tobacco, but with an unfamiliar scent of something else, a perfume.

Quick, grab the shoulder, back of the neck, trigger squeeze don't jerk.

A hand grasped his shoulder. Someone behind the door, so fast. A pistol. The nose of a heavy pistol at the back of his head, a click and a silenced cough then a blast of yellow fire, a screech of angels, no pain as in his last seconds Usher watched bones of his skull flooding towards the floor.

Recoil, don't drop it. Sounded like the bark of a distant dog. How he falls, folding, brains a fountain.

As the boards came up to meet his face all he could smell was dust and his own blood as Usher, traitor to the Irish nation, fell into splinters through the dark.

How he lies, a pool around his head, a miniature tide. Must be quick. Must move his feet from the door. Drag him in, smearing must not step in it. Where did the bullet go? I don't see it. He's finished. No mistake.

Twine took a life, professionally. Usher was a corpse on the floor. To have one Roamer less. He breathed deeply. It was easy. He enjoyed it. He wanted to do it again. But the gun was hot, and it left a scar inside the palm of his hand.

9 - To the River Hall

Twine did it again. And again, many times.

The Welrod was only the souvenir of a Service operation to bang up a Yardie gun-runner, not his weapon of choice. Twine had picked it up, with ammunition, and somehow he had neglected to take it to the Service store. He regarded it as his. In a globe where guns were all too common, to him it seemed impertinent not to have one.

But he was a bowman. To him, a gun was a lifeless thing. A crossbow and its arrows, they had life, and death. He was a bowman, but for now without a bow. What he had, was a rack of crossbow bolts, and that was what he used across the country to terminate those on the Dennison List, Roamers.

They were of all sorts - a shop-keeper in Wakefield, a teacher in Dumfries, numerous targets around London. He varied his angle of attack. Some he killed with a stab to the neck, some to the heart. Most he would finish with a knife, to make the gash of the arrow-tip less obvious. He never spoke, always hid his face, and dressed differently for every occasion, sometimes in jackets with a logo which would make him look on CCTV like just another hoodlum robber.

This did not fool everyone. In Scotland, Police urgently sought the 'Crossbow Assassin'. In London they called him 'Jack the Spiker'. Somehow, over a period of nearly ten years, Police north and south failed to compare notes.

Even if they had, there was no danger to Twine. For every occasion he had an alibi. Now that he had the ability to project, it was the matter of a moment to appear anywhere, back in his office or some other place with witnesses. No-one can be in two places at once.

*

Nonetheless, his absences from the security Service had been noticed, and Twine was summoned before a tribunal to explain himself. The two men and a woman who faced him across a polished table in a first-floor office near the Palace of Westminster were Chatham's people. He recognised them from the Lord Commander's night-time events. The result was an agreement that Twine had longstanding (but undefined) health issues, and that his working week would be reduced to three days. In the rest of the week he came to know more of the company of which his Lord Commander was Chairman, G-Range.

This company had thrust its tentacles into every area of business. Technology, financial services, property and pharmaceuticals led the way, particularly the last, with a product which Twine heard Chatham call 'Spice'. At the meetings across the City where Twine acted as secretary, when this matter was discussed, he and any of Chatham's squirrels in attendance were required to leave. They were replaced by heavy-jawed Slavic gentlemen in black suits who strode in as a team and strode out silently, eyes front.

This was a mystery, and Twine usually would be untroubled, but this was an affront - to be associated with squirrels, human low-life, and ejected.

*

On the morning of a Friday, Twine received a call from the on-duty secretary of the tenth floor. We have received an invitation from Mister Chatham of G-Range, she said, for Mister Twine to visit his company's headquarters to discuss a matter of strategic importance. Thank you.

Chatham stood by the window, his back turned, gazing out over the roofs of the neighbouring office-blocks. "Sit," he said. The long-jawed woman in the Modigliani print looked at Twine with an expression of gloom.

"There is a place," said Chatham, "that you do not know." He turned. "You do not know, Twine, because if its existence came to the attention of the authorities - such as the authority in which you are placed - our mission would be compromised." He sat at his table and looked sternly at Twine. "No doubt you would not reveal the existence of this place deliberately, but until now I could not take the risk of an accident. However, the time has come, Twine. I shall take you to it tomorrow."

Twine nodded. "We thank you, our master, for your confidence," he said.

"It is the one place," Chatham went on, "large enough to hold all of our people in this city at once. It is known as the River Hall. I have sent out invitations, and tomorrow we will gather, there. I shall make a speech, an important speech, and I want you with me. I shall be announcing a change of direction, a new strategy, and I want our people to see that it has your support."

"This is very exciting news, our master."

"We will have our little show tomorrow morning, eight o'clock. Do you know the Battersea Barge? Off Nine Elms Lane. There is a pier to the west of it. Meet me at seven-thirty sharp at the steps. Oh, and dress down. You might get wet."

*

The morning was bright but the breeze off the river brisk, as Twine tramped through river-side South London from Vauxhall, ahead of him the chimneys of Battersea Power Station. Early as it was, he was hot in the sun for he was dressed for winter, in a knee-length black raincoat and waterproof brown boots. He felt drops of sweat on his forehead even as he clung to the shadows. Half-way to the power station he turned right into a rubbish-strewn street lined with cars then into a dogleg alley which took him to the river, and a pier that stretched sideways along the shore. Barges were moored on either side, and the wake of river-boats sloshed around its columns

64

that disappeared into the murky water. Seagulls mewed above, whirling in a breeze that smelled of diesel.

Chatham stood by the steps of the pier, in a one-piece grey diving suit and black boots. He was speaking into a mobile phone, which he closed and dropped into a bag dangling over his shoulder. "Good morning, Twine," he said. "Are we ready?"

"Yes our master."

"Very well. We shall approach the venue by boat. Clears my mind. Follow..."

Twine followed Chatham up the steps then down a gangplank of uneven slats to a platform where a small wooden boat was moored. Alongside the sturdy barges of the Thames the boat looked fragile, its thwarts already wet. It had no oars, but an outboard motor. "Boats, Twine. I have a fondness for boats," said Chatham with a smile. "Take the bow seat."

Twine stepped down into the rocking boat and sat on the bow thwart as Chatham took the stern, dropped his bag between them, then turned and fired up the motor which whined, emitted a haze of black smoke and settled into a more comforting gurgle. He cast off, increased the motor's tempo, and steered the boat away from the barges, turning it east and out into the main channel. As they approached Vauxhall Bridge he said, "Happy?" Twine nodded. They sat very close, Chatham's eyes searching the water. Twine could not remember a time when he had been happier.

Chatham steered towards the rightmost of the bridge's yellow-painted arches. Overhead, the girders of the bridge passed by, reflecting the chugging of the motor. When they emerged, Chatham steered through an oily patch of water towards a pink arch of Lambeth Bridge. He frowned. People, students, were hanging out over it, dropping leaflets into the water. "I expect there's a Roamer up there," he said. "Scum."

Twine turned. Ahead lay Lambeth Palace on the south bank and to the north the Houses of Parliament, curiously beige in the early morning sun. "Need to be quiet here," said Chatham. "Eyes everywhere, including some of mine, and yours." They passed below Westminster Bridge in the main channel, as he scanned the water ahead. "Myths and legends, Twine," he said. "We ourselves, what are we? Spooks, actors. Impostors and frauds." Chatham waved a hand at the entire city. "Hundreds of people in this city only appear to exist. Images, projections. A remarkable thought, that they are gathering as we speak, our audience."

His brow furrowed. "Now, time for speed," he said, and he powered up the motor. The boat's wake spread out in waves as he threaded it through moored barges and the arches of the bridges. Twine felt unsteady and laid a hand on the boat's side for support. The breeze off the river was turning to a wind and banks of cloud loomed above the towers of the City, dark cloud, anvil-shaped thunder cloud. They called him the Gargoyle, and now Chatham had never looked more like one. Any trace of companionship had wafted away on the wind. He had a face of stone, hooded eyes that peered into Twine's soul.

"Remember, Twine," Chatham said, "those years ago when I killed Henry Chatham, how happy he was to see me. Isn't that fun? Sometimes I wonder if the Roamers would bring him back. But I suspect that their procedure for resurrection - like ours - is unpleasant." The boat rocked in the wake of a riverboat. Chatham appeared to move from side to side, lizard-like, snake-like. Nothing was fixed and anything was possible. He steered out into the main channel. As the boat puttered under Southwark Bridge he said, "But now we have news for our people, resurrected or not. A new beginning. The mission for which we were sent here. Finally."

He increased speed and turned the boat, following the bend of the river. Without a word, but with Twine's mind churning like the motor, they passed under London Bridge, then past HMS Belfast and under Tower Bridge, until the river turned north where Chatham decreased speed and said, "Here".

He slowed the boat to less than walking pace and steered to a wall of black and weed-spotted stone which supported the south bank. Above it, twin apartment blocks rose against a sky now grey with rain-cloud. Turning off the motor he guided the boat sideways against the wall, pulling it along with his hands through the flotsam of the wash until he came to a square stone at shoulder-height. He placed a hand flat on the stone, which swung back taking a section of the wall with it. The boat lurched forwards, sucked through the wall as Twine fell forward and grasped the boat's side, the wall closing behind them.

As thunder rumbled through the walls, Twine lifted his head. Over a channel of dark water the boat edged forward into a gloomy hall. Beneath a roof of stone the walls were stained with grime and on either side concrete platforms stretched for a dozen yards. On each of them stood two glass cloche bell-jars, metres high, lit in yellow from below. It was a wax-works. In each jar stood a fully-clothed figure, frozen in the attitude of a tailor's dummy. On the left platform stood Max the barmaid of the Griefer's Head, next to her a figure of Chatham himself in his dark-grey suit. On the right platform stood a tattooed bully-boy and a Police officer.

"Welcome, Twine," said Chatham, languorously waving a hand. "These are my images." He smiled, and moored the boat at the end of the hall. "Come. Our people are waiting for us."

Together they stepped from the boat. The wall before them appeared to be of solid concrete until Chatham laid his hand on it and an elliptical door opened. They passed into a tunnel, pit-props supporting a ceiling and walls of dried mud, the floor of pebbles and sandstone blocks.

"Disposition of the enemy," Chatham said.

Along the tunnel a male voice echoed, "Globe-wide and random, my Lord. Approaching two hundred thousand."

The path led upwards, with torches at either side behind silhouettes of mountains and of grotesque human heads, shadows leaping across what was now a tube which ended in a wall of steel, a wooden trunk to one side, its lid covered in dust.

"Assets," said Chatham.

"Two in the body," the voice echoed, "the first transfers. The rest, my Lord, are images, thirty-two hundred. Second Wing but with one hundred from the First. Disposition globe-wide, but targeted."

"Opportunities."

"You are our opportunity, my Lord. And your servant Twine."

At the wall, without a word Chatham took from the trunk a simple grey robe which he slipped over his head. From his bag he took the chain of the Lord Commander, and dropped the bag to the floor. He arranged the chain around his neck and laid his hand on the wall, which parted as if it were the door of an elevator.

They passed through into an apartment-block, which was no more than a shell. Without ceilings to divide them into storeys, walls rose high to a roof of pitched wood and all windows were blacked-out. Their feet rapped on flagstones as they advanced towards an aisle which ran between ranks of dark-wood pews, where men and women knelt in an attitude of prayer, heads bowed, hands clasped before them. There were many dozens of them, some looking as if they had just walked in off the street, others more formal as if they had stayed up all night after one of Chatham's gatherings, all of them quiet, expectant.

As Chatham approached the aisle, the unseen voice called out, "Welcome our Lord Commander! Bring on the day!" On either side the call was taken up by the congregation, together with a low humming, penetrated sporadically by the slap of hands on a pew. Chatham and Twine paced along the aisle, looking directly ahead to a dais of lighter, polished wood.

Behind the dais a statue stood in a niche, as tall as a man and buried in shadow. When they reached the dais, Chatham turned to Twine and said, "You will kneel." Twine knelt and bowed his head.

Chatham turned and spread out his arms. Light grew from the floor around the statue. Its figure was grey, and from its right hand the index finger pointed upwards. The face smiled, not a friendly smile, not a winning smile, but a smile which had the authority of a prince.

It was a statue of himself.

10 - The Address of the Lord Commander

Paper of The Ordinal (1)

Intercept for the information of Council

Author: The Ordinal

We have had this location under surveillance for many solar cycles. This event is unusual, for it sets out a new aggressive strategy. It appears that their Lord Commander is ready at last to begin the mission for which he was sent from the Gate. It also introduces Twine, whom their Lord Commander selected to be his servant. No doubt he chose so insignificant a figure only to enhance his own significance.

The name taken in this globe by their Lord Commander is Chatham. Hereafter I shall not dignify him by his rank but shall use the name he himself chose, which in the manner typical of him he stole from a glober he murdered.

A transcript of the session follows. Note that the grangels use the same term - 'sea' - as do we, for what the globers call a 'universe'. The 'Crossway' is our 'Gate'. All references to 'God' are to the Grey Angel, and not to the Presence of the Greater Sea.

*

My comrades

You know me as Lord Commander of the First Wing. All other commanders are subordinate to me.

Long ago, I came to this globe and I travelled far. I led armies which gave this place a new experience of war. But, I was needed for our assault on the fourth sea, and I was recalled to our Lord God.

Some time ago, I returned. In accordance with God's Will, I am projected here and my image stands before you. My body lies in the Vault, as do yours. This is not without risk, and my safety cannot be guaranteed. I am the living testament to God's Will to return this sea to its fundamental parts, to dust. In our success may lie my own destruction, and I welcome that.

As one, the congregation bowed. There is some mechanism in these creatures which - as a concerted action, bee-like - applauds destruction of the individual for the sake of the hive.

Of the fifteen inner seas, this is the sixth and is our God's target. Once, this was God's domain. It was a simple place, a place of worship. There was only dust, and rock, and those few of us guided only by God's logic stood before him face to face. The beauty and power of our God filled us. Our worship would be, as we thought, eternal.

Not so. The Roamers came upon us. Those homeless brigands swept through the Crossway and destroyed our perfect peace. Why? Was the Presence of the Greater Sea jealous? Were the Roamers despatched to send us into the aeons of wandering from which they were, for the moment, spared? We believe so.

Our lives became sour. We were consumed by the need for revenge. In every sea where we made landfall we found others of the same spirit. We learned of resurrection. Our God spoke. We gathered an army of the dispossessed. Where there had been death through the injustice of the Presence, we resurrected. Where there were Roamers, we drove them out. One by one the seas of the web fell to us. Our campaigns began in extreme complexity, over swathes of ever-changing space. Multiple worlds came before us, and all were overcome. We took from them what we need and left them without form. God was with us.

71

Now, in this most precious sea, our challenge is simple. Only one globe is defended. But those of you who have fought at the Crossway will know that we face determined opposition. At the very beginning, the destruction of God's Minister is evidence of that.

But now I declare a change of strategy. Why? It is clear to me and to God himself that our progress is slow. Yes, we have built an edifice of what passes for power in this place. Yes, we have acquired money, property, and access to the secrets of this globe. It is no accident that I and others have positioned ourselves in organisations of influence, where money and information are exchanged. To some, that may appear to be success.

It is not success. So far, our mission is a failure. Let us remind ourselves what that mission is.

Our Lord God waits at the Crossway. He cannot enter this sea until we have prepared his way. But, before him lies an intolerable stalemate. The Roamers advance. We throw them back. We advance, and the Roamers throw us back with their lightning and their mines. To and fro, to and fro, nothing is gained.

What has our strategy been? To use this globe as a diversion. To make so great a nuisance of ourselves here that the Roamers must act despite the risk. To draw them down into this globe, and so leave the Crossway less well defended.

How successful has that strategy been? Not at all. Through a simple genetic mutation the abomination who calls herself Mysul has created legions of new Roamers in this globe, to make it unnecessary to reduce the defence of the Crossway. Particularly, we have not made ourselves enough of a nuisance to attract those Roamers who are counted as senior, and destroy them or use them for God's purpose. That is failure.

Among their seniors, I must mention their Navigator. Yes, we have overcome their Navigator in the past, but at the cost of our own Minister, a loss equal to both sides. As God's Minister was the channel of his power into this sea, so was their Navigator the right-hand of Mysul, a key-holder and commander of channels, to whom nothing was hidden. But at this moment we know only of inferior Roamers barely worth turning. Certainly we have captured no Navigator. That is failure.

And what has been the focus of our attempts to entice Roamers into this globe? With what did this strategy expect to draw down their seniors into our trap?

Comrades, look at yourselves. You are warriors. You and I, we have seen service to our Lord God which brought us honour. Where is the honour in the money of this globe? Where is the honour in the destruction of this globe's memory?

For that was our strategy. Spice. Feed the globers spice. Destroy the memories of this globe's inhabitants, with spice. Feed them spice and watch them dement, stop their dreams, make it so that at their lives' end they have no memory. Memory is the Roamers' currency, the reason their Tower exists, the reason they exist. Destroy it at source and their Tower is fed by nothing. Then the Roamers must act, must be drawn down, to preserve the memory of the sea which they presume to call theirs. Spice, which destroys memory, was at the core of our strategy.

We have long been aware of our enemy's efforts in the development of pharmaceutical products. We also recognise with dismay that there has been violence from these grangels, these servants of the Grey Angel - murders, and the imprisonment of those we have chosen in the globe - but this is the first indication of the power and purpose of what they call Spice.

But what honour is there in that? Some of us have become rich with the globers' money, through selling our first generations of spice. Some of us have enjoyed the fruits of this globe as if they were globers themselves. I tell you now, there is no honour in that. Yes, the spice has value, and I shall not stop its production, but it is not enough.

I come as a warrior, under the command of our Lord God. Our failed strategy was passive, inviting the Roamers into a trap which was never sprung, but our new strategy is aggressive. Yes, one by one we shall seek out the Roamers of this globe, and destroy or use them where we can. Yes, we shall continue the search for their seniors, for they bring with them the keys to the Crossway.

But now this is war, total war. So rise up, and let the storm break loose!

Much cheering and rapping on seats. Loud shouts in that infernal mixture of tweeting and grunts which they call a language.

You are an army of the dispossessed. Nothing, no-one shall prevail against you. That is the Will of our Lord God. Our mission here is simple, to use or destroy. Use, or destroy.

We shall restore God's Minister, His most powerful weapon. Already we have discovered fragments of that weapon, in this globe, where the Minister fell when this sea was reformed. My secretary Saida is leading in that task.

It was our understanding that the Minister was destroyed when we Five came across. Not only (as we thought) did our Navigator fight that creature to the point of mutual destruction, it is difficult to see how either could have survived the pressures of a new, inflating sea. This statement, however, casts doubt on that understanding.

We shall open a new route into the Crossway. This is our most difficult task, but - when we succeed - the Roamers shall be caught between two arcs of fire. That task is underway, and I shall be leading on it.

As your General Administrator, I can assure you that every potential back door is closed.

And now it is time for us all to take on our new strategy. Its details will become clear to you all in due course. Firstly, I call upon all those of the Centre and Second Wings to return to the Crossway. You return with credit. Return now.

Most of the audience rose. Across the hall, for a second each reverted to its original form. From their squares, we see the cockroach insects, rearing on jagged legs, feelers waving, and the humanoid troops of the Black Army. We see the corpse-riders of their Wings. We do not see their spikers, which are capable only of limited independent thought and action. All vanished, leaving barely more than a dozen individuals, Chatham himself and his servant Twine.

We of the First Wing are the elite forces of our Lord God. With the other commanders we shall pursue our new, aggressive strategy across the globe and to the Crossway. I will now return this hall to its usual condition. Then I will outline our first step.

Chatham raised his arms and an orange light shone from his hands. Our Servator will recognise the effect. From above came a rattling and a clank, then another, as the ceilings and floors of the building returned to their positions. The lowest floor spread over the hall, sealing off Chatham and his confederates. Unfortunately our recorder was on the wall of the floor above, for otherwise it would have been conspicuous. We have no further record of this event.

11 - Englishmen in New York

Late at night, taking a route through Queens towards midtown, the black Mercedes limo sped from JFK airport into the centre of Manhattan within thirty minutes. It drew up in front of a block of apartments on East 48th Street, and its passengers climbed out. The driver unloaded two small bags, and the passengers walked under a green canopy into the apartment block.

"Wait here," said Chatham to Twine in the lobby. "Bring up the bags in five minutes." Twine nodded.

Chatham entered the elevator which took him to the top floor. Twine waited. Everywhere was the rumble of life, with a scent of roses overlaying the aroma of pizza from next door. Yellow cabs passed under the street-lights. The art-deco clock in the lobby had an infuriating tick, and the aircon was so breezy that Twine expected the pot-plants below it to be swaying, plastic though they were.

At the appointed time he summoned the elevator and - clutching the bags and frowning from the crackle of muzak - rose smoothly to the top floor. The doors parted and before him stood a young, thin-faced and bearded man whom he recognised as Stanley, regional commander for North America.

"Let me take those," said Stanley, pulling up the sleeves of his patchwork shirt. He grinned, took the bags and dropped them on the carpet by the door of a bedroom. "We're this way…"

"Good to meet you at last," Stanley said as they walked along the corridor.

"Very kind. Mutual."

"How was the flight?"

"We believe our master enjoyed the experience."

"Yeah. Probably the first time he's had to. From what I'm hearing I guess you're third sea?"

"We are. My poor soul and I."

"And you can't project, I guess."

"We can. We chose not to. This must appear to be a business trip."

They passed the open door of a room which contained only mannequins, plastic flesh in awkward poses. Most wore hats, trilbies and fedoras, but nothing else. At the end of the corridor, Stanley tapped in a code for the door and it swung open. They entered. Gazing out towards the lights of 48th Street, Chatham sat in an armchair whose purple plush was that of a throne. There was only one other armchair, which Stanley took, leaving Twine to stand by the door. The room was small, thickly carpeted and with modernist prints on walls which in daylight would be white.

"I like your new apartment, Stanley," Chatham said. "Are we safe?"

"Snooper-proof, Lord Commander. I got better protection here than Langley. But I sweep it every day."

Twine was conscious that in this room - as in so many around them across Manhattan - work was underway, new and thrilling enterprises planned, money changing hands under lights that burned all night, and that excitement made his eyes shine.

Chatham relaxed. "So, to the purpose of my visit, Stanley," he said. "We have something to show you. Twine, the photograph."

From his jacket Twine produced a small oval of golden metal, which he handed to Stanley with the reverence of a footman. To Twine it was a precious thing, for when he had found it among Usher's possessions his master had been so pleased that he had grasped his hand and called him a wonder.

Twine stepped back. He knew every detail of this object. It was a small, oval gilt frame, a cameo, and in it a black-and-white photograph, faded with age. At the bottom, embossed, was the logo of a photographic studio in Dublin, and at the top a title written in black ink, *From the Lady*. Its subject was a boy, on a stage, a curtain behind, and he stood by a potted palm with his hands clasped in front of him, facing the camera with a shy smile. His hair was a dark mop, his face very white. He was dressed in a black school uniform, white shirt, black tie, black socks that reached his knees, and shoes with a shine.

"What do you think?" Chatham said.

"I think," said Stanley, "it's a key."

"That was my impression," said Chatham. "I'd like you to confirm that."

"It's not the usual form," said Stanley, rising from his seat. "Should be a coin, or a medal. But we've seen something like this before." He strolled to the largest of the modernist prints - a wall-high square of randomly coloured squiggles - and laid a hand on it. Its surface shifted into a screen with a portrait of Stanley himself. "Keys of sea Four," he said.

On the screen appeared a picture divided into rectangles, in each the image of a round object, most of a plain colour, black or gold, some with a lightning-flash of silver. "B Two," Stanley said, and the screen zoomed to one of the images - a small oval frame of black metal, embossed with a design of stars around its edge. Its picture was of a parrot which had around its head a hand-written scrawl. "There," said Stanley. "From the Lady."

"Mysul," Chatham said.

"Typical of her," Stanley agreed. "Channels and keys. And this looks like a form of words she uses for - you tell me."

"Seniors," Chatham went on. "We know her Ordinal, her Cardinal, the Servator, and her Navigator. There may be others. Everywhere the Roamers go, through all the seas we've chased them from, their pattern is the same. You'd think by now she would have learned."

"My Lord, I don't believe that a Great Power will ever learn, as such." Stanley returned the screen to its picture of himself. He turned the photograph in his fingers, and stepped over to a desk in a corner of the room, where he switched on a banker's lamp and laid the photograph on the desk's surface. On the wall appeared a jumble of black numbers which scrolled down, stopping with words in capital letters alone on a line. "Material of sea One," Stanley said. "It doesn't belong here, that's for sure. Let's look at the code." Numbers scrolled further until the picture shifted to a network of black lines, which to Twine resembled the map of the London Underground. "It's a key, no question," Stanley said. "But it's incomplete. Look."

Chatham rose from his seat and peered over Stanley's shoulder.

"Half the code's missing," said Stanley. "It's tied to an identity. Single user. But it's one-way transfer. I guess you could use it to take whatever from the Crossway, but not take anything in. It's not the key to a back door."

Chatham ran a bony hand over the shine of his bald head and snorted. "That," he grunted, "is... disappointing."

"And..." Stanley went on, "you couldn't use it anyway, because it's tied to that single user. Looks to me like he or she was on the way to being a senior, but didn't make it. If you need to use it, then either you get whoever it is onside, or it has to be over-ridden, and for that you'd need a genuine Roamer senior. Have you got one? Where did you get this?"

Chatham returned to his seat, breathed deeply and sat. He steepled his hands on his chest and looked out over the lights of 48th Street. His expression was grim and his eyes closed. "Twine," he said, "tell Stanley."

*

The photograph came from the possessions of Sean Usher, the first Roamer terminated by Twine.

Stanley explained on that night in New York. "He stood out. Active when he was young, but something went wrong. He ended up alone for decades, a pointless life, as if someone had turned off his power. I've seen that before with Roamers, when they don't make it to senior. Lone wolves, self-destructive. Glad you checked him out."

Twine had done just that. After Usher's death, Service housekeepers had tidied up his possessions into boxes piled up in a back room of his cottage. They were still there, inside a bleak room with walls of stone in a cottage which had been abandoned by MI5 because it had no idea what to do with it.

Twine had rummaged through the boxes and cartons. Junk. Empty bottles, tourist junk, and musical instruments with broken strings. He returned to London with a few small items, just to prove he had been there, and one of them was the photograph in its oval gilt frame. When Twine laid it on Chatham's table, his master frowned, raised the claw of a finger to his nose, scratched it, and narrowed his eyes. He picked up the photograph. "I'm guessing this is a photograph of Usher as a boy," Chatham said. "I get a feeling from it. Twine, you may have found me a key."

"A key, our master?"

"It may not look like one. It may not be one. But I believe it is." He reached across his desk and grasped Twine by the hand. "Twine," he said, and there was a new light in his dark eyes. "You are a wonder. If you do nothing else in your service to me, you have done enough by bringing me this."

*

Usher had acquired a key to the Crossway. There, the Lord God waited until the tide of battle turned, until the stalemate before him was resolved. The delay was intolerable. As Chatham made it clear, limited though it was, in the right hands this key might, just might, unlock that stalemate, if not directly then by some alternative route.

It might, just might, unlock the gate through which the Will of the Lord God could pass into this misguided sea.

But now Usher was dead, how might the key be used? Only a senior Roamer could use it, and no senior had been identified, which is not to say they were not there. The priority was to find a Roamer who could use it, and could be made to use it.

Stanley stood before the picture of himself and said, "Plot Roamers younger than eighteen." He agreed that was an arbitrary number, but his reasoning was that anyone older should already have been identified as a senior or - as he described Usher - a 'busted flush'.

Stanley stepped back. Chatham stood at his shoulder. On the screen appeared a map of the world in shades of grey, and on it a pattern of yellow circles, large and small. "Remove known failures," said Stanley. The number of yellow circles dwindled, to a scattering of yellow dots. The number 1016 appeared in white at the bottom of the map.

"Too many," Chatham said. "Go further."

"Remove expected failures," said Stanley. The number changed to 47.

"We can live with that," said Chatham. "Copy that list to all regional commanders. Are there any who stand out?"

"I have a boy in Alabama who looks promising."

"I have another in mind," Chatham said. "The Andreyev girl. The mother had form before the Russians disposed of her. Lily… something. Twine?"

"Moss, our master," Twine said.

"Show Lily Moss," said Stanley, and on the map one yellow dot appeared on the southern coast of the British Isles.

"I'll take care of this one, Twine," said Chatham.

12 - Swivelhurst

Sussex, April 2009

On a cold morning in April, a flock of seagulls from the coast of Sussex dropped down through cloud over Swivelhurst to land on a corner by the railway station, where they began pecking around the skeleton of a spindle tree. They paid no attention to the black shoes of the man standing by the tree nor the pale face of a small blonde girl who was watching him from the upstairs window of a shop across the road.

Lily Moss sat at the window wearing her maroon-and-gold uniform, though she was not at school today but recovering from another of her 'turns'. The room was cold and these were some of her warmest clothes. Her desk was awash with books and papers. She was doing her homework, or trying to. It was Maths, when she would rather look out of the window with the radio burbling behind her.

She frowned. The window was filthy, and the road outside was a sheet of slime on this sun-and-showery day. It bothered her that everyone passed by and no-one stopped. It bothered her that no-one was buying anything, that her Dad's shop was slipping down the pan together with the rest of this village. She thought sometimes that she should leap out and drag people in through the door. She wished she could be older and bigger, for then she would stand in the shop's window and wiggle herself till someone came in. It bothered her most that there was a man on the pavement across the road, with seagulls at his feet, who should be a customer but could not make up his mind.

The only attraction of the Sussex village of Swivelhurst is its railway station, a junction, a place to pass through. The man had come from the station, passed the bus stop, and stood under a tree by the car park and second-hand car sales. He was even older than her Dad, his complexion pale, his nose prominent and bony, and he wore a black raincoat over a grey suit, with a black cap jammed over his ears. He looked up and down the row of two-storey shops which were neither modern nor old enough to have character. He looked around at the fake Tudor bank, the Estate Agent, and the Chinese restaurant. The comings and goings of the Co-Op store entertained him for a moment. His shoes were shiny, though, and his trousers had a crease, so there was hope there might be cash in his pocket. But he was frowning as his head turned towards her Dad's shop, because it was shabby, its window streaked with grease, and the paint of its woodwork yellowed and flaking away. Even the sign - Moss Auctions - needed repainting in a better red.

Come in, please. This is my Dad's shop and he is a lovely man and trusted by everyone. He was very high-up in the Army. We do antiques, auctions and house clearance. Did somebody die? We'll give you a good price for everything in their house, better than Paramount Auctions in Worthing who are a bunch of thieves. In our shop we offer antiques at prices which are very reasonable for the quality. OK we have a grandfather clock in our warehouse that we haven't sold in five years, but that makes it more antique, doesn't it? We also do keys. Come in. Please. We need your money, very badly.

Would this man stand and stare all day? No, for in a moment of decision he stepped out into the road, and hurried across as a Post Office van sped past. Then Lily Moss heard from downstairs a tinkle of the bell over the shop's front door. Refreshed, the seagulls flapped themselves up and off to the west.

*

In the back office of the shop, Riley Moss sat at his desk idly flicking through a motorcycle magazine. His years had not been kind to him, for he had not been kind to himself. Few who knew him in the Army and then Defence Intelligence would recognise the man who had lost his fitness and - some would say - his wits. He seldom made the effort to spruce himself up, but today he was expecting a visitor, so he had bothered to tame his awkward hair, and

83

had forsaken his ex-Army fatigues in favour of a loose-fitting white shirt and the trousers of his one remaining dark suit. Formality did not extend to his feet, on which were the leather boots of one who liked to walk in the countryside but not clean off the mud.

Traffic from Swivelhurst Road rumbled through the patchwork of carpet, and beyond the back window there were few cars in the public car park. The desk and chairs were cheap, the walls of breeze-block, posters of auction sales faded. From upstairs came the drone of a radio which was comforting, for it told Moss that Lily was at home and entertained. Otherwise, it was yet another dismal day.

The business was failing. He was living on credit. In the last year of his father's life he had taken the business on, because when he lost his job it was the path of least resistance, but his emotional connection to the family firm gave him even more pressure. To see it go under would hurt not only in his pocket but in his heart, even though he recognised that he was a parasite. Much of the business was probate work, house clearance, which depended on people dying. There was no shortage of death on the south coast, but nowadays the relatives were likely to take the lot to a car-boot sale. And the auction business was slipping away. Few dealers and fewer punters came to his warehouse down the road. As for antiques, customers were prepared to do without, or delay until the economic weather improved. Meanwhile, a small business like his could go to the wall.

Even his shop was full of rubbish. It lay on the main street of a village so small that 'High' for its street would be generous. Its premises consisted only of a front office which displayed a few knick-knacks from the warehouse - vases, pot-plants, a sideboard which pretended to be Georgian - a desk for the ordering of keys, a workshop behind, the back office (which served as a sitting-room in the evenings) and two bedrooms and a bathroom above a set of uncarpeted wooden stairs.

The shop had one employee, Percy Bee, formerly a Sergeant of Moss's regiment, whom Moss had employed (on minimal pay) because he had fallen on hard times. Percy was a kind-hearted rogue, useful for the heavy lifting, who minded the shop while Moss did creative work with antiques and keys. Physical work was soothing. The Riley Moss speciality was key-cutting, and to fill the air with oil and burnt metal to produce a perfect key was no great art, but the mechanical process kept all other thoughts at bay - especially the thought that both he and his daughter would soon be out of a job with no home to go to.

All he had left of real value was Lily, and she was under stress. Her 'turns' were more frequent. He was asking too much of her. Physically she was not strong, but she had other talents. To Moss Auctions she had become an asset - even more of an asset, Moss sometimes believed, than himself.

Lily was a little burglar, made of rubber but with fingers of steel, sniffing out the contents of a house as ruthlessly as a hunting dog. There was no window Lily could not open, no key to a door she could not find, no crevice, hole or chimney that she could not squeeze through. She had a grasp of what doorway leads where, what window overlooks what, how buildings connect with each other. Attics, secret rooms and passage-ways, nothing was safe from her.

Did a diamond hat-pin fall down behind a radiator? She would find it. Did anyone drop cash behind the cushion of that sofa? Yes they did, and Lily would stuff it into her Dad's hand with a grin. Did the owner of the house hide his booze under the floorboards? She would spot the fake nails, reach down and emerge triumphant with dust on her nose and a bottle of Chateau Petrus in each hand.

Then, from all the bric-a-brac she would filter out whatever had value. She knew little of antiques, but she would handle an object, think for a moment, and - with a far-away look which reminded Riley Moss of her 'turns' - declare that this thing had value for someone once, and perhaps it might again. The objects she picked out would always sell, and there was the profit.

Though he often wondered how he - not the slimmest of men - could have fathered this Saxon elf, Riley Moss knew that she had inherited a gift, an intuition, from her mother Anna, whom she so closely resembled. Even at the age of twelve she knew how the world fits together, what people like and how they think. And they were a team. Lily seemed to enjoy it. For every 'field trip' she would put on her bomber jacket, jeans and sneakers, and stand ready with her little mouth pursed, her eyes shining, and as tense with excitement as a thoroughbred at the starting gate. Yes there was a connotation of child labour, of Victorian sweeps shoving their kids up chimneys, and of infringing laws on the employment of minors, but Lily was happy to do it.

Happy, Moss pondered, for now. There would soon come a time when she would be the wrong shape to squirm through windows, less interested in helping her Dad and more interested in handling the rest of her life, the boys, the fashion, and God knows what other peer pressure, university perhaps, and how could he afford that?

Moss was roused by a ring of the bell at the shop's door, followed by a few words between the visitor and Percy. The door opened and Percy's close-cropped head leaned into view. "Visitor for you, Captain. A Mister Chatham," he said, leaning back and letting through the antique gentleman whom Lily had glimpsed from the road.

"Mister Moss." Chatham advanced over the carpet. "Glad you could see me."

"Good morning, Mister Chatham." Moss rose and shook the visitor's hand. In deference to Chatham, tall but not as tall as himself, he hunched, and so made himself look even more like a bear. "Take a seat. I recommend the one which has both arms. Would you like a tea, or a coffee?"

"Tea would be good. Thank you. Black, no sugar."

"Excuse me one moment." Moss sidled out into the shop, leaving Chatham to gaze at the posters, and turned into the kitchen where he cobbled together two teas in plastic cups with water from the Instahot boiler, and returned, handing a cup to Chatham who cradled it in both hands. The man had removed his cap, uncovering two prominent ears and a bald head which gleamed. His complete greyness reminded Moss of gargoyles on French cathedrals, and the hoods of his eyelids were so large that he seemed almost asleep.

Moss settled himself back behind his desk. Putting aside the magazine he said, "I hope your journey was not too tedious."

"Not at all," Chatham replied. "I had forgotten what the countryside looked like."

"So what can I do for you?" Moss asked. "I have to say, your secretary was vague on the telephone."

Chatham sipped his tea, then forced his jaw into a smile. "I may have a job for you."

There was something of the policeman about Chatham. The Met, Special Branch; Moss could not be sure, but the thin smile and the cold unblinking eyes reminded him of another man, years before, a man called Twine. "We are always happy to take on new work," said Moss. "Five days a week, and Saturday mornings."

"Am I right in thinking," Chatham said, "that you do house clearance?" Moss nodded. "Am I also right, that at some time you held a senior role in Defence Intelligence?"

"How do you know that?" Moss was taken aback, but restricted his surprise to a modest raising of his eyebrows.

Chatham leaned back and crossed his legs, obliging Moss to admire the stitching of his brogues. "I represent a company called G-Range," he said. "We are in the same line of business as yourself, though - if I may say - our clients are probably more substantial. One of those clients is Her Majesty's Government."

"Government? And which department of Government would that be?"

"I can say only that it is a department which normally requires security clearance."

"The security Service."

87

"That would be a reasonable assumption."

Riley Moss did not know whether to laugh or choke. Since that Service had lost him his job he had thought of himself as unemployable, persona non grata, disposed of in hazardous waste. "I'm sorry, Mister Chatham," he said, "but I prefer not to take on Government work, whatever form it takes. Sorry to have wasted your time. If you like, you can leave now."

As Moss rose to his feet Chatham stayed put. "Just think for a moment," he said.

"I did."

"Think again. It's just a job, Mister Moss. A week's work. Two thousand after tax, British pounds."

As this was four times what the shop was taking in a month, Moss felt his eyes widen but coughed to retain his composure. "Does it involve dropping my trousers?" he said, and sat down.

"Only if you must," Chatham said with the hint of a smirk.

He launched into a pitch aimed at Moss's pocket. As they both knew, the security Service owned properties in the south-east - offices, safe houses, even the odd airfield and manor house. But, in these cash-strapped times, budgets were cut and physical assets disposed-of. Even the Service was feeling the pinch. Many of its properties were off-limits, but some had to be sold off, and before that they had to be cleared, their contents valued and auctioned or otherwise sold. It had been decided by the Property and Procurement arms of the Service that a private company should be invited to do the work for an appropriate fee.

"That," Chatham said, "is G-Range, my company. But the job is too big even for us. So, we have to sub-contract. That is where you come in. We pay well, and on time."

"How much travel is involved?"

"Hardly any."

"I'm thinking about it."

Chatham leaned forward. "Look, it's simple," he said. "We have a customer with a property that needs clearing out, discreetly. Yes, that customer is the security Service, but it will have no direct involvement."

"I'm still thinking about it," said Moss.

"Very well," said Chatham. "Let me help with your thinking."

The property in question, he said, was a cottage in a poor state of repair. Its last occupant, now deceased, was an employee of the Ministry of Defence. This property was a luxury which the Service could no longer afford, neglected since the death of its last resident, except by a cleaner who went in once a month to dust and to fire up the generator. It had to be sold, but first it had to be cleared out, its contents removed and sold off.

"From what I remember of cottages in a poor state of repair," said Moss, "they don't have much in them."

"You might be surprised," Chatham said. "The last resident was quite the musician. There's recording equipment, and instruments, so I am told. Who knows? The man's personal effects were boxed up and stored in one of the back rooms. It could be a little treasure trove for all we know." Chatham paused, to let the word 'treasure' hang in the air. "Obviously we need an inventory," he went on, "but no-one will be too particular about what you do with that kind of stuff. Just sort out what's in the boxes, pick out anything worth selling, sell it and transfer the proceeds to a G-Range account. Take the rest to the tip. An easy job."

"I'm still thinking about it."

"I'll give you half an hour," Chatham said, with the flash of a more urgent self. "Is there anywhere a fellow can get a beer?"

"Try the Burrell Arms," Moss replied. "The other side of the station."

89

Money. A welcome visitor but quick to leave. Moss pondered, flicking through his magazine. Yes, his business was failing. Yes, he had no idea what to do about it. Shelf-stacking in supermarkets came to mind. Two thousand tax-free was a gift. But there was a factor they had not discussed, his daughter Lily.

"Well, Mister Moss?" said Chatham on his return.

"We need to agree something," Moss said. "Expenses."

"Paid within a week."

"For two. My daughter, Lily. She comes with me."

Chatham tilted his head to one side and asked, "Why is that?"

"She has a medical condition. I can't leave her."

"Not too serious I hope."

"She has fits, 'turns' we call them. I'm hoping she'll grow out of it. Meanwhile she helps me out, if she can."

"Well, I admit that's no surprise," Chatham said. "We looked at your customer reviews. All very good. What struck us was the mention of your daughter. That little girl helping her father, family firm. The sort of thing the Child Protection people would get interested in, if you're not careful."

"It's… an informal arrangement."

"Well, you'd have to take that risk. If you agree, there would be a contract between G-Range and you personally. The rest is up to you." Chatham added with a smile, "We could call her a consultant. What do you think?"

Moss weighed up the joy of money against the sorrow of having anything to do with Government, but the opportunity had to be grasped. It would keep Percy employed. "OK, we can do it," he said.

"I'll give you the address."

13 - The First Apparition

Jenkins Road, Sussex

It was a short ride by car. Lily Moss sat in the passenger seat concerned that her Dad had not told her everything about this field trip. He let out a rude word, which was unlike him, as he urged the old white Mondeo up hills it struggled to climb. They came up to a pub called the Hotspur where he turned right, down into Jenkins Road. Though the sun was doing its best, the road was gloomy even in mid-afternoon, branches thick with leaves hanging over it. Her Dad's mobile phone was propped up in the well of the handbrake. Texts and missed calls were popping up on it but he was ignoring them.

They drew up at the bottom of the road, by a track which led into the woods. Under a tree stood a woman - bushy dark hair, an ample figure, in a black dress and fake-fur coat. A yellow Fiat was parked further down the road, a man in its passenger seat. Lily stayed put as her Dad climbed out.

There was an exchange of words, with some volume from the woman - "Are you here to do something about the noise?" and "Is it true there was a murder in there?" - before her Dad returned to the car and let Lily out. Together they followed a muddy path, through a creaking gate and then on a dusty track to a wide wooden shack, single-storey, its timbers black with age and its tiled roof overgrown with algae. "This is a place fit for burning," said her Dad, pressing a bell loosely attached to the door-frame.

The door opened. Something inside Lily screamed for here was a creature as much lizard as man. It was the old man on the High Street whom she had seen from her window. But - now seeing him close-up - his skin was grey and scaly, his lips thin and black, his cheeks sunken, and his eyelids were hoods over dark eyes that peered at her with what Lily thought was envy. His ears stuck out like a goblin's. He was hunched, and he was sick, but this was a sickness no doctor could cure, but a great sadness which flashed into her mind like a dart.

"Mister Moss," the man said, in a creepy high-pitched voice. "And daughter. Welcome."

"Mister Chatham," said her Dad. "Is this a convenient time?"

"It is," said Chatham, and he stepped aside to let them in, closing the door behind them. It was a bare room, a low ceiling, one window, wooden floorboards and in the far corner a Victorian fireplace whose tiles drew her Dad's eye, but Lily could tell even from the door that they were too bright to be original. The only artificial light would have come from a black-spotted brass light-fitting just inside the door, but it had no bulb.

"Don't worry about that woman outside," said Chatham. "A busybody. Didn't you get my text?"

"No I didn't. She was talking about a murder."

"Was she indeed? Empty houses attract all manner of foolish rumours. I am sure we both would want to put a stop to such nonsense."

"And something about noise?"

"We will come to that. Where would you like to start?"

Her Dad turned to Lily. "What have you got so far, Lily?"

Lily took a deep breath. "Just scrap really," she said. "Fireplace might interest somebody. Three rooms behind. I don't think there's much in them. A room which has no windows. There's something there but I can't make it out. That's weird."

Chatham's eyes lit up. "Remarkable," he said. "And all without actually seeing it. I am impressed."

"Saw most of it from the path, sir," said Lily. "And the rest I kinda imagined."

"Imagined?" said Chatham with a grin that revealed sharp white teeth. He fixed his eyes on her. "Well, your imagination is spot on. The room with no windows is a special place. You will see."

Lily could tell that her Dad was uneasy. He was standing in that tense, upright way which meant he was on edge. His eyebrows were drawn together into a frown, his chin was up and he was looking down his nose as if the man smelled, which he did, of fried bacon. She wanted to tell her Dad that something nasty had happened right here by the door. She had a giddy feeling, a feeling of falling, but with a deep breath the giddiness passed.

Her Dad took out his notebook. "I will make notes," he said. "If you don't mind."

"I will let you get on with it," Chatham said. "But I must insist we all stay together." With a look directly at Lily he said, "No wandering off."

Off a central corridor they went from room to room, all decorated with plaster yellowed with age and crumbling. In the galley kitchen, and then in the bedroom whose single bed had been stripped and all other furniture removed, the damp creeping up the walls gave out a musty odour with a hint of cigarette-smoke. A curtain rail curved around a corner with pipework, where there was a sink and once a bath.

Chatham opened the wooden door to the room with no windows. He tried the light-switch and a single energy-saving bulb flickered on. "Ah, the mains is back on," he said. "So unreliable out here in the sticks." This room was different. Thick red curtains were draped around three walls, the fourth being of rough stone. A brown carpet covered the floor except in one corner where the floorboards were bare.

"What's this?" her Dad said. "It's damn cold."

"This, so I believe," said Chatham, "is what's left of a Saxon church."

Overhead, panels of white polystyrene stretched across the ceiling into the corners. A line of wooden crates divided this shadowy space, around them a scattering of suitcases, boxes and cardboard cartons, some with a coating of mildew. It was a disorderly collection of junk, and with a wave at it Chatham said, "Property of the previous resident. You might find this more interesting." After a quick survey her Dad estimated it would take a day to make an inventory and Chatham seemed happy with that.

Lily wrapped her arms around her bomber jacket. Something here was not quite right. Perhaps it was the atmosphere of this gloomy chamber, or the creepy presence of Chatham, but she did not want to take one step away from the door.

"The previous resident had musical interests," Chatham went on. "Folk music or something of the sort. He used this room as a studio."

Her Dad walked forward and took the lid off a crate. Dust twinkled in the dim light. Lily stayed by the door. "Come on Lily," said her Dad. "Poke your nose in. There's a tape recorder in this one, original manual. Very retro."

Lily was fixed to the spot. Her eyes darted from side to side.

"You might find that carton interesting, Miss," Chatham said, pointing at a box which had on it the word 'Jameson's' in red italic script. "Pictures, souvenirs, some from Ireland. You might visit Ireland one day."

Lily took a deep breath. The cardboard box lay flat on the floor and was already open, its lid in tatters, a good height for rummaging, should be safe.

"A couple of guitars," said her Dad, peering into another crate. "Cheap copies. Come on Lily."

Lily took a step forward. As her Dad was now on the far side of the room, Lily turned to Chatham and asked, "Do you know, sir, what 'Jameson's' means, on that box?"

"Oh, just an advertisement," Chatham replied. He stepped over to the box and separated its lid. "Take a look," he said, waving a bony hand over it.

Lily peered into the box, and saw only rubbish, but something was here. She could smell it as if it were a perfume in the dust. She brushed aside a layer of scrunched-up newspaper and rummaged. "Some of this is very old," she murmured, turning over souvenirs of Lourdes, plaster models of the Virgin, and junk, packs of guitar strings, drum-sticks in a plastic bag, wires and plugs.

"Let me give you a hand," said Chatham, and he cleared a space. Lily snatched back her hand, but saw that at the bottom of the box were rows of gold. She reached down and rubbed a finger over the gilt frames of pictures, photographs. She poked a finger between them and pulled one out. It was only a postcard of mountains, but something else was a magnet, and it drew her in. At the end of the row there was a gap. Something smaller was down there.

It was as if Chatham's hand pointed at it. Lily poked a finger down the side of the box and found something small and hard. She twisted a finger between the cardboard and the tiny object, and levered it gently upwards. It slid up the box's side until she could grasp it, and hold it to the light.

Lily looked up. Chatham was watching, his eyes narrowed. "Something interesting?" he said.

"No sir, not really," she replied, and she hoped he would not detect the burning in her cheeks. She pulled the object out and held it in the light, to be sure. It was an oval gilt frame, a cameo, and in it a black-and-white photograph. Lily made out a title written at the top in black ink, *From the Lady*. Its subject was a boy, on a stage, and he stood by a potted palm with his hands clasped in front of him. He was small, dressed in a black school uniform, with shoes that gleamed. His hair was a dark mop, his face very white.

She knew that face. A shiver ran through her from top to toe, the tingle of an anxiety she had not known and did not like. It was a face she had not seen since she was little more than a baby. It was a face from a dream, the face of a boy in a forest who wore that school uniform, who had only to open his mouth for music to pour out, who played with his animals, the rabbit, the donkey, in the imaginary place which she thought she had named - Roamers Cross. He was, or had been, real.

Best to say nothing. She turned her head, and clamped her mouth shut for she was sure her jaw had dropped, and she swallowed, hard.

It must be a coincidence. She looked more closely. Her reflection stared back in the glass, glinting in streams of white and strawberry red. Three pin-points of light glowed green.

In an instant her reflected self was far away, in the clearing of a forest where under a tree stood the little black-haired boy. He looked sad and held in his hand a dog's lead, which was red but there was no dog. Instead, over the undergrowth, a black balloon-like globe came bouncing towards her. It zoomed forward and spread over the glass. Then the gilt frame was warm, then hot, very hot and it would burn, scorching her fingers.

She tipped the gilt frame back towards the box but as she did there emerged from it a shadow, as if an oily rag were unrolling, and a spidery grey shape leapt out, fell to the floor, scuttled towards a corner of the room growing ever larger and more transparent, and vanished. "Oh!" she cried.

"Lily?" Her Dad's head poked out from behind a crate. "Are you OK?"

Lily tried to control her eyes. She knew they were wide, and she blinked. "It was just a sharp thing, Dad. I'm OK."

Chatham pursed his lips then said, "Dear me. I am so sorry about that. I didn't realise it had sharp edges."

Lily was breathing hard. She coughed. "I'm OK, sir," she said. "I just... well it is so hard to see in here." No-one else saw. It must have been just a shadow, but it was a shock. She had to leave this place before another shock came to burst her heart. There was danger everywhere, seen and unseen in the shadows. She looked around, nerves tingling.

Then she saw him. The little black-haired boy.

Her Dad emerged from behind the pile of crates. "My God," he said, "did someone open a door? It's got even colder."

"It has indeed," said Chatham, his eyes fixed on Lily.

Lily Moss saw a boy, in the shadows of the far corner of the room, a little boy, black-haired and white-faced. No reaction from the others. They could not see or would not. Had he been hiding? Was someone playing a trick on her? She blinked, but he was still there, his hands clasped in front of him. He was small, dressed in his black school uniform and polished shoes.

She knew she was staring. Was he a ghost? Was this a turn? This did not feel like a turn. She was not giddy. She was not falling asleep. In an instant there he stood, as still as if he had been cut from the photograph. And he was sad, Lily knew, very sad. She craned her head to the left, and the boy still faced her. She craned her head to the right and the boy still faced her. He had only two dimensions.

"Just a draught," said Chatham. "These old walls are full of cracks."

The boy's mouth moved. Several times he mouthed the same word, which at first Lily thought was 'Awful'. The blood was racing through Lily's brain and her heart was fluttering. Then she knew it was 'I fell'.

"Seen a ghost, Lily?" said her Dad. "You've gone a bit pale."

"No Dad. It's nothing. Just the cold." Lily blinked, and the boy was gone.

"Are you OK my darling? You're shivering."

"Yes Dad. Yes. Fine." She imagined it. The photograph had dredged up a memory that just as swiftly vanished. The atmosphere of the room was to blame, and the creepiness of this man Chatham.

The boy in the photograph might not be the little black-haired boy at all, just a boy who looked like him. Or was he a ghost? Scrooge had seen ghosts after eating a crumb of cheese. She had a cheese sandwich for lunch. If he saw ghosts after a crumb then she could see dozens after a whole sandwich. No, he must be an illusion, something she imagined, because of cheese. Her legs were trembling.

"Well, we're done for now," said her Dad. "What's out the back?"

Chatham sniffed and said, "You might want to look at the generator."

"OK, if you like. But it's probably worth keeping where it is."

"Noted," said Chatham. "This way…" Lily shivered and then was numb. To go, was such a relief. Chatham led them out through the kitchen and unlocked the back door. They stepped out into a tangle of undergrowth in the shadow of a thick bank of trees. The light was already failing. Lily stood quietly, trying to control her breathing and calm her thoughts.

A wooden kennel stood by the door. Chatham lifted its metal lid. Inside was the generator, a squat white box with a red button at its front. "Uses natural gas," said Chatham. "They can rely on that out here."

"Good make," said her Dad. "Maybe it just needs a service. Mind if I try it?"

"Go ahead."

He pressed the button. Instantly there was a whirring, and a grinding, then an appalling screech as if a hundred hands were scratching their nails down a blackboard. Lily put her hands over her ears. He pressed the button again. The screech stopped and the whirring subsided. "My God, what a racket," he said.

"That's the noise the locals were complaining about," said Chatham. "The generator. The cleaner fires it up once a month."

"Well. That goes right off my list."

The rest was mechanical, and Lily followed with a blank expression, mulling over what she had seen to convince herself that it was only a trick of her memory. She must have been half-asleep.

At the front, they walked to the road, where her Dad took Chatham aside. There was talk of a 'report' and 'recommendations'. He gave Lily the car keys and motioned for her to get in the car. The two men disappeared behind a hedge, with her Dad's hand waving up at the cottage's roof. Now she was alone in the car. No-one was under the tree. Lily was tense. What had she seen? Had she seen anything at all? It was a worry and she shook her head.

Suddenly at the car window a hand rose up, and Lily's heart jumped as her mouth fell open with surprise. A red fingernail tapped. The hand was followed by a broad face. It smiled. It was a woman, the woman who earlier had been lurking under the tree. She was crouching outside the car, and Lily thought her coat must be getting terribly muddy. "Hello dear," said the woman. "Can you open the window?" To be polite Lily opened the car door a few inches. The woman looked behind her then turned back and said, "What was it like in there, dear?"

"Very nice but quite cold," Lily replied to the broad face, which was heavily made-up. When the woman smiled her face cracked like the ground in an earthquake, and her eye make-up would not be out of place in a circus.

"Can you tell me some more about it, dear?" the woman said, her ruby-red mouth moving ever closer to the opening of the car door. "I'm a reporter. Maude Melly. I write for the Argus. You may have read some of my stuff."

"I'm sorry Miss, I don't read the papers. My Dad does, though."

"Your Dad? Is he the one with the dark hair? He's a hunk."

"Yes Miss."

"Moving on. Tell me, dear," said the woman. "What's your name? I might get you in the article I'm writing about this place."

"Lily Moss."

"Got it." The woman briefly looked down then up again. "So did you see the body, Lily?"

"What body, Miss?"

"The murder. There was a murder here wasn't there?"

"I don't know, Miss."

"But what about the noise? The terrible screams. The neighbours have been complaining."

"The generator, Miss. Just the electrical generator thing."

"And how do you know that, Lily?"

"I just do."

"You just do. You must be psychic."

"Yes Miss."

"You look psychic. It's the eyes. Quite distinctive. What a bright girl you are, Lily. Perhaps you can…"

At that moment, her Dad emerged from behind the hedge. The Melly woman stood up and Lily had the view of a broad backside that all-but filled the window, with a black handbag swinging from her hip. She heard her Dad say, "Can I help you, madam?" in a cross voice. "Maude Melly," the woman replied. "From the Argus. You must be Mister Moss. May I ask, are the Police in there?"

"You may ask all you like," her Dad replied. "But we do not talk to the Press."

The Melly woman whipped a camera from her handbag and held it backwards, pointing at Lily. "So, OK for a quick photo?" she said.

"No."

"Oh too late. Never mind." Her hips swivelled away and her broad face reappeared at an angle. "What shall we call this?" she whispered to Lily. "'Teenage psychic solves Sussex mystery'? Sounds like a cracker. Well cheers, darling. Be lucky."

With that, the Melly woman shifted her ample frame away from the car and set off down the road towards the yellow Fiat, her coat flapping. Riley Moss stared after her and glared. He climbed into the car and fired up the engine, grunting, "Busybodies. Let's get somewhere warm."

As they drove away, Lily heard a scream in her head, but not the scream of the generator, just a scream. It echoed in her mind as heat in the car began to seep into her and she sagged against the door.

14 - The Second Apparition

On the bus heading home from school, in the shifting mass of small maroon-and-gold bodies Lily Moss was interested only in two, her friend Swan who sat beside her at the window and - in the back seat - a blonde-haired boy with a ruddy complexion whose name was Chris Ormerod. As she climbed in she saw him sitting next to the puny Berthold. Chris Ormerod was not puny. He was a hero from beyond Time, usually described by Lily as an 'angel', often adding 'gorgeous' or with just a sigh. Fiddling with her bunches, and with an occasional backward glance, she barely heard what Swan was saying.

"Did you realise," said Swan, as the trees of Swivelhurst Road flitted past, "that the top score you can get on a dartboard is one hundred and eighty, which is exactly what the angles of a triangle add up to? And a dartboard is full of triangles. Isn't that totally amazing?"

"Mmm," Lily replied.

"You're not having a turn again, are you, Lily? You've gone a bit pale."

"Chris, at the back," Lily whispered.

"Oh, him." Swan glanced towards the back of the bus. "He looks a bit like you. I have a theory. First, people fall for people who are like them, but when they get older they fall for people quite different. My mother, for example, is fat and dark-haired. My father is thin and blonde. I think that's because they get bored with themselves. What do you think?"

It was certain that one day Swan would become a teacher. Thin, dark-haired and always pensive, Swan had a great many theories and was expert in Maths, not Lily's strongest subject.

"I think Chris is secretly romantic," said Lily. "Like Ivanhoe."

"Ivan who? Is he Russian? You look a bit Russian, now I come to think of it. Your mother was Russian, wasn't she?"

"Polish," Lily replied.

"Oh, that explains it."

*

At Swivelhurst station the bus disgorged its contents of swinging arms, legs and satchels. Many went for the station, tramping over chewing gum flattened by generations before them, and others - including Chris Ormerod, despite Lily's appealing glances - towards their homes in the village. With a farewell wave to Swan, Lily set off under the railway bridge and turned right into Hedge Lane. With the odour of newly-manured fields around her, she walked the few yards to the barn, the warehouse where her Dad stored his stock and held his auctions.

This was a long, low and draughty barn of Sussex flint, rented from a local farmer, with a roof whose tiles were continually falling off, leaving gaps between the cobwebbed rafters through which pigeons would fly in and poop all over the stock. The building was in three parts - at the front the auction room with a few rows of wooden seats, a stage and a table where her Dad would stand up and make the sales (with jokes at which Lily cringed), a desk where Percy would take the money, a front door of solid oak which at the moment was locked and chained-up, a wooden cartwheel in front of it to make sure, and a back door through which her Dad and Percy carried items for auction from the warehouse. Behind the auction room was the chamber of goods-in-transit, and behind that the warehouse itself, a shadowy stone treasure-house, though this was treasure only in the mind of her Dad. Whatever failed to sell ended up here in the corners. Stacks of chairs, three-piece suites so tatty no restorer would be interested, school desks scratched and riddled with woodworm, china vases with pictures of Dorset, amateur paintings lined up like the bellows of an accordion; and then there were the building parts, pots and fountains, that were supposed to interest the gardener or interior decorator, but did not. Every so often her Dad would clear most of it out, usually to dealers in Portsmouth, but sometimes it went to the car-boot sale at a racecourse nearby, where he would be happy to take a few quid for something worth even less.

Down a concrete track overgrown with tufts of grass, Lily made for the side door. Percy was already there, busily carrying boxes from the van into goods-in-transit. He waved and vanished into the building. Lily followed.

Percy Bee still looked like the soldier he had been for twenty years. Stocky, his hair cropped so close he might as well be bald, always in blue overalls which bore the badge of 'Moss Auctions' like a medal, his grin scrunched-up his weather-worn face as he said, "Your Dad's in the Burrell Arms, Miss Lily. He'll be along in a minute, I'm sure."

"Oh thank you, Percy," Lily replied, putting her satchel down by the door. She never liked to be called Miss Lily, but that was Percy's way, respectful and regimented, always with a crease in his overalls because Mrs Bee liked to ensure he was 'well turned-out'. It was a worry, though, that her Dad was in the pub at this time of day, late afternoon as the shadows drew in. "I'll just take a look at what we've got, if that's OK."

"It's all in, Miss Lily. I cleared out goods-in-transit so we could get a view. Doesn't look like much to me, but I'm sure you'll find something nice. You always do."

"What did you think of the place this lot came from, Percy?"

"Smelly, Miss. I know the cleaner, and she's supposed to go in there regular-like, but she doesn't like it. Spooky, says she. Folks do say there was a murder done in it. No blood on this lot, though. As far as I can see." He grinned and set about shifting boxes and crates over the dusty floor, arranging them in ranks with space to walk between. Lily inspected the parade. Nothing drew her eye, nothing said Take me, I'm worth Money, but her target was the cardboard box with the logo of 'Jameson's'. "What is Jameson's, Percy?" she asked. "Is it an advertisement?"

"It's Irish, Miss Lily. Whiskey, I believe. Not a drinker of spirits myself."

Percy stood back while Lily peered into the box. "Ah, Miss Lily" he said, "nearly half-four. I'm going to have to get back to the shop. Are you all right here?"

"Yes thank you, Percy."

"I'm going to have to lock you in, till your Dad gets back. Can't have prowlers getting in."

"OK Percy," Lily said, but she barely noticed him leave, with a turn of his key in the side-door lock.

She brushed aside the layer of scrunched-up newspaper and pulled out handfuls of bric-a-brac which she stacked on the floor. There were no valuables, nothing that would pay the rent on this draughty barn. It was getting cold, and dark. There was no electricity in this part of the building. Lily pulled her mobile phone from the inside pocket of her school blazer. It shed a pale light over the insides of the box where at the bottom she saw the rows of photographs, golden and shiny. Gently she picked out the photograph of the little black-haired boy and held it to the trembling light.

"Put that down!"

Lily froze. Everywhere was danger in the shadows. The walls were a church and who was buried here? The crates were a dark mountain that would swallow her up. She remembered the huge spider which had leapt from the photograph she held in her hand and she wanted to put it down but it was stuck to her fingers. Lily tried to control her eyes and she blinked. She was breathing hard and the blood was pumping through her brain. It was so cold, and dark in here now, except for the light from her phone. Who said that?

"You're a little thief!"

The voice came from the door to the auction room. Lily quivered as she looked around. A man stood in the shadows. He was tall and he stooped. His face was chalk-white and he wore a black suit. Lily turned the light of her phone on him but it barely reached. "No. No," she said, shaking her head. Was this what her mother died of, fright?

"People open doors that should be locked," said the man. "And they steal. Like you."

"No. Who are you?" Lily said, backing away towards a row of crates.

The man took a pace forward. "Sure it's your name the Police want to know," he said, "stealing people's private things."

"I work here."

"You work here?" His eyes were dark but there was a twinkle from the telephone light in them. "You, a little girl? What use are you?"

"I find things. And my Dad sells them. He'll be here in a minute."

"Your Dad is it?" he said, but to Lily it was more like 'Da'. This man had an accent, of Ireland. "So there's two thieves here then. What's that in your hand?"

"It's... a photograph."

"And is it yours?"

"Yes it is."

"You, are a little liar. Put it back in that box, or I will get cross." He said this in a voice that was not cross at all, but in the kindly way of a man instructing his dog. As if he had no care in the world, the man sat down on a crate and crossed his legs. Lily dared to take a step forward, and the light came with her, falling over the man's head and body. He was old but still dark-haired with a thin face; and he was smiling, his head turned away but with one dark eye fixed on her. "I seen you before," he said. "Would your name be Lily?"

"Yes." Lily slipped the photograph into the box and stepped back.

"Sure I thought as much. Tell me, how old are you, Lily?"

107

"Twelve."

"Twelve is it? Well, your Da's a lucky man to have such a fine grown-up daughter. This is his place then?"

"Yes it is."

"You can call me John."

At that moment Lily heard the rattle of keys at the side door and she looked away, feeling an overwhelming relief. As her Dad came in unsteadily with a torch she turned back to the visitor, but he was gone. The surface of the crate where he sat was empty.

*

She might be going mad. Either she had hypnotised herself with the light that had flashed over the photograph's glass, or she was hallucinating and that meant she was mad. There was no doubt that she saw him, a man who called himself John, a tall dark man, old but with something attractive about him, an elderly version of the boys in the Libertines, the band which made her friend Swan go silly. No mention of this to her Dad, for he would only worry. He was worried enough, entering goods-in-transit to find her with her mouth open and a dumbstruck expression, which she said was because she thought he was a prowler.

How had John got in? All the doors were locked. Perhaps Percy made a mistake with the front door, but the cartwheel would stop anyone. How had he got out, without a sound, with her Dad totally unaware? Perhaps there was enough time for him to get out the way he had come in, through the front door? But, it happened in an instant.

That night, as Lily sat on her bed, she examined the photograph which had caused so much trouble. It held no magic now. Obviously and logically, the boy resembled the musical boy of her dreams, but that was a coincidence, and anything else was the fault of cheese. Obviously and logically, the man called John was a homeless person who had been hiding in goods-in-transit, perhaps in a crate, and hid himself just as her Dad walked in. He might even be Jesus, though he didn't have a beard. Probably he was still there, in the cold and the dark. He might need something warm. Lily thought about soup. Chicken soup.

As she slid the photograph into a drawer, under the newspaper that covered her dream diaries, she decided to forget all about it. There was no time to take him chicken soup in the morning, and besides he would have gone to some place where they did have soup. With that comforting thought she kissed the photograph of her mother, slipped into bed, turned off the light, and drifted off to sleep.

15 - Lily Moss on Trial

"Traitor!"

It was an ugly face, which leapt into her mind between awake and asleep, pushing forward from some dark place and could be got rid of only by waking or by willing it away. If she woke then she would shiver, sweat, and not get back to sleep for hours. Lily tried to will it away, but she could only put something between herself and the ugly face - wire netting.

She landed in a cage of wire netting held up by pillars of iron. Through the netting the face peered at her. It belonged to a man, a stocky individual with close-cropped grey hair and a fat nose, under which a ginger moustache bristled, curling into extravagant whiskers. He wore a yellow uniform with a red sash and his expression was severe. In his right hand he carried a sheaf of papers. "The shame!" he hissed. "Her Eminence is going to boil your stupid little head in acid."

Her cage stood in a stone chamber lit by flaming torches. On a platform in front of her, three figures in jet-black robes sat like judges unmoving on gilded chairs, their faces concealed under black hoods. From the shape of their shoulders, Lily made out a woman to the left, a smaller woman in the centre and on the right a man, who was flipping a golden coin. Behind them arched a window of stained-glass panes, light playing in a spectrum of colours over its tracery as if outside there were trees shifting in a breeze. Two chairs, one at each end of the platform, stood empty. From the platform onto the stone floor hung a blue drapery with a pattern of globes, all silver except for one at the position of five o'clock which was gold.

In the shadows beside her stood the ugly man. Along the stone wall to her right, rows of women in smocks and woolly hats sat in a box of polished wood which had a gate open at its front. They were knitting, leaning over each other, gossiping, trading balls of coloured wool, wielding needles like knives. In an aisle between them floated trays of brown glass bottles. All seats were occupied except one in the front row which was higher than the others.

Thunder rolled from outside. On the platform, the smaller judge leaned forward. "Quiet," she said, directly to Lily's mind. It was a soft voice, of an old lady, and it was familiar but Lily could not place it. The hubbub diminished to a murmur. "Constable, proceed." She leaned back.

The ugly man stalked forward, fingered his sash and bellowed, "Be upstanding for the Court!" and the knitting women all stood with a great scratching and a clattering of boots. Some of them dropped their balls of wool and began to fumble on the floor in front of them.

"Court in session!" cried the Constable, and the knitting women sat down. He approached Lily's cage. His eyes were a deep brown, his eyebrows bushy, and his fat nose twitched. "Name?" he said.

"Lily Moss," she replied, putting on her most appealing honest face.

The Constable referred to a scroll of parchment. "The charge is as follows," he said. "The indictment holds the accused guilty of all the treasons, murders, burnings, spoils, desolations, damages and mischiefs to this place and the globes it defends, acted and committed in wars or occasioned thereby." Through a general mumbling in the audience the Constable persisted in a louder and higher tone, "Treason!"

As one the knitting women leapt up. Shouts and cries of "Monster!", and "Traitor!" filled the chamber. Needles were waved, bottles thrown at the cage, and Lily felt the value of the wire mesh as shards of glass trickled down it. The Constable held up his hands and the hubbub subsided. Turning to Lily he said, "How do you plead, guilty or not guilty?"

"Not guilty," was her reply.

"I will speak for the prosecution," said the Constable. "Who speaks for the defence?" He looked around. From beyond the knitting women a hand shot up. A woman stood. She was young. Her short hair was blonde. She wore a blue uniform dress. Lily gasped, and drew a deep breath.

"You are?" said the Constable.

"Mother of the accused, sir."

"Come forward."

Lily's mother stepped out until she and the Constable stood together before the judges' platform. "Prosecution first," said the old lady as the hooded man flipped his coin. Lily's mother turned and sat in the front row amongst the knitting women. She glanced at Lily with a smile then focussed on the broad back of her adversary.

The Constable approached the judges. He bowed to the old lady and said, "Your Eminence. We contend that, wilfully and deliberately, the accused committed an act of treason." He jabbed a fat finger in the direction of Lily's cage and cried, "Treason! For which we ask the maximum penalty." The level of hubbub rose, and another bottle flew from a distant seat and crashed into Lily's cage. "Do not be misled," he went on, fingering his sash, "by the appearance of the accused. How innocent she looks. But she has deceived us all. She is a traitor, the agent of our enemy." Puffing out his chest he declared, "The Grey Angel."

The name echoed through the chamber, and was taken up as 'Grangel' by the knitting women whose lips curled with a common hatred, then repeated slowly and with a gathering fury, until the Constable held up his hand to quieten the crowd. "Even now the forces of the Angel are descending upon us. How did this happen?" He stalked towards Lily's cage and pointed a finger at her. "She..." he said, wrinkling his nose. "She let it in."

Arms waved, and the Constable ducked as bottles crashed in a rain of glass down Lily's cage. The shouts made Lily cover her ears. She wanted to wake up. She cried, and she wiped her nose on the sleeve of her school blouse, which she knew was disgusting but there was no choice but to stand here and be shouted at, and accused of something she knew nothing about.

"Objection!" Lily's mother stood up. "Hearsay! Make him produce his evidence if he has any!" She sat down, and received a jolt in the ribs from one of the knitting women.

The Constable addressed the audience. "I have evidence," he said, "from eye-witnesses and from the Tower." From his sheaf of papers he pulled out a page which he threw in the air where it hovered. "One!" he bellowed.

Instantly Lily could see only the page. The Court, the Constable and the knitting women had all disappeared and she saw only a white sheet of paper with black handwriting, but still she heard the voice of the Constable as he said, "First. A report from one of our guards. It reads - 'Forest west of Tower. Enemy withdrew. Spiker left behind. Small blonde girl appeared from nowhere. Seen her in town. Spiker and girl vanished in trees before our eyes. Advanced to save girl. No body.' End one."

Lily's view of the Court returned, and she saw the Constable raise his eyebrows and peer around, as if searching for a monster lurking in the chamber. "The Spiker," he said.

Shouts of dismay came from the audience. "Some of you know that name," the Constable went on, and - jabbing a finger at every phrase - he said, "The Spiker. Springing from the shadows to smother, to pierce with its claw, and to suck out the soul of its victim. It vanished, suddenly. Where did it go? Surely, into the globe and let loose. The damage there cannot be calculated."

With a wave of his hand the Constable said, "Small blonde girl. Appeared from nowhere. Vanished. That is typical of... what?" A murmur of disquiet passed through the audience. Knitting women wrinkled their noses and pointed needles at Lily.

"A navigator," the Constable insisted, with a final jab of his finger. His eyes wandered in the direction of Lily's cage, and the rest of him followed, until he stood directly before her. Turning back to the audience, he looked around and raised his bushy eyebrows. "Is the accused a navigator?" he said, and answered himself with "Yes, she is. Two!" Again Lily could see only the page, a certificate with a red seal. "Evidence from the Tower," said the Constable, in a voice that had become unbearably smug. "Lily Andreyevna Moss, navigator level one. End two."

As Lily's view of the Court returned, the knitting women rose as one, their needles aslant like flattened stalks of hay, all pointing at her. "Witch!" they screamed. "Toads! Toads! Toads!"

Raising his hands to quieten the crowd, the Constable said, "We have the evidence of another eye-witness." In a voice which rang around the chamber he declared, "From the Tower I call... Sean Abel Usher."

The judge on the left shook an arm of her robe, and extended a hand whose middle finger bore a ring of gold with a bright ruby-red stone. In that hand lay a wand, a small bronze tube, and from it fizzed a stream of fire which settled on the floor in a sphere of undulating mist. The figure of a man emerged, dark-haired, in a black suit, overcoat and shoes, the only trace of colour being the pink of his lips in an otherwise chalk-white face. To Lily there was something familiar about him, and she frowned.

"You are Sean Abel Usher?" the Constable said. "Native of the island of Ireland?"

"I am, your Lordship," the man replied. "Where am I now?"

"Take your time, Mister Usher," said the Constable. "We understand you might be confused. You are summoned to this Court, as a witness."

Lily recognised him, John, the man from goods-in-transit. As his eyes swept the chamber and alighted on her she smothered a gasp with her hand.

Usher turned to address the Constable. "It's a dream, right?" he said.

"If it helps, you may think of this as a dream."

"This is all very odd, to be sure. So what am I a witness of?"

"Treason, Mister Usher. Have you seen this person before?" The Constable waved a hand at Lily.

Usher glanced sideways at her. "I seen her, yes, your Lordship" he said. "Twice. Once, in what used to be my home. The second time, I was in a building full of boxes and crates. She was standing there with my photo in her hand. Meant a lot to me, that photo."

"Ah yes," said the Constable with a leer at Lily, "the photograph. Here it is," and he bellowed, "Three!" All Lily could see was the photograph, the image of the little black-haired boy. "A photograph of yourself as a boy, is it not?" the Constable asked. "End three."

Usher nodded, and flashed a smile at the rows of knitting women.

The Constable puffed out his chest and addressed the judges. "It was by means of that photograph," he said, with a majestic twirl of his whiskers, "that the accused, wilfully and deliberately, transferred into the primary globe a spiker, the aforesaid monster which will create havoc among an unsuspecting population. There is no doubt that... "

"Constable." The old lady leaned forward. "One moment," she said. "I have information for the Court." The Constable bowed and withdrew a few steps.

"This photograph is a key," the judge went on. "It is the key to a channel into the sea, and only into the sea, in one direction only. It was my gift to this man when he was a boy, when we had high hopes for him, hopes which - for reasons I do not care to mention - came to nothing. None of us thought it necessary to retrieve this key. Its power is severely limited, and only one of exceptional talent could over-ride its security. It appears that the accused has that exceptional talent. You might say, in the language of the globe, this was an accident waiting to happen." The judge to the right of the old lady flipped his coin and caught it in a fold of his robe.

"An accident, your Eminence?" said the Constable with a frown. The old lady replied, "It is for you to prove otherwise."

115

The Constable turned towards Usher, who was making eyes at the knitting women. One of them blew him a kiss. "Mister Usher," he said, "you may return to the Tower."

Lily's mother stood. "Not yet, if it please the Court," she said. "I have questions for this witness." Her Eminence nodded and Lily's mother sat down.

With a grimace, the Constable scanned the rows of knitting women. "So..." he said, striding along the front row of seats, "what are the consequences of this action by the accused? Not long ago, intruders came through the Gate. Monsters, hideously deformed, savage creatures. These intrusions happen occasionally, and we deal with them, as you know." There were nods from the audience. He halted at the middle of the front row. "They had no discipline. We expected them to turn tail and return to whichever sea of damnation they came from. But they did nothing. They waited. For what?" He paused, hands on hips. "They waited for an act of treachery by... someone," he said, glancing at Lily's cage. "Then, their master showed its face. At the Gate its shadow appeared..." He bellowed, "Four, Gate!"

In a flash, Lily's view in three dimensions was of a mountain-top, a cliff of scorched and blackened rock. Dark vapour swirled from boulders at its base as from a volcano's slopes, immense shadows leaping into twists of smoke that rose into a bank of cloud where lightning crackled. Above the cliff as if carved from some higher precipice, against a swirl of yellow vapour a silhouette loomed through the clouds that framed it. It was the silhouette of what would be a man, were it not for the head of a bull, the eyes flashing red through the clouds, and the wings, outspread from each shoulder like grey curtains gathered to points where claws flexed their fingers. One claw held a silver staff which the bull-man raised and lowered in a slow rhythm. This was a statue that moved, an automaton.

Lily knew she must wake up. The image's power was like the electric current she had felt by accident in her school's laboratory. It hummed, tingled through her and must wake her up, but nothing could release her from the horror. She had seen him before,

116

glimpsed in her nightmare, but now she felt him, now from below she knew that he could not be conquered, that he was Death.

Stunned, she did not reply when the Constable said, "The Grey Angel, your master. Immortal, marshal of an army of savage creatures from dead worlds, loyal as only the resurrected can be. To our knowledge it has laid waste three seas already, reduced them to chaos, to dust. End four."

The knitting women were aghast. Mouths open, some fell sideways in a faint, others chewed on their knitting needles.

"The Grey Angel," the Constable went on. "Once, it was a dreadful myth. But now, it has come. Why? Because, wilfully and deliberately, someone let it in. Someone gave it hope. Someone opened a channel into the sea through which one of its creatures passed. If one can, then so can more. Someone gave the Angel hope, that it could pour its forces into the sea without interference by us. I wonder, who could that traitor be?"

Among the knitting women a murmur began, "Li... Lee, Li... Lee."

The Constable turned to the judges. "That act of treachery," he continued, "began the war. Now, many thousands of its creatures are ranged against us." He let his gaze wander towards the ceiling, but lowered his head and said directly to the knitting women, "This was treason. Many of you have fathers, mothers, brothers, sisters, at the front. For them, for the security of this place and of the globes which we defend, this Court must find the accused guilty."

Turning to the judges and with a low bow he said, "The prosecution rests." He grasped the hovering white page and stuffed it back into his sheaf of papers.

Lily's mother stood and stepped forward. The Constable sat, to a tumult of applause, and looked around with a satisfied smirk. Knitting women patted him on the back and presented him with woolly hats, which he gracefully accepted and piled up on his lap.

"You may question this witness," said the judge.

Lily's mother bowed and turned to face the witness. "Mister Usher," she said, "I am sure that we all regret that you were robbed of life before the expected time."

"I appreciate your sympathy, madam," Usher replied.

"But I would like to make something clear. You did not see the accused, Lily Moss, pick out from your possessions the photograph given to you by Her Eminence, did you? If you had, I am assuming you would have said so."

"That is correct, madam. I didn't see the girl do that."

"I am sure, Mister Usher, that all this talk of keys must be confusing. But, if I were to say that your photograph was the key to a door, you would say that you did not see the accused use that key, nor did you see what came through that door as a result?"

"Quite true, madam. I saw none of that."

The Constable leapt up, scattering woolly hats in all directions. "Objection!" he cried. "Leading the witness!"

Her Eminence leaned forward. "Over-ruled. A sensible line of enquiry," she said, as the Constable did his best to gather the scattered hats and resumed his seat with a face full of fury.

"And Mister Usher," Lily's mother continued, "on the occasion of your first meeting, at your home, was the accused alone, or with others?"

"With others, madam."

"Was this one of the others? Open!" Suddenly Lily was looking at the back room of the cottage in Jenkins Road. She saw herself, and by her side the old man, Chatham, who was guiding her hand towards the photograph of the little black-haired boy.

"Yes madam."

"For the information of the Court," said Lily's mother, "we have evidence from the Ordinal that the man standing by the accused is a senior agent of our enemy. As you can see, he is clearly directing her towards the photograph in question, the channel key. Close!"

The Constable jumped up. "Proof!" he cried. "Proof… of treason!"

With a shake of her robe the judge said, "Nonsense. Obviously she did not know what she was doing."

The Constable lifted his chin and said, "Is your Eminence directing the jury?"

"Damn right," the old lady replied. The Constable sat, fuming.

"Mister Usher," Lily's mother went on, "I take you now to the occasion of your second meeting. Please, hold in your mind how the girl looked to you. Did she look like this? Open!"

Suddenly Lily was looking at herself. All she could see was the interior of goods-in-transit as she held John's photograph, the light from her mobile phone playing across it. Her mouth was open and her expression distraught. She heard John's voice - "Exactly, madam," and then that of her mother - "Give us a general impression, if you will. Close!" Lily's view of the Court's chamber returned.

"Alarmed," Usher replied. "Surprised."

"Guilty, would you say?"

The Constable began to rise from his seat, but Her Eminence waved a hand at him and he sat down.

"Struck by horror, I would say, madam. If she did any wrong then she did it without knowing."

"Then there must be doubt that - whatever she did - she did it wilfully and deliberately. Do you agree?"

"I do."

"So, if any harm was done it was accidental. Do you agree?"

"I do, madam."

"Thank you, Mister Usher," said Lily's mother. "You may step down." John suddenly looked hunched and old. A mist gathered around him, collapsing into a ball of blue fire which faded away.

Lily's mother scowled at the Constable as a ripple of sympathy spread through the audience. "Oh poor child!" one knitting woman exclaimed. The Constable shifted uneasily in his seat. Two knitting women stood up. They looked at each other then cried together, "She was tricked!" Another stood up, her knitting needles whirring over a ball of yellow wool. "I am knitting!" she shouted, "a hat for Lily! Yellow for innocence!"

Her Eminence held up a hand and said, "Sometimes I despair. One moment you throw bottles at this child, and then she is all innocence. Neither is correct. Reflect. She opened the door to the most dangerous adversary we have met since the beginning. Sit down."

Lily's mother took in a deep breath and in her silvery voice - which had in it some pride - said, "Your Eminence, judges, I do not dispute that the accused unwittingly allowed into her world one of our enemy's creatures. But I dispute that this was an act of treason, wilful and deliberate. The evidence is circumstantial. I ask you to declare the accused innocent of this charge as it stands. The defence rests."

With a bow to the judges, Lily's mother smiled then walked back to her seat beyond the rows of knitting women who began again to clack with their needles, looking at each other sideways to identify who was responsible for what none was quite sure was a mistake.

Her Eminence spoke briefly to her colleagues on either side then stood. "The verdict of the Court of Council is this," she said. "On the charge of treason." She paused. The chamber was silent. "The accused, Lily Andreyevna Moss... is declared... innocent." Hats were thrown in the air, and knitting women jigged about in the aisle. "But!" The hubbub subsided. The knitting women stopped their clacking and their jaws dropped. The Constable leaned forward.

"On a secondary charge," the old lady went on, "she is declared guilty. Ignorance."

Everyone looked around. No-one knew what this meant. There was much frowning and fingering of ear-lobes. In her cage, Lily looked out at the audience through a mesh of wire, and decided that it was good not to be a traitor, but bad to be ignorant, and ignorant of what?

On either side of the old lady the hooded figures vanished, leaving her alone, leaning forward. "Lily Andreyevna Moss," she said. "In your world there are many destructive forces. You have added to them. Do you understand?"

All Lily could do was lower her head and nod.

"Ignorance is not a crime," said Her Eminence in a soft voice. "But this Court shall address it. You shall be taken from here and made subject to a course of instruction. But…" She paused again. The quiet was absolute. "We also demand that you strike back at our enemy, to restore the balance you have upset."

Lily's mother marched towards the platform. "Objection!" she cried with an anxious look at her daughter.

"Too late for that, Anna dear," Her Eminence replied. "As you know, we have kept our eyes on your daughter throughout her short life. We have visited her in hospital, where we left her flowers from our own garden. We have seen her at home, where her father has been caring for her as she has grown into the charming but foolish girl we see today. But the time for foolishness is past."

Her Eminence turned back to face Lily. "There will be danger," she said, "which you must face bravely. The ability you have is a power which might be misused. Your loyalty must always lie with us. Do you understand?"

Lily Moss nodded.

With a wave to the Constable the old lady cried, "Take her down!" The Constable advanced and with a leer on his grizzled face unlocked the metal cage and roughly grabbed Lily by the shoulders.

121

As his face dissolved and the bars of the cage flew away, Lily felt herself falling and her breath return.

She opened her eyes, as an owl hooted from the other side of Swivelhurst Road. She had a memory of her dream but it was fading fast. Her mother was there, John from goods-in-transit but called Sean, a man with an ugly face, and judges in black robes which hid their faces, one of them an old lady whose voice she was struggling to remember. Lily got out of bed. The clock said it was three in the morning. She reached into the drawer, pulled out her red book and picked up the pen. On the next clear page she wrote one word, because she hoped that in the morning she would remember from that enough to write the rest. That word was - Ignorant.

16 - Portsmouth

"Do help yourselves to the Montrachet."

On a calm night, in the private room of a restaurant in Portsmouth, high up in a building of metal and glass overlooking the dockyard, three men and three women sat at a table loaded with utensils and wine-glasses on a white cloth, the dim light giving a sparkle to glass but a comfortable glow on the faces of the diners. Roses stood in crystal vases next to white-labelled bottles whose corks lay below them, delicately poised on napkins. Conversation was muffled by thick red curtains around three walls, the fourth being a picture window through which, far below, lights twinkled along the waterfront and on the ferry to Gosport where apartment blocks stood up like luminous blocks of Lego.

At the head of the table sat a man in a black dinner jacket with lapels so glossy they reflected his bottle-blonde hair. Airily he waved a hand around the company of his guests and turned back to his neighbour, a black-haired woman in a purple sari. The wine flowed. There was chatter. There was anticipation. The man stood and tapped a wine-glass with a spoon.

"From Asia," said Twine, bowing to his neighbour, then looking clockwise around the table. "North America." A young blonde-bearded man in blue overalls. "South America." A large brown woman of middle age in a tight dress of shocking pink. "Africa." An intense, bald and bespectacled black man in a white dinner jacket who sported a purple bow-tie. "The Far East." A tiny Chinese woman in a flowery red-and-white cheongsam who giggled as Twine's gaze fell on her. "As host this year," Twine went on, "I am delighted to represent Europe. I do so with the full authority of the Lord Commander."

There were nods around the table, which Twine was pleased to see. Each region had its commander, and there could be jealousy.

"Welcome to you all," Twine went on. "We are delighted that you have travelled so far to attend this, the annual general meeting of G-Range. But before we dine, to business." He smiled. "Jacob, the financial summary."

Twine sat down, and the representative of Africa stood. He swelled in his white suit, rubbed a pudgy hand over his head and coughed. In a deep bass voice he said, "Expenditure, two point zero nine billion US dollars." He looked around the table. "Mainly research and development, Africa region, and production, Far East. Income, fourteen point eight billion US. A bumper crop. No tax." The Chinese woman at his side put a hand to her mouth to stifle a laugh. He fingered his spectacles and grinned. "Mainly from technology and insurance services, and consultancy in the military arena. From the sale of health foods, including the garnica spice, five hundred ninety million. Property portfolio stands at twenty-nine point three billion. Reserves one hundred thirty-nine point four billion. Thank you." He sat down, re-arranging his white jacket.

"Thank you, Jacob," said Twine. "A bumper crop, as you say. Saida, please report on our search for the Minister."

His neighbour stood and ran thin fingers down the folds of her sari. She blinked, and in a high and grating voice said, "Gentlemen and ladies, what I have to say is not much different from what I said last year."

She took a sip of water. "We have found seven fragments of God's Minister, who threw himself into the Crossway at the beginning," she went on. "That was a stupid mistake, but the damn fool did it anyway, and we pick up the pieces. What we have so far are virtual components, and we have housed them in my monastery. They are useless until we find physical fragments. We believe those exist somewhere in this globe, because that was his direction of travel, but we can get nowhere till they are in our hands."

Saida made to sit down, but Twine raised a hand. "Meanwhile," he said, "what resources are in place, and what do you need?"

124

Saida straightened. "I have fifteen images of the Second Wing," she said, "working day and night to investigate every sighting of more fragments. Hauntings, poltergeists, ghosts, you name it, wherever there is someone with a tale to tell." She sniffed and took another sip of water. "So far," she continued, "every one of these so-called paranormal events is either total rubbish, or only an example of how inefficient the Roamers are at managing death. Lost souls, remnants, memory that loses its way, it's a mess. Their Tower is not the fortress of memory that they think it is. If we had more images we could work faster, but the energy needed to project them would be too much. Anyway, we will continue as we are. Thank you."

Polite applause rippled around the table. "So," said Twine. "Stanley, please give us our position on the Roamers."

The representative of North America stood. He wrinkled his nose, rubbed his beard, sniffed and from the pocket of his blue overalls produced a scrap of paper from which he read, "Sixteen hundred up on last year. The list is nearly two-fifty thousand, world-wide, around two hundred thousand alive. Two thousand are on our payroll. The rest will have to be put down. So far we have no evidence of an active senior, unless Europe knows better." He sat, raised an eyebrow and looked directly at Twine.

Twine gave a gentle cough and smiled. "Seniors, yes," he said. "I have news. We have transferred a first-line resource, a spiker, one-way, out of the Crossway. Via a senior Roamer. The first time." Applause followed from everyone at the table, ranging from a hearty slap of the hands from Africa to a delicate patter of fingers from the Far East. When it subsided, Stanley asked, "So, is it a navigator?"

Twine nodded and replied, "She was identified at the age of two. We held our fire for ten years, until we could be sure she was useful. Whether she can be used reliably, though, remains to be seen."

"Why's that?" said Stanley. "Don't you have this freak locked up yet?"

"No," Twine replied. "We expect she will draw out others on our patch. A honey-trap, if you like. We've kept her in the wild."

"Jeez, that's risky. The old ones could pull her back."

"We have plans to deal with that, Stanley. Meanwhile, think what this means. We've transferred a spiker and it survived. We can transfer others. It's slow, but we've made a start. Eventually perhaps we can transfer even you. No longer images, but yourselves, fully and permanently in the game. You'll taste the Montrachet just as the natives do."

"If you behave like warriors, and not members of a gentlemen and ladies' dining club."

The voice came from behind a red curtain. Heads turned. A skeletal hand pulled aside the curtain and Chatham stepped forward in the grey robe of the Lord Commander, his chain of office twinkling in the dim light. Into a gathering of people assembled for a comfortable night he strode uncomfortably, urgent and with an expression of disdain. All stood, and wine from a tipped-over glass spread over the white table-cloth.

"Pardon my intrusion," said Chatham. "But there is business to be done. Not the business, Jacob, of which you speak so... confidently. Be seated."

Chatham walked forward and ran his hand around the rim of Twine's chair. "It has come to my attention," he said, looking around the table, "that there have been... irregularities, in the way that the business of our organisation has been conducted. Let us look at one of them."

He extended his right arm, and the grey robe hung to the floor, its folds like the bones of a bat's wing. Above the gold ring on his right hand appeared a hole in the air, which expanded and cleared to present a blank, black screen. At first fuzzy, an image on that screen came sharply into focus.

Chatham lowered his arm but the screen remained, at shoulder-height. "CCTV," he said. "From a bank in Lagos. Who is that at

126

the counter? Why, it is our Jacob. And what is he doing?" The image zoomed in then froze on Jacob's hand as he pushed papers over the counter. "Clearly, he is transferring money. Between what accounts? Why, from a G-Range account into his personal account. Seven million US dollars. And where in our accounts do we find that money entering the G-Range account and then leaving it? Nowhere. Obviously it never happened. Obviously, what we are seeing is an illusion. I wish it were, Jacob, I wish it were."

The Director of Finance twitched in his seat and fingered his bow tie. "Expenses," he mumbled. "And... Director's drawings, unforeseen... I shall certainly talk to our accountant about this... you have my..."

"We have your body in the Vault, Jacob," said Chatham with a smile, "and your image here." The screen shrank and vanished. "How safe in the Vault is that body? Oh dear, not safe at all. Now that I have ordered its destruction."

Jacob's mouth fell open, and his eyes widened, their pupils darting from side to side.

"Sadly, I do not have time to make this interesting," said Chatham. In a blast of white fire from the palm of Chatham's hand the image of Jacob dissolved into multi-coloured pixels, which dropped over his seat onto the floor, sparkled for a moment, then vanished.

"And you, Jingfei and Leonora," Chatham whispered, leaning on the table and fixing his eyes on the two women. "Jingfei, what have you done for us in the past year? How are your nails? Very pretty. You spend so much time on them. And how is your new swimming-pool, Leonora? Olympic size, so I am told. How wonderful that must be for you, so relaxing."

Both women pushed their chairs back, shivering with alarm, but before they could get to their feet they were enveloped in fire from Chatham's uplifted hands, and their images crumpled in fragments to the floor.

Chatham smiled, walked around the table, and sat in what had been the chair of his Director of Finance. "Thank you Twine, Stanley and

Saida, for your information. Twine, you will inform all regional commanders of what has happened here. This is now a time for action. Indolence, corruption, will not be tolerated. Make that your message."

*

When Stanley and Saida had returned to their regions, Chatham and Twine remained alone at the table with the view over the dockyard before them. Chatham sipped delicately at his glass. "You did well," he said. "They were unprepared. We shall find another Director of Finance. I have one in mind."

"As you command." Twine felt inside a pocket of his jacket. "We have received a gift for you, my master, from a regional commander. We had reservations about her loyalty, but we take this as a peace offering." He produced two photographs, which he slid over the table to Chatham, who picked them up and examined them.

"There he is," Chatham said. "Henry Chatham. A back view there, and part of his face there. Tourist shots, Italy. Now it really is time for dinner." He reached over the table for a book of matches, flicked one and held the photographs over it. The flame spread, and Chatham let the black ash fall into a side-plate. He dipped a forefinger into the ash then sucked on it. "An image feeding on images," he said. "Twine, if you also had this ability, you would feel the pleasure I feel at this moment." He sniffed, and downed the contents of his glass in a single stream.

"When we arrive at the Crossway, our master, will we remain an image?"

"No Twine. We shall leave the Vault, and then you shall have your bow. And, you shall see our Lord God. Then, you will understand. He is beautiful, more beautiful than you can imagine. He is Beauty itself. My heart swells at the memory of him."

"Bring on the day, our master."

128

"But now, tell me about the girl. Stanley was right. We need to do something about isolating her. And retrieve the key. Have you had ideas?"

"Yes our master. This poor soul has made a plan. It is underway."

"Good. If you need my help, ask. The time has come when I must be away more often, but I am delighted to see you take on more of my duties. Soon your hunt for Roamers shall be over. I shall find others to take that on. A grander task awaits, Twine. For that, you shall be at my side."

"We live to serve, our master."

Chatham sniffed the air. "I am called," he said. "But before I go, we must be certain of the spiker. It is outside, waiting. You know that it homed to me on its arrival. I shall now re-home it, to you. But it will follow you around like a useless dog unless I give you authority over it, and I am happy to do so now."

"Thank you, our master."

"Take my hand," Chatham said, stretching out his right hand.

Twine took his hand. He felt a tingle and when they parted he saw that the scar inside his palm which had been made at the killing of Usher, and had been the purple of a bruise, was now a pale red.

"The spiker is yours," Chatham said. "Its loyalty to you will be absolute, and it will follow when you leave this building. Preface all your orders to it with its name, spiker. It will decide from its own resources what needs to be done. I recommend that you find a target for it soon. It must feed within three days."

"We shall, our master. Bring on the day."

Chatham rose, pulled back his chair, and moved sideways. Twine saw as if obliquely in a mirror the body of his master vanish and he was alone, with a sparkling view and a bottle of Montrachet. He had been expecting trouble, but it was a good night after all.

129

When he left the building Twine looked around. The alley was a canyon between the backs of hotels and apartment blocks. It was empty but for a line of rubbish bins, its rain-wet cobbles reflecting the light of the moon and of an antique streetlamp. From a hotel came a muffled stream of pre-war jazz, a slow and sensual tune led by an alto sax and picked up by a clarinet whose notes soared into the night air and were carried off by the breeze.

He walked on for a few yards. Between two rubbish bins a plastic bag rustled. It was orange, and it bore the logo of a supermarket.

As he passed, the letters of the logo peeled off and fell into shadows on the cobbles. "Spiker," he whispered. "Follow."

He walked on. As he went towards the lights of the waterfront, Twine looked back over his shoulder. Behind him an arrow of scuttling shadows stretched out in his wake. To be the servant of the Lord Commander, such trust, such purpose. He walked on with a lighter step, chin up, chest out, and a smile which brought light to his eyes.

17 - Julian's Hotel

Moss. GR contract signed. Fee paid. New property, Julian's Hotel, Southsea. Same terms for further week. Contact Mister Tote, Tote Lettings Albert Road. Absolutely essential any time today or tomorrow. Reply asap. Chatham.

Moss replied, 'OK today. Moss,' and slipped the mobile back into his jacket. As he rounded the corner by the Co-Op he smiled for the first time in months, now his cash-flow was in rather than out. With a cheery cry of "More from those G-Range people, Percy. Mind the store," he dashed into the back office, threw aside his jacket, donned his Argyle sweater and called upstairs, "Field trip, Lily." He paused. "Are you ready?"

"No," was the answer.

"Hurry up," Riley Moss shouted.

"OK Dad. Wait." Moments passed. There was a rustling, then a clatter of boots on the narrow stairs as Lily threw herself down clutching at the handrails. "Ready!" she cried.

"Inspection," her Dad said, and made a play of inspecting her bomber jacket and jeans before scowling at her black leather boots. "Muck," he concluded. "You, Corporal Lily, have been rolling in muck again, like a little piglet. Look at these boots. Can you see your face in them? I can't."

"Dad," Lily replied. "People nowadays do not look at their faces in boots. They have mirrors for that."

"Ah, but I remember when I had to take a hot spoon to my toecaps. My old Sergeant would have killed me if he couldn't see his nose-hair in them when he looked down."

"Dad, someone has invented polish since the 1940's."

"Cheeky girl. You can peel the potatoes tonight."

"Oh Dad."

"With a knife, not a peeler."

"Sadist."

"Do you know what that means?"

"A follower of the Marquis de Sade, Dad. Do I get promoted?"

"OK. You can be a Brigadier and boss me around."

"Oh Dad, must I? Oh, all right." Lily puffed out her chest. "Captain!" she cried, and then, "That sweater is disgusting. What is it?"

"Disgusting."

"Disgusting what?"

"Disgusting, Brigadier."

"It smells. Eyes front when I'm talking to you!" Her Dad obliged, and then she began marching on the spot. "To the cleaners, quick march!" she cried. "Left right left right left right left!" till her Dad tapped her on the head, grasped her by the shoulders, turned her round and propelled her towards the door.

*

Southsea should have been only a half-hour away along the A27, but his Mondeo spluttered and all-but died at the Tangmere roundabout, so Moss drove like a pensioner till he was obliged to scythe across the traffic at Farlington onto Eastern Avenue and then into town, with rain in the air, parking in a side-street off Albert Road.

At first sight the office of Tote Lettings could be taken for just another junk shop. Furniture was piled up on the pavement in front of it. Sofas, chairs, and floor lamps, together with an assembly of bicycle parts and pictures in wooden frames, conspired to prevent any passer-by from passing anywhere but into the office, to whose open door a path had thoughtfully been cleared. This office could be distinguished from the bric-a-brac shops on either side only by the fresh paint of its shop-front, made whiter by sheets of A4 paper plastered over the window. Riley Moss scanned them as he went in, Lily trailing behind and eyeing the clutter. Most were the details of student lets, in the rows of terraced houses which give Southsea and the rest of the southern island its character of a lively and in parts dilapidated warren.

Behind a desk with his feet by an electric fire sat a berry-brown man who overflowed his chair. His chins were numerous, and onto the desk spilled his belly, contained only by a red t-shirt which bore the logo of a heavy metal band. With one hand he clasped a mobile telephone to his ear. In the other he held a cigarette. He waggled his head, ponytail flapping, and looked up. "Be with you in a moment," he said, then swore into the phone, fumbled with it and slammed it down on the desk. "How can I help?"

"Mister Tote?" Riley Moss enquired.

"That's me," Tote replied. "Unless you're from the Revenue, in which case I am someone else sitting here by accident. Who are you and what do you want?"

"Moss is the name, Moss Auctions."

"Oh yes." Tote struggled to his feet and extended a hand. "Mister Chatham said you was on your way. Maybe the little girl would like a seat."

Moss shook his hand. There was only one chair on his side of the desk and Lily self-consciously sat in it. "Chatham," said Moss. "Know him well?"

"Never met him. Does his business by 'phone. Anyhow, you'll want the keys of the hostel."

"Hostel? I thought it was a hotel."

Tote grinned. "Not much difference in that street. Hostel it is, for the moment I guess. Social services, resettlement of homeless guys. Chatham's company has held the lease for years. Seems they want it cleared. I could do that, says I, but it seems you're lucky. If there's anything worth having perhaps you could pass it by me first, if you catch my drift. OK?"

"Doesn't sound promising."

"You never know. Oh, and I've got something for you. Some creepy guy brought it in." Tote reached down and brought out an orange-plastic supermarket bag which he dumped on the desk. It contained coils of wire and lengths of plastic pipe. "There's a problem with the boiler. The engineer will be over later, but he needs this bag of parts. OK for you to take it? You can leave it in the basement."

*

It took five minutes to drive along the sea-front, on Clarence Esplanade and into a side-street flanked by terraces of three-storey Victorian villas in stages of decay. Moss parked the Mondeo in front of the hostel, above its door a panel of glass with 'Julian's' in a red script.

Seagulls mewed as Moss locked Lily into the car then made his way past the bins and up concrete steps to the main door, which was ajar. He went in. Immediately the smell hit him, from a damp carpet, from cigarette-smoke and from bags of rubbish lining the hall. Ahead was a wooden staircase, painted white, and behind that a view of saucepans piled up in the kitchen's sink. On his left a door led into a sitting-room. He poked his head in. The room was whitewashed, its walls and floor bare, and in the bay window an aspidistra threatened to overbalance from its wicker stand onto a sofa.

An old man sat in a deckchair by an electric fire. "Are you Moss?" he said.

134

"I am," Moss replied. "And you are…?"

"Most people call me the Old Git." He chuckled. "The name's Bolney." The old man made no attempt to get up. Swathed in a red dressing-gown, still in his pyjamas and with tartan slippers on his feet, he was slight and bony, with only a few wisps of white hair. His brown eyes twinkled but he was deathly pale, and it seemed to Moss that the old man's future in this world would be brief. "The agent telephoned," Bolney went on. "Said you were on your way. We're not used to visitors. What is your business here?"

"Just a survey, Mister Bolney."

"Pity. What we need is a heating engineer. The central heating has packed up. Is that your business?"

"No." Moss stuck out his chin. "Antiques are my business."

"Sorry. I'm not for sale. Did I say that? No I didn't. It was someone else, not me. Carry on."

"I will, thank you." Moss walked back out into the hall, and out of the hostel. He unlocked the Mondeo, and Lily climbed out.

"There's something odd about that bag," said Lily, pointing at the bag of boiler parts on the back seat. "I'm sure it moved of its own accord. I heard it rustle."

Riley Moss rolled his eyes. "Lily," he said, "bags do not move of their own accord. Must have been the vibration of the car. Here, I'll take it."

By the main entrance a set of stone steps led down to a door. They walked into the basement. "Tanked," said Moss. "Damp-proof, more or less." He switched on a light by the door, and had to stoop under the low ceiling. Shelves filled the dreary space, on them tins of beans, tins of paint, and packs of toilet paper. In the far corner the white box of a boiler was fixed to the wall.

Moss threaded himself through the shelving and deposited the bag by the boiler. "Heavy-duty boiler, this," he said, studying the

135

control panel. "It might help if it was turned on." He flicked the mains switch, and the boiler started up. The pilot light was lit, the main burners came on and the fan whirred in a steady rhythm. "There's nothing wrong with it," said Moss. He flicked the mains switch off, and the boiler calmed down. "Not our problem," he said.

They tramped up a set of wooden steps and emerged under the main staircase, turned into the hall, then up the dog-legs of two staircases to the top floor. Here were doors to bedrooms and a bathroom with blue linoleum and bare walls. Moss opened the doors, looked in and made notes. Lily peered around him and saw only tatty old furniture, and they already had too much of that in the warehouse. By the bathroom door a ladder was propped against the wall, below a hatch in the ceiling.

"Hold the ladder, Lily," Moss said. He climbed up and pushed the hatch open, levered himself up and disappeared into the roof-space. After a few minutes he returned and climbed down. "Only a pipe that goes out through the roof. Nothing there."

The four bedrooms on the next floor were all cheaply furnished and rank with sweat and stale cigarette-smoke. They stayed in each room only long enough to examine the fireplaces, and to get a view of the weed-infested patio at the back. On the ground floor, Moss poked his head round the door of the sitting-room and asked, "Is that your room at the back, Mister Bolney?"

"It is."

"Do you mind if I take a look?"

"Be my guest."

Moss stepped into the back room, leaving Lily in the hall.

"Girl!" Bolney called from the front room. "Can you get me a glass of water please?"

Lily paused. She was not used to dealing with old men. "Yes, sir," she said, and went down the hall to the kitchen, picked up the cleanest glass she could find and put it under the tap. Her Dad appeared from the back room. "Thirsty?" he said. "You'll get a good shot of bacteria from that tap." Lily replied, "It's for the old man in the sitting-room. Is that OK, Dad?" Her Dad thought for a moment, but nodded, and headed out through the kitchen door to inspect the rear of the hostel.

In the front room, Lily handed the glass to the old man. He felt in a pocket of his dressing-gown, pulled out a pack of pills and popped two of them in his mouth then took a deep swig of water. "That's better," he said. "Much obliged. Heart." He tapped his chest. "Not long before I'll be six feet under. Could be any time now."

"I'm sorry to hear that, sir."

"You're a polite little thing," he said. "How old are you? Eight? Nine?"

"Twelve, sir."

"Twelve? Goodness me, soon you'll be all grown up. Stand by the fire so I can take a good look at you." Lily obliged, but awkwardly. "I had a kid once," the old man went on. "But I hit the road when I was fifty. It was never the same when the broadsheets went tabloid. You should try sleeping under tabloid newspapers, draughty as Hell, pardon my language. I thought I'd die under a bush somewhere. But those busybodies from social services picked me up, and here I am."

"I'm glad to see you better, sir."

"And you can stop calling me Sir right now. It's annoying. You can call me Silas."

"Yes. Silas."

"And who are you?"

"Lily," she said, remembering just in time not to say Sir.

"Nice name. I've been waiting for you, Lily."

"You have?"

"I want to give you a present." From a pocket inside his dressing-gown he pulled out a leather pouch. Even that minimal effort left him breathless and he panted for a few seconds then held out his hand. "Take it," he said. "It's my memory."

"Your memory, Silas?"

"Before I lose it, I want you to have it."

Gingerly, Lily took the pouch from the old man's hand. He smiled and rubbed his jaw. "That's better," he said. "Just in time. Open it up. Take a look."

The pouch was a square of brown leather with a flap that fitted under a strap. Lily pulled the flap away and poked a finger inside. She felt something hard and round, and tipped it out into the palm of her hand. It was a penny, an old brown penny. On one side was the head of a man with a beard, on the other a seated woman above the date, 1929. She looked up at the old man. "Look after it," he said. "Put it under your pillow. It's good luck."

"That's very kind… Silas. But I'm not sure I should."

"Nonsense," the old man said with a flash of anger. "It's yours now. Rude to refuse a present, don't you think?"

"Oh yes… Silas. Yes of course."

"Do you girls have pockets nowadays?"

"Yes I do."

"Well, put it in your pocket, and don't tell a soul about it. Mum's the word." He tapped his nose with a bony finger and smiled. "And don't spend it either."

"No I won't."

"Good girl. Now run along, your father's coming back. He could do with a diet. Pity he's not a heating engineer."

"Thank you, Silas. I will look after it. Your… memory."

The old man sniffed and with a wave of his hand said, "Make damn sure you do, child. It's a precious thing. Be off with you. I need to sleep."

"Yes Silas. Thank you," said Lily and she made for the door.

Back in the car, Moss turned to his daughter and said, "What was that about?"

"He just wanted to talk."

Her Dad frowned. "Well as long as that's all it was. You know what I've said about talking to strangers."

"I'm not seven, Dad."

"And you're not twenty-seven either. All right, Brigadier. Back to camp," he said, and accelerated towards the seafront.

*

That night, Lily lay in her bed looking up at the ceiling, with the old man's penny under her pillow. Long ago, between awake and asleep she would float up through that ceiling to the forest of Roamers Cross and the little black-haired boy. When she was seven she climbed up the ladder of a man who came to paint the staircase, opened the hatch - just as she saw her Dad do today - and climbed into the roof-space. Nothing there. It was just a triangular space of dusty air, timbers, some fabric that was rubbery, and yellow prickly stuff she later learned was insulation. Now, the streetlight that spilled from above the curtains and made patterns on the ceiling was a mockery. Time to move on, Lily. Nothing there.

As she drifted off to sleep, though, her in-between state returned. Something was moving in her head and it came in pictures.

Often when she went to sleep she would see faces, that flashed before her eyes and grumbled and cajoled, and she rejected them. She would say Go outside, you are not welcome. Now, she could not reject them. They passed before her as on a strip of film, faces of children and of men and women; a room with brown wallpaper where a toy fort lay under a Christmas tree; horses, and buses with curly staircases that drove along streets where people wore old clothes and bowed to each other; small shops in rows, each of them selling something different, fruit in baskets and fish in trays, eels that wriggled; the back of a soldier's head, his green cap above a shaven neck and the barrel of his rifle poking up; a whistling overhead that was dreadful as artillery shells exploded in the sea behind; crowds, of people along streets with tall grey buildings, people who were not English, laughing, singing, and waving flags; the face of a pretty nurse with a white cap; a body lying under newspaper in a forest.

These were faces and places that she had not seen, that were not in her memory. She observed someone else's life, detached, watching as it unfolded and discharged itself, as she slipped into a deep but troubled sleep.

*

The basement of Julian's Hotel was pitch-black. No-one, even if standing beside it, would have seen the twitching of the supermarket bag under the boiler. There was a rustle, though, as the letters of the supermarket's name peeled away and dropped to the floor. That became a patter as they scuttled up the wall, clung to the boiler's exhaust pipe and climbed up through the crevices of the building. In the attic space they formed a rippling line of spidery shadows, then one by one they slipped through the gap around the hatch, clung to the wall and came down. Some headed into the bathroom, and others slipped under the bedroom doors. The rest headed down the staircase, a cascade of grey shadows on white wood. On the landing all but one scuttled under bedroom doors. The remaining one slithered and hopped down the staircase to the hall, where it waited.

Silas Bolney was awake in his back room. Still wearing his dressing-gown he lay in bed, propped up on a pillow. Light from outside made a dusty white slice between him and the empty fireplace. He heard what sounded like a crab on the staircase, then

140

nothing as whatever it was landed on the carpet of the hall. Most likely a rat. He was not afraid of rats, and decided to leave it alone. But it would not leave him alone, for he heard something slip under his door, and then the patter of claws on his floorboards as the rat came towards him.

He lifted his head but saw only a grey shadow. He hissed at it, and it halted. For a moment he wondered why there should be a shadow cast by nothing.

In that instant the shadow leapt onto his bed and inflated to a sphere that flung itself at his head, encircling it, clinging to his mouth, its vapour choking him as Bolney tried to raise his arms but was paralysed, his eyes staring at light through the window which suddenly was grey, split by pulsating veins. He felt a claw at the back of his neck, and a spike that pierced his skin. It pierced further, but it was a feeling without pain, a thin spike penetrating his brain.

So that is what a spiker does, he thought, goes for the hypothalamus, nasty mind-sucker, and then he began to forget.

As his consciousness slipped away into a fog of oblivion, finally, Silas Bolney forgot how to breathe.

18 - Mystery Virus Kills Southsea Man

Frank Dennis, Inspector of Hampshire CID, shoved the newspaper across the table of the Moss Auctions workshop and jabbed a finger at the headline. "No virus, Mister Moss," he said. "I am investigating a murder. And you were the last to see him alive."

"Except for the murderer," Riley Moss replied.

The Inspector was a crow looking for meat, Moss had decided, young and sharp. His Sergeant, a woman, wore the uniform of Sussex Police, mid-twenties, long straight black hair and a face he could lose himself in. The uniform did not suit her. He did not like the way she wandered off, flirted with Percy, disappeared into the office then returned to plant herself by the doorway, but everything else about her was just fine, especially her smile.

Dennis looked around. "Tools," he said. "Very orderly. A lot of wire. Heavy duty wire. What's it for?"

"I make keys."

"You don't make keys with wire, Mister Moss. You have blank keys and that machine of yours. I bet that's noisy as hell when you're running it. Gone a bit deaf have we?"

"Not yet. I do repairs, bicycles, furniture. The wire comes in handy."

"And the bit you cut recently off that straight wire. What did you do with that?"

"Pinned the leg of a chair. Where are you heading with this?"

"I ask the questions, Mister Moss." Dennis blinked. "If you remember any more about the last moments of Mister Bolney, you

will let us know, won't you? And I hope you don't mind if I take a
piece of that wire. Just routine."

"If you must. I want it back."

*

In an office of MI5 high above the rumble of London's Victoria
Street, Twine was concerned that his biscuits were not fresh. Two of
them, bourbon biscuits, sat in a saucer on a table under the window.
The office was plain, small and all-but empty, a threadbare carpet,
beige walls without decoration, a yellow light-bulb without a shade.
There was a distinct whiff of paint and sawdust. To some this would
be an admirable example of economy. To Twine it was a sign of the
times. Cuts in the funding of the public sector had reached even to
the secret services, and he was glad he would be getting out when
there was still carpet on the floor.

He turned, to face the young woman sitting in the only chair in the
room, who wore the uniform of a Sergeant of Sussex Police.
Amanda by name, dark-haired, lissom; Twine wondered for a
moment whether she was a Roamer plant, but immediately dismissed
the idea. She loved him, for his position, so superficial, so liable to
gaze at him with an expression of vacant wonder. She would be
disappointed physically, but meanwhile it was good to have a slave.

"So Amanda," he said, silhouetting himself against the window in
the manner he learned from Chatham. "How was the secondment?
Learn much from Police work?"

She shifted in her seat, working her hair, stroking it, letting it fall in
appealing curls over her throat and down to what had no appeal for
Twine. "Yes sir," she breathed. "I learned that it's not for me."

A laugh grew somewhere inside Twine but surfaced only as a
broadening of his smile. "Just as well," he said. "We need you here,
Sergeant."

143

The beam of delight on her face could have lit a small town. "I did as you required, sir," she said. "I hid the box under the target's bed, under a piece of carpet actually. No-one would know it was there unless there was a totally thorough search, or someone told them. And I attached the tracking device to the girl's jacket. That will be hard to find. Our colleagues in the Police will really have to know their stuff."

"Good girl," Twine said. "Now we'll see whether they're up to scratch. It's a pity we have to go through these exercises, but that's inter-service operation for you. Keeping them on their toes. Just one of our many tasks. Well done anyway. I'm pleased."

Amanda replied, "Thank you sir!" with an eagerness that Twine finally found appealing.

*

Inspector Dennis was not having a good day. First he had lost his own Detective Sergeant to an investigation in Winchester, and instead had to put up with some uniformed woman seconded from God knows where who knew as little about his patch as he knew about hers, and now the theory he had formed in his mind about the murder of Silas Bolney was crumbling into ashes.

"Not wire," said the pathologist, a grey-haired Scottish woman. "I'll print you out the report, in an hour or two."

"Damn it," said Dennis, standing under the blinds of a mortuary in Southampton. "What is it then?"

"A series of strokes," the pathologist said. "Damage to the brain over wide areas, in a pattern that's new to me. Considering your man's age, I could just say Dementia and move on, but… when you stack that up against the perforation at the back of his head, well, then it's time to look again, and I did. Whatever it was, it was long, thin and triangular. Hollow. And it delivered a shot of acid, melted our man's brain."

"Jesus."

"Not sure Jesus would do that."

*

Moss said nothing to Lily about the Police. Together that evening, perched on chairs in the back office which at night became their sitting room, they went through the attachments of the email from the Lodge, which Lily had received on her laptop from the school where Lady Meizel was a Governor. Three documents with one picture, they were hand-written and scanned-in.

"So we get one chance at this, Lily," said Moss. "Then they get deleted. Is that right?" Lily nodded. "Very strange," her Dad went on.

"Miss Chesterton says it's all OK."

The writing was spidery and old-fashioned, with a great many embellishments which for Lily made it hard to read, but no problem for her Dad for that was the writing he was taught as a child. After a while he said, "It's all rather vague. Are you sure you want to give this a try?"

"Yes Dad."

"But what happens if you have a turn while you're there?"

"They can phone you, Dad. And look, it says that if the student or the parents are not happy with the school they get their money back. That sounds very fair."

"But we're not paying a penny."

"Not one penny."

19 - The First Friday

The first Friday arrived. From what Riley and Lily remembered of the email from the Lodge before it deleted itself, new students were to wear their normal clothes on the day, and a school uniform would be issued on arrival. They were to carry nothing into the school, and nothing out. Lunch was provided.

From Lily's bedroom window, Moss watched her standing by the post-box. Another rite of passage, into the unknown. The sky was grey but she had refused a raincoat, insisting on her bomber jacket and jeans. It was warm, though earlier than she was used to, seven in the morning, and the train that brought so many of the local school's children would not arrive for an hour.

A white bus drew up in front of the Estate Agent's office, smaller than a coach but larger than one of the Army trucks of his youth. Now it was her turn. Other faces were at its windows, and it opened at the back, where a black boy in what looked like a military camouflage uniform helped her up. And then they were gone.

Moss turned from the window and walked across the landing to his bedroom, where he opened his wardrobe, took out the case of his guitar and laid it on the bed. He opened it, took out the guitar and tuned it by ear, then sat on the bed and quietly began to play, disappearing in his head to somewhere in the Mississippi delta.

*

"Hi noobie!" came a cry from the front of the bus, the driver. "Name?"

Sitting in the back seat, Lily thought this must mean her, so she yelled back, "Lily!" and two lines of faces turned, about a dozen in all, an equal mix of boys and girls. Her face reddened. "Sit back!" the driver cried. "It's only a short hop from here!"

Across the aisle, a black boy with a grin said, "Hello. I'm Theo. Where are you from?" He had an American accent, and he wore a patterned, multi-coloured uniform like a soldier. All the other boys and girls wore the same. They turned their heads and faced front, leaving it to the boy to interrogate their new companion.

His question, though, to Lily seemed daft. They knew where she was from. "Swivelhurst," she replied.

The boy frowned. "Ain't never heard of it," he said. "Is that in the north some place? Boston?" Behind his head the landscape flashed by. The morning had become foggy and the window was misting up.

"Sussex, Theo," Lily replied. "England. South."

"Oh, England, yeah," said Theo. "You know Benny Hill?"

"Sorry, no."

"Hehe, he's cool, funny man. I watch him on TV all the time. You like TV?"

"We don't have one, Theo."

"You what! Wow, so weird! But cool. Uh oh, time for a hop. Sit back. It gets bumpy."

Lily Moss had never before travelled in a bus that hopped. It was difficult to see in the fog, but she could tell from the rumbling that the bus was picking up speed over a rough road, and then the rumbling stopped so the road must be smooth. For a few moments she felt sleepy with the smoothness of it, until the rumbling began again but quieter.

"Everyone OK?" the driver cried out. "Noobie Lily, you OK?"

"Yes, thank you," she yelled back, as the fog began to clear.

She did not recognise the landscape but it was probably East Sussex, for the bus had headed east. It was all very green, and as the fog cleared she could see that the bus was slowly traversing a field over a track of white stone which led in a straight line to a building. She craned her neck to the right and looked forward, past the driver. She recognised it from its photograph, the school, the Lodge.

"Ain't it just the prettiest place?" sighed Theo.

It was a mansion, a stately home of grey stone over three floors, with porticoes of arches that ran along the lower two floors, at one end an octagonal tower topped with a gracefully curving roof and weather-vane, at the other end a wider square tower that rose high above the red-tiled roof. Everywhere was decoration, crenellations along the roof-line, balustrades, windows, some as bay windows letting out into the porticoes, finials poking skywards from every corner, sculpture wherever there was space to sculpt. It would have been a castle if it did not somehow keep the character of a home, a very gracious home, all behind railings that reminded her of Buckingham Palace.

The bus drew up at a wrought-iron double-gate. Statues stood on brick pillars, on the left a young girl, dress billowing and flowers in her hand, her head uplifted in ecstasy. On the right, an old man stood hunched and bony, his face downcast with a grimace of despair. "The one on the left," said Theo, "is how you feel going in. The one on the right is how you feel after Science class with Miss Servator." In front of him, two girls giggled.

The driver honked his horn, the gates opened and the bus puttered through into a wide semicircle of white gravel. This place was huge, and Lily wondered how big the building must be, somewhere behind it, of which this was only the lodge. They stopped by a projecting portico with grey columns, and Theo was the first out, giving Lily a hand down, which was embarrassing but she smiled as her boots crunched into the gravel. She looked up. The mansion towered above her like a decorated cliff, and on the pediment of the portico, around a sculpted shield, ran a phrase which she knew was Latin but did not know what it meant - *caelum non animum mutant qui trans mare currunt*. She made a mental note of it, in case anyone might ask, but wondered what currants had to do with horses, and the 'mutant' was a worry.

"Moss, Lily!" came a man's cry from inside the portico. The others filed past, looking her up and down, most smiling, some of the boys with their noses in the air. Around from the front of the bus came the driver. He was young and his dark hair was tied back into a pony-tail. Hands on hips he eyed her for a moment. He looked Indian, American Indian, a hawkish nose, a weather-beaten brown face and his taste in clothes was bizarre, a lurid purple tie-dye t-shirt above black trousers with a ludicrous flare that belonged to her Dad's generation. He was chewing on something gold, a coin. "You better hurry, Lily," he said. "Ordinal takes no prisoners."

"Come along, come along. I don't have all day." A man emerged from the shadows of the portico. "Lily Moss," he said. "You are Lily Moss?"

"Yes sir," she replied.

"I know you are. I don't know why I asked. It must be Tuesday. Cardinal, don't you have something better to do than stand around gawping?"

The Indian, Cardinal, rolled his eyes and with a smile wandered off through the flower-beds to a gate in a hedge.

Ordinal was no older than middle-aged, but could be the twin of the old man Lily met in Southsea, Silas. He was bald but for a few wisps of white hair, and so bony that his bottle-green suit hung off him like melting spinach, but his complexion had colour, and there was a twinkle in his brown eyes. "You will refer to me as Ordinal," he said. "That's because I keep young tykes like you in order. I prefer THE Ordinal, but people never have the time to say it. Discipline, Lily Moss. Perhaps you are not used to it." He peered at her with his eyes wide. "Now," he went on, "to your induction. This way." He stalked off into the portico with the tails of his green suit flapping, and Lily followed, struggling to keep up.

They entered a rectangular hall panelled in dark wood, whose ceiling was as high as a cathedral's. At its centre, on a plinth of black stone,

149

a sculpture slowly revolved. It comprised a number of white spheres, inter-connected, all inside an egg of translucent material which looked like plastic. "The Omnium," Ordinal said. "Don't touch."

Ordinal's boots rapped on the stone floor as he ushered her to a door under a grand wooden staircase. "In there," he said. "Light-switch on the left. Find a uniform that fits and put it on. Your clothes in one of the bags on a peg, look for your name. I will stay here discreetly. That is only polite. We are very polite here, no gender business at all. There are many genders in the sea - the Universe, I mean, you haven't done Cosmology yet, have you? You'll enjoy that, though we've got you down as a navigator, maybe THE navigator. We lost him, you know, when we came across. All a bit of a mess. SUCH a hurry. He navigated himself somewhere and we have no idea where. That's why I have to run the navigation course, and I'm not cut out for it. There. In you go."

To Lily this was an incomprehensible babble, and in some alarm she allowed herself to be shoved into darkness underneath the staircase. She felt for the switch and flicked it on. When she emerged, now in the military uniform of the others, Ordinal clasped his hands and eyed her from top to toe. "Very good," he said. "But you are rather small. Not sure the uniform fits, but it will do. Take your belongings back home with you after school, and the uniform, and nothing else. Every time you return - oh, it must be Friday after all - you wear that. Understood?" Lily nodded.

"Come," Ordinal said, with a wave of his hand, and he strode off towards the bottom of the staircase. Lily spotted a purple rope slung across a corridor off the hall. "Private quarters," said the Ordinal. "You never go there. The school is here. In the tower."

This was the square tower Lily had seen from outside. A wide polished-wood staircase, decorated with carvings of cupids and flowers along its entire length, stretched upward through a series of clockwise doglegs. Some could be seen from below, some vanished into the shadow of upper floors. Ordinal pointed towards two iron-studded doors to the left of the staircase. "Outside in the garden, for lunch," he said. "No rain. We don't allow it."

"No rain, sir?" Lily said. "How do things grow?"

"They don't. If something dies I replace it from the Tower." Ordinal set foot on the red-carpeted stairs. "Come," he said. "First stop, Public Administration. One of mine."

They tramped upward, past square windows of leaded glass, and turned to the right, to another iron-studded door, which Ordinal pushed open with a cry of "Put that away!"

In a cramped schoolroom with a single lozenze-shaped window a half-dozen military-clad students, mainly girls, were bent over their desks, writing furiously. Bookshelves overflowed with box files and stacks of paper tied with ribbons, and on a filing cabinet stood a glass bowl where a goldfish meandered. On the blackboard was written, in a spidery hand, 'Discuss the impact on the population of a rural town of merging Health and Social Care services. One hour.' The students were all older than her, she was glad to see, for she had no idea where she would start with a subject like that. Ignorant. Ordinal ushered her out, with a cry of "Transport!"

Up they went to the next floor, and a door which Ordinal ignored. "Test in progress," he said. "We will return to that later."

Up they went again, around the dogleg to a storey whose walls were of beige stone perforated by arrow-slit windows, at its centre a cube of glass with an open door. In that cube sat four students at black metal desks. Theo was among them and he gave Lily a wave.

"Focus!" hissed a lady in a white robe. Her hair was long and black, her face thin and her black eyes piercing. Theo turned his head towards the teacher who - on a long wooden table laden with curious tubes, retorts and bubbling saucepans - was bashing a pestle into a mortar from which fumes of purple rose. Behind her a whiteboard was covered with long strings of formulae of a kind which were to Lily no more than black squiggles. "No interruptions, Ordinal!" cried the teacher. "Or we might have an accident."

Ordinal bowed, and took Lily by the arm to a narrower staircase at one corner. "Miss Servator," he whispered. "Science, Mathematics, and anything to do with computers. Very famous, and very tetchy."

The next floor was much as the first, a schoolroom with panelled walls and a window that gave out onto a view of fields and hills. Bookshelves were laden with leather-bound tomes and the light was speckled with dust.

Three girls and two boys sat in a curve, pondering a sculpture which rose high above the red carpet and was a copy of that in the entrance hall, inter-connected spheres inside an egg of translucent plastic. The whole structure slowly revolved, and the students stared at it with empty faces. Every so often a sphere would change colour, from white to green to red and then back to white, and the pipework between them glowed through all the colours of the rainbow.

"Wake up!" said Ordinal, and heads turned towards him. "First one to predict red correctly on level three gets a chocolate orange." The heads turned back. "Martha," he said, gesturing at the girl who looked oldest, more woman than girl. "Keep score. I'm busy."

Ordinal again took Lily by the arm and they ascended a still narrower staircase towards an opening in the roof. "Navigation, that was," said Ordinal. "Another of mine. Often I have to be in two places at once, which is inconvenient, but that is what navigation is about. Ah, here we are."

They stepped out onto the roof of the tower. Through its battlements the view was of green fields and of hills fringed with forests. Ordinal drew a deep breath and patted his chest. The Lodge sat in a bowl of the hills, blue sky above with a scattering of cloud which Lily thought close enough to touch. The nearest to this she could remember was on a school trip to Stratford, where the sky seemed strangely close, though there it stretched off into the distance, whereas here it enclosed, as if the Lodge and its surroundings were at the centre of an immense blue and green bubble.

"Here we hold classes in Cosmology," said Ordinal, "the organisation of cosmic forces and bodies. Mysul holds those, and she is always busy so they hardly ever happen. You have met Mysul, I believe."

"Is that Lady Meizel?"

"Meizel? Interesting," Ordinal replied. "Yes. And if she were here - and in a good mood - she would tell you a thousand interesting things about this Universe of yours. I shall think of an example."

He blinked, sniffed, extended his right fore-finger and waggled it in a curious manner. "If I were to tell you that your Universe has a gate, to other universes," he said, "would you be surprised?"

"Yes, sir."

"Don't you know that your Universe has a centre? That it was from that point that the Universe grew? Haven't you wondered what might still be there, at that point?"

"I haven't really thought about it, sir."

"Then you have not wondered enough. Your horizon is limited. Expand it, girl. Expand it!"

Ordinal raised his arm and his fore-finger began to rotate. As it did so it appeared to Lily that behind him the sky stretched back, the clouds became bigger, thinner and darker until all she saw above her was night and a field of stars, and one of those stars grew, a blue dot which expanded, around it a haze of orange; but when he curled the fore-finger back into his palm it vanished, and again the sky was a blue bowl with a scattering of cloud.

It was a wonderful illusion. Lily had heard of hypnotists who could do tricks like that - make people bark like dogs, and put all kinds of strange ideas into their heads. Ordinal was a hypnotist. She wondered whether he could teach her that trick. She wondered. Then it came to her - he was teaching her, to wonder.

"There is much you have missed, Lily Moss," said Ordinal with a frown. "With a mind like yours you should have missed none of it. We shall do something about that. Now, let me show you what we missed on the way up here."

They descended, past the curious sculpture of spheres, past Miss Servator who was busy squiggling on the whiteboard, to the second floor, where Ordinal knocked on the iron-studded door, opened and put his head around it, then ushered Lily in. The bus driver, Cardinal, stood at a table with a book in his hand. In front of him, three students sat cross-legged on a red rug. To Lily's eye the students appeared to be levitating, as if someone from the floor above were raising and lowering them on strings.

"Welcome," Cardinal said. "For your information, we are discovering whether meditation is an aid to memory. In the context of the oral tradition of sacred texts. So far, it seems not." He pursed his lips and looked at his students with disapproval. "Because they keep jigging about."

"The Comparative Religion class," said Ordinal to Lily. "Very relaxing. Thank you Cardinal. I hope to see you at lunch."

"I may be asleep," Cardinal replied.

Back on the ground floor, Ordinal gestured towards one of the two side-by-side doors at the foot of the staircase. "Ancient History class," he muttered. "Door on the right. I never know what I am going to find down there." He pushed open the door, which swung back with a squeak, revealing an iron spiral staircase which led down through a tube of dark stone into shadows. He went first, clutching at a handrail.

They arrived in a chamber which Lily had seen before but could not remember when. It was of solid stone, flagstones on the floor, lit by flaming torches. A low platform lay below an arching window of stained-glass panes, light playing in a spectrum of colours over its tracery as if outside there were trees shifting in a wind. To the right, a long box of polished wood stretched along the wall, and in it were rows of seats.

There one student sat, a plump little girl with an oriental face. She was gazing intently at the gilded chair on the platform below the window, where a fat man in a yellow uniform, with a red sash, gold braid on his shoulders and brown riding boots, was asleep, his gingery moustache and whiskers trembling in the snores from his bulbous nose.

"Chun," whispered Ordinal. "Has the Constable been asleep for long?"

The little girl blinked. "For a few minutes, sir," she replied. "He was most interesting before that. His description of the battle of Salamis was very dramatic."

"I'm glad to hear it," said Ordinal. "I doubt, though, that we will get much sense out of him for an hour or two. This is Lily Moss, by the way. Say Hello." The girls exchanged greetings, the oriental girl standing up and delivering a deep bow. "I have had a thought," Ordinal went on. "Chun, come here please." She stepped from the box and trotted over, delivering another bow and a smile. "Chun," said Ordinal, "this is Lily's first day. Do you remember your first day?"

"Yes I do, sir," Chun piped up. "I was so happy to hear everyone speaking perfect Mandarin."

Ordinal looked down at Lily. "That is one thing you need to understand, Lily Moss. I expect you think everyone here speaks English."

"Yes I do, sir. It's all I have heard."

"You have heard it, young tyke, because of our automatic translation. Everyone hears in their own language. A remarkable invention of Miss Servator's. Look at Chun's lips while she says something. Chun, please say, 'What a nice day it is."

Chun obliged, and Lily could see that the movement of her lips bore no relation to the words she heard. "Now Lily," Ordinal went on, "Say something for Chun. 'Yes it is a nice day'." Lily obliged. "Did that make sense to you, Chun?"

"Yes sir," Chun replied. "Perfect Mandarin. Though there are movements of the body which would make it more perfect than perfect."

"Quite so," said Ordinal. "Lily Moss, this is a most crucial part of your induction. Our students come to us from across the globe. We

155

put huge effort into making all of them feel at home. Be prepared for occasional confusion. For example, sometimes you will see students stepping over objects which you do not see. But as a whole we rub along. I am sure you will get used to it, in no time at all. And talking of time, it is time for the morning break."

Lily had no idea how he could know that, for she had seen no clock, no means by which he could tell the time, except perhaps by the workings of his insides. They climbed back out of the chamber, leaving Chun to collect her books. When they reached the top of the spiral staircase, the howl of a hooter rang around the entrance hall, followed by a patter of feet on stairs. With an immediate right-turn, Ordinal opened the other door at the foot of the staircase and let Lily through, into a corridor of stone walls with a pitched roof of glass and metal struts, one door off it to the right with the label of 'Ablutions' and another to the left - 'Housekeeper'.

"Let's say Hello," Ordinal said. "She is bound to be in." He unlatched the left-hand door and they stepped through.

In a pine-panelled room, lit from the ceiling, an old woman sat at a wooden desk. Her booted feet were well off the floor. Above a dark-lined face from which two beady eyes peered through round spectacles, her hair was grey and tucked up into a conical woolly hat. She wore a smock of coarse brown wool that hung around her high chair like a curtain. Behind her one door bore the sign of 'KITCHEN' and another of 'STORE'. "Ordinal," she said in a reedy voice, "and who is this?"

"Lily Moss, a new student," Ordinal replied.

"Is she clean?"

"Very."

"Then she may approach."

Ordinal shoved Lily forward. "Very pleased to meet you," said Lily, putting on her most honest face.

156

"Really?" said the old woman, wrinkling her nose. "Ordinal, is this girl mad?"

"Not as far as I know."

"That makes a change. Girl," she said, leaning forward over what looked like a dusty book. "My rules are simple. Bring nothing into the school, except the uniform. Take nothing out, except the uniform. Eat what is put in front of you. Clean up after you. And always be polite to the mechanicals. Do you understand?"

Lily nodded and said, "Yes, my lady."

"I am not your lady. I am the Housekeeper and Head of Mechanicals. Ordinal, take her away. I am devising the lunch menu, always a challenge." She waved a hand, and Ordinal guided Lily back into the corridor.

There, Lily asked, "Excuse me, sir, what are mechanicals?"

"You will see in a moment," he replied. "This way to the sitting room, where people… sit."

The corridor opened into a conservatory of glass and white wood. Through its windows Lily made out a group of students on the grass outside running, jumping and then standing on their heads. Chun and another girl were sitting on wicker chairs in a corner. At their side stood a woman much like the Housekeeper but younger, similar in features and in dress, and so was probably a relation. The two girls were talking to her, and then she bowed and glided past the Ordinal and Lily out into the corridor.

"A mechanical," Ordinal said. "Taking an order for a refreshing break-time drink and a biscuit. Remember, always be polite to mechanicals. They are easily distressed. You, though, will have to do without a break, because I am pressed for time and need to show you where to have lunch. Here…"

The outer door of the conservatory led to a circular platform of stone in the shadow of oak trees. On it stood two trestle tables, each with a table-cloth and utensils already laid-out. It was a warm morning, and from the trees Lily expected the song of birds and the chirrup of insects, but there was only the sound of students engaged in their unusual play of running for a few paces, jumping, and then standing on their heads. Lily and the Ordinal watched them for a moment.

"The Game of Nouns," said Ordinal. "The girls are usually better at it than the boys. They are practising. Don't ask me what the rules are. They are too complicated. I am sure you will grasp it very quickly. Now…" He took Lily by the arm and they sat at one of the trestle tables. "A few words." He sniffed and patted his chest. "What are your thoughts so far, Lily Moss? Confused? I would be."

"Yes sir, Ordinal."

"This is no commonplace school. We do not teach what to think, but *how* to think. Our age-range is only from twelve to fourteen, but these are important years. We set you on a path. Deviate from it and you will fall into the mire of mediocrity. Embrace it, and *per ardua ad astra* the worlds are your oyster."

He raised a bony finger and pointed upwards, with wide eyes and a gleam in them which in other circumstances might be that of a madman. Not for the first time, Lily frowned with concentration, for she was unsure what he meant.

"Today is only your induction," he went on. "We expect nothing from you, today. But from your next visit we expect improvement. For the rest of the morning, you will join the class of Comparative Religion, with Cardinal. This afternoon will be Science, with Miss Servator. When you have experienced all the classes, you will choose your special subject. Do you understand?"

Lily nodded. "Good," Ordinal said. "Now, your first test is to remember where the class of Comparative Religion is held. Break is over. Run off, and do not annoy the mechanicals. Off with you now."

20 - First Classes

Ordinal waved a hand and Lily stood. She passed through the now-empty sitting room and corridor, back to the grand staircase. It was quiet, with only a gentle hiss from the Omnium sculpture as it revolved. She climbed the staircase, took a right turn, and climbed again, till she stood before the iron-studded door of her first class. She knocked, gently. From inside came a cry, "Knock harder! Try again!" She knocked harder, so hard that she felt a splinter in her knuckles. "Come in!" was the cry.

Cardinal stood before his blackboard, still in his tie-dye shirt and flares, but now four students squatted on his rug, one of whom - Lily was glad to see - was little Chun, the only student who was smaller than herself. "Everyone," he said. "This is noobie Lily. Lily Moss, isn't it?"

"Yes sir," she replied. "Lily Andreyevna Moss."

"Oh, an Andreyev," he said, his eyebrows raised. The other students turned their heads. "It's been a long time since we had a Russian."

"My mother was Polish, sir."

"So your father was Russian?"

"English, sir."

"Impossible. One or the other was Russian. But enough of that. Our subject is paganism. This is a cool one. Look at me, you dimwits. Noobie Lily, I would say Take a pew, but there's only the rug. At the back, if you don't mind."

Lily squatted awkwardly, half on the rug and half on the cold stone floor. On the blackboard the word 'Paganism' was written in large white letters.

"Do you have fairies at the bottom of your garden?" Cardinal asked. Heads shook. An older boy, plump with a shock of black hair, pursed his lips and blew out, making a noise like a ruminating cow. "Any more of that, Robert, and you will go before the Housekeeper, on the mat." The boy rolled his eyes. "Fairies," Cardinal went on regardless, "are one example of other-worldly creatures who live in natural habitats, hedgerows, ponds, trees, and mess about with people like you, sometimes for good, often for bad. Who knows what a kelpie is?"

Little Chun's hand shot up. "A water horse, sir."

Cardinal nodded. "Right. I hope you never bump into one of them, a kelpie, a shape-shifting horror. A resident of rivers, streams, pools. And remember when we read of 'divers djinns' in the Arabian Nights. That was not, as you believed, Robert, an alcoholic drink for divers." Robert scowled, as Cardinal went on, "No, they were genies, as in Aladdin, often the inhabitants of pools."

Cardinal went on to list numerous mythical creatures in whose existence a pagan might believe. To Lily the kelpie sounded the worst, a horse that could appear human, and dragged people down into the depths of the water to eat them alive, leaving only their innards at the water's edge. Robert and the boy sitting next to him approved of that, but were disappointed that it could be overcome simply by putting a bridle on it. A captured kelpie would be a wonder, to Lily's mind, a horse that could carry its rider through seas, through the air like Pegasus, just about anywhere, but there was no such thing as a kelpie.

Druids, pantheists, the Wicker Man, the Green Man; Cardinal ranged over a wide field of pagan beliefs, leaving Lily's head numb with it. As the hooter downstairs howled he concluded with, "For homework, read up on Hinduism and be prepared to explain to me, next time, why it is *not* a pagan religion. Now get your lunch."

Outside, Lily sat by Chun and found Theo and the obnoxious Robert sitting opposite. Four women in woolly hats and smocks, the mechanicals, bustled about. One deposited in front of Lily a bowl of mince with pasta and a sprinkling of cheese. "You watch out,

160

Russian," said Robert with a smirk. "It's got chili in it. Your throat will swell up and you'll die."

"Don't be silly," said Chun. "There's salad too."

"Crawling with slugs," said Robert. "In Singapore, we give slugs to the staff for breakfast."

As lunch went on, Robert prefaced much of what he said with 'In Singapore'. Lily wondered why. She had said nothing for some time, but could not stop herself from blurting out, "Why is it always, 'In Singapore'?"

"Because," said Robert, "that is where I am from. But I live here now, full-time. I'm not a bursary student like you. My family pay for a private room. It's very expensive. And my sponsor is Miss Servator herself."

"Your... sponsor?"

"That's right. And who's yours? One of the mechanicals?" Robert's laugh was more of a gurgle as a gobbet of chili tangled around his tonsils and he spat it out on the grass. One of the mechanical women scooped it up with a tissue.

"I don't know," Lily replied. "Lady Meizel I suppose."

"Who? Mysul?"

"I suppose so."

The expression on Robert's fat face turned from pride to alarm in a second.

"Excuse me, Lily," said Chun. "Mysul has not sponsored anyone before. Are you sure?"

"I don't know. It was Lady Meizel who offered me the bursary, herself."

"Wow," said Chun. "That's a first."

Theo chipped in with, "Mysul's your sponsor, Lily? What is she like? I never met her."

"Oh, just an old lady. Very intelligent, I thought."

"Jeez, girl, just an old lady," said Theo, and in a sing-song voice, "I don't think so. Coz she's up there." He pointed up at a cloud. "Even upper, I reckon, sure thing."

"What, she lives in the sky?"

"You know what I mean," Theo said, but Lily did not.

Robert had gone quiet, and began furtively to glance at Lily with something like fear, or jealousy. His piggy eyes were scrunched-up, and Lily heard no more of Singapore until Theo said, "Hey, no pudding!" It was true. The mechanicals were tidying up the plates and marching off.

"In Singapore, we had pudding after every meal. Klaus," said Robert to the blonde boy sitting next to him, "find out what's wrong. I pay for pudding."

Lily and the others left Robert waiting for news about pudding, and Lily made her way up the staircase to Miss Servator's class-room, the glass room-within-a-room. It contained only four desks of black metal, and Lily sat in the desk nearest to the door of the glass cube, anticipating an afternoon of Science or Mathematics, which she dreaded.

Miss Servator's whiteboard was clear of squiggles, but Miss Servator herself did not look friendly. She glowered. Her face was thin and sallow, beneath a curtain of long black hair, through which her black eyes twinkled like the headlights of an oncoming train. Her robe was pure white, decorated at the neck and cuffs with a gold meander pattern. From the middle finger of her right hand shone a golden ring in which was set a bright ruby-red stone. All she needed to complete the impression of a white witch would have been a broad-brimmed pointed hat.

"Moss," she said, "this will be new to you. I want no nonsense. Listen and learn."

In came a tall ginger-haired boy with his chin in the air. He smiled regally at Lily and wandered to the front, to a desk directly facing Miss Servator's table. "Miss Servator," he said, in a high-pitched drawl, "a pleasure to be with you again."

"Don't get smarmy with me, young man," Miss Servator replied. "Your last paper was a disgrace. Ninety-one is not a prime number."

"A slip of the keyboard, Miss Servator. Maths, not my strong point. It's what we hire an accountant for."

Miss Servator drew a deep breath but her reply was cut short by the arrival of Robert and his associate, Klaus, who parked themselves in the middle desks.

"Now we have all made the effort to turn up," Miss Servator said, narrowing her eyes, "I shall begin. This afternoon, we shall go in-depth into the study of compression algorithms and digital storage. That will be thrilling, yes?"

Seeing an appropriate number of nods, she went on, "For the afternoon, instead of pudding, our Housekeeper has come up with milk and her special brownies, which are very delicious. Take one when you feel hungry." She waved a hand in the direction of a table adjoining her own. "Robert, if you take more than three you will stay behind for a Biology practical. Frogs."

Robert pulled a face, and whispered to Klaus next to him, "In Singapore, I can eat what I like when I want to."

Lily wanted to whisper to him, "That's why you're so fat," but merely thought it.

"Klaus," muttered Miss Servator. "No gossiping. Now… compression…"

What followed was, to Lily, a mystery. Miss Servator was clearly a difficult woman teaching difficult subjects to students who were not interested. If - as Lily had believed - students chose their subjects, then she already knew these were subjects she would not choose, and was surprised that the other members of the class had chosen them, for they showed no aptitude for them whatsoever. It was as if Miss Servator were teaching - or reminding - herself. She drifted off into a world of whiteboard squiggles, pacing back and forth, muttering, while the boy at the front put his feet on the desk, and Robert persuaded a reluctant Klaus to hand over his share of the brownies. Lily dared to fetch one for herself, and received from Robert a look which was part glare and part a wistful appeal.

After one hour of this, Miss Servitor came to a halt. "Marco," she said. "Your feet have been on the desk for fifty-seven minutes. I have said nothing before, because I realise that the distance between your head and your feet is such that you occasionally require some time to get re-acquainted with them. As punishment, I expect from you for next week an analysis of the set partitioning in hierarchical trees compression algorithm. Is there anything there you don't understand?"

The ginger-haired boy removed his feet from the desk and slumped over it in a posture of misery.

"Now," said Miss Servator. "Digital storage."

Here was something that Lily hoped she would understand, for it was about computers, but again she was disappointed. This was A-level when she had just begun to study for GCSEs. Probably it was beyond even that, for Miss Servator stalked about, mumbling to herself about protein chips and the price of gold, coaxial neural synapses and the transfer of human memory, data backup to 'the cloud's cloud' and all manner of exotic technologies which meant nothing to anyone else in the room.

By the end of the class her whiteboard was black with squiggles and her table covered with an array of equipment, some tall and glassy, some small and brightly-coloured, all of it whirring, steaming, marking a line of demarcation between a teacher in a world of her own and a class which - on a warm Friday afternoon - was mainly asleep. Lily came to her senses only when Miss Servator said, "And the result is… this."

Above Miss Servator's right arm hovered a bubble of glass, in which images flickered at high speed. It was a hole in the air, a round screen whose images settled into a colourful scene of palm trees, a beach and blue water.

Robert woke up and blinked. "Oi!" he cried. "It's Singapore!"

Miss Servator glowered at him. "It's from your head, Robert. Holiday memories. I hope you don't mind my borrowing them. As you were asleep I decided you would not miss them. Stay behind after class. It will be frogs."

This to Lily was a miracle. She put up her hand. "Excuse me, Miss," she said. "Could you just explain, how you did that?"

"No," Miss Servator said. "I have just explained at great length how I did that, and if you missed it, you will have to catch up next time." She flicked her fingers and the bubble vanished. "It is only a matter of technology, devised by myself. Of course the grangels have stolen it, but then they steal everything. And if you don't know what grangels are, ask your fellow students. I have important work to do. Class is over. Goodbye."

All except Robert stood and left the glass cube, as the end-of-class hooter sounded. They ambled downstairs. "I thought that went rather well," said the ginger-haired boy. "Your servant, Miss Lily." He bowed graciously and wandered off to the purple rope, which he unhitched then ambled into the shadows of the private quarters.

"You want to watch out," hissed the blonde-haired Klaus. "Robert is unhappy with you."

"Perhaps he is unhappy with himself," Lily replied.

"You want to watch out," Klaus repeated, and strode off to the private quarters, not bothering to hitch up the purple rope.

From all sides students gathered. Lily manoeuvred herself into a gaggle of girls who were chatting in excited tones about events of the weekend, Lily nodding as if she understood. All were older, except little Chun and one or two of the quieter girls. "Anything planned, Lily?" Chun whispered. "I think I have to write something about Hinduism," Lily replied. "No, I mean, are you going out anywhere?" "I don't know, I don't think so." "I'm going to a birthday party. It's a long way from Beijing but it should be fun." "From Beijing?" "Yes, my home." "You are going there now?" "I go there every evening after school." "But it's miles!" "Yes it is, and I always go to sleep on the way." "My goodness. Chun, what is a grangel?"

The conversation around her stopped. "What did you say?" said the lanky blonde girl whom Lily had glimpsed in Navigation class, Martha, and who towered over the others. "Who are you anyway?"

"Lily."

"What did you say, Lily? Did you use the G word?"

"I just asked what a grangel was."

The tall girl looked disgusted. "Vicious thieving scum, Lily. We don't mention them in school. OK?"

"Yes. OK."

Shame-faced, Lily followed the students heading outside for the bus. She sat at the back and was pleased to see Theo in the seat opposite. "All OK?" he asked. "You gone a bit pale."

"I used the G word in school."

"Oh. Well you didn't know. I bet there's a whole lot you didn't know. Must be mighty weird, but - hey - you get used to it. Took me a few weeks."

Lily smiled, as Cardinal climbed into the driver's seat and with a cry of "Homeward bound!" fired up the engine.

*

Explaining the day's events to her Dad was difficult, because she wanted to be positive, but there was much that left her unsettled, partly because she understood so little of what was going on, but also because some of the students were not as friendly as she had hoped. Looking back, though, they were no worse than the pupils of Swivelhurst School by and large, so she did not think she was lying when she said she had a good time, had eaten her lunch, had learned something, and it was worthwhile going on with it. Her Dad particularly approved of the uniform, which he said would make a 'right little soldier' out of her.

That night, she took the red exercise book from the drawer, found the right page, and after the word 'Ignorant' wrote a question mark.

21 - Malbury

May 2009

West of Salisbury, in a tangle of countryside where foxes roam, lies
the village of Malbury. It is a place with history, of witch-finding, of
rebellion by the lower orders. Roman legions have passed through
it. Roundhead cavalry trounced the King's army over its hill.
Today, though, it is a shadow of itself. There is no railway station,
and only one bus stop, for a bus which passes twice daily. The main
road to Salisbury is so distant that it might as well be in Japan.

None of its residents would call Malbury picturesque. It has its
duck-pond, fringed with reeds and willows, but the water is muddy
and smells of manure. No-one plays cricket on its green, which lies
on a slope so steep that a ball delivered at pace might end up in
Somerset. On a narrow tree-lined lane it has its pub, the Goat and
Bucket, which claims a Queen Anne date despite a façade of the
1930's and the honest modernity of the red-brick shop next door. Its
streets are few and winding, lined with slate-roofed cottages which
hold each other up along steep lanes to the church, their chimneys
issuing a fragrant layer of wood-smoke through day and night. Only
the church has some distinction, for in the past it served not only
Malbury but also its neighbouring villages, and so it is bigger than it
needs to be, a Gothic thing whose black spire sticks up from the
woods all around and can be seen from as far away as Yeovil.

Once, the village and its surroundings were a grand estate. Now
buried in the woods lies the Great Hall, built in the 1850's to a neo-
classic design for the tenth Lord Ellsworth. His Lordship did not
take up residence, for he and his collection of Italian marbles
perished in a shipwreck off the coast of Brittany while the Hall was
under construction. After him came a succession of short-term
owners, whose rapid departures defined the reputation of the Hall
and its grounds as a place unloved and even sinister. It is now the

property of a charity, the Malbury Trust, and to that Trust the Vicar of the parish is an adviser. Great Hall though it was, today the villagers of Malbury call it only the 'House Over-There' and it is empty and generally shunned, as a place to which no-one in their right mind goes.

Visitors to Malbury are rare, and so it caused some talk in the village when - late in the afternoon of a Saturday in May - a black taxi drew up before the village shop. From it sprang the driver, a young man dressed for tennis. Into the shop he plunged, swerved around a stack of tins, and confronted the shop's owner, Mister Aldsworth, who stood tapping his fingers on the counter as if ready to serve a long line of customers, of which there were none.

The young man blinked, collected his wits and said, "Good afternoon."

"Afternoon," Aldsworth replied, the time of day just occurring to him.

"The Hall. I'm looking for the Hall. Could you point me in the right direction?"

"Is that so?' Aldsworth mumbled. "Which hall is that? The Spiritualist Hall? You don't look old enough to be a spiritualist, if I may say."

"Malbury Hall. I think I went past it on the road from Luffham."

"Let me think about that. Can I interest you in these packets of jelly-beans which are on offer?"

"No thanks. I am in rather a hurry."

"Is that so?" Hurry meant nothing to Aldsworth. Sixty years in the village, barely larger than his pinafore, his face weathered more by alcohol than by fresh air, Aldsworth had learned that Time is relative, to the season, to the person, to whether he could be bothered to get out of bed, which on some days was not at all.

"The Hall," he mused. "Maybe a mile west. There's a sign to the left. If you're back in Luffham you've missed it. You'll be wanting some bottles of water for the journey, I'm thinking."

"Good afternoon," the young man replied and departed with similar haste.

"Afternoon to you, indeed." With a frown, and musing on the rudeness of youth, Aldsworth peered from his window at the departing taxi. All he could make out of the passengers was the black hair of a man in his middle age, and the face of a little girl, who looked like one of the angels of Malbury church.

*

On the steps of the Hall, the Vicar of the parish paced nervously back and forth, his overcoat flapping as he peered into the gathering shadows. The sun was setting over the hills at Luffham, and a cold evening breeze rippled through the trees which surrounded this desolate spot. Above him loomed a colonnade and the dormers of a roof growing dark as if the Hall were closing its eyes. He was expecting visitors, and unwelcome visitors at that, a girl called Lily Moss and her father.

It began at the monthly meeting of the Malbury Trust. The Chairman of the Board had come across an article in a local newspaper which had fired his enthusiasm. 'Teenage psychic solves Sussex mystery' was its title. It was wrong on two counts. Firstly the girl was twelve, so no teenager. Secondly, it was hardly a triumph of psychic power that she had uncovered the cause of other-worldly noises from the cottage described in the article, which was - a faulty electrical generator.

After lunch in a public house at Barn Elms, the Board met on a Friday afternoon in the Committee Room of the Town Hall, a dark-panelled room overlooking the High Street through a series of casement windows, in the air an aroma of ancient tobacco-smoke and leather bindings. Around a long mahogany table the members of the Board and the Vicar sat in red-cushioned chairs made long ago for men of larger proportions, this being farming country. At their head sat the Chairman, Julius Ballantine. He was a Tory of the new sort, a man of business, sharp-suited and aquiline, and no fool. As he looked around the table, members flinched.

No journalists or members of the public were present, for this was a private meeting with a difficult subject. There were two outsiders, however, who had such influence in the town that they sat alongside the Board members. These were the Bishop of Luffham - an individual of modest size but impressive countenance, wearing a black suit and purple shirt - and the one woman in the room, Mrs Amelia Urquhart. Much had been written in the local Press about this woman. On the one hand she was the overbearing pink-rinsed fat lady who made more noise than she should. On the other hand, she was a defender of the Labour faith, a no-nonsense socialist who stood up for working people against the tyranny of the Upper Class. Mrs Urquhart was Chair of the local hospital Trust, and if anyone would stand up to Ballantine it was she.

Ballantine rose to address the meeting. He adjusted his tie, coughed modestly, and welcomed the members and their guests. His scribe took notes. After some minutes running through the perilous state of the Board's finances, and elaborating on the success so far in disposing of its property - five stately homes closed, brownfield sites sold off to local developers (which caused a murmur of satisfaction around the table, at which Mrs Urquhart merely blinked) - Ballantine got to the point.

"Malbury Hall," he said. "We have a valuation but no serious bidders. Does anyone disagree with the valuation?" He looked around. There was no reply. "Very well," he went on. "The valuation of two million pounds is accepted by the Board. But... no serious bidders. Why is that?"

"Because," Mrs Urquhart piped up, "it is a ruin falling apart on land so marshy it would take a team of divers to develop it. I wouldn't give you tuppence for it."

"On the contrary," Ballantine continued, with a faux-deferential smile at his Labour antagonist, "it is a very desirable property, a splendid example of early Victorian architecture standing on a hillside which - given sufficient clearance of trees - would offer outstanding views to the west. It requires only an effort of restoration. Failing that, it could be knocked down and the site used for - let us say - an out-of-town supermarket."

Mrs Urquhart grumbled and shook her head. "Is there anything in the Trust's Constitution," she asked, "which prohibits personal profit from the assets of the Trust?"

Ballantine coughed. "Not as such," he muttered. "The matter has not arisen."

"Well there should be," said Mrs Urquhart, and she crossed her arms in a gesture of defiance.

"But I repeat my question," Ballantine went on. "What is preventing its sale? If no-one has any ideas, then I can offer one of my own."

"Its reputation." This came from the Bishop, to whom the Vicar gently deferred. "A load of nonsense. Haunted, it is supposed to be. Poppycock." The Vicar backed him up with, "That is the reputation in the village. And the villagers are always keen to give graphic descriptions of what this so-called haunting is. Some female ghost, apparently. Poppycock."

"That is my understanding," Ballantine said. "A sinister reputation, for an old house standing empty on a hill. Haunted. Gothic. It is that reputation which has attracted intruders, hippies, thrill-seekers. There have been fires, broken windows, damage to the property of the Trust. And it is the people of the village themselves who - with their stories about the Hall - are indirectly causing that damage, and preventing its sale. But, I have had an idea." From his briefcase he produced sheets of paper which he shuffled over to the Board members. They were copies of an article in a Sussex paper - 'Teenage psychic solves Sussex mystery'.

"What is this rubbish?" complained Mrs Urquhart.

Ignoring her, Ballantine addressed the Bishop. "Is it true, my Lord Bishop, that exorcism by the Church may reinforce the reputation of a place to be infested with spirits and so on? In the case of Malbury Hall, would an exorcism not acknowledge, officially, that the place is haunted? And the locals would leap on that."

"Possibly," the Bishop replied. "It is not a service we would offer lightly."

Ballantine smiled. "So," he said. "If we are to address this superstition spread by the villagers, which has its impact on the saleability of the Hall, we might look for some alternative method, which we might call - private enterprise?" This raised a series of grins and chuckles from those members of the Trust's Board who had made their fortune in the private sector.

"I am not entirely happy with that," said the Bishop, and he looked towards the Vicar, who chipped in with, "It is the spiritual welfare of my parishioners, Mister Ballantine, which must come first. No-one is better placed to be responsible for that than a servant of the Church." The Bishop nodded.

"That is your business, Reverend, and I agree of course. However, consider for a moment. What does it do for the spiritual welfare of your parishioners to spread these tales of ghosts and whatnot to all and sundry? Surely this is something which you would like to stop. I am aware, Reverend, of your own efforts to close the Spiritualist Hall in your village. Surely that is in the same category."

That was true, at least. To the Vicar, Spiritualism was bunk. His opposition to it had been forthright, and well known. The Vicar was a man of Science. Nightly he walked through his churchyard, and though its shadows might inspire visions in those already unhinged, his shivering would be due only to the cold. No ghoul had jumped at him from behind a tombstone. No hand had risen from its grave and waved. The dead in his churchyard stayed where they were put, which was the correct order of things. The miracles of his religion he consigned to a box called Faith, which was a useful box which he opened every day and closed every night when he looked at the News on television.

"My suggestion is this," said Ballantine. "That we engage the girl mentioned in this article to... discover the cause of these ghostly sightings at the Hall. In the case described in the article before you, it was an electrical generator. There must be something in the Hall which - perfectly naturally - is creating these illusions. She will find it, and we will make it known to the villagers that she has found it. And the nonsense stops there."

The Bishop cleared his throat. "But what if she finds nothing?" he said.

"Oh she will, my Lord Bishop. Be assured of that."

*

Of the members of the Trust's Board it was the Vicar who was most critical of Ballantine's plan. He resisted it to the end, but the end was agreement by a majority that the father - and by proxy, the girl - should be engaged as a consultant, on a contract for one week at a cost of three thousand pounds (at which the Vicar flinched, thinking what that could do for the church roof). The contract would contain a gagging clause, to ensure that the Board could offer to local people and the Press a satisfactory report of its result. As what seemed to the Vicar to be penance, his task was to welcome this child and her father, and offer any assistance they might require.

So it was that he found himself in the shadows of the Hall on an evening cold for May, waiting for two people he had no desire to meet.

Between the trees a black taxi emerged and drove around to the steps. A stocky but tall, dark-haired man in a patterned sweater and jeans stepped out, and behind him a small blonde girl in what looked like a school uniform. The man carried a suitcase and the girl a rucksack. Off the taxi sped, leaving them standing in the twilight. Together they mounted the steps to the portico where the man stuck out his free hand and said, "Reverend, a pleasure. Say hello to the Reverend, Lily."

"Good evening, Reverend," piped up the little girl.

"Good evening," the Vicar replied, with the smile he reserved for the simple-minded. Such a small, sweet thing she seemed to be, in her school uniform of maroon and gold. Her father, on the other hand, was a rough sort, a man of middle age with a tangle of black hair, a broad face, and the physique of a fairground boxer. His name, the Vicar knew, was Riley Moss.

"Welcome to Malbury," the Vicar said. "I see you have come directly from school, child."

"Yes sir. It was all very sudden."

"Can we go in?" said Riley Moss. "It's freezing. Lily will have a turn."

"Oh," the Vicar replied. "This way…" At first the Vicar was not impressed by the brusque, military manner of this urgent man whose eyes had narrowed into an expression which could only be called challenging. There was also a whiff of alcohol on the man's breath, and the Vicar, being teetotal, had already decided - from the redness of his nose - that this fellow must be terminally alcoholic, possibly unfit to be in charge of so fragile a daughter.

He led them through the front doorway into an echoing hall, the grand staircase curving up into shadows, and then into a low-ceilinged chamber whose floral-papered walls were stained with grime, and where rats had nested in its fireplace. There he stopped, and pulled a cluster of keys and a sheaf of papers from his overcoat. "I have here," he said, "floor-plans of the Hall. This was the ballroom. I am not sure where and how you want to conduct your… investigation, shall we call it?"

"Our task, Reverend," said Riley Moss, "according to Mister Ballantine, is to find what is making your villagers think the place is haunted. We are as much surprised about this as I expect you are. We are not ghost-hunters. We have no thermal imaging equipment, or whatever it is they use. This all came about because of an article in a local paper which was a lot of nonsense. Reading that, I could believe that Lily wore a turban and performed acts of necromancy on

Bognor Pier. It's nonsense, but if Mister Ballantine wants to give us a big fee for doing not much, I am not going to stand in his way."

The Vicar began to warm to the uncouth but straight-talking Mister Moss. He looked down at the little girl. She smiled back with sparkling white teeth and violet-blue eyes of pure innocence, her blonde hair falling in bunches around a thin and pale, almost Slavic face. So this was the notorious Lily Moss, skinny in her school uniform, maroon jacket, gold crest, white shirt, grey skirt and shiny black shoes. It was hard from this innocent appearance to conjure up the image the newspaper gave her - Lily Moss the psychic, Lily Moss the bridge between this world and the next, Lily Moss who did several impossible things before breakfast. She was just a little girl who had a rucksack at her feet and looked around with an enquiring mind, small for her age, but bright and unusually healthy. "And what do you think about this… Miss…"

"Lily, please," she said.

"Won't you be afraid in a creepy house like this … Lily?"

Her father butted in with, "We're taking no risks, Reverend. We're out of here as soon as it's dark. I have made that clear to Mister Ballantine. The cab is booked."

"Then you won't have long here this evening. Do you have rooms at the inn?"

"We do. We'll make a quick survey tonight, and carry on tomorrow. I have taken a week off work, and it's half-term, so no problem for Lily."

"Then I will leave you to it," said the Vicar, handing over the keys and floor-plans. "The key with the blue tag is the key to the front door. If you need me, the telephone number of the Rectory is there. I have arranged with my canon for him to conduct my services tomorrow, so I expect to see you here in the morning."

Moss nodded. "Not a problem," he said. "We had better get a move on."

As he cycled away from the Hall, through the shadows and whispering trees, there came into the Vicar's mind the paganism he was trying to eradicate from his own village, the nonsense that drew his parishioners into the Spiritualist Hall when by rights they should be worshipping in his church, nonsense spread by people who impressed others because they were marginally less ignorant, so-called wise women who lived at the edge of the village and dispensed life-threatening cures made from bat droppings and poisonous plants.

It seemed to him then that this innocent creature, Lily Moss, was in danger. If she found a natural cause for the curious tales told by the villagers, then she might become hardened to the genuine wonders of the world, or she might fail, and that would only increase the superstition in her mind and in the minds of the villagers. Either way, she might end up in the hands of people exploiting her youth and natural goodness to make a show of paganism, for a television audience feeding itself on crisps and warm beer.

22 - A Shopkeeper's Tale

"They call this the House Over-There," Riley Moss said. "And the Great Hall. But not that big, is it?"

"It is creepy, though, Dad," said Lily, and her father nodded.

After a quick change of outfit by Lily, they stood at the base of the Hall's steps. Around them the light was failing. No birds sang. In a circular forecourt of gravel stood the wide cylinder of the fountain, its water rippling. The plaster-white statue of a mongrel figure rose at its centre, with scaly hindquarters and the top half of a long-eared goblin, bearing on its head a stone saucer and a spout. If there was a pump it was out of action.

The four columns of the portico towered into the evening sky. On either side, wings of the Hall extended through the gathering gloom. Its rendering was long gone, and the brickwork was stained coal-black and swathed in ivy. Each wing was wide enough for only one room below and above, the frames of their casement windows scarred by rot and panes cracked. The only sign of maintenance was black plastic pipework which ran up to an overhanging roof, whose dormers Moss had glimpsed on their way in, one each side, heavy and dark.

"We have about one hour before the place is pitch-black," Riley Moss said, looking down at his daughter. "The cab will be back then. So, Lily. Now we pretend to be ghost-hunters. We are told that people break in and do damage, because they want to see the ghost. Where would you go if you wanted to do that?"

"Around the side," she said, with such certainty that Moss could believe she had been here before.

She hared off to the left and Moss followed, crunching over the gravel. He turned onto the path at the side of the house and side-stepped a bramble patch, finding Lily in the remains of a flower-bed pointing down at a ground-level window, a single large pane of glass in a wooden frame. "There," she said. "Look how rotten that is. I bet I could get in there in two seconds."

"I expect you could," Moss agreed. "We'll look at that tomorrow. But while we've still got some light let's make a quick spin around the outside and go in by the front door."

"OK Dad," Lily said with a frown. "That's boring."

"You can have your fun tomorrow."

They walked along the path between the Hall and its outbuildings, sheds of wood and stone in stages of collapse. Lily declared these to be 'stinky' and was sure that 'something's dead in that one'. As they came onto the overgrown lawn and stepped up to the French windows, and then fought their way around the other side of the Hall over a path so thick with brambles that Moss had to go first and trample them, Lily - despite her father's continual "What do you feel here?" and "Is there something odd about this?" - found nothing to make her stop and stare with the peculiar intensity which to Moss was her sign that something was not quite right.

Side by side they climbed the front steps of the Hall. Moss fumbled in a pocket of his jeans and brought out the key-ring. He thrust the key with the blue tag into the lock. It turned with a click and locked. Unlocking was not so easy. A determined shove forced the door open, and it swung back, the evening air flooding through with a sigh. Inside, was quiet.

"Dark, isn't it?" Moss whispered. "There's no electricity. We'd better be quick. This is the hall."

The oak-panelled hall was empty, and the boards of its floor were bare and dusty with patches of damp. To the right, a staircase against the wall rose to a landing. Up there four doors were closed.

"A quick spin around the ground floor," he said, "then it will be time for the cab."

Moving clockwise, they passed through a series of echoing rooms, their windows grimy and cobweb-infested, fireplaces spilling ash and soot, floors of bare and splintered boards. A corridor ran along the back of the Hall, French windows set at its middle and a door at each end. Light now came more from the moon than the evening sun, which had slipped down into clouds beyond trees at the end of the garden. He pushed open a door at the end of the corridor to find a set of rough wooden stairs, leading down into moonlight on a stone floor. He went down, and Lily followed, sniffing. "That is disgusting," she said. "It's like cabbage soup a rat died in."

"Whiffy, that's for sure," her father replied. "This is, or was, the kitchen."

"Look there, Dad. That's the window that was all rotten. That's where people get in. Oh my God I'm glad I didn't try that. I could have broken a leg."

This was a cavernous space, the grey plaster of its walls pock-marked, and stained black where there had been ovens. Moonlight fell on flagstones, through a window set high on the wall and a grille of glass blocks by its side in the rough-plastered ceiling. The smell that rose from the flagstones was of decay and animal dead, a stink that made Moss cough and put a hand over his nose. "I think, Lily," he said, "it's time to leave."

Lily walked over the stones to the centre of the kitchen. "Wait a moment, Dad," she said, and she began to pace in a circle. Her breathing was heavy. Moss had not realised how cold the air had become until he saw the plume of her breath rising in the moonlight. Lily had surprised Moss before, but this time it raised the hairs on the back of his neck to see his daughter so intense, so sure she was close to something which he preferred not to imagine. Around and around she travelled in the gloom, until she stopped, and moved some paces away into a dark corner.

"It's here," Lily whispered. "Whatever it is, it's here. But I can't see."

"Careful, my darling," said Moss. "We need better light. Leave it for now. Tomorrow, this is where we start."

*

The Goat and Bucket is the only pub in the village, and claims to date from the time of Queen Anne despite its mock-Tudor façade. Its downstairs bar is antique in an oak-beamed and brassy fashion, and the dinner menu works best for those who prefer minimal style with maximum gravy. Its rooms are spartan, with oppressive low timbered ceilings. Riley Moss and Lily were used to sharing a bathroom, but it was a relief that there were no other guests.

When Lily had settled in her room and gone off to sleep with no fuss, her blonde locks spread over the pillow, Moss tramped downstairs to the bar, perched himself on a stool and ordered a pint of whatever the barmaid recommended.

"An Old Toby," she said. Riley Moss nodded, and was impressed by the skill with which a lady of her age could draw a pint with just enough exposure of her considerable chest.

"Don't have too much of that," the man on his left whispered, "You'll go blind."

"Aldsworth, you are a caution," the barmaid said, tossing her red curls and flashing a smile that said *All my own teeth.*

"I am that, Missus Peeps," Aldsworth agreed. "And you can set me up another of them, if you don't mind."

"That will be the fourth," the barmaid said. "Shop must be doing well."

"Can't complain."

"You usually do."

Aldsworth grumbled into his beer, and said, "You wouldn't be from Salisbury would you, Mister…?"

Riley Moss realised he had become the focus of attention. "Moss," he said. "No, from Sussex." He turned to face his companion, a small fat man in a brown shirt and grey pinafore, with a leathery complexion, a sprinkle of white hair, and the beady brown eyes of a hamster.

"Mister Moss," Aldsworth went on. "Pleased to make your acquaintance, I'm sure. Saw you earlier, in a taxi. You was on your way to the Hall?"

"I was, Mister Aldsworth. I have been asked to take a look at it."

Aldsworth scratched a chin which had not seen a razor that day. "Is that so, sir?" he said. "Take a look, is it?"

"By the Trust that owns it. There have been break-ins, so I hear. I have been asked to do something about that."

"Ah," Aldsworth said, returning to his pint. "The Trust. Them's posh beggars, Ballantine and his crew." Aldsworth sniffed and gulped down most of his beer. "Don't suppose you'd be interested in some garden furniture?"

"If you want to do business, Aldsworth," the barmaid interrupted, "you do it in your shop. I don't know how many times I've told you that."

Aldsworth grumbled into his beer. "And there I was thinking you'd come to see the ghost."

"The ghost?"

Aldsworth shrugged. Behind him a picture of huntsmen hung above a fireplace whose log fire crackled and was in danger of going out. Horse brasses on black leather strips hung on each side, where two straight-backed armchairs were positioned for occupants to warm their feet. To Moss the empty chairs told a story of others, who listened, watched and no longer had feet to warm. "There's them who says the Hall's haunted, sir," Aldsworth went on. "No-one from the village goes up there now. There's been too many frights.

182

Even Barney up the hill won't dare, and he's on an anti-social for being drunk."

A shadow fell over Aldsworth's face, but it was only that of the barmaid hanging up glasses. "Frights?" Moss said. "Surely, there's always a scientific explanation for that sort of thing."

"That's so true, sir, so true," said Aldsworth with a grin. "And no doubt Mister Ballantine has told you all about it. But he's not seen the world, not like you, sir, if I may say. You have a touch of the Services about yourself. Navy, was it?"

"Army."

"Ah that's well and good. But tell me, sir, who was the little girl you brought along? Your daughter perhaps?"

"Lily, yes my daughter. She comes with me on these field trips."

"Lily Moss is it? That rings a bell, sir." Aldsworth frowned. "Would that be the Lily Moss I seen in the newspaper?"

"Perhaps," Riley Moss replied, surprised that the reach of a Sussex paper should be so wide. "But what newspaper was that?"

Aldsworth slapped a hand on his thigh. "Ah, I thought as much, sir," he said. "Lily Moss, and no mistake. Famous, she is. I seen her with me own eyes, in the Luffham Gazette it was, one of them Ballantine rags. And that was something about a murder and a ghastly screaming ghost, if I'm not mistaken."

"There was a scientific explanation."

"That's well and good then," said Aldsworth. "Lovely looking little girl, if I may say. You must be proud."

Moss nodded.

Aldsworth waggled his empty glass. "If there's something ghosty about that Hall I'm betting that girl of yours will find it. Am I right, sir?"

"Well, if we get the chance to clear up any mystery about the place, we will do so, Mister Aldsworth. There is something, though, you might be able to help me with. Are you ready for another pint?"

"That is very civil of you, sir, very civil I'm sure."

"Then perhaps we can discuss it over there by the fire."

"Always happy to oblige, sir, happy to oblige."

With both settled in the armchairs by the fire, Aldsworth pulled out a briar pipe, stuffed it with tobacco from a tin, and lit and drew on it with an expression on his face of extreme pleasure.

"What I'd like to know, Mister Aldsworth," said Moss, "is why people bother to break into the Hall. What do they expect to find?"

Aldsworth needed no time to think. "The ghost, sir. Folks from Barn Elms," he said. "Vagabonds and hippies. I've got no time for 'em. They bring a bit of business for the shop, though. And we could do with more of that."

"The ghost. And what ghost is that?"

"Missus Peeps," Aldsworth called over to the bar, "have you got that paper, the one about the Capsticks?"

The barmaid replied, "Somewhere. Wait a moment."

"I'll say what I knows, Mister Moss," Aldsworth went on. "And you makes up your own mind."

*

The history of the House Over-There according to Aldsworth was two hundred years of bad luck. "There was always something strange in that place, sir," he said. "And they disturbed it. They woke it up."

184

The first casualty was the builder, the tenth Lord Ellsworth, who died before he could take up residence. His estate was split up, and the Hall and its land were sold to a succession of individuals and families, some of whom left in a hurry. In more modern times, Aldsworth remembered a man called Southey, an artist who lived alone in the Hall.

"He was a painter, and mad as a bicycle, if you want my opinion. I think it was the drugs," said Aldsworth, turning back to knock out his pipe on a fireplace log. "Ran stark naked all the way down the hill shouting out 'She's 'ere! She's 'ere!' What a sight that were." Aldsworth leaned forward and narrowing his beady eyes said, "He drowned his-self in the pond. Had to fish him out, dead. Staring eyes, tongue hanging out, hair full of weeds. Horrible."

Southey was succeeded by the Capsticks, Peter and Marjorie. By then the woods had grown around the Hall and it had become a dark and sinister place, shunned by the village. 'Sinister' was the term used by Aldsworth for Capstick himself, along with 'squirt'. His wife - to the disapproval of Mrs Peeps registered in a series of clucking noises - he called a 'stuck-up baby doll' and a 'tart with more money than sense'. They were too grand for the village. Mrs Capstick was one for Society of the higher sort, playing the field in London while Capstick himself drove around in a Jensen motorcar which was too young for him, wheeling and dealing, putting his face in the local papers, but always saying his home was in Barn Elms, where he had a flat, for that town lay in the parliamentary constituency which he hoped to inherit from the Tory incumbent.

There was no pity in Aldsworth's tone even when he came to the death of Mrs Capstick. She had been ill for some time. Some said it was cirrhosis, some cancer, and some a depression whose cause was unknown. What is clear is that, on a dark winter's day, in a shed, an outbuilding of the Hall which her husband used as a darkroom for his photography, she pulled a strip of electrical flex from a hover mower and slung it over a beam. Then she hanged herself.

"And now she haunts the place," said Aldsworth.

"Mrs Capstick?"

"Right you are, sir. Suicide, you see. A lost soul. Weeping and moaning. Heard it meself."

"When you was pissed," the barmaid added.

"That's as may be," said Aldsworth. "Some says they seen her, plain as day, by the shed where she hanged herself. But me, I heard her, on that path by the House, when I was walking to Barney's up the hill. A terrible feeling came over me, sir, terrible. Like a big black hand pressing down on me head. And then I heard it, whispering - oh the language, sir, I can't begin to say. Foul it were, horrible. A soul in torment. I ran downhill like the hounds of Hell was behind." Aldsworth raised an eyebrow and sat back, sniffed and refilled his pipe. "Oh that was her all right," he said. "I knew her, and I knew her husband too, that nasty little squirt who fetched up in a pond."

"In the fountain," the barmaid insisted.

"That's 'im," Aldsworth went on. "And he was a guilty soul, if ever there was one. But it were what she found in that shed what did for 'er, I reckons. Missus Peeps, you found that paper?"

"It's here somewhere, Aldsworth," she replied, rummaging under the bar.

Some - including himself, Aldsworth admitted - had said that it was the photographs in that shed which tipped Mrs Capstick over the edge, that they were of her husband and another woman in his Barn Elms flat. The photographs were explicit, mementoes of a man who struck lucky with a woman half his age and made the most of it. Whatever the cause, Capstick's behaviour after the death of his wife showed an extraordinary devotion. Her cremation in Barn Elms was a grand social event. For the primary school at Luffham he paid for the Marjorie Capstick swimming pool. Were these the offerings of guilt? To Aldsworth, yes. He had seen Capstick driving through the village, bent over the wheel, tears in his eyes. Sinister squirt he was, but there was a soul in there somewhere, a guilty one. "Sold 'is soul to the Devil, sir," Aldsworth insisted.

Then, as Aldsworth knew from his suppliers in Barn Elms, Capstick turned to drink. Deliveries were made daily. Around him the Hall was falling into ruin, but Capstick drank the day away and piled up his empty bottles in a bin which refuse collectors called 'Capstick's hat', for there was more sense in it than in its owner's head. "Then Capstick popped his clogs," Aldsworth concluded, "and everything in the Hall was sold off. I got meself an ormolu clock for next to nothing. Are you interested in ormolu clocks, Mister Moss?"

"Only for next to nothing."

Aldsworth guffawed. "A man after me own heart, sir, after me own heart."

"But what happened to the man, Capstick?"

"Drowned." Aldsworth sniffed and drew heavily on his pipe. "And a sorry sight it were when the postman found him, with a look on his dead face, big staring eyes, blood trickling out of his ears, well it doesn't bear thinking of. Horrible."

"There," said the barmaid, and she dropped a rolled-up newspaper in Aldsworth's lap. "Don't never say I don't give you nothing."

Aldsworth unrolled the newspaper and handed it to Moss. It was a local paper, the Luffham Gazette, and its headline was 'Landowner drowned on own property'. It concerned Peter Capstick, found dead in the fountain of Malbury Hall on a winter's morning.

There were two photographs, one of Capstick's wife, a dainty dark-haired woman with a touch of the 1920's screen goddess about her, and the other of Capstick himself. Moss suspected the photographs were flattering. Capstick was a thin-faced, white-haired man with metal glasses, a weak man pretending to be strong. A weasel would look more honest. He wore a light suit, and a tie with a pin. He was connected. Regrets came from the County Council, from the Health Authority, from a Masonic Hall at Luffham, and from the Malbury Trust of which he was a member. It was presumed that Capstick, after a night on the tiles, tottered into the fountain, hit his head and drowned.

"Interesting. Would you like a nightcap, Mister Aldsworth," said Moss. "A scotch?"

"A brandy would hit the spot, sir, and very generous too. A double would fit the bill something admirable."

Mrs Peeps supplied two brandies. Aldsworth put his pipe aside and downed a mouthful of brandy with the bravado of the already drunk. "You's wanting an explanation of that, sir? Drowned in his own fountain?"

"If you can."

Aldsworth leaned forward and fixed Moss with his hamster eyes. He blinked, breathed deeply and his expression in the flickering light of the fire was grim. "I'm saying 'twas the House what killed him. There's something in that place that goes way back, and that's what did for the Capsticks, and the others. Eats 'em up and spits 'em out. You can say what you like about Science, sir, but there's something there what Science don't know about."

Moss frowned.

"You'll see for yourself, sir," Aldsworth went on. "There'll be rain tomorrow. That's when it happens."

"When what happens?"

"The House wakes up, and Missus Capstick walks. It's not safe when the rains come."

"I think we can look after ourselves, Mister Aldsworth."

"I'm feared for you, sir, and for your little girl specially," said Aldsworth with a final drain of his brandy glass. "If you goes in that place when the rains come, well I don't like to think what you'll find. Or what finds you."

23 - Underground

The next day was a Sunday, and the bells of Malbury church rang out as Riley Moss and Lily walked up the hill from the village towards the woods surrounding the Hall. It was a fine morning, and quicker on foot than by cab. To his 'field trip' clothes of the day before Riley had added a knapsack containing two bottles of water, a torch, and packed lunches. On the path described to them at the pub they passed by the cypress trees of Malbury's churchyard, then by hedgerows buzzing and chirruping with the life of late spring, through ploughed fields already showing signs of the harvest to come, and over streams and brooks gurgling from wooded slopes, all under a blue sky whose only blemish was a steep bank of black cloud, anvil-shaped, rising above the hill to the south-west.

It had been warm and bright and the air fresh, which made the transition to the woods all the more eerie. Here the cold began, and a mist swirled between tall and tangled trees, birch and pine, at their roots the twisted carcasses of their forebears decimated by storms and lying where they fell, rotting but alive with fungus. Their path rose between the trees, and in minutes the Hall was visible through the mist. They tramped over nettles and brambles until they stood on the gravel of the forecourt, above them the columns of the portico and the roof's unblinking dormers.

"I didn't spot that last night," said Moss. He pointed at a grey box fixed on the balustrade to one side of the steps. "It's a water detector. There's one in our warehouse. In the base there's a sensor and when water hits it the alarm goes off. But this one is upside-down. Look at the label."

Lily peered at the box. "It will catch the rain," she said.

"So it will." Riley Moss frowned. "And why would anyone want to do that?"

"So they know when it's raining, Dad."

"And I suppose looking out of the window would be out of the question?"

"Maybe they're underground."

"Who? The people who need to know when it's raining? Let's find out."

Breathing heavily after the walk uphill, Riley Moss led the way up the steps, unlocked the door, and dropped his knapsack in the hall. He bent down and took out his torch. Together they made their way to the back of the hall, through the rear corridor and down to the kitchen which, Lily declared with a grimace, was "Even more stinky than yesterday".

Moss switched on the torch and shone its light over the soot-stained walls. "Now where was that spot you found?"

Lily stood, hands on hips, on a flagstone in a far corner. "Over here!" she cried. Moss approached, his torch lighting her face in a ghoulish grin. "I'm standing right by it, Dad."

Moss directed his light over the wall. "There's a crack," he said.

A vertical crack in the wall's plaster stretched from floor to ceiling, and another a few feet to its left. "It's more than a crack, Dad," said Lily. "It's got holes in it." She thrust a finger into one of the little black holes. She sniffed at it. "I don't like the look of it, to be honest," she said. "And I don't like the smell of it either." She ran her fingers up and down the crack. "Turn off the torch for a moment, please."

Moss turned off the torch.

"That's funny," said Lily. "I was sure I'd see a light. Just a feeling."

"Well there is a little light, from the window." Moss looked up. "It's getting very grey up there." He turned on the torch.

"No," said Lily. "From through there. There's a light not switched on. Dad, can you see a switch?"

"I can hardly see a thing with you jigging about." Moss flashed the torch-light over the walls of the corner. "Can't see one. It wouldn't work anyway. No electricity."

Lily stood up. "There is something behind that wall, Dad. I can feel its eyes."

"An animal?"

"I don't know, Dad. I can't see…"

Moss took his turn to feel inside one of the holes in the wall. He waggled his finger around, and put his eye to the hole. "Can't see a thing."

"Whatever it is, Dad, it's making me feel… not good. Dad…" Lily came close to her father and clasping him around the waist buried her head in the folds of his sweater. Riley Moss knew what was coming. He put his arms around her and held her head in his hand.

"Hold me, Dad," Lily whispered. "I need to sleep."

Clasped together, they stood in the almost dark as the rain began to patter on the grille above their heads. What Moss did not say, as Lily clung to him, was that the holes were wider on the other side. It was from that other side that the holes were made. The thought came to him then that the wall was there not to keep anyone out, but to keep something in.

*

In the Council House, Lily Moss sat at the end of a long and brightly-lit corridor whose carpet led to a door bearing in italic gold letters the word 'Clerk'. A bald, lanky man in an undertaker's black suit, his spectacles awry, rushed up the corridor with a sheaf of papers in one hand, some of which he spilled as he came to a halt with a look of alarm and gasped, "Lily Moss! What are you doing here?"

Lily put on her most appealing honest face. "I have no idea, sir," she replied. At first his name did not come to her, but then she remembered this was the Recorder and his name was Misser because - though his job was to record the decisions of the Grand Council - he was a daydreamer and missed most of them. Despite this, the Council was pleased with him, for it changed its mind so often that the decisions he remembered, which were few, were usually right. "I was called, Recorder. That's all I know."

"All you know," said Misser with a frown. "Then you are a dimwit. What are you?"

"I am a dimwit, Recorder."

"Well said. You will go far, Lily Moss. But not beyond that door until I tell you. Is that clear?"

"Yes, Recorder."

"Must dash. Dish dosh." So saying, the Recorder picked up his papers, turned the door knob and shimmied into the office of the Clerk without leaving enough space for Lily to peer through.

She waited. A minute passed. Through doors along the corridor came sounds of conversations and the hum of machinery. Another minute passed, and another. The door opened and the bald head of Misser appeared. "Still here, Lily Moss?" he said. "Why?"

"I don't know, sir."

"Then you'd better come in. Hippity hop."

Lily Moss rose from her seat, smoothed down her school skirt, and followed the Recorder into the office of the Clerk. Across a sky-blue carpet, and in front of a window which was a single immense pane of glass, stood a timber scaffolding, at its front a tapestry on which a succession of optimistic mottoes appeared, glowed, then vanished. 'Nothing too much', 'Failure is success delayed', 'Do more with less' came and went as if on a ticker-tape. At its top, up by a black ceiling in which tiny lights twinkled, the head and shoulders of a man poked out. He had flowing grey hair and seemed to be wearing a dressing-gown. Through the window Lily saw that it was day-time as usual, but dark clouds rolled over the distant hill where the Great Tower stood.

"Misser!" the man shouted. "Bugger off. This ceiling is in a terrible state."

"Yes Clerk sir, toot sweet," the Recorder replied, and he sidled back out clutching a now even larger sheaf of papers.

"Dog!" the man shouted. "Come up here!"

"I am not a dog!" Lily shouted back. "I am a Lily."

"Come up here this minute!"

"How?"

"In the dog basket!"

The tapestry parted and out popped a basket, into which Lily climbed. The basket jerked upward with a squeak, and Lily clung to its side, until it arrived under the ceiling at a platform of shiny wood on which stood the Clerk. A stocky, portly man, his face was brown, his grey hair unkempt and topped by a pillbox hat with a blue ribbon. What Lily had taken to be a dressing gown was a robe of dark green which billowed around a body which suggested its owner liked a good lunch. Around his neck dangled a heavy gold chain bearing a crystal which he fingered, looking at her with tired, gloomy eyes. She climbed out and the basket squeaked downward.

"What are you?" said the Clerk.

"A girl, sir."

"You look like a dog."

"My name is Lily Moss, sir," she said, blinking and putting on her most appealing honest face.

"Oh. Yes, Lily Moss. Do you do carpentry?"

"No sir."

"Damn. Did I call you?"

"I believe you did, sir."

The Clerk frowned. "Well, I wonder what that was about," he said. "I do lose track of things sometimes." With a twist of his crystal there rose from the platform a black screen, which flickered into life. "Lily Moss, navigator level one. How did you manage that? Did you cheat?"

"I have no idea sir."

"Oh dear. Then you don't know what a floater is."

"A floater? Is it something people have in a bathroom?"

"Try again."

"Something fishermen use to catch salmon?"

"Getting close."

"I don't know."

"Then you had better find out, because you are about to meet one. That is why I called you. This is a matter of training."

"Thank you, sir."

"You're welcome." The Clerk raised his dimpled chin and turned away. "Look outside, Lily Moss," he said. "See how Grangel is surrounding our Tower. It is trying hard today."

Beyond the roofs of the town, lightning flashed from the clouds swirling over the Great Tower on its grassy hill. From the earliest days in which Lily had dreamed herself into this place, the Tower had been the focus, the landmark of Roamers Cross. Early on, she could only glimpse it through the trees, a craggy square monument, walls of flint and buttresses of white stone topped with a grey spire as high as the sky. Only later, as she landed ever nearer to the town, did she realise that everything here revolved around the Tower, that it could be viewed from every window in the hotel, and through the doorways of the town's houses, that the business of the Grand Council was to keep safe whatever was inside it, and Lily did not know what that was.

Around the Tower billowed a cloud of luminous egg-shapes, in each of them a creature, some of a grotesque animal form, some human, some no more than puffs of black writhing smoke. By the thousand, they swarmed from behind the Tower and through the trees. The screen zoomed to a human figure, a girl skirting the tree-tops, around her a translucent porcelain-white shell. She was a little dark-haired girl, no bigger than Lily, travelling fast but inside her bubble her movements were slow, the tatters of a blue dress flowing around her like water-weeds, so fluid she could have been underwater, drowning. Her face was pale, expressionless, and her brown eyes wide and unblinking. As if knowing she was watched, the little girl turned her head towards Lily and stretched out a hand, and Lucy knew this was a shivery thing that would turn her into a skeleton, this was a horror. On instinct she jerked back to the edge of the platform.

"The creature of a lower sea," the Clerk sighed. "A shellfly, a poor dead thing Grangel has given a short and miserable life." With a flash which filled the window a bolt of lightning struck the girl's bubble and she toppled wriggling down the Tower's wall, returning to smoke which dissipated and vanished.

The Clerk turned back, his expression mournful. "Our defence holds," he said. "But we cannot protect our Tower against legions such as these forever." He twisted the crystal and the black screen slid down into the platform. "You have seen the Grey One, Lily Moss," he said, "so your record tells me."

"Yes, sir. Twice. But I escaped. I think I was lucky."

"Lucky? You were, child, you were. If it had reached out for you, then that is what you would have become, a shellfly, of a type which - as you are of human form - we call a floater."

Lily whispered, "You mean… one of those creatures?"

"A floater, yes," the Clerk went on. "Floating in your little shell, dead but alive by the will of the Grey One. From the seas it has conquered it has gathered a vast army of them, cannon fodder in this place. But in your world, they can be exceptionally dangerous."

"Floaters can get into my world?"

"Indeed they can. In nightmares, through channels which - for its own amusement - Grangel steals from the Presence itself." The Clerk turned to face her, a frown on his face. "Mysul tells me, that a floater is close to you, in your world, at this moment. You must know what to do with it. One false step will be fatal."

Lily gasped, "Fatal?"

"To you and to those with you. Your floater is an ancient thing, a shadow of Grangel itself, which entered your Universe at the beginning. It is close to you now. As a citizen of this place, Lily Moss, it is your duty to face it, overcome it, and dispel its malign spirit. I will give you guidance."

"Understand," the Clerk went on, raising a finger. "Your floater is trapped. It has trapped itself, deliberately, because it is hiding something. It may be treasure, something shiny that has drawn the floater's eye. Or, it may be an object of power, a weapon perhaps. It may even be a person, or a ghost, a lost soul denied its lawful rest. That plays to your advantage. The floater will not move, or at worst not move very far. But it will try to entice you towards it, and it will pounce."

"Pounce?"

"The result is painful, and fatal. A physical attack is pointless. To dispel a floater, the technique we advise is to shine light on it."

"Just light?"

"Bright, white light. That must be brighter than the floater's shell. Only then is its defence weakened, and that will happen gradually.

The floater will moan, it will make promises, but finally its shell will break, and the floater will melt, and dissolve in whatever atmosphere surrounds it. Then, when the floater is destroyed, what it was hiding will be revealed. Lily Moss, have you understood?"

"Light," she replied.

"Yes. That is your weapon. If you succeed, you will have done what Mysul asked of you, to restore a balance that you have upset. If you fail, you will be only a memory. Your life is in the balance. Do you understand?"

"Yes, sir Clerk."

"Remember what I have said. Be brave. Remember."

*

The Vicar cycled rapidly over the gravel of the Hall's forecourt in a state of panic, for - deceived by the bright weather of early morning - he had not bothered with a raincoat, and now it was raining, hard. Above him, a steep bank of black cloud towered above the Hall, gusts of rain breeze-blown over it, sploshing into the fountain, cascading down the colonnade, dribbling into pools through which he splashed to the steps and then to the front door. He stood in the hall, dripping. "Hellooo!" he shouted, his voice booming through the house. "Hellooo!" Spotting that the door to the rear of the hall was open, he advanced, and called into the stair-well, "Hellooo!"

From below came a cry of "Down here, Reverend!" from Riley Moss, and the Vicar descended the steps to the kitchen, seeing through the gloom that Moss and his daughter were holding each other up in a far corner, rain splashing on the grille of glass blocks above their heads. He saw Lily wriggle in her father's arms, then grab at the back of his sweater. The Vicar advanced towards them as Lily's eyes opened and she looked up at her father. "Oh Dad," she said. "Oh Dad, that was awful."

"You've been asleep for only a few seconds," said Moss. "Was it a dream?"

"Yes Dad." She let go of him and breathed deeply. "Just a dream. Not a turn. Better now."

Only then did the Vicar realise how appalling was the stench in this cavernous space. It was sulphurous, choking, and he put a hand over his mouth and nose. "Are you all right?" he mumbled. "Goodness, it's not exactly fresh in here."

"This is where your intruders get in," said Riley Moss, pointing upwards at the window with rotten frames. "You need to do something about that."

The Vicar looked up. It was a square window, set high-up on the kitchen wall. He saw through it to the sheds on the path outside. Its inside catch was missing, and the whole window trembled in the rain cascading over it. "Yes," he said. "That looks like a job for the maintenance company. Perhaps we should block it."

"Good idea," Moss agreed. "Talking of a block, we might have some sort of door here, but we can't figure it out. No door-knob, just a bunch of what might be keyholes. Here, in the corner, these cracks in the wall..."

"Oh yes," the Vicar said, stepping to the wall and running his hand down the plaster. "This was constructed in Capstick's time. I remember he had to get the agreement of the Trust."

"So is that a door?"

"Indeed it is. Let me see. Dear me, where did all those little holes come from? Well, one of them is a key-hole. Would you mind handing me the keys?" Moss produced the key-cluster from a pocket of his jeans and handed it over. "Now, which key?" the Vicar continued. "A mortice, definitely. And the keyhole - should be a little to the left and at keyhole height, I suppose..." The Vicar searched up and down the crack in the plaster. "If I remember correctly," he said, "the key had a red tag. Would you mind giving me more light, Mister Moss?" Moss directed his torch-light onto the

Vicar's hand. "Ah, that's the one," the Vicar said, as all the keys but one slipped away from his fingers down the ring. He poked the key into a hole, to no effect. He tried another hole.

"Wait," said Lily. "What's that noise?"

From beneath his feet, the Vicar heard the sound of rushing water, and from beyond the wall a gentle thumping, the beating of a heart, faint but insistent. "What the Hell is that?" said Riley Moss, stepping back and all-but bumping into the Vicar. "Pardon me, Reverend. Do you hear it? Where's that coming from?"

"I suspect," said the Vicar, "there is something beyond this wall. It sounds like a pump. And something else, voices I think, faint, can't quite make it out."

Moss put his ear to the wall. "Yes I hear it. Are you sure there is no electricity here?"

"The switchboard was disabled, years ago," the Vicar replied. "To stop intruders running up electricity bills."

"Well, something's alive in there."

At that instant, beams of light shot from the holes in the wall. They all backed away. "Gracious!" the Vicar cried. "What is that?"

Lily retreated till her back was flat against the kitchen wall, streams of coloured light playing above her head onto the kitchen window.

"It's OK," said Moss. "I think I know what that is. Vicar, keep trying. It's OK. Nothing to worry about."

Lily backed even further away. "Dad," she said, "I don't think it's a great idea to open that up."

"Ah, success," the Vicar said, finally finding the keyhole. He turned the key, but nothing happened.

Moss thumped the wall, hard with the flat of his hand, light from the wall flickering over his sweater. No result. "Reverend, your thoughts?"

199

The Vicar's first thought was to pray for guidance. But there was no need. Of its own accord, a floor-to-ceiling rectangle opened in the wall. It swung back, scraping over the concrete floor of a further room, as a light blazed out which made all three blink and hold up their hands against the glare. "Well," said Moss. "Would you look at that!"

The room which opened up before them must once have been a storeroom or scullery, wider than it was deep and white-plastered, a floor of concrete blocks with a red Persian rug at its centre. From the far wall two fiery eyes glared at them.

On a table whose green baize cover flowed to the floor sat a twin-lens video projector. It was whirring, its two lenses at odds with each other, the light of one focussed directly ahead through rising dust, the other slanted so that its rays flooded up and into the kitchen. Beside it lay an empty wine-glass, an ashtray with the butt of a cigar, and trays of video cassettes. By the table, the cushion of a black-leather armchair still showed the indentation of its last occupant, and on the floor an indistinct grumbling came from two small loudspeakers. In a far corner the floodlight from a movie studio of the 1920's stood unlit and tilted on a brass tripod against the wall.

Moss stepped forward, and the Vicar joined him, light from the projector flickering over them, as the heart-beat pulsed beneath their feet.

"That sounds like a pump, no question," said Moss. "Reverend," he said, "I have to accuse you of theft. Stealing... electricity. This equipment, and the pump, must be on a circuit ahead of the switchboard, taking power directly from the grid. I think there's a law against that."

"Oh dear."

"Did you spot the water sensor by the steps outside?" Riley Moss went on. "The grey box?" The Vicar nodded. "Well, this room is right under the steps and the fountain," Moss continued. "When it rains, it's my guess the sensor opens a circuit, straight off the grid.

200

The pump fires up and fills the fountain with rainwater. The equipment here is on the same circuit, and someone left the projector running. It's showing whatever video was last in it, looping through it. Spooky or what?"

It was difficult to see what that video was, for light flooded out into the kitchen, then up through its window, fragments of a picture, moving together but unclear. The sound was indistinct, muffled, though occasionally words leapt out, words which were coarse, in the voice of a woman who seemed to be in the middle of an argument.

"Lily, close your ears," said Moss. "It's all right, Dad," she replied. "I hear worse at school." Moss raised an eyebrow.

The Vicar put a hand to his mouth. On the wall he made out a face that he recognised. "Mrs Capstick," he whispered.

"Sure?" Moss said.

"That's her."

The two of them edged further into the room. "Come on, Lily," said Moss. "It's only a home movie." Across the white-painted wall a woman walked. Her image was unfocussed, as tall as the wall, and streaked vertically with what looked like streams of undulating glass, but clear enough to make out a dark-haired woman with bright red lipstick, her face in profile, wearing a black pencil dress that belonged to the 1940's. As she came to the end of the wall, she vanished, but her walk began again. She was doomed to an infinite loop.

All three of them watched. "There, Vicar," said Riley Moss with a flourish of his hand, "is your ghost. On video. With a soundtrack, the voice in the background. You could hear that from outside, on a quiet night. And you'd see it on the walls of the sheds out there. Spooky, if you were in the right mood."

The Vicar sighed. "I can just see Capstick, sitting in his chair, playing videos of the wife he loved…"

201

"Getting himself drunk…" Moss intruded. "And falling in his fountain."

"Tragic," said the Vicar.

"And no ghost."

"No ghost." The Vicar brightened. "Excellent!" he cried, with a clap of his hands.

"That's your culprit, Vicar," Moss said. "Capstick's private cinema. And just a little spooky, right now. It'll get more spooky in a few minutes if it stops raining and we're left in the dark. So I suggest we get out of here."

As they mounted the stairs, the Vicar was overjoyed. There was a natural explanation behind the tales of the chatterbox Aldsworth, and with pleasure he anticipated the look on the shop-keeper's face when he told him.

Lily followed on, with backward glances, for she was not pleased. It was fun to discover the reason for something, but that was not the something she expected, the something which was underground but had not shown its face, if it had a face.

24 - On the border of Bhutan

Chatham stood with the world at his feet. The monastery clung to a mountain above a river-cut valley on the Indian side of the border with Bhutan, snow-capped mountain ranges to the west, and its courtyard extended far out from the cliff edge overhanging a precipitous drop through swirls of cloud to the foaming rocks below. Dragon-claw pine trees shaded one corner where - for the visit of the Lord Commander - Saida had moved her map, and the team of black-clad young women who supported it, down from her stupa on the mountain's peak.

Twine was expected but not immediately, for he had business in Itanagar. Meanwhile, lunch in the shade had improved Chatham's mood, and here - amongst Taoists, Buddhists, and renegades from China - his grey robe was comfortable and appropriate.

On the red stones of the courtyard the map lay before him. It was a twenty-metre square of black wooden panels, with countries outlined in yellow, and suffered in translation from three to two dimensions. Everything looked too close to everything else. But, this was not an aid to navigation. This was the record of Saida's search for the fragments of God's mightiest weapon, his Minister.

Saida stood beside Chatham, in a purple sari whose hem she stroked with long thin fingers gleaming with rings and jewels of every colour. Black hair framed her wizened pale face. She raised her dark eyes, and the whiteness of her teeth was a shaft of light as she said, "My Lord, shall we begin?"

With a nod from Chatham, Saida motioned to the line of girls on the other side of the map, her nuns, each in a stark body-hugging uniform of a black as deep as that of their hair. All were very similar, fashioned in the monastery. It was for Saida to determine how they looked, and if that were the form she approved - which was probably how she looked in her youth, before so much of her expanded - so be it. With a word from the Lord Commander she would make them monkeys, boys, green-faced dragons, but that word would not come. After the cull of his organisation's middle order, Chatham was left with those he could control, and to them he granted the comfortable illusion of free will.

The nuns arranged themselves around the map, and squatted at its edge, drawing out keyboards from its sides. They began to pummel at the keyboards, chattering and calling across to each other, as one by one seven lights spread across the map.

"This view, my Lord," said Saida, "is of locations where we have found fragments of the Minister. Random, as far as we can tell. It's hardly credible that the Minister could allow himself to be so dispersed. This shows how shattering was the blow he received at the beginning. The component under the Pacific Ocean was found only by accident. On the other hand, there are many locations which we might investigate." She waved a hand, and now lights lit up world-wide. "So many," she said. "So-called paranormal phenomena, disturbances in the fabric of this globe, lights in the sky, ghosts, and so on. If resources can be found, my Lord, I suggest they go to the regions, because we would need their help."

"That, I will consider," said Chatham. "It is our duty to seek out Roamers and deal with them, but to restore the Minister is a more urgent priority. Saida, you already know which are the two most promising locations, do you not?"

"I do, my Lord. Here…" She waved a hand and the map cleared to display two lights, one on the west coast of Africa, the other on the south coast of the British Isles' mainland. "That is real-time data, from our tracking devices. I gather that your servant Twine has news about the location in Africa. Let me focus on the one to the north." She waved her hand in a circular motion, and the nuns typed furiously for a moment then sat back. "It is the senior," she said. "She is very close, within twenty metres of the site. It may be nothing. We can't tell without being there."

"It seems, Saida, that those who own that place have taken the bait, so carefully laid by your team. Isn't that fun?" Chatham smiled and twitched at his robe. "Teenage psychic, indeed. The senior has moved quickly. It pleases me that she may do our work for us."

Saida nodded and said, "The site has potential. From what we know of it and of the Minister's direction of travel at the beginning, it is highly likely that there is a fragment of the Minister right there. It may be virtual, in which case it goes into the pot with the others. But if it is physical, then we can make a start. Do I have your permission to project?"

"You do. I can think of no-one better."

With a smile, Saida vanished.

25 - In the Cellar

My Lord Bishop

In reply to your letter of June 6th, I herewith attach my record of the event at Malbury Hall about which you enquired at the weekend. I hope that it is sufficient explanation of my request for leave of absence for two weeks. Canon Southgate is an adequate replacement.

I remain, sir, your humble colleague in the service of Christ,

Thomas Ellis, Vicar of Malbury

*

Pride comes before a fall.

You will remember, my Lord Bishop, that I and the Mosses, father and daughter, identified the cause of apparitions witnessed at Malbury Hall by my parishioners. Rain was the culprit, rain that turned on the power for Capstick's private cinema. Mister Ballantine was correct: there was no ghost here.

Together we ascended from the depths of the Hall in a spirit of celebration, even gaiety. Rather, two of us did, the father and myself, but the daughter not so. She was sullen, distracted, muttering to herself. Her father asked why her mood should be so low, and she replied in a sharp tone that their work was not done, that underground in that building was something which we had missed.

I cannot tell your Lordship how affecting was the sight of that little girl, so sweet in manner and angelic in appearance, troubled. Her father, though of a rougher nature, was moved, as was I. His question as to what it was we missed was met by a blank look and a confession that she did not know, but she was sure it was dangerous, very dangerous, and might be the cause of those other incidents over the years, from before the time of the Capsticks, indeed dating back to when the Hall was built and even before. Her evidence was only a feeling, and the memory of a dream, the dream which I had interrupted earlier at my arrival. To the father, who presumably had witnessed other examples of her intuition, this was persuasive.

I also was of a mind to investigate further, not because of the girl's so-called intuition but because she was right in reminding us of those earlier incidents (I am thinking here of the artist Southey and of others who left the Hall, often with disturbing tales), and there was the matter of value for money. The Trust was paying a great deal to these people, and to call their work of a few hours sufficient when they had been hired for a whole week would be irresponsible. If nothing else, the father could have been useful in helping with the underpinnings of the Vestry.

So we returned to the kitchen, a dingy and malodorous place, as I described it to your Lordship at the weekend. The light now was only of the torch held by the girl, Lily, and as much daylight as came wanly from the kitchen window. The door of Capstick's private cinema was open, and there was no sound of pump nor projector, only of water below coursing through the rife which runs under the Hall, fed by the rain and from springs further up the hill.

Down there were four rooms, for that was the number agreed by the Trust in Capstick's programme of rebuilding. Of those rooms we had investigated only two. I had the keys for two others. It was clear where the door to one of those rooms must be, for at the far end of Capstick's cinema was a door, an ancient blue-painted door hanging off its hinges. Cautiously all three of us passed through the doorway. Moss took the torch from his daughter and went in front.

This was a large chamber, its walls of black stone, on its left-hand wall a metal door, shut, which must lead to another basement room. The ceiling was low, of rough plaster supported by thick pillars of concrete which stood in a line across the flagstones of what looked to be a cellar. Moss ran his light around the walls, which dripped and twinkled with a greenish slime. The smell here was even more foul, the cold even more bitter, and our breath blew in plumes through an atmosphere which seemed not to hold sufficient oxygen.

With the rushing of water below us now very audible, Moss turned his light onto the far wall of the cellar, to a cylinder of grey brick, topped by a thick layer of green metal. "Looks like the lid over a well," he said. "I suppose," said Moss to his daughter, "you want us to look down that well." She nodded, anxiety visible in her face even in the dim light. "Vicar," Moss said, "this might take two of us." I rolled up my sleeves.

The lid of the well-head was so heavy, so corroded, green and slippery with slime, that it took the efforts of both Moss and myself to shift it even one inch, the feeble light spilling over our faces as over wrestlers, grunting and puffing.

As we struggled with this well-cap, we became aware of a further light, from below, which shone up from the small gap we had made between the lid and well-head. It would be remarkable that the sun had penetrated those depths, was my first thought, but even more remarkable if the sun itself was down there and coming up to meet us, for the light moved, as if a man were climbing up inside the well, a miner's lamp on his head.

Brighter shone this thin shaft of light, brighter than the torch-light, right to the ceiling of the cellar. I made out what gave the greenish tinge to the walls - insects, small beetles, green scarabs scrabbling upward through islands of algae to escape the rising light. And then what horror it was to feel the well-cap turning in our hands, of its own accord, that heavy metal twisting easily as it unscrewed, rising from the well-head. We took our hands from it and stepped back in alarm, and Lily stumbled back with a cry against one of the cellar's supporting pillars.

Gas, a visible gas twisted in wreaths of cold steam from around the well-cap, with a stench of excrement so strong we choked and covered our mouths. What is there in the human mind that freezes, that paralyses the legs while the heart races, that keeps the eyes fixed on something they do not want to see? This was the matter of a moment but it was terror, as the lid of the well, which had been so heavy, spun from the well-head with a clank onto the floor.

Lit from below, choking steam billowed around the well-head and through the cellar in a grey haze. We stepped further back, all of us, Lily by now behind the pillar. Our minds were telling us to run, but the steam, the gas was everywhere, swirling, irresistible.

"Born."

The voice was low and slow, as if an echo from a far-off place. It was one word, whispered, which I did not hear but rather felt, one word, which was repeated. "Born."

There was movement at the far wall and I turned my head. Through curls of grey steam a figure emerged, long-legged, its head lowered to the floor. Whether it came through the wall or through the floor I could not say.

Its head swayed from side to side, the head of a horse.

It was a stallion, coal-black. Steam parted around it as it turned and raised its head, on that head a white mark, a star. The ears pricked up. The horse raised a leg, a powerful sinewy leg, and brought its hoof to the floor through tissues of steam with a mighty thud. Warily its eyes scanned us.

The horse turned away from the wall. "Born," I heard again.

It was the motion of a beckoning finger, the horse lifting a hoof and drawing it back, its head turned towards the pillar where Lily was hiding. It came forward one step. Sensing danger to his daughter, Moss came alive, and threw himself against the horse's side, grabbing at its mane. The horse twisted aside and kicked out, dashing a hoof against Moss's head. He fell to the floor, blood streaming from a wound to his scalp. The horse lowered its head and licked at the blood. "Sad time," I heard. "Many time sad."

I backed off towards another pillar, my eyes fixed on this beast, its eyes fixed on Lily's pillar where she was flattened against its other side. The horse took another step. "Sir," Lily whispered to me. "Is my Dad... alive?"

I saw a movement of her father's foot, and a tremor around his shoulders. "Yes," I replied.

The horse stood above the prostrate body, and snorted. It was a living creature, for breath streamed from its flaring nostrils and swirled through the haze of steam. If its arrival from nowhere were not remarkable enough, what followed was even more so, for the horse bowed. It bowed, bending one foreleg, extending the other, and lowering its head to the floor. "Born," I heard distinctly and, "You." From this position it lowered the rest of itself to the floor, bending both forelegs beneath it, twisting its rear to the side and extending a leg alongside the now moaning Moss. For some moments its head remained up, but then with more of a sigh than a snort the neck relaxed, the ears flattened, the eyes closed, and the entire body of the animal lay flat. It seemed to be asleep.

"The horse is our friend," Lily whispered. "What happened was an accident. Our enemy, is the floater."

What she meant by that I soon discovered. At first this was just intuition on my part, a feeling that there was something in the light of the well, indistinct, feeding off it. But slowly above the well-head there formed a sphere, whose light grew in intensity until beams of it flashed through the steam as from a lighthouse on a night of fog. It was an egg of light, translucent, and inside it, floating in some milky liquid, a little girl, barely more than a baby. But a monster. Who but Satan himself could have fashioned so misshapen a body, a carcass, pencil-thin and disjointed, the head lolling to one side, the webbed hands outstretched? The face was from nightmare, wide staring and bulbous black eyes, a little girl's skeleton in a flowing robe of green but a woman's face, grey, cracked with age, ghoulish, the mouth agape, the teeth of a saw. The sight struck me dumb. My fingers felt for the pillar behind me, and I wormed my way around it, my back to its back as I breathed again.

"I see pretty," I heard. "Pretty hides. Bad pretty."

"Reverend, please," I heard Lily say. "Can you help?"

"Yes," said I, still gasping. "What can we do?"

"What can we do?" the creature echoed. "Bad pretty, come. I have treasure, pretty things. Come."

Lily had been peering around the pillar but now she flattened her back against it as had I. "Please. Put water on the sensor outside," she said. "Can you? I must have light."

"I can't."

"Oh bad man," the creature intoned. "He can't. I say to pretty, not to man, set me free, and I give pretty treasure. Many time I wait and say I kill pretty but no pretty. Now pretty come and I give pretty treasure. Come."

"Don't listen," I said. "It is the voice of Satan."

"Can you do it, Reverend? Please. It can't move. You can."

"How do you know?"

"I know."

"You are sure?"

"Yes."

"Oh bad pretty. Come. I give you my treasure. And horse to ride. All for you. Set us free."

Without looking towards the well-head, I leapt across the cellar, past Lily Prometheus-like on her pillar, racing through the kitchen as if the creature were on my heels, up again and out, into clean air. To fire up the projector I had to activate the sensor, I must pour water on it, but the rain had stopped, and I saw nothing to carry water. I had seen, though, a knapsack by the door, and there I found two full water-bottles. I dashed outside once more, and poured water gingerly over the sensor so as not to waste a drop. As I returned through the ground floor I was rewarded with a gleam of light from

211

the kitchen over the walls of the sheds, faint now, for the watery sun's light was too strong even for Mrs Capstick. With a deep breath I hurtled downward, down into the kitchen, as light from Capstick's projector beamed through and hit me in the face.

Lily was there, moving the projector on its stand so that its light shone fully through the open door to the cellar. She twisted the errant lens, so that both lenses together focussed in a single tight beam between the pillars and onto the creature in its shell of light. How bizarre was that effect, of Mrs Capstick projected in glaring light onto the vaporous shell of that hideous creature! In a second, Lily had found how to stop the video's projection, and there was clean white light, very strong, against which the creature held up its webbed hands.

"Pretty!" it moaned from beyond the doorway. "Bad, so bad!"

More, Lily grabbed the floodlight and - having flicked its switch and setting it upright on its tripod - step by step advanced through Capstick's cinema holding it, through the door and into the cellar, side-stepping the light of the projector, until the length of the floodlight's cable was exhausted and prohibited her from going any further. I could not leave so tender a child undefended, so followed, and stood inside the cellar gasping, but I saw that this was no longer my affair. This was a battle of light, between the monster and Lily.

Writhing in its liquid the creature began to smack its webbed hands together, and flattened its ghoulish face against the wall of its shell, black eyes wide and staring as if in agony. "Pretty!" it moaned. "No, no! Come closer! Closer!"

Lily stood by the cellar wall with one hand on a hip. She was not afraid. The look on her face in the reflected light, my Lord, this was determination, this was valour in a twelve-year-old girl, this was Joan of Arc. I could believe that light flooded from her eyes, so fierce was her expression.

"Come pretty!" wailed the monster. "Come we go find treasure. I give you all. I give you all…"

Its shell of light cracked. Whatever the milky liquid was, it spilled out and fell to join the waters of the rife beneath. Its light vanished, leaving a writhing mass of green slime atop the well-head.

"No!" This was a new voice, a male voice deeper than the well from which it came, booming, echoing around the stone walls. "Scum. Roamer scum. No beginning, scum. We finish it. Here!"

I saw the disquiet on Lily's face, even as the light of the projector and floodlight began to fade. I stepped forward. Surely, there could be no danger from the creature's remains, but I was wrong. Claws sprung from it, on spindly arms that reached out as it hopped from the well-head onto the floor and scuttled through the dust towards the girl. Now in the nearly dark she pulled from her jacket a mobile telephone, and turned its light onto the creature, which pulled back, held up its claws and with a final shout of "Come!" melted into the dust.

All that remained of it was a speck of black dirt, a fragment of coal, as the steam in the cellar coalesced and with a monstrous hiss was sucked back down into the darkness of the well.

As Lily bent down to examine this last evidence of her opponent, the horse rose from the floor, opened its eyes and shook its mane. I heard it clearly. "Roamer," it said. "Take me home. My bridle is below. I beg you. Take me home."

In the flickering light, the horse turned towards Lily as she paced across the floor towards the well-head. For a moment she looked down upon the prostrate but now stirring body of her father, and with no further delay she shone the light of her telephone into the well. She reached down, and as she pulled back her hand I saw in it a tangle of leather, a horse's bridle.

Again the horse knelt, and Lily dropped the bridle over its head. In a single motion, and before I could utter a word of protest, the girl climbed onto the horse's back and took hold of the reins. The horse lifted its head, and with a whinny so loud that dust rained down from the ceiling it leapt forward and jumped.

Both horse and rider vanished.

My Lord, I can record only what I saw and heard. I believe that there was in the atmosphere of that place something which affects the mind. Certainly, in the days since this event I have doubted my memory, even my sanity. I was convinced that I had peered into the Abyss, the abode of Satan.

The girl and the horse had escaped, disappeared, jumping through the ceiling as if it and the rest of this building were made of air. Where had she gone? Should I call for an ambulance? Or Police? Had she tumbled down the well? Had I pushed her? Had I hit Moss over the head with… something? Had I pushed Moss against a pillar then thrown the girl down the well? Was the horse the invention of my own mind, a phantasm to explain a sudden fit of violence, due to stress? Am I mad? I did not feel mad, but then mad people probably do not. My mind whirled and I put out a hand against a pillar to steady myself.

Mad or not, it seemed to me that something approaching normality had returned. But the miasma of the cellar was still in my veins. My hallucination continued. It was not normal for the figure of a woman to coalesce there, in the middle of the floor. She came from nowhere, her head lowered, her hands together as if in prayer. Indian, I believed, quite small, her hair long and dark, in a purple sari that billowed around her as if in a breeze. She lifted her head and I saw her face, not Indian, but pale and thin, with black eyes which glowered at me and a curl of disdain in her thin lips.

Swiftly she bent down. Her fingers closed around the fragment of coal and lifted it. She turned. Now with her back to me I heard her cry out, "Minister!" as into the well she flung the fragment of coal.

Thinking her cry was for me, I stepped forward, but the woman disappeared as swiftly as she had come, as if she had been only another of the images from Capstick's cinema, turned off with the flick of a switch.

What had been a faint light around the well-head thickened to a lurid yellow. Something was coming. As before, the light brightened and shone to the ceiling. I edged away, along the wall and towards the doorway. But Moss still lay there. Whatever was coming might consume him. A Christian soldier must defend the vulnerable. I lifted my chin, swallowed hard, and stepped forward.

It was right to be wary but I must not be afraid. I had no defence other than the cross around my neck, no experience of Satan or his demons whatsoever. I could only trust that the powers of Good were at my side, for I was in no doubt that what was coming up the well, inch by inch, was evil. Already I heard mutterings, in that deep voice which growled at itself, and rumbled as if the body it came from were far away, deep down. Whatever I was to confront, it must take me as I am, or I would take it, and throw it back into the Pit. I stepped over the prostrate body of Riley Moss, cleared my throat and began to speak.

"In the name of…"

"Don't give me names. You have no power here."

This was not heard, but felt inside my head. My mouth dropped open but I forced out, "… the Lord…"

"Our Lord God sees you."

Up from the well-head rose what looked to be a grey cloth, a sheet of grey which twisted into multiple corners, spikes of cloth each glittering in the yellow light of the well.

"Our Lord God gives me power."

It seemed to me that there was on the cloth a face, skeletal, impassive. But before I could study it further, the cloth swirled into a tube which flew like a rocket downwards as the yellow light faded away.

The girl re-appeared in seconds, bending over her father's body and helping him to regain his feet. This occurred so quickly that I was left by the wall with my mouth hanging open, amazed.

Of these events the father remembers nothing, believing that he hit his head by accident on a pillar. The girl herself says little, following her father's lead. I had from her only a curious look and the words, "That was a nasty accident, Reverend, wasn't it? I do hope Dad will be all right. I'm so glad there was nothing in that well to worry about."

In the circumstances, my Lord Bishop, I humbly suggest that I have become subject to a temporary illness, related to stress. I am sure this is due mainly to my worry over the lack of funding of necessary improvements to the fabric of this parish's church. With the permission of your Lordship I will apply for a stay of two weeks at the centre in Bournemouth, from which I am sure I will return fully restored.

26 - Roamers Cross

Lily had never ridden a horse. They were scary big animals with jaws that chomped, and people fell off them, even with saddles. Horses belonged in fields safely out of the way. This horse had no saddle. Her knees clung to its ribs as if glued and the reins in her hand pulled so hard she thought she might lose her fingers. It was madness to jump onto it, but that is what it wanted, what it needed, and she knew it would take care of her, come what may.

What came, as the horse leapt through the cellar's roof, was the bed of a sea, stretching into a blue gloom over white sand dotted with black boulders and waving fronds of seaweed. The horse took off at an alarming pace, grunting and snorting, foam from its mouth streaking past Lily's face as she bent over its neck. Shoals of silver fish turned tail and flashed aside. If there was water, then it did not impede the horse, which careered between rocks and over under-sea gullies as if following a well-known track. If there was water, then Lily should drown, but she was not aware of breathing at all.

Ahead loomed a wall of rock, with a curve at its centre which led up from the sea-bed. The horse made for it over a channel of sand, until with a grunt it reached the surface. Here was a river, sparkling in the sun as it flowed past, on either bank clumps of mangrove, tall swaying palm trees behind. The horse paddled to a sandy shore, then took off along a dusty track, palm fronds whipping past Lily's ears, upward until they stood atop a rocky cliff, above them only sky.

The horse stood panting. Lily felt its heart pound between its ribs. "Roamer," it whispered. "Your name?"

"Lily."

"Thank you, Lily. I have energy for one last jump. Are you willing?"

"Yes. But what do I call you?"

"Navigator. Clasp your hands around my neck. Our course lies upward."

The horse reared on its hind legs and pawed at the air. Lily clung on, her face buried in its mane. With a tremendous leap they took off, vertically, the horse's forelegs outstretched, Lily's hair streaming back as her bunches unravelled. The speed was terrifying, through a cloud layer in seconds, into a blue sky, a white sky, then no sky but only stars in a black night, and then no stars at all for in a blinding flash horse and rider stood at the edge of a valley.

To one side was nothing, sheer black though with a fast-disappearing arch of purple light. On the other side beneath a blue sky lay a valley, rocky but with a scattering of bushes, at its bottom a stream meandering through the rocks. Twisted rails of iron ran along the valley's other side, the remains of an ancient railway. "The Safe Gate," the horse panted. "An awkward jump but… safe. Safe."

"Where is this?" Lily also panted for she felt drained, as tired as she could remember. "Is this home? Your home?"

"It is," Navigator replied. "Be patient. I must call." The horse let out a whinny which echoed around the valley. It pawed the ground, raising dust.

Above the opposite side of the valley appeared a white haze, as if beyond that hill bonfires were burning. It expanded along the valley's edge, growing as thick as cloud, and in it sparkled shafts of light, then patterns of stars that revolved and twinkled in what became a mist which spread over the valley's side but in a moment flashed into a small conical shape that advanced upward towards them on their side of the valley, picking its way through rocks and bushes. It was a woman in a white robe, sandals on her feet, her hair grey and tied back in an elaborate bun, and her face pinched but luminous, the face of Lady Meizel.

The horse bowed. Lily slipped down over its side to the dusty ground. "Mysul," the horse panted. "Your servant."

"Rise, Navigator," said the old lady. She advanced, and gently stroked its head as it rose, unsteadily. "Faithful Navigator," she said. "What was lost, is found." She turned. "And Lily Moss. Child, you have gone where you should not, and seen what you should not. There must be a reckoning for this."

"I needed her, Mysul," said the horse. "There is nothing left of me. After such time…"

"Yes, Navigator, faithful friend. But you were unreachable, beyond my sight."

"I cannot say, my soul, how painful was our separation," Navigator groaned. "When I was caught at our crossing by that devil - how I fought it, struggled with it in the vapours of the Gate. I took on every form. If I were a lion, the devil would be a pack of spear-throwing hunters. If I were a tree it would be men with axes. If I were a cloud it would be a thunderstorm. Only when I became a horse, and it became my rider, could I pass through the Gate and shake it off. I thought myself safe, that the devil had been blown apart by the crossing, for it had no course to follow through your inflating sea. But no. It clung to me, biting and cursing, dragging me into its pit, and… so much sad time."

"That is over, Navigator. You are home."

"But you must release me, Mysul. My heart fails. My time is done. I must find my home in the Tower."

The horse lowered its head. On the old lady's face was a look of utter sadness. "To find you and to lose you, in a second," she said, "is unbearable."

"Nothing is lost," Navigator replied.

"Nothing is lost," the old lady repeated. She paused, looking at the horse with tear-filled eyes, as it swayed and its forelegs sank to the ground. "Go then, faithful friend," she said. "Your time has been beautiful. Live again in your time."

With the last of its strength the horse pulled itself upright, but bowed, extending one foreleg, then rose onto its hind legs, pawed at the air, and froze. Its image grew, expanded until it towered over the hill in a pattern of twinkling stars, and faded.

The old lady was overcome with grief. Her head was bowed, and tears fell as she clasped her hands. "You cannot understand, child," she said, "what this means. But I thank you. Our Navigator thanks you. One mystery is understood. No doubt there will be others."

Lily shuffled awkwardly in the dust. "My Lady. Mysul. May I ask… where am I?"

"You know where you are, child."

"Is this Roamers Cross?"

"That is your name for this place. I have another name, but so be it."

"But I come here only when I am asleep. When I dream."

"You are not asleep now, child. You are here. At the Gate."

"The Gate, yes."

"And where we stand is the mirror of a valley in your world. Your people believed that beyond this hill are other worlds, the world of ancestors, worlds of demons. Through this mirror many have passed into our horizon. Navigator built a gate here, the Safe Gate. I permit my Navigator to build gates, and control the paths in your universe which we call channels. You may do that yourself, one day. But now you must return. Do you remember where you were?"

"Yes, my Lady."

"And was that where Navigator began his last journey?" Lily nodded. "Then take the Navigator's key. It lies at your feet."

Lily looked down. By her feet lay a disk of gold. It was shiny, and looked like a coin. She picked it up and wiped away the dust. The only feature on the disk was a small silver star at one edge. "A key, my Lady?"

"A key. Follow."

The old lady stalked further up the valley's side, to where the sheer darkness began. Lily followed. As they approached the edge, Mysul turned and said, "The key in your hand must not be lost. In the wrong hands it will bring danger to this place. You have already seen what a key can do, for you have used one already, without knowing. The key you hold is the most powerful. It is the Navigator's key, and I trust you with it now. Do you understand?" Lily nodded. "So," said Mysul, "we shall open the gate."

She raised a hand, and around them a mist gathered into the hemisphere of a sparkling blue wall, curving behind them and to each side. At the edge, between light and dark, a block of basalt rose from the ground, a metre-high cube of glistening black stone veined with white. "Forward, to the stone."

Lily stepped forward until her feet touched the stone.

"Lay the key on the stone."

Gently Lily lowered the golden disk onto the stone, which slipped down without sound into the ground as the disk rose back between her fingers. Ahead of her a sphere of cloud rose and grew from the edge of the darkness, and through that a path over the dark, a dusty track, unrolled towards an archway, vapours of white and purple hissing and swirling within it. "Forward through the gate, Lily Moss, no looking back," said the old lady. "Guard the key with your life. It is our secret. Our Navigator thanks you. Until we meet again."

Breathing hard but with a steady pace, Lily traversed the path into the archway. As she entered and the vapours swallowed her, she felt herself dissolve into a mist of rainbows, and then she was in two places at once, to choose. Her choice was the cellar of Malbury Hall. And there she stood, by her father's prostrate body.

*

Leaving the Hall was no easy matter. The Vicar was in a daze, and only slowly and blank-faced, muttering to himself, he led the way up through the kitchen, as Lily supported her father up the stairs.

Out in the fresh air, with a new energy Riley Moss took Lily's hand and all three headed off past the fountain towards the path to the village.

As Lily looked back at the Hall, its façade was like a human face; dormer windows like eyes, a pediment like a nose, and columns like teeth in a grinning mouth. In front of it a man called Capstick had been found dead in his fountain. The Hall killed him. She wondered whether she would ever return, and - if she did - whether it would kill her.

27 - The Second Friday

Sitting on her bed, just after six in the morning, Lily Moss was in a quandary. She knew that Roamers Cross existed. She had doubted it, for it was a dream, but she had seen it, and survived. Whether it existed as she dreamed it, whether there was a Mother's Hill where her mother lived, she did not know, but she had seen what she should not have seen, and gone where she should not have gone. Meizel was Mysul and she was real, super-real, and did what in Lily's world was impossible but what in Roamers Cross - like leaping over craters on the Moon - was natural.

The horse, Navigator, was no dream. She rode him, and she remembered the gleam of his flanks and the smell of sweat in his mane, the grunting and snorting, the raising of his head and the courtly bow. Besides, she had evidence, the key, the gold coin with the silver star, which - in the cellar of Malbury Hall - she had dropped into a pocket of her bomber jacket.

Her quandary, was what to do with that coin, Navigator's key. For the whole of half-term week she had kept it in her purse, with the Silas penny, and that purse had not left her side. Today was her second Friday. Today she was due at The Lodge. She had to wear a uniform with no pockets, and could take nothing in and nothing out. Somewhere, she had to hide Navigator's key.

She had not expected to be at home that week, but with her father she had returned on the Tuesday to face a barrage of questions. From Swan - 'Teenage psychic? Lily, is that you in the paper? How could you let them do that to you?' From Nathalie, 'Teenage what? Sicko?' From Miss Chesterton, 'Lily, would 2pm on Monday be convenient for a chat about the article about you in the local newspaper?'

She replied to no-one, not yet. She kept her head down. She could talk to no-one about what had happened over the previous weekend, for her Dad - who still had a plaster over his scalp - remembered little about it (though he remembered enough to be pleased about the improvement in his bank account), all her friends would think she was making it up, and the only other witness - the Reverend - had wandered off shaking his head and was probably, secretly, annoyed. Only at the Lodge might she find someone to talk to, but she did not know who, Ordinal possibly.

Meanwhile, there was only one place for her purse with the key and the Silas penny, and that was with the photograph of the little black-haired boy and her dream books, under the newspapers in her bedside drawer.

*

"Orders from on high," Ordinal said, taking Lily by the arm and guiding her across the hall of the Lodge towards the grand staircase. "From here on, navigation is your subject, like it or not. Up you go."

With a wave to Chun who was heading down the steps for more Ancient History, Lily climbed the staircase, a throng of students around her, laughing at first then more serious as they dispersed. Near the top, Lily turned into the Navigation classroom. The tall ginger-haired boy from last week's class with Miss Servator was standing at the window. He turned. "Ah, Lily," he said with a grin. "Delighted. Marco is the name." He advanced over the red carpet and with an unexpected bow extended a hand which Lily shook. "Father's in the City, Bogota. Do you have family?"

"Yes, Marco."

"Charmed. And what does your family do?"

"Antiques."

"Oh, do you do Meissen? We have it all up the stairs. I've broken a few. And three Lowreys. Marvellous to see how the lower classes live."

"I'm sure we do Meissen."

"How wonderful. You must give me your card."

"I will." Lily pondered how she might smuggle a card into the Lodge. This was obviously a boy with Money. Though she had no idea what Meissen was, she was sure that her Dad could make some.

Other students entered, without the obnoxious Robert; but in came the more-woman-than-girl who had told her off for using the G word, Martha, all teeth, blonde hair and hips. Marco stepped back and cleared his throat. In came a small brown-faced boy with spectacles, who peered around like a mole. "Wezza wotsit?" he said.

"I beg your pardon, Sidney?" Marco enquired.

"Wotsisname? You know, him. Oh. OK."

In came Ordinal, with a swish of a black academic gown which clung to his spinach-green suit as if paint had been splashed on him by a mischievous toad. "Carpet time," he said. There were no chairs, only the red carpet. Around the walls, bookshelves were piled high with dusty volumes, but the focus, on the carpet, was the sculpture of spheres and pipes all inside a translucent plastic shell, which reminded Lily of an egg with veins. The Omnium. At any moment she expected a heart to beat, blood to flow, and a chicken to pop out.

"Let us remember the basics, for Lily's benefit," said Ordinal, striding over the carpet as his students squatted in a curve.

The basics of Navigation, as defined by Ordinal, were to know where you start, where you end, and what you have to do in-between, unless you were exploring, and then you need to know where you started and where you had been on the journey, so that if everything went horribly wrong you could find your way back.

This made sense to Lily, until he called out "Pipe six," and one of the spheres inside the egg turned from white to green. She counted them. There were fifteen in three layers, four on top, seven in the middle, four at the bottom, all arranged around the central sphere of

225

the middle layer, which was number One. Each had a number or letter, from One to Nine and then A to F. Around them, the encasing egg of clear plastic had no number. Sphere Six lay at the edge of the middle layer, and was now green. All others were white.

"Pipe six, seven," Ordinal called out, and another sphere, next to Sphere Six on the same layer and also at the edge, turned red. Between them a pipe twinkled, then turned orange and then green. The red sphere turned green. "Simple route," Ordinal said, "from one habitable sea to another. Now let us try another. Pipe clear. Pipe six, five, two."

All spheres were white, but Sphere Six again turned green, and two directly below on the bottom layer red. Pipes between them twinkled, but turned red. "Sidney," said Ordinal, "explain why that route is impossible."

"Ummm..." Sidney peered over his spectacles. "Owned by, you know... it. The G word."

"You skilfully avoided a penalty point there," Ordinal said. "Now let us try this. Pipe clear. Pipe six, D, E, F. Martha, what is the problem with that?"

Again Sphere Six turned green. On the top layer of the egg three spheres turned red, and the pipes between them turned orange, but then red.

"D and E are seas without Time," she replied, as if everyone knew.

"Precisely," Ordinal agreed. "And we don't want to go there, do we? What would happen to us?"

Students looked at each other. Lily looked straight ahead and blinked.

Sidney spoke up. "We'd get frazzled?"

"Wrong answer, Sidney," said Ordinal. "Will you ever learn? Martha, the correct answer please."

"No-one knows," she said.

"Exactly. Navigators have made the attempt, and not one has returned. It is hard for us who live in Time to imagine a place of such stillness, no getting hotter or colder, entirely static. If any of you ever become navigators, perish the thought, you will avoid seas D and E, as you see in red here. Pipe fill."

Every sphere now took on a colour. Three on the bottom layer turned a muddy brown with one green, all green in the middle layer, and on top two green and two red. "That is not to say," Ordinal said, "that there is no perfectly good route between those two seas. This, young Lily, is where true navigation begins. Meanwhile, let us cheat. Pipe clear. Pipe six, one, F recast."

The result was a chain of green spheres on the top two layers, linked by green pipes, all avoiding any contact with red spheres D and E. "There," Ordinal said, "quite safe, though that will require hopping about between gates. I hope, young Lily, this is now clearer than mud."

To Lily this was not clear at all. She put up a hand. "Excuse me, sir," she said. "The round things. Why are they seas?"

"Why?" said Ordinal. "What a good question. Clever child. You are one to watch. Why? Because they are, and that's an end to it."

"They look like little eggs," Lily went on. "And there's a big egg all around them."

"Eggs is it? Well let me tell you, clever child, those little eggs are what you call universes."

"Whole universes?"

"Obviously. Many of them are only dust, not as interesting as this one. Ours is the sixth sea, by the way. That's something for Cosmology."

"But what has the big egg got to do with it?"

"The big egg?" Ordinal tilted his head to one side. "Ah, the Greater Sea. That also is something for Cosmology. You will have to wait. Any more questions?"

"Gates?"

"Dear me, you know that already. You've used one, Lily Moss, don't you remember? The Navigator's gate, the Safe Gate of... oh bum..." Ordinal shook his head and sighed, "I didn't say that. You didn't hear it. It never happened." But it was too late. The rest of the class turned their heads towards Lily wide-eyed and open-mouthed.

"Hey!" piped up the bespectacled Sidney. "You been through a gate, Lily? Well cool. Did's you get all fizzled up?"

"I... well, I don't know," Lily said, blushing a red as bright as one of the forbidden spheres. "Maybe. By accident."

Ordinal butted in with, "Rumour has it, and so on and so forth. I shall say no more about it. And neither will you, Lily Moss." He looked at her with a penetrating gaze.

"Did you..." Martha stuttered, "did you... have a key?" But Lily made no reply.

"Of course she had a key," Ordinal went on. "You don't open a gate without a key. Oh bum, there I go again."

"But," Martha continued, "It takes a level-two navigator or one of the Five to do that. Lily, are you one of the Five?"

"Obviously she isn't," Ordinal could not stop himself from saying. "Now. To proceed..." He set them a test, to plot a course between seas five, on the bottom layer, and C, on the top, which was safe and required no more than one sideways movement. Marco said that it was impossible, but Ordinal had no time for debate. "I will test you on my return," he said, "except Lily, who obviously knows little of the subject."

He stalked out, and Lily - sitting nearest to the door - heard from outside a stream of rude words, seemingly directed by Ordinal at himself.

*

The test - which Martha passed, Marco failed, and Sidney did not complete - saw them through to break-time, when the class joined the others in a tramp downstairs to the sitting-room.

"Wozzu stretched till you was nearly busted?" said Sidney, pinching at Lily's elbow as they passed the Housekeeper's quarters. Lily jerked her elbow back and said nothing, but gave him the briefest of smiles. In front of them, Martha kept looking back with a worried face, and in the sitting-room set off for a corner where the older girls had gathered around a steaming pot of tea. Lily spotted Theo sitting with some younger boys, and he waved her over.

"Hey Lily," said Theo. "This is Fred and Barney. Our cartoon twins." They were not twins, for one was dark and plump, the other thin and blonde, but both nodded, picked up glasses of lemonade deposited by a mechanical in a yellow smock, and sipped on their straws.

"Settling in?" said Theo. "I guess it's all still pretty weird."

"Yes it is," Lily replied, smiling at the mechanical who - unsmiling - laid a glass of lemonade and a tray of biscuits in front of her.

"I guess you seen some weird stuff yourself, though," Theo went on. "I mean, we all have. That's why we're here. Even fat Robert. I think he's ill."

Fred, the dark plump one, chipped in with, "He ate a mechanical and it disagreed with him." Barney chuckled at his side.

"Is that why we're here?" said Lily. "Because we've seen... weird stuff?"

Weird stuff, said Theo, was what he saw in his dreams, back home in Alabama. He suffered from fits, and when he had fits he had dreams, and when he had dreams he went to a place of cobbled streets where balloons bounced around and had to be avoided at all costs, a hotel from which he was always being thrown out for not paying his rent, dark houses where people whispered from the other side of walls and held wild parties through which he drifted like a ghost, talking horses, cars with square wheels and policemen who would somersault across the street and begin dancing on the sidewalk.

That was weird stuff, and Lily could identify some of it. "Yes," she said, "I have dreams like that. And I get what I call 'turns', like fits I suppose. Can be really nasty. I have something called a DVA, in my head."

"So do I," said Theo. "And me," said Fred. "Me too," said Barney.

"We all do," Theo went on. "We're Roamers. That's what makes us different from regular folks."

"Navigator called me that. I thought it was just someone who roams around."

"Who called you that?" said Theo with a frown.

"Oh. Just a friend."

"Well," said Theo, "you're a fully paid-up member of the Roamer clan now, Lily. But it's not a word the staff use."

"They call us idiots and morons," said Barney.

"It's kinda traditional," Theo went on. "It's a name we call ourselves. Roamers. We roam the Universe, well, bits of it anyway. Did you say Navigator?"

"I can't talk about that. Sorry."

"Whoah, big mystery. Anyhow, we're all off after break. It's a sports day for some of us, including you."

"Oh, that will be fun."

"Yeah it will, won't it?" said Theo, and beside him the cartoon twins laughed over their lemonade.

*

They went in two white buses, one driven by Cardinal and the other by Miss Servator. Lily sat at the back of the Servator bus, which was the safer place to be, for she drove slowly, following the Cardinal bus along the stone track into the forest, but soon losing him as he sped off into the distance.

Miss Servator grumbled. She could not get into a gear higher than second, and she slapped the gear-stick muttering about the Housekeeper with cries of 'murder' and 'idiot'. Lily knew none of the students within earshot, and they were all quiet, more so as the journey continued. As they reached a bank of fog over a stream's bridge, one by one, starting at the front, the students slumped and Lily herself felt a comfortable numbness, then an irresistible need to close her eyes.

She woke in sunshine under a sky of hazy blue, hot and steamy. The buses were parked between walls of crumbling orange-red stone. They were high up, above a dusty plain dotted with spindly trees. "Out!" yelled Miss Servator. "Girls on the right, boys left!"

Lily followed the girls from both buses behind the wall on the right. Over the wall came a barrage of black and red t-shirts and shorts, followed by a consignment of woolly hats. It was too hot for a hat, and not knowing what the colours meant Lily chose a hybrid - red top and black shorts. The other girls, though, chose a single colour and changed, tidily folding their uniforms, then trooped off up a ramp. Lily followed, until she was yanked back by her elbow. "Not you, Lily Moss." It was Miss Servator. "Today you are a lexicon. Follow me."

The students, Cardinal, Miss Servator and Lily arrived at a garden, a rectangle of green grass with an edge of rose bushes, around it single-storey buildings and balustrades of pink stone, domes upon thin columns rising above them into the sky. An aroma of spices tickled Lily's nose, the aroma she remembered from the Indian take-away in Swivelhurst. Some students leapt onto the grass and began exercises of bending and stretching. Lily trotted behind Miss Servator wondering what a lexicon might be, up into a wide and flat courtyard. On every side were the halls and pavilions of a palace, of a style which Lily had seen on Brighton sea-front, but these were of pink stone and weathered red brick, walls with windows that had no glass, balustrades and onion domes on stalks of columns.

There, grey panels in the courtyard's floor made a pattern of eight squares by eight, a chess-board.

Miss Servator came to a halt. "Here, Lily Moss, emperors played chess with live chess-pieces, slaves. When one was captured, his head was lopped off. There are students here I would gladly do that to. This way. To the Porch."

In the shadow of a pavilion, the Porch was entirely of pink stone, its four square columns supporting a meander frieze and a cupola. What it offered was shade, which Lily was glad to see, for the sun - though past its zenith - beat down upon the courtyard with a hot, flat hand. Four chairs were arranged in the shade, around a rickety table bearing glasses and a jug of lemonade. The back seats were raised on a wooden step, where Cardinal sat flipping a gold coin. Miss Servator sat at his side and motioned to Lily to take one of the front chairs. Lily turned, and there, in a column's shadow, sat Robert. Her heart sank.

"Hello Lily," said Robert, in a feeble, wheedling voice. "We're lexicons today. I'm not well."

"I'm sorry to hear that, Robert," Lily replied. "I hope you get well soon."

"Thank you."

"Miss Servator, what is this?" said Lily, pointing to a book which lay on the dusty floor between her and Robert.

"The lexicon," Miss Servator replied. "If there's any dispute about what a word means, then one of you looks it up in that book. That's your job."

Cardinal leaned forward. "Don't worry if you don't understand anything, Lily," he said. "We'll help you out. This is only a memory game, a game of strategy. We call it the Game of Nouns. It confuses most people, me included."

"Nonsense," said Miss Servator. "It's as easy as pie. Oh, here they come."

Two lines of students strode up from the garden, one line in black, the other in red. Rather, it was the leaders of these lines who strode, one being the almost-woman Martha in a black hat, the other a tall blonde-haired boy whom Lily had not noticed before and who marched with a military swagger. Behind the leaders, their teams - all with numbers pinned on their backs - slouched and waddled. When the leaders arrived at opposite ends of the chess-board, they unrolled long mats of their colour at their feet by the board, and over the files on each edge. Team members assembled on the mats at each end, so that the two teams now faced each other across a chequered pattern six squares across and eight deep. The team leaders stood in the middle of the teams, on the same file like the kings of chess.

Cardinal stood, and walked towards them, carrying two rugby balls, red and black. He tossed the black ball to Martha, and the red ball to the boy he called Michael. "Begin with black. At my signal!" he cried. He walked back, sat, and waved a white handkerchief.

"Butter!" Martha yelled.

Robert leaned forward. "That rules out food," he said. "That's a shame."

"Martha is such an aggressive player," whispered Miss Servator. "We can look for slants from her."

"Wall," yelled Michael, his voice echoing around the courtyard.

"I don't have a problem with that," Cardinal said. "If anyone's ever made a wall of butter I've not seen it."

"Agreed," said Miss Servator, and Cardinal waved his white handkerchief, dropped it, and picked it up. He held his other hand aloft.

The team leaders turned their backs and whispered along the lines of their teams. Lily heard only, "Five, forward two," from Michael.

Cardinal lowered his hand. Simultaneously, the girl next to Michael moved two squares forward onto the board while, at the other end, a boy at the far end of the black line advanced one square. "What did I tell you?" whispered Miss Servator. "She's going for a slant already."

"Cockroach!" cried Martha. "Tree!" yelled Michael.

Miss Servator and Cardinal colluded, and decided that there was no relationship between cockroaches and walls, and between trees and cockroaches, though Cardinal thought he might once have seen a cockroach in a tree, but was not sure. He waved his white handkerchief, and this time a girl of the black team advanced two squares, and Michael himself moved forward three squares. "Passive aggression," Cardinal whispered. "Typical Michael."

Moves such as this continued for some time, and Lily found herself nodding off, until there was a shout from Michael of "Ponderosity!"

"What?" said Cardinal. "What?" Robert echoed. "Lexicon," said Miss Servator. "Ponderosity."

"You do it, Lily," said Robert, sipping his lemonade. "I'm too ill."

Lily picked up the book. It had a cover of rough brown leather. She opened it. The script was all squiggles and made no sense. "Ponderosity?" she said, and instantly the script changed to one she could read. On the left page was written, 'Enquire within upon everything', and on the right, 'Ponderosity' with a definition. "The quality of having weight," she said.

Cardinal pulled out a black handkerchief and waved it. "Penalty for red," he shouted. "All... previous... have... weight."

Michael slapped a hand against a thigh. Miss Servator whispered, "That's a blow. Serves him right for showing off. He'll have to sap."

By now, Lily had worked out some of the rules. Before a team could make a move, its leader had to shout a word which had no connection with a word which had been used before. At each simultaneous move, one member of each team could move forwards, backwards or sideways depending on the leader's command. The rest, though, was a complete mystery. Martha's black team were now arranged in two slanting lines, but she and a boy at her side still stood on the first rank. Michael's red team, though, were in a square pattern, and he stood at the front of it towards one side of the board.

Lily could not see why anyone had been bending or stretching, for this involved no exercise at all. But then, Martha gave a command which Lily could not hear, and a girl moved forward two squares, making a triangular line across the board from one corner towards the centre and a square occupied by Chun. "The slant's on," whispered Miss Servator.

The boy next to Martha, a long-legged and dark-haired individual, took several paces back from the board. He ran, he jumped, his legs cycling in the air, and he landed with the poise of a diver on Chun's square. Chun wrinkled her nose at him and waddled off the board. Instantly Martha threw him the black rugby ball. "New shouter for black," cried Cardinal. "The idea, Lily," he whispered, "is to get the team's shouter - that's the boy with the ball - onto the other team's mat. Watch how they do that."

"Sapping!" cried Miss Servator. Michael performed a handstand. He wobbled. He wobbled even more as the panel beneath him sank down, till only his feet protruded, clinging to the edge of what was now a dark hole in the courtyard. Those on each side of him jumped into the hole and stood on their heads, so that four pairs of feet now dangled over the hole's edge. "Martha's left the back board open with that slant," said Miss Servator. "It's a matter of time now."

"Poppy!" the black team's shouter yelled, and "Drain!" from down the hole. Martha stepped forward from her back rank. "Very appropriate," whispered Cardinal. "That's what they're in. Very dark and smelly, but with the advantage that all four can move at once, and the other team can't see what they're up to." All four pairs of feet vanished, and there was the sound of scrabbling from below.

"Unicorn!" and then "Shoe!" Clutching his rugby ball, the black team's shouter was now on the last square before the red mat. But, as he pondered which word to shout out next, another hole opened, one square away from the black mat, next to Martha, and Michael's head popped out, the red ball in his upraised hand.

Miss Servator stood. She narrowed her eyes and called out, "Crossing!"

"No, Miss Servator!" Michael cried. "I took all the moves."

Miss Servator sat. "A risky strategy," she said. "That seems to have paid off."

With final cries of 'Goalpost!" and "Wheelbarrow!" the black team's leader stepped onto the red mat, and Michael levered himself out of his hole onto the black mat. Both held their rugby balls aloft.

"A draw!" Miss Servator cried. "Spirited offence, and sneaky defence. Well done! Again!"

The teams repeated the game, several times, as Lily tried to work out what was going on. Holes opened up, and balls were thrown. There was jumping, leaping in all directions. If a jumper landed on someone's square, or jumped around someone as in draughts, that someone was out. How far players could move depended on the numbers on their backs, which Lily worked out to be one square for players one and six, two for players two and five, and three for the players in the centre, three and four. But, if there was a diagonal of at least two players of the same team - or a 'slant' as Miss Servator called it - then a player could leap to the end of it from the back line, if they could reach it. And a shouter could move any number of squares, up to three. That mattered at the end, because shouters had to move exactly the right number of squares to land on the opposing team's line, or they would be stuck.

Finally, the black team, Martha's team, were two games up, and Miss Servator called a halt. "Now… the run," she said, turning to Cardinal. "Your turn, I think. Lily, join the others."

There followed a run around the gardens of the palace, Cardinal leading but then slipping back into the shadows of a doorway. It was warm, and the jostling throng of students soon divided into athletes and also-rans, of which Lily was one, puffing her way beside Chun around lawns, pools, through corridors, back to the courtyard then off again under an arch to another lawn and a garden filled with roses, around through long and dusty halls to another courtyard, until the athletes followed by also-rans turned sharp left under an arch to the first courtyard, where they all stopped, panting.

Waiting for them was a table with a white cloth, loaded with glasses of lemonade. Lily spotted Martha and Michael together, the almost-woman with the almost-man. It was loathsome, the way she waggled herself and ran fingers through her hair. At any moment she would lay a hand on his chest, so obvious. Michael was having none of it, Lily was glad to see. There was something of a grown-up Chris Ormerod about him, she decided, blonde hair, a gentle face, shoulders that the red t-shirt exaggerated, and he was tall, much taller than Chris Ormerod, who Lily was beginning to think was only a passing fancy; but Michael, Michael was special. Could he feel anything for a girl so much smaller and only twelve? What had Swan said? That people fall in love with people like themselves, but when they get older they get bored and go for someone totally different? Perhaps she would have to wait.

Theo sidled up to her. "I…" he said, "am totally puffed. How about you?"

"Totally," Lily agreed.

"Bus!" yelled Miss Servator. "Hurry up, or you'll be in India all week."

"We're in India?" said Lily to Theo.

"Sure are," he replied. "But we better catch that bus right now. Miss Servator has left people behind before."

"But I thought we were in East Sussex," said Lily as they both hared off across the courtyard.

"East, for sure," said Theo with a laugh, and he scooted around the back of the wall to pick up his uniform. Lily went behind the wall and changed with the other girls, then took her place at the back of the Servator bus.

Every week, the impossible was happening. In the bus, as she drifted off to sleep, she wondered what she could tell her Dad - that she had found a boy she really, really liked, that she had been to India - no couldn't say that - that she was doing Navigation and it was all about whole universes; that...

*

"Dad! I'm home!"

As she came through into the office from the shop, Lily found Mrs Bee and a young uniformed policewoman standing by the desk. "Lily!" cried Mrs Bee, "Lily, oh Lily!"

"What's happened?"

Mrs Bee, a dumpy dark-haired woman in a pinafore and round spectacles, wrung her hands and looked down. "It's terrible," she said, "terrible. They's been taken to Chi and it's terrible. What's to do? Terrible."

"What is?" So much ran through Lily's mind. There had been an accident, a death. She would never see her Dad again. There had been a fire in the workshop, but no, there was no smell of fire.

Mrs Bee lifted her head and in a tone of disbelief said, "They's been arrested, both of them!"

It must be about money. Her Dad had robbed a bank. Percy was the driver. Or fraud. They had sold an antique that was a fake...

"You are Lily Moss? Your father is Riley Moss?" said the policewoman. Her dark hair was tied back in a bun, a serious face with an upturned nose and brown eyes. Lily nodded. "Not good news, I'm afraid," the policewoman went on. "Your father has been taken to Chichester. I must ask you to come with me to Chichester Police station. Are you ready to go now or would you like to pick up a few things?"

"But the poor mite hasn't had her tea!" protested Mrs Bee.

"I'm sure we can find her something at the station."

"Miss," said Lily. "What has my Dad done? What is he accused of?"

"Murder."

28 - The Arrest

Inspector Frank Dennis was pretending to be a Detective Sergeant. It was rare for Hampshire CID to piggy-back on a Sussex case, but he had a good reason. Despite his disappointment that the wire in the Moss workshop failed to match whatever it was that did for Silas Bolney in Southsea, Dennis was sure there was something shifty about Riley Moss. Officially he was there to pick up any pieces which might lead to an arrest.

He sat in the passenger seat of an unmarked car parked facing the wrong way in front of the premises of Moss Auctions, his counterpart from Sussex CID next to him. A female officer was in there to collect the girl. It was early evening on a Friday, and punters from the Co-Op passed by with the occasional worried glance at the two guys in suits. No doubt his counterpart knew a few of them.

This was not his case, so he had to mind his manners. This was about a routine search of the premises of Moss Auctions, stolen goods suspected, thanks to a tip-off, all pukka, warrant produced. What they found was a gun, hidden under a carpet in the man's bedroom. It was no ordinary gun, a Welrod, a hitman's weapon. What a fellow like Moss was doing with a weapon like that, his Sussex counterpart at first had no idea, until he ran it past Special Branch, who ran it past other undisclosed sources and came back with the news that the weapon had been used for a murder in the vicinity, some time ago, a murder of which Sussex CID knew nothing, but which had - in the words of his counterpart - 'implications for security'.

His counterpart was Inspector Aspel, a broad-beamed man close to retirement who - from the pile of wrappers under his seat - had an appetite for pork pies. "Finally. Here they come," said Aspel, as the policewoman emerged from the shop, a blonde-haired girl at her side. There was something strange about the girl. She was small, dressed in a bomber jacket and jeans, her hair in bunches, but it was the eyes. They were very bright, knowing, not still for a moment.

"In here, dear," said the policewoman. "Nothing to be afraid of. I'll keep your mobile safe," she said, opening the rear door and helping the girl in.

Dennis turned his head and smiled. "Lily, is it?" The girl nodded. "Hello Lily," he said and turned back.

Aspel manoeuvred the car out onto Swivelhurst Road and they sped off to the A27 without a word. Dennis had expected a direct route to Chichester, but with a grunt Aspel turned off at Tangmere where he drew up in a lay-by behind a black Mercedes. "Out you get," Aspel said to the policewoman. "Check there's a woman there."

The policewoman stepped out and went to the kerb-side window of the Mercedes. There was an exchange of words, and a hand appeared through the window holding a wallet. The policewoman nodded and came back to Aspel's car. She opened the rear door. "All OK, Boss," she said. "Lily, come with me please."

Dennis was confused, as the girl climbed out and went with the policewoman to the rear of the Mercedes whose door opened, and she climbed in. He looked over at Aspel, who tapped a forefinger against his nose. The Mercedes growled away, as the policewoman walked back. "What was that?" said Dennis.

"As I said," Aspel replied. "Implications for security."

*

Lily sat strapped into the back seat of the Mercedes next to a woman in a purple sari. In that dress, the woman should have been Asian but she was not, and Lily suspected that she wore it to hide the bulbous body which lay below a thin, pale face framed by long black hair. There was still a hint of glamour about her, though, with her lips too red, her eyes coal-black, and her scrawny hands covered in rings.

241

"My name is Saida," she said with a smile. "And you are Lily Moss?"

"Yes Miss. I am."

"Very good. Sit back, Lily Moss. We are not going far. And we have a very careful driver."

"Are you taking me to see my Dad?"

"Yes, Lily Moss. Don't worry. We're sure this is all a mistake, and both of you will soon be home."

Trees flashed past. As the evening light faded, in the rear-view mirror she saw the face of the driver, whose eyes flicked up at her. He was small, blonde-haired and looked harmless. Someone else was in charge, possibly Saida, but the way that she kept sticking her finger into a little bottle of black powder and licking it showed her up as someone who was dependent on something - and probably someone - else.

They drove past Chichester, westward along the A27 under gantries which said Portsmouth, and Lily began to be even more anxious. She tried to get her companions to say more about what had happened, but their replies told her nothing. Carefully she fingered the door handle. It was locked. They sped along under the lights. "Where are we going?" she asked. "Look, over there," Saida said, and Lily turned her head towards the lights of Portsmouth.

She barely felt the syringe which Saida jabbed into her neck.

Lily woke and everything was hazy as if she was looking through misty glass. The door of the car was open, and with yellow light behind him a man bent over her. She knew him, the grey man from Jenkins Road, the goblin.

"Lily Moss," the goblin said in a high-pitched voice, as from behind Saida grabbed her by the arms. "How marvellous to see you again. Thank you, Saida."

"My pleasure, Lord Commander."

29 - Anna

Storaye Gorkolovo, Russia

In the evening of a warm day, Sister Klara emerged from the front door of the Hospital at Gorkolovo in a state first of excitement, then of confusion, and then fury. Typically for a person in a hurry, she was the victim of an accident. The rosary on her wrist had caught on the iron knob of the Hospital's front door, and had so yanked her back from the front step that she was certain something had come undone (*'... lest the shame of your nakedness be revealed'*). She muttered a rude word, then peered around to be sure that no-one had heard.

Others less charitable would call her fat, for twenty years of Hospital food had rounded-out a body already intended by Nature to be large. Klara's size and billowing habit - that of an Orthodox nun, but white for the most senior of nursing staff - were suitable for stately motion, but being urgent by nature she was always getting caught on the spikes that protruded from the architecture of this Hospital, a villainous Gothic pile which was the only building in Gorkolovo left unscathed by the Germans in the 1940's, presumably because it reminded them of their own.

Sister Klara drew a deep breath to calm her nerves. The air was tangy with salt and a hint of wood-smoke. Gorkolovo lies on the shore of the Baltic Sea, in Russia and close to the border with Estonia. Its climate is mild, its shoreline is attractive to sea-fishermen, and the woods around it are popular with mushroom-pickers in autumn and with school-children who come from as far away as Petersburg for botanical field-trips. It remains rural, a village where everyone knew Sister Klara and where Sister Klara knew at this moment that the wood-smoke was the work of the Hospital's gardener, an Estonian whom she suspected to be in league with The Devil.

Satisfied that she was intact, Sister Klara gathered up her skirts and set off at speed through the gardens to a picket gate which led to the hill overlooking the village. There, too confident in her ability to swerve, she slid sideways on a patch of manure left on the path by the gardener, who was if not Satan himself then certainly one of his minions, a view expressed forcibly by Sister Klara into the green and prickly bush in which she found herself. Undaunted she rose up and set off again puffing and panting, then flapped from stone to stone up the path which ran through a channel of pine-trees above the Baltic shore, until she came within shouting-distance.

"Anna!" she bellowed. "Anna Andreyevna! Anna!"

Ahead of her, sitting on a wooden bench, a woman slowly turned her head. She was not young, though there was still something of the girl about her. Blonde hair curled around a face that was delicate and sallow as if a stranger to the sun, and her violet-blue eyes were unnaturally bright but her expression vacant, whether uninterested or simply drugged. She sat demurely, hands folded in her lap, and she wore the blue uniform of a long-term patient.

Raising dust, Sister Klara came puffing up the hill until, hands on hips, she stood before her target. "Anna Andreyevna," she panted. "I have news."

"It is too warm a day," the woman replied, "to be so excited, Sister."

"But wait till you hear," said the nun. "I just heard on the telephone. Yes it is warm isn't it? I shall sit, if it is no inconvenience to you."

"Not at all. Please do."

Sister Klara lowered herself gently onto the bench. Apart from the rustling of some small creature in the long grass, it was quiet. The evening sun sparkled on the waves of the Baltic and if there were birds then they were minding their own business. "Where is nurse Meri?" she asked. "She knows you are not to be alone."

"The nurse? She is up the hill, behind a bush."

"Behind a bush? What is she doing there?"

"I am not interested in what the nurse does behind a bush."

Sister Klara frowned. "But!" she said. "Listen to this. You will be excited too, I'm sure." She puffed for a moment, gathering herself for a moment of climax, then summoned up a deep breath and declared, "Anna. Your case. Your case will be reviewed!"

The patient called Anna said nothing, but turned her head back towards the sea.

"Reviewed," Sister Klara persisted. "Anna. Do you know what that means?"

Anna replied calmly, "Nothing happens."

"But this time," the nun insisted, "it will be different. Doctor Georgi has gone. The politicians, the military, all gone. And you will be discharged. I am sure."

"Then I will be allowed to go home."

"If that is what you want. I expect so."

"And when will this happen?"

"First we must do something about your medication. I will ask the Superintendent, but I expect, perhaps a few days. Then, we will go to Petersburg for the review. Isn't that exciting? We will go together to Petersburg. I've never been."

From somewhere up the hill there came a rustling and a snapping of twigs. "I know Petersburg," said Anna. "It was where I arrived. They kept me in a cage, like a mouse. Can you see the mist?"

Sister Klara followed Anna's gaze out beyond the rocky shore, through a pack of wheeling sea-birds soundless at this distance, to the north. On a clear day you could see Finland, but now, though the sun still sparkled on the waves, there was no Finland, but a solid bank of grey mist far out to sea. Sister Klara felt the salt air and moisture on her glowing cheek which meant to her that the mist would be closing in, just as the sun was going down and the warmth of the day began to be replaced by an evening chill. "Mist, yes," she said. "It will be over us before dark. Where is that nurse? We must get back. Did you say she went up the hill?"

"She is already here."

Sister Klara looked around.

"Behind the tree which was split by lightning."

Sister Klara turned to look up the hill. She saw the tree, a birch tree split into two pale spikes and overgrown by bushes. Of the nurse there was no sign, but Sister Klara was certain that she was there, if Anna said so.

Sister Klara had known for years that the patient called Anna had a gift, which the superstitious would call The Sight. Sometimes she would say what she had no right to know. She knew of events before they happened, even of people's thoughts before they had them. There were peasants in the fields around Gorkolovo who would make a Wise Woman of her, and priests in the history of Sister Klara's own church who would have burned Anna as a witch. The scientific, among whom Sister Klara included herself, would say that this is a woman of extreme sensitivity, and would be worth a study; not that there was any chance of that in the Hospital. For all the good intentions of its founders, the Hospital remained a prison.

"Nurse Meri!" Sister Klara called. "I do believe you are hiding. Come out of there this minute!" There was a rustling in the bushes around the tree.

"She is embarrassed," said Anna. "But she will come out now."

Above a bush by the birch-tree, a face appeared that was broad and white, its tiny mouth puckered in apprehension. Round spectacles flashed in the evening sun. Then out came a young woman nearly as wide as she was high, wearing a brown robe tied with a rope.

"Sister," said the young woman. She padded through the long grass which was swaying gently in the breeze from the coast. "Good evening. I was…" she said, with her eyes downcast, long brown hair falling forward, "I was…"

"You were behind a bush, doing the Devil knows what," said Sister Klara, rising from the seat. "When you are supposed to be here, with our patient."

"I know. But… I think it was something in the soup."

"I see. You are not well, nurse Meri?"

"Something like that, Sister."

In Sister Klara's long experience of this area of rural Russia, being 'not well' for a peasant like this nurse would mean - pregnant. That was not good news, considering how staff were hard to find, now that so many girls were flocking to the cities. She frowned. "I am sorry to hear that, nurse Meri," she said, and looked up into the tree as if for guidance, then down at the quivering nurse. "Naturally," she said, "we shall take care of you. Let us discuss this later."

"That is very kind, Sister."

"But now we have to get our patient back to her room. She has had some exciting news, and I am sure she will want to rest."

"Yes, Sister."

"Come, take her arm. I will lead the way."

As she flapped downhill over the stones of the path, Sister Klara mused on the marvel of God, how He was inclined - when you had solved one problem - to set you another. The problem of Anna would be solved. She was a relic, and would be tidied up. On the other hand, a pregnant nurse would be a challenge. But of the two, there was no doubt in Sister Klara's mind that the nurse belonged in the Hospital but Anna did not.

She remembered the snow-laden night of December, ten years before, when Anna arrived in a car from Petersburg. Her clothes were strange, foreign and impractical, their fabric flawless, and they fitted unusually well. What Anna had done, where she came from

247

and what life she had before, Sister Klara did not know, and she could not ask. Only the Superintendent would know, but he was a grizzled old Soviet thug and what he knew he kept to himself. Obviously Anna had been heavily sedated, for the driver and the Superintendent had to carry her in on a stretcher.

Anna Andreyevna, as she became known to Sister Klara, was subject to the regime for Politicals, which meant drugging them to oblivion. In places like Gorkolovo, far from the centre, the old Russia survived for years after the collapse of the USSR; no more so than in psychiatric institutions like the Hospital, where a diagnosis of schizophrenia could usefully contain the outsider, the dissident, or even the mildly odd. Through the light and dark of the Hospital's halls and corridors, in her slippers and uniform - white for the first three years, then blue - Anna had shuffled with no mind of her own, drugged and sluggish. But as the years passed, and Russia changed, so Anna began to wake up. Her medication was reduced. She was allowed out, though it was still a rule of Doctor Georgi that no Political could go out unattended: they might escape, throw themselves into the Baltic, head for Finland, drown, and be useless.

Anna was sane. Sister Klara did not doubt it. But as she reached the picket gate at the bottom of the hill, Sister Klara warned herself against the sin of Pride, for resurrecting a person of such promise, a person whom she, Sister Klara, had brought from the dark into the light. Just as her own Church had suffered and had risen again, so would this poor woman rise, and perhaps - with her gift - take up some lofty position in the Church. She may even be a Saint.

The three women walked on arm-in-arm down the last slope into the garden, as the mist began to roll over the Hospital's dark towers, and lights came on one by one in the mullioned windows. When they mounted the steps and the light over the front door blinked on, their welcome was an aroma of cooking, of oil and a meaty dish, and the clatter from inside of the nuns and kitchen staff setting out dinner trays.

As they walked into the Hospital, Sister Klara saw in the face of the patient called Anna something she had not seen in the ten years she had known her. A smile. But this was not the smile of someone suddenly made happy. This was the smile, with narrowed eyes, of someone who thought only of revenge.

30 - Have we had fun?

Raw terror rose in her like an electric current and shocked open her eyes. Lily Moss woke. She could not move her legs. She could not move her arms. Her body quivered and she tried to gasp but around her neck a rope, anchored somewhere behind, pulled tight and cut into her throat. She was upright, in an office chair, her ankles bound to its legs, her arms cuffed with leather straps to the curving steel of the chair's arms. Ahead of her, a metal door was shut, and on the black wall a flat-screen TV displayed a News channel without sound. That was the only light.

Her eyes flicked from side to side. Shadows moved in corners. Around her, stacked up by the walls were penny-in-the-slot machines, in one corner the glass case of a puppet, a black-haired wizard in a red robe with a wand that trembled. By the door another case held the puppet of a sailor in a blue suit and white cap. As if there remained in him some spark of mechanical life, the sailor opened and closed his grinning red mouth and twitched on the pinion which held him up, with a shake of his uniform and a creaking of gears. Reflections passed over the glass of the puppets' cases like ghosts coming and going.

Lily was hungry but fear kept the hunger at bay. Panic would be useless. Panic would make her want even more to pee. She controlled her breathing. At least she still had her clothes. At least she was alive.

As she sat in the dim light, helpless and drifting with whatever these people had put into her system, there surfaced in her memory the dream of Ignorance. She had been accused of treason. John whose name was Sean was called from the Tower. Unknowing, she had used a key, which worked only one-way, from Roamers Cross into her world. Unknowing, she was a navigator, and she thought and worried about what that could mean. But whatever was in her system took a grip on her again, and she felt herself drift away.

When with a jolt she woke for a second time she was not alone. Two silhouettes stood between her and the TV, the driver and Saida, rainbows of light sparkling around them. She could not see their eyes.

"Don't be fooled, Twine," said Saida.

"She is awake," said Twine.

Saida bent forward. Now Lily could see the whites of her eyes. "Lily, dear Lily Moss," said Saida. "Hello. I'm sorry, but this is for your own good. The Lord Commander insists."

Lily could not speak. Tape was over her mouth. Saida peeled it off. "There," she said. "We want no harm to come to you. Trust me."

Twine stepped forward. "Shout as much as you like," he grunted. "The nearest house is a mile away. No-one will hear you from down here."

Lily said only, "What do you want?"

"To help us, that's all," said Saida. "When you've done that, you go home."

They kept her alive with water and cereal in a wooden bowl. That night and into the next evening, all that changed was that her arms were released, and every so often - when she cried out - she was allowed up, into a corner of the room to use a bucket which Saida covered with a towel and took away. Twine tied her legs back to the chair.

But in those moments Lily glimpsed what was beyond the door, another room, and she recognised it - the cellar of Malbury Hall. She saw its black walls tinged with green slime, its concrete pillars, and in the far corner the well-head with its lid lying on the stone floor beside it. It was on that floor that her father had fallen, from that floor that she had jumped on Navigator on her first journey to Roamers Cross.

She asked what was going on, what they wanted with her, how was her Dad, what are we waiting for, but all she heard was Waiting for the Lord Commander, who is so busy, just wait, and then you go home.

He came on that second evening. Lily was strapped to the chair enduring the flickers of the soundless TV when she heard the door from the cellar open, and a thump of feet on the floor. The door handle turned, and in the dim light stood the goblin of the day before, but now in a grey robe, around his neck a curious chain which had a flashing mirror at its heart. He paused on the threshold, turned, and closed the door behind him.

"Lily Moss, brave little Lily," Chatham said, in a cracked and high-pitched voice, the robe hanging off him like the wings of a vampire bat. As he lowered his face towards hers, in the light that issued from the mirror around his neck Lily made out the greyness of his face, the hooded eyes, the bone of his nose, the hollows of his cheeks, and a mouth with black lips drawn back over sharp white teeth. "Lord Commander to you," he said. "When you were two, I let you live. Now look at the brave little girl you have turned into. I'm impressed."

"You... let me live? Did you...?"

"I took your mother. Do you want to kill me?"

Lily's hands were twitching. They were free, and they could close about that goblin neck but she had no strength. His face was less than a foot from her own, and then he stood. With a wave of his hand the TV turned off, but there was still light, from his chain and from under the door. "But I'll make it up to you," he said. "I'll give you a choice. You navigators are all about choice. To go or not to go, to take that route or another, all about choice. Your choice is, to help us or not. That's simple enough, isn't it?"

Lily said nothing.

"Dear me," said Chatham. "Nothing to say? Mysul will be unhappy. Oh dear. I will give you some good advice. Choose to help us, and you and everyone you know will be safe. You go home

252

and everybody says Well Done. Otherwise, people, your people, will die. Who will die? Every time you disappoint me, girl, one of these will die…"

Chatham stretched out his right arm. Above it appeared two windows in the air, round screens just as Lily had seen in Miss Servator's class, port-holes of coloured light, in each a picture, of her friend Swan, bent over papers on a school desk, and of her Dad, sitting mournfully in a grey prison cell. "Or perhaps…" he said, "this one." Closest to his neck a third window opened, in it the picture of a woman, standing by the rails of a ship. "Someone you won't remember. But I do. Your mother. Anna."

Lily said nothing. Her mother was alive. Something in her always knew that. Her Dad had not said she was dead, only 'lost'.

"She is alive. Isn't that fun? Shall I kill her? I could have done that, ten years ago, and we are tracking her now. Perhaps I should have killed you. But I prefer to keep you alive, for now. You're a little soldier aren't you? And a navigator. We all need navigators. I love navigators, truly. So, which shall it be? I will make it clear. Help us, and they all live. Isn't that wonderful? What do you say?"

Lily said nothing.

With a flick of his hand the images disappeared. Chatham leant forward. "Can't decide? Let me help you make up your mind."

He stepped back, stretched out his left arm, and opened the palm of his hand. A stream of orange light issued from it, directed at Lily's knees. "One thing you must understand, Lily Moss," he said. "All animals have predators. I am the predator, and you are prey. Do you understand that? Probably not. But welcome to the world of inferior animals." His eyes widened, as the colour of the light changed to red and focussed on Lily's right knee.

It started as a burning in her knee, through her jeans. The heat grew, and she expected to see smoke, even flames as the pain spread across and down her leg, then following a stream of nerves all on fire up her leg to her hip.

She screamed.

"No-one to hear you, darling," Chatham whispered. "Only my people. Do it some more. It's music."

Across her hips, to the base of her spine the agony crept ever upwards. She arched her back. In seconds it would be at her heart and she would be dead. But it stopped.

"Shall I do that again?" Chatham whispered. "It's such fun. Have we had fun? I have. Let's do it again."

"No. No," Lily moaned as her breath returned and she slumped back into the chair.

"No?" The goblin face pressed forward between her eyes. "No what?" it said. "No my Lord, is what I expect. No my Lord. Try it."

"No… my Lord."

"Good girl, but No is the wrong word. Bad girl." Chatham stepped back. "Shall I burn your face now? No, such a pretty face. We might need it one day. Let us be elegant."

From his right palm the light streamed onto her left foot. Inside her boot she felt the heat, boiling, but the pain moved to the underside, to the sole. This was a spark of pain that leaped directly to her head. This had to be Death. It was a white fire which removed all thought, which detached the spirit, so rapid her mouth fell open but she could not breathe. The light faded. The shock passed. Her eyes closed. She was dying, until a slap to her face twisted her neck and her eyes flicked open.

"You know," Chatham said, his voice distant, "I could kill you with one hand. But I won't. I have always wanted a navigator. So useful. Your mother, though, such a fidget. She might take two hands, but there would be nothing left of her, not a scrap. Is that what you want?"

"What… do you want…"

Again before her eyes swam the obscene face. "Something simple, darling," it said. "Something you have done already."

"What…"

"The key. Use it. You remember, the photograph. I have it here. We knew where to find it, in your room. Who would ever guess this awful thing is so precious? Especially when everything else in your little room was worthless rubbish. But such interesting reading, your books of dreams. I had to laugh out loud quite often. Roamers Cross indeed. So where are the Roamers now? I see only one. You. Now you are all alone. Isn't that sad?"

Lily felt a claw-like finger under her chin.

"You will use the key, Lily Moss, as you did before," the goblin went on. "Hold it, use it. You will pick up and bring to me whatever you find waiting for you. Easy, for a navigator. The next word I hear from you is Yes, or someone dies. Be careful."

Through the ache of despair came a glint of hope. They had not found Navigator's key. All they had was the photograph, and that was only a one-way ticket, out of Roamers Cross but not in. Lily drew a deep breath, then exhaled. In a tone of voice she hoped was feeble she whispered, "Yes."

*

When again she held the key of the little black-haired boy, the cameo in its gilt frame, when Saida put it into her hand and Lily looked into it, trembling, through wisps of white and strawberry light and then twinkling green lights, and in a few seconds allowed herself to be in two places at once, it was John as a boy she saw, standing in his school uniform under a tree, a dog's lead in his hand but no dog. It was his key. She was shocked to see the misery on his face. As a boy he had been her friend, talking in music, with his animals. As a man, she had wanted to give him chicken soup because he was cold and alone. Now, like her, he could not escape the treachery that had been forced upon them.

255

As before, a black globe bounced from the undergrowth, and again it made the photograph so hot that she had to drop it in her lap, as in the room a spidery shape fell to the floor, began to be transparent and scuttled away, but was grabbed by Saida who said, "Spiker, sleep," scooped it up and thrust it into a plastic bag which she kissed and carried out.

Then it became as mechanical as breathing. Hour after hour, strapped to her chair in the cellar of the Hall, with the puppets twitching before her, Lily Moss lived in two worlds at once, flicking between them, but to one she was bound to return, strapped into the chair.

Whatever waited for her in the forest of Roamers Cross, and leapt into her arms or just stood in the bushes, she brought it back with her into the basement of the Hall - monsters, nightmare creatures, things that should be dead but lived on; spikers, the spiders that fell to the floor, grew into globes and scuttled around with a clacking of claws; human corpses, mindless white naked bodies scarred and misshapen, which she had to hold by what passed for a hand, not looking into what remained of their eyes; insects bigger than people, with feelers that swayed and jaws that crunched; above all the mosquitoes, giant mosquitoes which pulsed and hummed. One would all-but fill the room, glistening and dripping saliva, its thin jointed legs scraping on a tube which hung down to the floor. Riding them from Roamers Cross was a blasphemy, their bodies humming beneath her, and she could not rest till Saida had thrown over each of them a grey sheet and dragged them out. It was a relief when all she had to pick up was a metal box, so black that if you left it out at night you would not see it.

But each transfer left her exhausted and numb, as the little black-haired boy stood mournfully under his tree while one by one, hundreds of them, these creatures and things passed through her hands.

She could do no more. Even Saida recognised that and withdrew. Twine entered and swore at her, and slapped her around the face, but she was spent. She had to sleep.

"Mum?"

"Hold on, baby. Be brave. We are coming."

"You were lost. But you're alive."

"Yes, I am now."

"Oh, Mum."

No longer was this Mother's Hill. This was a small green-walled cabin, which rocked gently from side to side. A port-hole gave out onto a night of shining stars. Her mother sat on the lower of two bunk beds, around her a hum of engines. Her uniform dress, which was all that Lily could remember, was gone. Instead, she wore a blue overcoat and her blonde hair, tied back into a pony-tail, had grown almost as long as Lily's.

"I can see you, baby," said Anna. "On the floor by the wall. You're grey. But I know where you are. You have a key, two keys. I know where you are."

"It's horrible, Mum. I can't begin to say."

"I know. We tracked them, from the Gate and into the forest. It had to be you. In the whole sea, I mean the Universe, all the other keys are safe..."

"I know about seas, Mum. But I get mixed up with a sea meaning a universe, and the sea we swim in."

"So did I, once. Where did you learn about seas?"

"At school, Mum, the Lodge."

"The Lodge." Her mother sighed. "So many years since I was there. But quickly, tell me, who is there with you?"

"A woman called Saida, a man whose name is Twine, and a man who calls himself the Lord Commander."

Her mother narrowed her eyes and winced. "I know them. Grangels. And Chatham. That devil," she said. "Has he hurt you?"

"Yes Mum. But I'm OK."

"One day," said Anna, looking to one side, "there will be the end of him. I can promise you that."

Never before had Lily heard that tone in her mother's voice, a snarl. "What can I do, Mum?" she said.

"I must talk to Mysul. Wait." Anna closed her eyes but in a few seconds opened them. "Do you have Navigator's key, the…"

"Gold coin, with the star. Yes I do. I've hidden it."

"Hidden it so you can get it again?"

"Yes Mum."

"Good. We're coming, my darling girl. Be brave. Hold on."

31 - Spice

From all the many locations in the globe to which he had projected himself, this - on the edge of Bhutan - was the place which Chatham had chosen for his new eyrie, where finally he would plan his campaign. After a night of thunderstorms and torrential rain, he sat under a canopy in the great hall of the monastery, watching as water cascaded over a window arch. At his side, a spiker had taken on the pink colouring of the walls and was rolling around in a wicker basket, happily feeding on filth.

He was beset by failure. The strategy which preceded his arrival had failed, and he knew why it had failed - because it had been put in the hands of idiots, who had been seduced, corrupted by the pleasures of this globe, gone native. It was too slow, and passive. To attract Roamers into this globe and deal with them here was wishful thinking. Instead, the number of globe-grown Roamers was increasing. Even their juvenile navigator, the pathetic Moss girl whom he had left in the hands of Twine and Saida, was a glober, a strange one admittedly, but born here. The edifice of power his predecessors had built - the money, the property, the access - was wasted, and its result was trivial. But, there was one element of that failed strategy which worked, and Chatham was minded to keep it. Spice.

The garnica spice. Regrettably, this was not a matter of military action. This would not set the world ablaze, quite the opposite. It would set the globe asleep, a dreamless sleep, the waking sleep of a zombie world which had forgotten its past, its identity, its purpose if it had ever thought it had one.

Many years of research, and many millions of development dollars had been spent in perfecting the garnica spice. At first it was yet another drug, addictive for its amusing recreational effects; but now, tests of its latest generation confirmed that in a few days it erased the memories of these creatures, bringing on what would be mistaken for dementia. The new spice, marketed as a healthy alternative to salt, had been picked up by distributors across Africa and India for use in care homes and hospitals as a cheaper substitute for low-sodium products, a major step forward but only the beginning, of a Great Plague of oblivion.

Spice, a marvellous development of G-Range Pharmaceuticals, Chairman Henry Cornelius Chatham, now a resident of India, his office contactable on Facebook and LinkedIn. Adapted from garnica previously known only to natives of South America for its health-giving benefits, but now adapted as a saline substitute thanks to its filtering through a solution of Pureday Miracle, patented world-wide. Today Chatham would authorise further distribution, and sign off the strategy of his new Director of Finance. It did not feature in advertisements that Pureday Miracle was modelled on the venom of a spiker.

Spice destroyed memory. Why bother? Because memory was precious to the Roamers. Whether that memory existed in earth, air, plants or animals the Roamers saw themselves as its protectors, even its owners, such foolishness. Especially the memory of human animals. The dreams they had, and what remained of their animal memories at their lives' end, all fed the cursed Tower of the Crossway, which the Roamers fought so hard to defend.

Strike at the source; that had been the core of the previous strategy. Dry the supply. If their channels were impenetrable, their keys unobtainable, their navigators more slippery than eels, what did that matter if the entire structure of the Roamer defence existed only to protect a well which day by day began to run dry? It was better, as the Lord God himself commanded, to ignore the memory of your worthless life, for he carried in himself all logic, and all could be deduced from him. Memory in this globe was pointless, but any threat to it would draw the Roamers out like rats from a hole, and then they would be met in a fair fight - rather, an unfair fight because they would be out-numbered and squashed like maggots on the corpse of a cow.

Chatham decided to keep the spice. Passive though the tactic was, it had value as a distraction, and if in the general plague which the spice would cause it disposed of Roamers, then that would be fewer Roamers to deal with. And, if any wind of this had reached the ears of the Roamer hierarchy, then they would be surprised by the new, more aggressive strategy which he had in mind. Besides, it was too late to stop it. As he sat under his canopy, a grim smile on his grey face, pallets, containers of the garnica spice were filtering across continents. If the rate of dementia increased, well, that was a lifestyle issue. People forget. If they no longer had dreams, that was a blessing, for what would fill their dreams other than the routine of a life in care, the sounds, the smells, the idleness which made their lives not worth living?

Chatham frowned and scratched his chin. The atmosphere of the monastery and its dusty columns, distant chanting and ancient crumbling walls, were distracting him. He was there to make a difference. It was his nature - and his mission - to introduce that new aggressive strategy, to break the stalemate at the Crossway. It was his nature, the nature of a Lord Commander, to drive forward, to move quickly, and he had waited long enough.

It was time to take the initiative and strike back at the Crossway behind the Roamers' lines, through a back door which he knew must exist, somewhere. Twine had done well, returning from Africa with new information from the regional commander of that continent.

Now Chatham knew where a back door might be found, but he had to tread carefully. He would have to deal with regional commanders who had been here for many years longer than he had, who had networks in this globe which might lose their value if those commanders were humbled, commanders who had their own privilege in the eyes of God Himself. These were the early transfers, entirely physical and not images, God's scouts.

Even if he found a back door, what did he have to pass through it? All he had to hand was a rag-bag of munitions, a few hundred, too many to hide under a blanket but too few to set the sea ablaze, for now. Meanwhile, they had to be fed, and exercised. There was only so long that they could survive on a diet of farm animals. Already spikers had lost their colour, and some had evaporated. Twine was still on the hunt for Roamers, and it was too much to ask him also to be these creatures' chef and physiotherapist.

It would be different if the Roamer girl had been more useful, quicker, but no. Spikers, white riders, hoverflies; barely enough for one small circle, and no officers, no intelligence. The spikers and flies would breed, but the white riders could not. Spies, the shellflies from the sea where the Minister was created, he could do without. There were enough spies in the globe already.

What was missing was the heavyweight punch of a Black Army, the tidal mass of resurrected bodies in the armour of their conquered worlds, a horrific and infinitely pleasing sight as they swarmed over the enemy, stabbing, stinging, crushing, through their sheer weight and persistence destroying all will to resist. But unless God's Minister could be restored, he had too few munitions in this globe to make much of an impact anywhere. Saida continued to gather fragments of the Minister, and she was close to success, but vital parts eluded her grasp.

Nonetheless what he had was enough to make a statement, somewhere. Every day he received pleas from regional commanders. Mine is the perfect candidate, each would say, for the Lord Commander to begin his campaign. We can send ships, container trucks, aircraft, leave it to us. Chatham decided that today he would select a short-list of those regions, but with one proviso. Yes, we can begin the campaign, and its aim is to leave this sea without form and without history, without any trace of what preceded the entry of our Lord God into this misguided place. The proviso is - find me back doors, ways back into the Crossway which are behind the Roamers' lines. Only then can the Lord Commander unblock the stalemate of the Crossway and open this sea to the Will of God.

It was such a waste, a war of attrition. There were so few Roamers and so many in God's army but their losses were equivalent, pointless. The Roamers' advantages were their flexibility, their independence of thought and action. Compared to them, the myriad resurrected creatures of God's army were mindless idiots. They might have nothing to lose, but they understood only the most primitive tactics. And they were physically disgusting. Chatham himself, born in the second sea, was human in appearance, for this was the dominant species of that sea, but the creatures under his command were debris, mistakes of Nature.

He remembered how his Lord God had been worshipped when he entered the second sea, for he too was human in appearance, but all-powerful, immortal and beautiful, the very image of the Presence. There had been no resistance but an all-encompassing hatred of any who might resist him. It was gracious of the Lord God to bring into the sphere of his revenge all the creatures of his army, but a grace which Chatham did not find in his heart.

As the image of the Lord God flashed through his mind, Chatham knew what he had to do. There was a risk, but it was necessary. He stroked his chain of office, then rose from under the canopy, grinning, and stalked across the flagstones to the window arch, where a lotus flower swam in a red stone pool. He scooped up the flower, advanced to the window and threw it out into the rain, which carried it down over the rocks and out of sight.

32 - At High Table

Paper of The Ordinal (2)

Recommendation to Council

Author: The Ordinal

It is recommended to Council that all channels between the Lodge and the Gate be closed immediately. Evidence for this recommendation follows in two parts, the first being a report from a source close to one of our enemy's senior officers, the second being an interview between that officer and his Lord Commander, known in the globe as Chatham, transcribed from video and translated with commentary by Silas, Ordinal.

Our conclusion is that the enemy is preparing an assault on the Lodge, as a means to enter the Gate behind our lines.

To avoid reprisals, the identity of this source must be protected.

Sir

As I communicated to you earlier, the Master of my College invited to attend our Founder's Feast one Henry Cornelius Chatham, Chairman of G-Range Pharmaceuticals. The Feast is always a grand event, and I and my staff strain every sinew to make it grander every year. This year, the arrival of so wealthy a donor to the College - and a person whose true identity I know - gave our preparations an extra urgency, and not only did we roll the red carpet out over Front Court we rolled out a few purple ones too.

I should explain that our Master has a particular interest in pharmaceuticals. As you may know, the Master of a College is likely to have had an illustrious career - in politics, the Arts and Sciences, the City, and so on. In the role of Master, some regard themselves as retired but with skills and experience which remain valuable. Others think of their role as managerial at so high a level they become invisible.

Our Master made his name in the Health Service, then in Industry, and then in Cambridge, where for many years he managed a department for medical studies as a visiting Professor. He knows his drugs, one might say. Some say that he tries them out on himself, and it is true that - never a man of solid physique, being small and squat in stature, grey of hair and beard - in recent years physically he has gone downhill at a rate of knots. The fact that he is an impostor, that his so-called discoveries have come from theft, and that he has for years used the cloak of Master of this College - and the invisibility it can confer - to focus on entirely different pursuits, is known to me and to you, but not to the general population.

It was on Thursday 24th of this month that Chairman Chatham's limousine arrived at the side gate, and we processed through Front Court towards the ante-room of the Dining Hall. He seemed to me a slender fellow, bald-headed, tall and skeletal, with hooded eyes and a greyish complexion which spoke of too many hours in the dark. It is a look I have noticed in some of our students, those who spend too long at their studies, or drink too much. He wore a long raincoat of black leather with deep pockets, just such as I remember seeing on the Stasi guards at the Berlin Wall.

I followed Chatham and his entourage, the Master, and a gathering of our more influential Fellows into the ante-room and ensured that all had their sherry. When we obliged him to wear an academic gown Chatham at first demurred, but was persuaded by the Master that on this night - the most important in our College's round of feasts - it might be wise to wear it, for form's sake, even though it might conceal the magnificence of his suit.

All agreed with my suggestion that the Dining Hall had never looked better. Others might regret the admission of female students so many years ago now - and I remember the upheaval of it - but I personally welcome the colour they bring to any occasion such as this. Black academic gowns are smart and historic, but that was pleasantly outweighed on this night by the colour of the ladies,

265

which made my job easier, for I could save a few pounds on the bill for table flowers. All wood panelling and the tables were brightly polished, all silver was our best, and the portraits of former Masters and our Founder which adorn the walls had been carefully cleaned. High Table stretched from wall to wall above the salt in a condition of immaculate tidiness and splendour. Some sixteen diners took their places there, and after the saying of Grace by the Dean of the College, we were off, and I kept a keen eye on our serving staff throughout.

As organiser of this event I placed myself opposite the Master. On his left sat Chatham, and on Chatham's left the infernal busybody Maude Melly, a former scholar of the College and now a woman of the world, who has made a name for herself in that most despicable of professions, journalism. Chatham had brought her with him, presumably to make some record of the event. I cannot say how loathsome was her conversation, spiced with innuendoes and plain bad language, at which I was obliged to smile. She is a hag, a black-haired overweight witch, and I am convinced that she is another of that gang to which Chatham and our Master belong.

After the soup, I conversed with a Classicist who talks a great deal and to whom I listened with one ear, with the other ear concentrating on what was said on the other side of the table. Much of that was *sotto voce*, between the Master, Chatham, and Melly, but this is the substance of what I picked up.

Chatham once called the Master, 'Commander'. The Master twice called Chatham, 'Lord'.

Chatham was concerned that the Master should support a product of his company, which he called 'spice'. (It is normal for donors to expect something in return, but not good form to conduct business at High Table so overtly). The Master seemed unhappy to do so, considering his reputation in the field of pharmaceuticals, but was happier with the proposal for a new Fellowship of Memory Studies to be funded at the College by Chatham's company. The Melly woman volunteered ideas for how the Media might be involved.

At one point, during the main course (venison, from our own grounds in Scotland) Chatham grew exceedingly agitated, jabbing his finger on the tablecloth. The subject seemed to be an 'insider' at the Lodge. I know the Master's Lodge well, and it has its staff, not normally called 'insiders'. The reference may be to an entirely other Lodge, of which I have no knowledge. Just as likely, though, Chatham was concerned that the secrets of his business might somehow be compromised by someone at work in the Master's Lodge.

There was one remark over pudding which seemed to me odd, something about a 'minister'. I wondered at the time whether I might encourage our Dean to join in, but soon realised this was not a servant of the Church, for Chatham balled a fist, scowled and used the words 'crush' and 'overwhelm' in a most aggressive tone. It may be that these gentlemen, both with political connections, might be at loggerheads with some person in a high political office, and had hopes of success, for the Master's reply was, 'Bring on the day'.

Finally, after several rounds of our best port and madeira wine, the diners withdrew to the ante-room, and the Master and Chatham made off to the Master's Lodge. What followed is unclear, and there has been speculation about it in the newspapers, but not by Maude Melly nor by the newspapers to which she contributes, even though she was so close to the event. Chairman Chatham and his crew left about one hour later.

That was the last time I saw the Master alive.

In the Master's Lodge

For several SCs, as you know, we have been aware of the identity of this so-called Master. It was he who supplied a reference for Chatham's servant, Twine, when he applied for a position in the security service of this division of the globe. The Master is one of the few who exist fully in the globe, and are not images.

The recording begins when the Master enters his study followed by Chatham. Though one might expect the study of an academic to be overflowing with books and in a state of general untidiness, this is a

small and minimalist office, with a view out over the Fellows'
Garden. It is remarkable only for the number of African artefacts on
the walls and shelves - wooden masks, pot-bellied women,
ornaments and decorative sculptures of all kinds.

Master: My Lord, please take this seat. You will find the view more attractive.

Chatham: Thank you, Commander. But, to business. You have an insider, do you not? In their Lodge, the Roamers' training establishment?

Master: Perhaps, my Lord, you might care to tell me who gave you that information?

Chatham: I would not. Do not in future answer my question with another. Yes or No.

Master: You are well informed.

Chatham: And that individual has been the source of those toys and trinkets created by the Roamers which this individual stole, gave to you, and are the basis for your reputation as an original thinker. Am I right?

Master: In principle, my Lord. Of course, I have added to them what one might call my personal stamp. The source, the person to whom you refer, is only the most recent of a long line of informers. All dead now. We hold his parents. And he is well compensated, financially.

Chatham: And who is the 'we', who hold the parents of this source?

Master: The informer was identified in the first place by your regional commander for Africa, under the guidance of your previous Director of Finance. I was under the impression that you knew this.

Chatham: I did not. To me this smacks of a conspiracy, for personal gain.

Master: I can assure you, my Lord, I was assured by your regional commander for Africa - a continent close to my heart - that he had reported our activities to you as a matter of routine.

Chatham: I will be generous, Commander, and believe for the moment that you are not the prime mover in this conspiracy. However, that does not excuse you from making a report yourself, independently.

Master: I understand, Lord Commander. I will be more careful in future.

Chatham: Very well. You know, Commander, that for some time I have been looking for the region which would be the ideal place to begin my campaign, with the resources at my disposal. You have applied to be that region. I will say this to you, as I have said to others - provide me with the support I require, and you shall be that region. There is one item I particularly need - an insider, in the Roamers' Lodge. It seems you can give me that.

Master: I am not sure that I can, my Lord.

Chatham: And why not? This is an order. Do you refuse to obey?

Master: The situation is complicated. I am not sure the timing is quite right. I can explain.

Chatham: Well?

Master: The identity of my source among the Roamers is my most carefully kept secret. It has accelerated our research in many fields, brought us discoveries which we have been able to patent, and substantially add to our - your - income. I am sure you will agree that our protection of this asset must be entirely fool-proof.

Chatham: Are you implying, Commander, that I am not capable of protecting this informer of yours?

Master: Not at all, my Lord. But there are around you certain persons whose... integrity, whose... ability to keep a secret might be questioned.

Chatham: Such as?

Master: The Melly woman. If I might be so bold, I would say she is a blabbermouth.

Chatham: Intriguing turn of phrase. So, must I conclude that you are unwilling to reveal the identity of this informer? Would that be because of your suspicion of this female - or rather, could it be that this source and those who preceded him or her have brought you a considerable reputation, a position in this glober society, and that is what you wish to protect?

Master: No, my Lord. My loyalty lies with you and Our God, always. But, I must insist that I present myself in person before Our God and get His agreement.

Chatham: Oh, you do? You think Our God can be bothered with such a trifle? Very well, while we think about that, perhaps we might try that bottle of Armagnac I brought you. Always goes down well after a dinner as magnificent as that we just enjoyed.

Master: Of course. And I will pass on your compliment to our kitchen.

The Master rose from his chair and stepped to a sideboard, where he poured out two glasses of the amber fluid, handed one to Chatham, and sat himself back facing his 'Lord'.

Chatham: You, Commander, were one of the first to arrive in this globe in a fully human form. The power required to move a channel here from the third sea, effect your transfer and then replace that channel, was immense. It led to our current strategy for projection, less demanding by far. We have invested a great deal in you.

Master: Yes my Lord, and I am grateful to have been chosen.

Chatham: And you repay us by making difficulties.

Master: I do not seek to be awkward, my Lord. I see it as protecting the interests of both of us.

The Master took a large sip of his brandy and smiled nervously at his 'Lord'.

Chatham: That, Commander, is arrogant. Your position has gone to your head. What were you before? A commander of the Centre, quartermaster, adopted from the third sea. Am I right?

Master: Yes my Lord.

The Master finished his glass of brandy. Chatham had not touched his.

Chatham: I have heard other reports of your activities, and lack of them. Money from the patents went into your pocket. You have lived a life of idleness, waiting only for something new to arrive from your source for which you can claim the credit. The best thing you have done in twenty years is provide a reference for Twine and bring him to my attention. Apart from that, you have been useless.

The Master appeared frozen in his chair.

Chatham: It is time to die, Commander. Perhaps, like Socrates, you can feel the poison creeping through your body, the body it took such power to create. That is the garnica spice, the spice that eats your memory. In your brandy is a concentrated solution of the spice which gave you such concern. Because it was not one of your own fraudulent inventions. Dementia beckons, Commander, and then a quick death. You are lucky. Do you feel it at the back of your head yet?

The Master did not reply. His mouth hung open, his eyes were half-closed and watery.

Chatham: Ah, I see you do. Our God smiles at the death of incompetents.

Chatham stood, picked up the glasses and stepped to the sideboard. Into the bottle he poured the brandy from his glass, then slid the bottle and glasses into pockets of his raincoat. We hear the sound of a door closing, as the Master's breathing quickens, then stops.

271

Conclusion

1. In our Lodge, there is an informer, identity unknown. Through bribery and blackmail that person and persons before him have been obliged to provide information and our Servator's inventions to the regional commander, the so-called 'Master'. This will have contributed to the exponential growth in the power of technology which we have witnessed in the primary globe in recent SCs.

2. Chatham has identified the need for an informer inside our Lodge. Why? I suggest that the most valuable information which could be supplied by an 'insider' is that of channels into the Lodge and between the Lodge and the Gate. Chatham would seek to make use of those channels to introduce his forces into the Gate, behind our lines.

We hope and expect that the Council will adopt our recommendation that those channels into and between the Lodge and the Gate be closed, if not with immediate effect then at least as soon as possible.

Decision Notice

Meeting of the Grand Council, as dated

Author: Misser, Senior Recorder

Summary:

On the advice of the Constable, supported by the Head of Mechanicals, this recommendation is *not* adopted. The disruption of the Lodge's day-to-day business would be unacceptable to staff and students. Rather, our effort must be put into identifying who this 'informer' might be, and then feeding to this person incorrect information sufficient to damage the enemy, for example to provide inaccurate numbers and positions of troops and other assets.

The Ordinal's concern, however, is noted, and the whole episode is yet another fine example of his thoroughness in surveillance and generally in Public Administration. Those operating channels between the Lodge and the Gate are asked to agree with the Head of

Mechanicals staffing sufficient to close down all such channels should the need arise.

33 - The Wrestling Match

'It is a pleasure to me to fight the fool-mad oppressors'.

So said one of the graffiti on the wall of a warehouse overlooking the shore of the Atlantic Ocean. Tunde Thompson admired its sentiment. There was an innocence about it which made him smile, and if the writer were before him he would probably shake his hand, and only then order his execution.

Tunde, a tall black man with close-cropped curly hair, a graduate of Lagos, was never seen in anything other than a black suit, white shirt and black bow-tie. This he believed appropriate for his new position of Director of Finance, though in the stifling heat of the West African coast he looked back with nostalgia to his role in Logistics which required no more than a t-shirt and jeans.

He stood in the shade under a portico of wooden posts which flanked the warehouse, below him a sun-baked hill that led to the beach, a fringe of palm trees and the rollers of the Atlantic's sparkling blue ocean. Beside him stood the Lord Commander, who on his sudden arrival in Banjul had changed into the white-linen suit which some would remember as the uniform of a colonial oppressor.

Behind them the warehouse was alive with machinery, a dragging of crates and cartons, and the continual traffic of trucks from across the west coast. This route was no longer suitable for distribution of the garnica spice, and the trucks - with GR in gold letters on their sides - were conspicuous as well as unreliable. Tunde knew that there is a point to which self-interest should be encouraged. This was his home territory, and that had given impetus to the first phase of this operation, but even he knew that it was time to move on.

"We will be scaling up, Director," Chatham said. "I assume you are ready."

Tunde coughed and said politely, "My Lord, we end first phase. The result is clear. Where spice is used, the rate of dementia is sky-high, and always blamed on some small thing - water supply, bush meat, aluminium in tea. Now, all regional commanders are ready, with one exception as you know. Funds are ready to go world-wide, if that is your command."

"See to it. Target water supplies, the military, Government and the media. Then, universities and financial institutions. Move quickly. The time is upon us. We must catch in our net as many Roamers as we can."

"Yes my Lord. Bring on the day."

"Dispose of the spice where you think fit. Dump it in reservoirs. Increase the concentration. We shall move faster than these creatures can respond."

Tunde nodded, and said, "On the other matter..."

"The exception. Is he ready?"

"Yes my Lord. Waiting."

*

Their driver took Tunde and Chatham downhill towards Banjul, but turned towards the shore into a scene of chaos. Parking the limo was no problem, for there were no other cars, only a heap of bicycles and a battered coach whose tyres were shot and which bore a placard - 'Today Mister Godzilla'. Black bodies heaved to and fro, raising the dust, slouching, scampering, all in a riot of colour, some in scarlet caps, and jeans everywhere. Most were male but a group of well-padded ladies in flowing white dresses fanned themselves delicately in the shade of an awning. Smoke, of cigarettes and of a barbeque drifted through the palm trees. The noise was terrific - whistles, drums, shouts, applause, a stamping of feet on the baked-hard ground, and intermittently a cry from the public-address system, its loudspeakers slung from the branches of palms and a baobab tree.

275

Tunde led Chatham uphill, where on a plinth of baked earth a wide and open white tent overlooked the crowd. Below, ranks of seats were arranged in a square around a patch of open ground where pairs of black bodies gripped each other, wrestled, stood apart, came together, tussled and strove, feet raising the dust, until one threw the other down, to loud applause and shouts from the gesticulating crowd.

In an aisle between the seats a procession was underway, at once solemn and chaotic. Its focus was an immense black man in a white robe, who shuffled through the dust and occasionally raised his arms so that the sleeves of his robe fell back to reveal muscles which glistened in the sun, every time bringing cries of wonder from his audience. In front of him capered a misshapen dwarf, the counterpoint to the physical perfection of his master. Behind trailed three drummers, hammering a thunderous rhythm on drums of decreasing size, the last, the bass, booming at a speed to quicken the heart.

In the tent stood three wooden chairs in a row. To the left, one was empty. In the middle sat a young boy in a blue robe hemmed in gold. To the right sat an old man, his eyes rheumy, around his neck a string of cowrie shells, at its centre a diamond of black glass, and in his left hand he held the bleached skull of a monkey. The red head-dress and white robe from which bony arms protruded gave him the look of a cockerel, as he beat his bare feet on the ground to the rhythm of the bass drum. He gestured with a fly-whisk, and Chatham sat in the empty chair. Tunde withdrew to the back of the tent.

"The marabout gives you greetings, sir," said the boy.

Chatham paused, then said to the boy, "Tell the marabout that I am honoured to be in his presence, and that I bring him gifts, of money and tobacco."

The boy turned to the old man and whispered in a mixture of pidgin and a dialect that Tunde did not recognise. The old man nodded, flourished his fly-whisk and kept his eyes on the wrestling.

276

"Tell him also," said Chatham, "that he will be dead before nightfall."

The boy said nothing. He stared at Chatham wild-eyed. No-one speaks to the holy marabout, the shaman, in that way. With his fly-whisk, the old man poked the boy in the ribs and gestured for him to move. The boy stood and retreated to the back of the tent.

The marabout sniffed. In a thin, cracked voice, but with the precise diction of one educated at one of the more prestigious English public-schools, he said, "Lord Commander, do you threaten me, your host?"

Chatham turned his head and the marabout gazed directly at him, but with no obvious sign of alarm. "I asked all my regions for their assistance," Chatham said. "You offered none. Why was that?"

"I am sure others are more capable."

"I disagree."

"Why do you bother me?"

To Tunde this was an unthinkable request, and he could tell that it annoyed his Lord Commander. By the arching of an eyebrow, narrowing his eyes, lifting back his head, shifting in his seat to face his opponent, Chatham looked ready to pounce, but in a calm voice he said, "Firstly, information. My servant Twine has had his people around you for some time. I gather you have been talkative. Something about a contact inside the Roamers' training establishment, which they call the Lodge? You will give me the full details of this person."

"I have no idea what you are talking about."

"Secondly. You have around your neck an ornament, a black diamond. How did you come by it?"

"It is a gift from the sea."

"You stole it from a fisherman, whom you killed. It is the origin of the powers which your followers call supernatural. My Saida has

investigated this gift of yours. It excited her a great deal. We know
- and you know - that it is a fragment of God's Minister. There can
be no debate. You will give it to me."

"I will do no such thing."

"Then you will die before nightfall."

"That, my Lord, would be a serious error."

"On the other hand, if you are still capable of obeying an order,
which I doubt, then your life, such as it is, will be spared. You will
lose your so-called powers, but then you would be no different from
the other charlatans of this coast, all of whom I'm sure make a
perfectly decent living."

"Lord Commander, this is my region. These are my people. You
are not safe here."

"Let us walk. We need some words in private." Chatham rose from
his seat and looked down on the marabout, who turned his head
away. "I am sure we can come to some arrangement," Chatham
went on, "which will suit us both."

The marabout wagged his head and scratched his jaw. With a deep
sigh he gathered himself up and rose to his feet, clutching the
monkey skull. "This way," he said. He paced unsteadily to the back
of the tent, where his boy opened a flap. The marabout and Chatham
passed through the tent's back wall and onto a flat circle of hard
ground enclosed by rocks and bushes.

Tunde and the boy peered after them. The conversation of their
masters was animated but they could not hear it, only tell from the
jerking of the marabout's arms and from Chatham's pacing around
that it was not going well.

Chatham took hold of the right arm of the marabout, who cried out.
From the bushes leapt four men, tall, muscular, each with a knife.
They circled Chatham, who let go of the marabout's arm and turned.
Tunde stepped forward but the boy grabbed his arm. Tunde heard a
click and felt something hard poking at his ribs. He looked down.

Grinning, the boy held a pistol. Tunde took another step forward and the boy fired. The bullet passed straight through Tunde and lodged in a post of the tent. Tunde turned and slapped the boy to the ground. "Missed," he said.

In the few seconds it took Tunde to deal with the boy, the Lord Commander had summoned his defence, full battle-dress, and stood at the centre of the marabout's circle of toughs in grey armour, a helmet sparkling in the sun, gauntlets over his arms. He was taller, for his boots raised him from the dust. The gauntlets terminated in circlets of silver metal, which shone as he held them up, turning to face each of his assailants in turn. They drew back. Two ran off into the bushes. The Lord Commander whirled around and sliced down on the arm of another, severing the hand at the wrist. The man yelled, and screamed as his companion dragged him away, gobbets of blood spurting in an arc from the wound, leaving the severed hand in the dust, still clasping its knife.

Raising his head, the Lord Commander stretched up his right arm. The silver circlet and his gauntlet wrapped back. From the palm of his hand a red light grew, and in a flash extended further into the sky than the eye could see. Around him grew a mist and after a few seconds the light collapsed back into his hand.

The man Chatham had returned, in his white-linen suit, his grey face sombre, his eyes on the marabout spread-eagled in fear against a bush. Chatham leaned over and grabbed him by the shoulder. The marabout quivered, eyes staring, legs slowly giving way until he knelt in the dust. Chatham bent over and whispered in his ear. The marabout responded, but so feebly that Tunde could not hear. From the man's neck Chatham tore the necklace, breaking its string, its cowrie shells scattering on all sides, leaving the black diamond in his hand, then he walked slowly, casually, back into the tent. The marabout's boy dashed away, yelling.

"We have what we need," Chatham said to Tunde. He stalked out of the tent downhill and Tunde followed. The crowd parted, whispering, and began to gather around and threaten them as they reached the limo.

Chatham smiled. "Dispose of that fraud before nightfall," he said, "and find a replacement that does not stink of fish." To the driver he said, "Hotel."

34 - The Prisoner

"My wife, Reverend, is an angel."

They all say that, men who have a decent relationship with their wives. "Well, of course," said the Vicar of Malbury.

"No I mean it," said Riley Moss. "She is. Really. An angel."

It was eleven o'clock at night, and the Vicar had tried to shut up shop. His clerical garb was back in the wardrobe, and to ensure a mood of relaxation he had put on his golfing gear - the lozenge-patterned sweater and red trousers which his wife had given him for Christmas. The miracles of his faith were safely in their box till tomorrow, and he was not in the mood for angels, especially those who do impossible things and flap around with messages for people who should know better. The angels that support the altar of Malbury's church, which once had been of a porcelain complexion that briefly entertained Pevsner himself, were now pock-marked and surly. Their restoration would cost thousands, which the Church did not have, and so those angels would soon be on their way to the great rubbish-dump in the sky.

Meanwhile, the Vicar was dealing with an apparition, the appearance on the Rectory's doorstep of Riley Moss, bearing with him nothing but a small bag of toiletries and the clothes in which he stood - a blue t-shirt, jeans, and blue plastic shoes. Once, the Vicar might have been amused to see this rough fellow reduced to essentials, but no longer. Self-important he might be, but the Vicar had decided that Moss was a brave man. Since the moment he saw him throw himself at what he thought was a danger to his daughter - that horse, the horse which jumped through ceilings - the Vicar had a new respect for him, a respect which had survived the weeks of counselling and respite between this night and the events of Malbury Hall, which the Vicar had tried to forget, for such things happen only to people of unsound mind, of which there are many but none in the service of the Church. His conclusion was that he had been gassed. There had been something in that cellar which turned his mind, temporarily. Riley's act of bravery may have been an illusion, but he gave him the benefit of the doubt.

Now Riley Moss claimed sanctuary. The Vicar had to point out that sanctuary had not been available for nearly four hundred years. Riley suggested the Vicar might be able to put him up for a night or two, while the business of the murder was sorted out.

"The murder, Mister Moss?" the Vicar had said.

"Can I come in?"

The Vicar's wife showed her usual generosity of spirit by retreating upstairs. Visitors at all hours were not uncommon, people in trouble, parishioners with ideas to impart or grouses to air. The Vicar settled the obviously agitated Riley Moss in an armchair of his study and closed the door. He sat at his desk and said, "There has been a murder, Mister Moss?"

"You can call me Riley. People do."

"As you say. Riley."

"I am accused of it. The whole thing is ridiculous."

Riley Moss outlined his situation. Police had searched his shop looking for stolen goods, which was shameful for so respectable a business. He would never live it down. They found a gun under his bed, a gun which was used for a murder not so long ago. How it got there Riley had no idea. It might have fallen out of a job lot of house contents, but how it wormed its way upstairs then hid itself under a piece of carpet was a mystery. According to the Police, he used a gun he had never seen to kill some chap he didn't know, for no reason at all.

"But," said Riley, "there might be an explanation."

"And what is that?" the Vicar said, as kindly as he could but with one eye on the clock.

"I have been set up," Moss replied. "Someone wants me out of the way, and Percy my assistant too. He's banged up in Chichester. Why? To leave my daughter, Lily, with no-one to protect her. She's the key to all this."

"I see. But if so, why are you here? Surely you should be back with Lily?"

"I don't know where she is. The Police picked her up too. Some idiot of a policeman mumbled something about 'implications for security'. Besides, if I go home they'll arrest me again."

"But if you were arrested... Riley, how did you get here?"

"My wife, Reverend, is an angel."

"Well, of course," said the Vicar.

"No I mean it," said Riley Moss. "She is. Really. An angel. She rescued me. I thought she was dead, you know? But she rescued me."

His arrest, in full view of the High Street, was one of the most shameful episodes of Riley's life. Handcuffed to a police constable and with an Inspector looking on, he was led head down to a Police car, its driver a Sergeant from Chichester. Into a second car Percy was dragged, protesting. They sped off along the A27 to Chichester's custody centre, where the Sergeant booked him in and gave Moss a blanket, a mattress and a pillow and bundled him off into a cell to await an interview. They took his shoes, and issued him with blue plastic slippers. He was to be held there over the weekend, for the next court would be on Monday morning.

He sat quietly on the bed in his cell. It was cold. He needed a sweater. Every so often the peep-hole would open and an eye would peer around, in case he had hanged himself from a hook which wasn't there by a belt or shoe-laces he didn't have. Hours passed. There was no phone call, no solicitor, only a boisterous drunk who was dragged along the corridor outside and was briefly entertaining. The cell was of a good size, and more comfortable than his barracks in Belfast in the '70s, but reeked of disinfectant. He paced around.

He re-arranged his pillow, several times. There was no mirror, so he had no idea what to do with his hair. He was accused of murder. In the past he could be hanged, which was ridiculous.

It became night. He knew that by the darkening of the concrete wall beyond the barred window. He lay on the bed. Sounds of people having a life drifted across the town, the distant squeal of brakes, the laughing. He got up and paced around. This was dull, so dull he would almost welcome a hook and a belt or shoelaces.

He stopped in mid-prowl. He blinked, looked away then looked back. His jaw dropped. In the middle of his cell a light had appeared, a will-o'-the-wisp. The light grew, from a white centre like a drifting light-bulb, and then a cloud, and then a figure, a ghost, but the ghost took on legs, navy flat shoes, and a body in a blue overcoat, a head and blonde hair, and a face.

"Anna," said Riley Moss, and he fell back against the wall. "My God."

The shock of his arrest, his half-asleep state and the lateness of the hour were affecting his wits. The wife he had not seen, had not held, for ten years, stood in the middle of his cell with her overcoat wrapped tightly around her. "Riley, my love," she said with a broad smile.

Riley blinked. "I have had a heart attack," he said. "I'm dead."

"No you are not. And neither am I."

"Are you a dream?"

"I don't have time to explain it, Riley."

Moss took a pace forward. "I'll never let you go again. Anna."

"Riley…"

She was real. She was warm, and the familiar scent filled his head as he took her hand, kissed it, held her, and their lips met with a passion he had not known for a decade. They stood, clasped together, eyes searching the face of the other, for moments which

284

neither believed would come again. With tears in his eyes Riley said, "Don't wake me up."

"Riley. This is not a dream."

"Must be. People don't just appear. It's not scientific."

"You men. We don't have time for that. I have to get you out of here, quickly. You're not safe."

"This is a nice dream."

"Riley, be serious," said Anna, detaching herself. "Have you heard of a place called Malbury? Be quick."

"I have. Lily and I were there the other week. Why?"

"That's where she is. In the Hall. Trust me, I know that from someone who has eyes everywhere. We have to get her out."

"Is she in danger? Let's get on a magic carpet and save her."

"Is there anyone there you can trust, Riley? We might need their help."

"The Vicar, I suppose. In the Rectory by the Church."

Anna stepped back and drew from a pocket of her overcoat a copper coin. Riley peered at it. "What's that?" he said, "An old penny?"

"Yes. I got it from Lily's room. And thank God it was still there."

"Can't we go somewhere romantic? How about Bermuda?"

"No. I'm no expert with one of these things. It took me two hops just to get here. I landed in the car park. It was embarrassing. Wait." Anna turned her head and closed her eyes. Then she opened them, and began tapping on the coin. Old copper coins are not supposed to have lights in them, but this one did, white and red, as she tapped and paused, then tapped again. After a minute of this - for she obviously made mistakes, and muttered to herself - the lights were green. "Hold my hand, Riley," she said.

"Yes, my angel."

Landing in a prickly bush by the pond on Malbury green was unpleasant. "Damn," said Anna, disentangling herself. Riley was upside-down with his nose inches from the water. He grunted. With difficulty he righted himself, and brushed the mud from his t-shirt. "What the hell was all that?" he said.

"A sideways transfer by personal key," Anna replied. "If you must know. How do you feel?"

Riley patted his stomach. "Sick. It's bloody cold," he said. "But my brain's still in my head."

"Is this the right place?" Anna said. "Where's that Vicar of yours?"

It was a short walk uphill through the village to the Church and then the Rectory, Anna striding ahead and urging Riley to hurry up. At the Rectory's gate she pulled from inside her overcoat a plastic bag of toiletries which she shoved into Riley's hand. "Got them from your home," she said. "Not the sort of thing you'd think of, Riley, unless you've changed in ten years."

"My love for you, my darling," he replied, "is stronger than ever."

"Enough of your nonsense," she said, though in the light from the Rectory's porch Riley could see she was pleased. "I'm away, Riley. This is the longest hop of all. Get it wrong and I could end up breathing nothing. I need to focus. Get yourself indoors, my love. I want to see you safe."

Riley protested. He would never leave her again. Wherever she was, there he would be, but she was having none of it, held up her hand and looked down her nose at him which was the look she always used when argument was useless. They kissed at the gate, and Anna withdrew behind a tree while Riley made his way up the Rectory's path, in a dream.

The Vicar did not believe a word of it. "Mister Moss," he said. "This is most improbable. Tell me. What was it like to travel, as if by magic, from one place to another without the benefit of public or private transport?"

It was, said Riley, exhilarating and at the same time terrifying. As it appeared to him, he and his wife flew hand-in-hand from his cell up some gas-filled pipe, which opened in the ceiling then twisted and turned through a field of stars, and was highly discombobulating and sick-making. Then, as if floating up from a sewer, they both popped out into a lavishly-furnished room, a thick carpet, walls papered in red flock, portraits of ancient worthies in gilt frames on the walls, a golden mirror above a log fire in an open fireplace, and the furniture was heavy, Victorian, yellow plush everywhere, with thick red curtains which obscured the view. Anna in her overcoat was lengthwise on a sofa, and he sat in an armchair by the fire, a cigar in his hand. "And believe me, Vicar," Riley said. "I do not smoke, and never have." He could not say the same about the glass of brandy which he held in the other hand.

The Victorian room was very odd. Riley was aware that though he could direct his gaze around the room, his eyeballs remained fixed in his head. Also, the fire in the grate was just a bright picture of flame, static. The wreath of smoke that rose from his cigar was a spiral frozen in the air. And when he or Anna spoke no lips moved, but they heard each other nonetheless. When they laughed or frowned, it was inside his head, for there was no visible sign of it. And, he did not appear to be breathing, though he did not think he was dead. "My God," he said. "What is this place?"

"We are in-between," Anna replied. "I wanted to stop here because I want to hear about Lily, and you. This was the only way I could do that. The Ordinal let me have his room."

"The who?"

"The Ordinal. Silas. He tells me you met him once, on the coast somewhere. Do you remember? An old man called Silas."

"Silas? Mister Bolney?"

"Possibly. Every so often he likes to be a human being, so he can remember what we are fighting for."

"Are we fighting?"

"We are. A war that is about to get very serious, and for that we need Lily."

"What?"

"Perhaps I didn't mention, my love, that you are the father of a wolf."

"My God."

"An Andreyev, with five thousand years of war and conquest behind her. You think of her as a baby, and so do I. But inside her is a creature of the steppes, a wolf. I love that wolf. I am not worthy to be that wolf, but she is."

"Anna, please. She is just a twelve-year-old girl. Well brought-up too, as well as I, we, could manage. An ordinary girl."

"She is not ordinary, Riley. She is an Andreyev."

"And a Moss. Polite, well-spoken, shy even, I would say. Well-mannered."

"Screw that, Riley. If I say so, she's a wolf."

"Whatever you say, my love."

They talked. Time had stopped. So they talked for hours. Anna had been in a hospital. The Head Nurse, who was some sort of nun, was convinced Anna was a Saint, which made Riley laugh. Lily had grown up, and was doing well at school, though she had a fixation on some boy, which made Anna laugh, and some boy had a fixation on her, which made Anna cough. The shop was a disaster, and Riley would have closed it, but Percy had no other job to go to and it would be letting the side down to put him out on the street, and Mrs Bee, and the two little Bees. Anna spoke about the gardener in the hospital who kept setting traps for the Head Nurse so she would fall over, but Riley was concerned that so large a lady might hurt herself, and so not be fit to look after Anna. At this Anna snorted and said she was perfectly able to look after herself, thank you very much, though she had missed everybody and you especially, Riley, but they had fed her drugs for years and only recently had she got her brains back. Meanwhile, she had been talking to Lily often, in dreams.

"In dreams?" said Riley. "Like this one?"

"We're not dreaming, Riley. We are just in-between."

"In-between what?"

"Two hops, darling. One from your cell to here, then one from here to wherever it was you said, the Rectory. I have the coordinates now, and they're in the key. Configured for launch in about three minutes. Sorry to rush you."

"All this hopping makes me giddy. What key was that? That old penny? Didn't look like a key to me, and I should know. I've been making keys for nearly ten years, and people say I'm good at it."

"I'm sure you are, darling. Yes, the old penny is a key, a key to this room and others. Silas gave it to Lily, but she didn't know what it was. Luckily, no-one else did either. If it had fallen into the wrong hands, I don't like to think what might happen. The war is going badly enough as it is."

"Who exactly are we fighting? Will I need my Army uniform? I still have some of it, in my wardrobe. I clean my boots sometimes."

"I'm sure that will be useful. But, darling, we are fighting something so awful it is hard to describe, but I will try."

Anna asked Riley to imagine something that could - and wanted to - destroy everything there is; the world, every star in the sky and everything between them, black holes, energy, galaxies and constellations, squeezed to nearly nothing and left as a speck of lifeless dust. This thing was as old as Time, and could not be killed, but it was hateful, it was Hate itself. Why this thing should exist, Anna could not say, but it must be some sort of test. Those who resisted, would survive and grow stronger. Those who gave in, would simply cease to exist or had to join its army of dead things.

"Army of dead things?" Riley said. "Lily said that, from a dream. When she had one of her turns."

"Yes she saw it. That was an accident, and I blame myself for scaring her, but she saw it. And now she knows what her enemy is."

It was not a man, nor anything that could live in a well-made universe - and for that Anna thanked something called 'Mysul' - which was why it could go no further than the Gate, the door of the Universe, but its victims called it an angel, not Satan though if it helped to imagine it that way, fair enough. But it didn't live in fire, or up to its belly in ice, nothing like that. It roams the universes - yes, Riley, there are more than one - with an army of the dead, savage creatures it brought back to a kind of life and sends wherever they can do most harm. They are here too, Riley, in our world, spies, images, looking just like people, with histories, good reasons to be here, sparks of the Grey Angel. That is what we call it, Riley. Wherever you find people who have a spark of the Grey Angel in them you will find hate, deception, brutality. You have probably met some already.

But Time returned. For a second, the fire flared up, and Riley's cigar-smoke curled up towards the ceiling. He found himself in the twisting and turning sewer-pipe once more, holding tight to Anna's hand, and then he was upside-down in a bush by Malbury's pond, and very prickly it was.

The Vicar was appalled. He was in the presence of one who was not only suspected of murder, but mad with it. It was necessary to be kind, while he considered his options.

"Ballantine," said Moss. "He's one of them. An image. He's not actually real."

"I see."

"Forgive me Reverend, but you do not. Anna told me. He is an insect."

"Ah yes, of course. An insect. Would you like cocoa, or perhaps Ovaltine?"

Before Riley could reply, there came a knock at the Rectory door. With his wife upstairs, the Vicar knew he would be expected to answer it. "Pardon me one moment," he said, and looking back at Moss who now sat in a less agitated - and presumably safer - state in front of the desk, the Vicar darted into the hallway and opened the door.

Outside stood a blonde woman in a blue overcoat. "Excuse me, sir," she said. "Do you have Riley Moss in there? I am his wife, Anna."

35 - In the Rectory

"Mrs Moss," said the Vicar. "This is something of a surprise."

"I'm sorry to bother you, Reverend," said Anna, standing on the door-step of the Rectory, "but we don't have much time, and there is something you must know. May I come in?"

Giving time for the Vicar only to give a cursory nod, Anna pushed past, looked around the hall and spotted her husband in the study. The Vicar followed, urgently, in case there should be a domestic dispute in his very own house.

"Anna!" cried Riley, getting up from his chair.

"Riley, my love, you are in danger. We are all in danger. You too, sir," she said turning towards the Vicar.

This was a very attractive woman. In her late thirties but with a bloom of youth on her cheeks, she was slim, her thick blonde hair tied back, and eyes of a violet-blue that the Vicar had seen only in her daughter Lily. Her blue overcoat hung well on her. Why so exotic a creature should have married rough-looking Riley Moss the Vicar could not fathom. "Danger?" he said, eyebrows raised.

From outside came a rumbling. It was a truck, or a heavy car, moving slowly up the street and coming to a halt with a faint squeal of brakes.

"I blame myself," said Anna. "I was in too much of a rush. Riley, are those your clothes, or did someone give them to you?"

"I… well… they're mine," Moss replied. "Sorry, standards have slipped since you… since you were taken from me. Oh, some chap at the prison gave me the shoes. No laces. In case I hanged myself. What nonsense."

"The shoes. Damn. There must be a bug in them, a tracker. I had one in my coat. I threw it in the sea. The shoes, that's how they found us. I didn't think of the shoes. Take them off right now."

"A bug? How do you know?"

"Take them off."

Embarrassed, Riley took off his shoes, blue plastic sandals that he poked together on the carpet with a foot. "How do you know?" he repeated.

"Carefully, darling," said Anna, "crouch down and look outside. There's a car, with a woman in it. I saw it coming and then I saw her face. I know her. She's here to make trouble, serious trouble."

Riley crouched by the window and parted the net curtains an inch. He peered out. Beyond the Rectory's fence a black car had drawn up. From the car's near side a man stepped out, light from a street-lamp flashing from a mop of blonde hair.

"I know that man," Riley said. "It's Twine."

"Who?"

"The man who took you from me. Secret service. Twine. What the hell is he doing here?"

A head and then the face of a woman appeared on the car's further side. She stood stock-still, her hair shifting in a light breeze, as Twine moved to the right and out of sight. Perhaps it was the breeze which made the rustling outside, leaves from the trees. Moss stood and walked back across the room. "There's a woman," he said. "Is she Indian?"

"No," said Anna. "Her name is Saida. Not Indian. Not human."

"Excuse me," the Vicar said. "How can that be?"

"I think, Reverend," said Anna, "in your terms, you might call her a demon."

"Goodness me."

"Is there anyone else in the house?"

"Only my wife. Upstairs."

"Call her please. There is something you both should know."

The Vicar was perplexed. Moss had been an Army man, and so might be better able to deal with such matters, but for the Vicar to involve his wife was a step too far. "I'm sure, Mrs Moss," he said, "that would not be wise. My wife is of a nervous disposition and I would not want her troubled."

"Would you want her dead?" said Anna.

The Vicar's eyes widened. Anna advanced over the carpet and looked at him squarely in the face. "My daughter, Reverend," she said, "has been kidnapped. By people who do not care what they do. Two of them are outside right now. We need to move, and quickly. No-one in this house is safe."

"Kidnapped?" the Vicar said. "Then this is a matter for the Police."

"No time," Anna replied. "Call her."

The Vicar cleared his throat. "If you insist," he said. He stepped into the Hall and called upstairs. In seconds - as if his wife had been listening with one ear to the floorboards - she descended, and came with the Vicar into the study.

"Good evening," said the Vicar's wife - whose name is Rosemary - looking around the room. "Is there some debacle?"

"Do you have a coat?" Anna said. "You will need it."

"I beg your pardon," Rosemary said. "Are we going somewhere? Why?" It was true that she was not dressed for an expedition, but in beige slippers and a dressing-gown of an attractive yellow which well suited her small but womanly form. Her brown hair was in curlers, but that in no way diminished the beauty of her perfectly oval face.

294

The Vicar took her hand. "This, my dear, is Mrs Moss, and her husband. You will remember that it was Mister Moss - and his daughter - who were with me on that day in the Hall."

"When you came back babbling about ogres and monstrosities and such," said Rosemary, eyeing Riley Moss with a glare.

"Their daughter," the Vicar went on, "is in danger, so I am told by Mrs Moss. Kidnapped, in her words. I am also told that we too are in danger, and must leave this house immediately."

"Danger, my rear end," Rosemary replied. "We're more in danger from the bleach which you use so liberally in our bathroom, Thomas, truth be told."

Anna held a hand to her mouth and muttered what to the Vicar sounded like 'square'. Before he had time to assess the meaning of this, Anna advanced towards him and in a commanding tone said, "Vicar, hold tight to Mrs Ellis's hand."

"Are we praying for guidance?" said the Vicar.

"Something like that," Anna replied. "Riley, take hold of the Vicar's other hand." Across the room, Riley took a step forward.

"Mrs Ellis ... " Anna said, but got no further.

At that moment, the window of the study smashed. Shards of glass scattered over the net curtains. Rosemary gave out a yell and put her hands to her face. The Vicar flung his arms around her.

A grey ball bounced over the carpet.

"Grenade!" cried Riley.

The grenade lay between Riley and the others. For precious seconds Anna stared at it. She could not get to Riley, nor he to her.

"Get out!" Riley yelled. "Now!"

With a grimace of despair Anna tapped furiously at her key, then grasped the Vicar's free hand.

In a column of light Anna shot up from the floor, dragging the Vicar upwards, his wife clasped to him. Riley Moss threw himself to the floor behind the sofa.

At lightning speed the three of them hurtled upward in a chain, the Vicar holding his wife tightly as the Rectory fell away, their last view of Riley Moss being of him tilting the sofa over the grenade, which burst into light.

Twisting and turning as if in the insides of a worm, pin-points of light flashing past, the Vicar had no time to think nor even to breathe as they shot through an arch of purple light into a whirlwind of dust.

The dust cleared. The Vicar breathed. His first thought, as he surveyed Roamers Cross for the first time, was that it looked rather like a small town in the Alps.

36 - Sealed In

Spikers, bleached-white corpses, insects, mosquitoes, black boxes, and something new - men of huge size in black armour which shone like the carapace of a cockroach - one by one Lily ferried them from the forest of Roamers Cross into the basement of the Hall.

The new arrivals had a human shape, but Lily could not see inside their armour. Between the grinning puppets either side of the door, the giants would shuffle together and stand shoulder to shoulder, the wings of their helmets connecting, flashes of grey appearing at eye-level. When three stood together, Saida would lead them out and close the door. Then, above her head, Lily would hear an engine start up, and a truck drive away.

It was dark in the basement but for the light of the soundless TV. Behind her she had glimpsed light through cracks in the black stone of the wall, but that was visible only by day. It might be a door. It might be nothing. It would not be easy to get to, for the wooden cases and broken parts of slot machines were piled up in front of it. If anything could be worse, it would be to have a false hope.

She had been in that chamber for two nights, a day, and now a morning. Her fingers tingled from the constant burning of the cameo, the key, which every time became too hot to hold. That night, she had been so tired that she could not remember whether she had dreamed. Her mother was on her way. That was a comfort, but had been the dream of the night before. Strapped into her chair, she knew that she could not survive for long. The atmosphere was biting into her, acidic, sulphurous, and her head swam with it. As the hours passed, her strength was ebbing away.

Then, suddenly there were no more monsters. Twine arrived in the basement and opened the door. He scowled at her, drew a finger across his throat, and left the door open.

As Twine stepped back into the cellar, Lily felt a tremor beneath her feet as if some mighty engine beneath the Hall had come alive. The floor trembled, and she heard a roar as of an avalanche, the bursting of a dam, of water gushing from all the streams below uniting into one foaming white torrent which would shoot up from the well and drown her. But it was mud, not water. It was brown, not white, and it came not from the well, but from the ceiling.

A stream of waxy mud flowed down over the walls and the open doorway with the whoosh of a hundred opened taps, across the ceiling and over the floor, lifting Lily's chair with a jolt. It sealed her in. It had the smell of a petrol filling-station and froze solid in an instant. She stared at it. It was dark brown but translucent, except at the door, which had become a sheet of opaque brown plastic.

Why seal her in? Were they going to gas her to death? The puppets were half-in and half-out of this shell, even more life-like and macabre.

The tremor subsided and now there was quiet, all sound from outside deadened by the insulation of this plastic mud. To see whether the door still worked, Lily called out that she wanted to use the bucket. A door-shaped rectangle shifted up onto the ceiling to let Twine pass through. He untied Lily, and turned his back. In those few moments, Lily could see that Saida was crouching over the well, scraping at its inside with a trowel. Every so often she flicked the contents of the trowel into a vase, from which issued wisps of black smoke and a pale yellow light.

Finished, Lily stood, and Twine tied her back in her chair. With a grimace he removed the bucket, left, but after a few moments returned, replacing the bucket inside the door.

"That's the last time you'll need to do that," he whispered.

298

37 - Return to the House Over-There

The blast blew the sofa backwards, and Riley Moss with it. He landed with a tremendous thump against a sideboard, his head feeling as if it were loosely attached to his neck and his legs sticking out at an ungainly angle.

Much of the explosion had been smothered by the sofa, a heavy leather-bound antique. Ball-bearings and shards of metal had penetrated even its back and sides, and as Moss pulled himself together and crouched he had to take care not to lacerate himself on what had become the quills of a metal porcupine. There was a ferocious whistling in his ears. He calmed his breathing and peered over the sofa. Its cushions were ablaze, and thick smoke rose to the ceiling. If these people had any sense they would follow that up with a spray of machine-gun fire, but no shadow appeared on the blown-out windows, no gun-barrel poked in. Amateurs.

What was the point of that? To Riley Moss it was an invitation. If you're still there, come and find me, do your best. You're an amoeba, unemployable, disposed of in hazardous waste. Anger rose in him. If he had a gun he would have used it, but as he heard the car drive off at speed he knew they did not have the balls to be targets. They had his daughter and he would get her back. Lily, I'm still here, and I'm coming.

Riley dared to creep around the sofa, stood, shook himself and checked that his limbs were in working order. With a cushion he smothered the sofa's flames, and fanned away smoke billowing through the room. Even in the dark he could see that the room was destroyed. Every item of furniture except the sofa and what had been behind it was shattered, by the blast and the ball-bearings that came with it. Now at least there was no fire, only an oily smoke which was gushing out through the windows. Lights were coming on one by one in the windows of cottages across the street.

The smoke was dissipating. It was safe to leave. Common sense stopped him from going out through the front door. But as the adrenalin wore off, the chill of the breeze through smashed windows began to seep into him. He needed clothes, something warm.

He made his way in a daze through the ruins of the room back into the hallway, then upstairs where, in the Vicar's bedroom, he closed the curtains and switched on a bedside light. This was an old-fashioned man's room - a heavy bed, antique wardrobe, and a dressing-table. Framed photographs of clerics lined the walls, bishops and saints, and in the air lingered an aroma of pomade now with the addition of a bitter smell of burning. From drawers of the dressing-table Riley took out an Argyle sweater which reminded him of his own, stout corduroy trousers and precious thick brown socks.

He changed, descended the stairs and stood in the hallway. It would have been quiet but for the whistling in his ears. From under a hat-stand he grabbed the Vicar's boots, which fitted with the merest wobble. The Vicar had a bicycle. It was out the back. Along the corridor he paced, then through the kitchen, where he opened the back door and stepped out into the night.

He wasn't thinking. He went too quickly. Amateur. Didn't check the shadows. A pistol-barrel crunched on his skull and knocked him down onto the concrete track. As he fell he glimpsed the white face of a small man in a dark-grey suit, the face of the man who had stolen his wife. Twine.

*

Everywhere was green. Riley woke on a mat, looking up at a green ceiling. He turned his head, and the pain shot through him like a lightning-strike. He winced. He rolled onto his front, gingerly pushed himself up, stood and rubbed his head. He was alone, standing inside a shell of green plastic which filled the room. It was a room he knew, the ballroom on the ground floor of Malbury Hall, the House Over-There.

Through the green walls of the plastic shell he made out a fireplace, and windows through which came an eerie early-morning light. He jabbed a heel of the Vicar's borrowed boot into the plastic beneath him. It skidded and made no mark on the waxen surface. Whatever this substance was, it was tough. He stepped unsteadily towards a window and rubbed his hand over the shell between him and it. Very smooth, translucent but a dark leaf-green. He blinked and looked down at himself as a relief from the deadly green. The Vicar's boots reminded him of the night before.

"Ah. Up I see," came a voice from behind. Riley turned from the window. An oblong of the shell's green plastic had swung up by the ballroom's door, and through that space came Twine, in his right hand a pistol, and in his left a bowl. "Stay right there," Twine said, as with a sigh the oblong closed behind him. He took a pace forward.

Embarrassing, to let this lightweight get the better of him. A smaller man, his dark-grey suit without a crease, a baby face, blonde hair thick and under control, black shoes that shone, and a pistol held steadily forward. Riley sniffed. "So," he said. "Twine. Is this another MI5 operation or are you moonlighting?"

Twine's smile was fleeting. "A minor deception, Moss," he said. "On the mat. And sit, if you don't mind." He waggled the pistol in the direction of the mat.

Riley blinked and estimated his chances. Five metres away, too far. Slowly, with his eyes on Twine, he paced over to the mat, and sat cross-legged.

Twine laid the bowl on the floor. "Eat when you like," he said. "You'll appreciate it later. Pee or whatever in a corner. Welcome to our world."

"Is Lily here?"

Twine pursed his lips. "That's for me to know and for you to find out," he said. "Your daughter. Such a pretty girl, and so useful. But we have decided after all that she needs a little encouragement. You can give her that."

"Like Hell."

"I suppose it must be. Eat. We will see you later." Twine stepped backwards, and the oblong doorway opened. Riley made out a further opaque green door which would lead to the hall. The oblong closed behind Twine and Riley heard his footsteps but could see nothing of him.

Leaning on the green wall of the shell precisely where Twine had left, Riley Moss saw no trace of the doorway, not the slightest crack or seam to suggest it had ever been there, but he heard sounds, of a door opened and closed, of heavy feet on the hall's floor, and then the sound of a truck's door, opened, closed, and its engine as it drove off. He hammered on the curving wall, but his fists bounced off it. Now there was only quiet. He yelled, but his voice merely echoed around the walls in a deafening crescendo, then died.

38 - A Watcher

BOOM BOOM BOOM

The booming of the bass drum echoed around the walls of the town, followed by a braying of horns which the Vicar recognised to be music, but of an uniquely cacophonous kind. Between a black-timbered house and a bank-like building of classical style there stretched a banner. 'Welcome Home Our Defender' it said in large red letters on white cloth.

"Goodness gracious," said the Vicar, his insides churning in a disagreeable manner.

They had landed at a junction of four streets each lined with small shops whose awnings were of various colours, some striped. On one corner, the broad white steps of the bank building led up to columns and an empty pediment, glowing in light which came not from a sun but seemed to come from inside itself. On the opposite corner, a square red-brick building identified itself as a 'Recruitment and Training Centre'. In the distance against a backdrop of black mountains, the Vicar made out the tall spire of a white tower which he concluded must be a cathedral.

Ahead under the banner, people swarmed around a band composed of women in smocks and woolly hats, each of them puffing and blowing on brass instruments which made an infernal din, all to the beat of a bass drum wielded by an impressively moustached gentleman in a yellow uniform. In front of him stood a smaller fellow, plump and grey-haired, wearing a pillbox hat and a green robe. Around his neck dangled a heavy gold chain which singled him out, in the Vicar's mind, as the Mayor. The people of this welcoming committee - of all ages, colours and sizes - looked normal for a provincial town out of the mainstream of fashion, though many wore military camouflage uniforms, and some carried long staves and bows.

303

The Mayor stepped forward and raised a hand. The band stopped playing. "As Clerk of the Council," he cried, his voice echoing around the square, "I welcome the return to the Gate of our glorious Defender, never defeated in battle, never defeated in Court, messenger from the Council to all peoples of this world and the others!" In a quieter tone he added, "Oh, and two others I don't know."

The band struck up again with a mighty crash of cymbals and an appalling blare of horns. Anna stepped up to the Clerk and embraced him. There were shouts from the crowd and hats were thrown in the air. Anna held up her hand, and in the quiet that followed, she cried out, "My friends! We thank you for your kind welcome! And now, let us have... breakfast!"

To a universal shout of "Yes!" the band and the people surged forward across the square carrying Anna and the Clerk with them. They all trooped into the Recruitment and Training Centre, past the Vicar and his wife, who looked at each other in amazement.

"Thomas," said Rosemary. "How did we get here? Is this a dream? Are we dead?"

"I don't feel dead, my dear," the Vicar replied. "You don't look dead. I remember flying and feeling rather sick. It was all very quick. It seems to me that someone has invented a method of instantaneous travel. I suspect, the Russians."

"But do you think this could be Heaven?"

"My dear, I am not sure. That may depend on the quality of the breakfast."

*

At a trestle table in the echoing hall of the Recruitment and Training Centre, the Vicar sat with his wife and Anna Moss to one side, and on the other a studious bald-headed individual in a green suit who had introduced himself as Ordinal.

304

The Vicar was unsure why the Centre deserved its name, for there was nothing about recruitment nor training in it. It reminded him of his village hall, an antique construction of wood panels with beams arching overhead, but whereas his hall was usually empty throughout the year (except at the Harvest Supper, which this year had been abandoned through lack of interest), this hall was packed with the residents of this unusual place, and the table at which he sat was squeezed by a wall with numerous other tables spread across the planks of the floor.

At one end, under a round window the Clerk sat in a plush high-backed armchair. Every so often he would rise, straighten out the folds of his robe and deliver a few words of praise to one or another of the crowd, who would applaud and hoot. It seemed to the Vicar that the Clerk liked the sound of his own voice, which was pleasant and carried far.

The crowd was of an extraordinary variety. Men, women and children sat and slouched at their tables, many in costumes which belonged to bygone eras, some in a military uniform, on a cream base but mottled in yellow, green and brown. Between the tables moved an army of women in smocks of various colours and woolly hats. Their appearance was regimented, all as similar as if they were from one family, and they bustled about with trays bearing brown bottles and bowls of soup.

A bowl of soup landed in front of the Vicar. It was a plain white bowl, containing a green liquid which bubbled and issued an unpromising aroma. "May I ask," he said to Ordinal, "what is this?"

"Frog," Ordinal replied. "I am told it is delicious, but I don't eat it myself."

The Vicar gulped. At his side, his wife attacked the soup with gusto, her spoon rattling against the bowl. "God's beard and whiskers," she said eventually. "Such a good stock. Tres francais. I always keep a pot of stock bubbling on the stove. Don't you?" She said this to Anna, who raised an eyebrow and with a flat hand refused her bowl.

305

Nonetheless the Vicar was encouraged. He dipped his spoon into the soup and tried a mouthful. It was an extraordinary sensation. He had only once tried frogs' legs, in a hotel in northern France, and found them like chicken but with the after-taste of a ditch. But this soup, though suspiciously green, had a flavour which the Vicar could describe only as beautiful. It flooded his taste-buds, it reached up his nose and tickled every atom of his being. One spoonful, and he needed no more. It filled him up, and as he looked around he saw the same on all sides. The smock-wearing women were already clearing up the bowls. No-one here seemed to eat much, and there was no water, no liquid other than what might be in the brown bottles, and the Vicar had none of that. Neither was there any smoking - which, despite government legislation, still infected the atmosphere of his village hall. Though this town had the aspect of an Alpine village, its inhabitants had none of the habits of such a place.

Anna leaned forward, frowning. To Ordinal she said, "I have to go back. Now."

Ordinal took a deep breath. "I understand," he said. "Your daughter, and your husband..."

"I don't know if they're alive or dead. I have the co-ordinates. If I can use your key again..."

"No point," Ordinal replied. "They are alive. Our Servator does not record entries to the Tower from that location. They have not died."

"Thank you, Ordinal. Then my husband will be in the Hall. He will be looking for Lily."

"Ah yes, the Hall. That would be the Great Hall of Malbury, west of Salisbury and a little to the south. You would find nothing there. Not your husband. Not your daughter. Nothing."

"But..."

"I have dispatched a watcher to make sure, and am about to receive his report. But, as I see it, the Hall is completely empty."

"It can't be."

"So it appears. But to me, that building is all-but invisible. To me, whatever is inside that building is not of this sea. Some power - and you can guess what that is - has removed the inside of that building from this universe."

*

Over the last two days, an unusual vehicle had been passing Aldsworth's shop in Malbury. To and fro it went, towards Luffham and then back to the main road to Salisbury. It was a green three-ton truck with a large GR in gold on its sides. Aldsworth knew all the delivery vehicles. He had one himself - a small white van, unmarked, which he used - in a car park of Barn Elms - to pick up supplies which could not be delivered directly to his shop. These were supplies by which the Revenue would not be troubled - cigarettes, rolling tobacco, wine, beer and brandy - for in a triumph of individual enterprise they came over the Channel from France in a private car thoughtfully adapted to carry goods in secret compartments slung under its chassis. But the GR van was new.

Aldsworth also knew that the Hall had new occupants - a man with a woman who was too old for him. There was talk in the village about this new arrangement, and about another man who had been driven to the Hall and then to Barn Elms in a Mercedes limousine. Could these people at last have the funds to make something of the Hall? Make it a tourist attraction perhaps? Bring employment to the village?

That morning, Aldsworth had not given this much thought. It was that one morning in the week when he was due at Barn Elms, and the clock was against him. He took off his pinafore, adjusted his spectacles, slung on a raincoat, turned the sign on the shop's door to Closed, stepped out and waddled around to the side alley where his van waited.

Only on his way back, with his packages securely strapped together in the van, did the idea pop into his head that it would save him a journey if - at that moment, right there, just as he drove towards the signpost to Malbury Hall - he were to make the acquaintance of these new people, new customers with funds and friends who were driven in limousines. Already he could offer an impressive discount on two cases of brandy which were maturing from Fine to Vintage at that very moment in the back of his van. So, he turned off onto the track which led to the Hall, drove through the parade of pines and poplars which was all that remained of the grand avenue, and came to the five-bar gate which swung back with a mournful creak as he tumbled back into his van and drove onto the gravel of the forecourt.

There were no other vehicles. This was dispiriting, for he had expected one Rolls Royce at least. He levered himself out of the van, and set off towards the steps and the portico with its four columns reaching up to the grey sky. At the front door he rang the bell. He heard only a faint clunk as if the bell were covered by a sock. He knocked on the door. No-one came. Being no respecter of private property, he tried the door handle. The door opened a few inches, but was stopped by something. Aldsworth inserted a hand, and the tips of his fingers bounced from some invisible obstruction. He peered more closely and tried again. Inside the door was something solid but invisible. As he looked in, though, he detected a faint green light around the doorway to a side room, and then up the stairs another light, pale blue.

He frowned and his face crumpled like an old leather handbag. Was there no end to the mysteries of this place?

His conclusion - from what he had seen on television and from private reading of his own - was that aliens had landed on Malbury Hill, and had parked their spaceship inside the Hall and put a force-field around it.

This would not be the first time that Aldsworth had blamed aliens for the mysterious events of the Hall, but now he was on firmer ground. He was already constructing the tale he would tell in the Goat and Bucket that evening, and convinced himself so well that he trotted fearfully back down the steps and to his van without a backward glance. There, he manoeuvred the van around and sped off back to the village without bothering to close the gate behind him.

*

"Aliens," Ordinal said to Anna. "Did I say that? Surely not. It was someone else, not me."

"Aliens!" Mrs Ellis had overheard, and clasped a hand to her mouth, eyes wide in horror.

The Vicar said in a kindly tone, "Please let Ordinal continue, my dear. They may not be aliens of other-worldly nature, but perhaps only visitors from abroad who might need our assistance."

Ordinal frowned. "I have to say, sir, that according to my report they are indeed of other-worldly nature, very. If you are interested, I can give you sight of some of my paperwork. I'm sure you will find it thorough, and even enlightening."

Mrs Ellis went pale and slumped in her seat.

"That would be helpful," the Vicar said.

Ordinal turned back to Anna. "It appears," he said, lines of worry creasing his forehead, "that the grangels have installed inside that Hall a peculiar structure. I am informed by my watcher that it is an alien spaceship. Whatever that is."

"That doesn't sound likely," Anna replied.

Ordinal gazed in an absent-minded manner at the rafters of the ceiling. "That is how my watcher describes it," he said. "You must give me a moment while I interpret his findings." He closed his eyes, and his nose began to twitch in a manner the Vicar found curious.

Those at the table eyed each other. Mrs Ellis looked at her husband with wide eyes. Anna kept her eyes on Ordinal. The Vicar looked at the two women, one after the other, while behind them the smock-

309

wearing women bustled around tables, and the Clerk let loose another volley of praise at a gentleman in a yellow uniform who stood, bowed, and sat to a tumult of applause.

Ordinal opened his eyes. "Remarkable," he said. "It appears that the grangels have constructed an Omnium. Inside that building, a replica of our Omnium. Just such as we use at the Lodge in Navigation class. The colours are the same, and the levels. Our spheres are represented by shells of some plastic material which fill up the rooms of the Hall. They have turned the inside of that building into a reflection of all the universes. Quite extraordinary. I must see Mysul about this."

Ordinal pushed back his seat, and with a great flap of his spinach-green suit stalked away and out of the building.

Mrs Ellis had assumed a state which would be catatonic but for the rapid flickering of her delightful brown eyes. The Vicar leaned over the table. "Could you possibly explain that?" he said to Anna.

"No," she replied.

"Oh," the Vicar said.

*

Anna watched Ordinal leave then - frustrated that there was nothing she could do - drew a deep breath and took more notice of her companions. The Vicar's wife was a well-padded little woman, curlers in her hair, a dressing-gown draped around her. The Vicar, on the other hand, was dark-haired and aquiline, in a white shirt and lozenge-patterned jumper, and red golfing trousers which would have been bought for him, probably at Christmas.

"Excuse me, my dear - Anna, isn't it?" said Rosemary. "Is there somewhere possibly I could acquire clothes more appropriate for this place? I realise I must look rather odd, coming out without my going-out clothes."

"You don't look odd at all, Mrs Ellis," Anna politely replied. "I can assure you, clothes are not a priority here."

"Well you can say that, but you are so elegantly attributed. Fabulous. I feel dowdy by comparison."

"Not at all. You look perfectly sweet."

"Why thank you, my dear. But I have my eye on one of those smocks. Very fetching."

"I'm sorry, smocks are only for the mechanicals."

"Excuse me, Anna," the Vicar interjected. "Those women are robots?"

"No. But they perform mechanical tasks, mechanically. And sometimes they sit on juries."

"Juries?"

"Yes I suppose it must all be very confusing," Anna said. "Why don't you go for a walk around the town? I recommend the shops. You don't need money. If you need something, take it."

"Heaven," Rosemary breathed.

"And you could try the hotel. Very comfortable, I'm told, if you want a room. And the proprietor, Mister Humbert, is full of information. But shouldn't I be getting you home? I'm sure it's safe now."

"Not at all," said Rosemary. "Shops that don't charge. Heaven. Delicious soup. Marvellous."

"I too would be interested in learning more about the mysteries of this place," the Vicar said. "Ordinal did promise me that paperwork. And, I can always say to my parishioners that I took some time off to visit my sister in Fernhurst. Meanwhile, my canon can hold the fort."

"It may take some time to get that paperwork from Ordinal," said Anna. "He's always busy."

"Then we shall stay here... forever!" cried Rosemary with a clap of her hands.

*

The Vicar and his wife emerged blinking into the light of the Square. Its cobbles were flat, as were those of the four streets which led off it, and offered no hardship to the feet. Grandest of the buildings in the Square was that which to the Vicar looked like a bank - with a colonnade and a pediment, all of gleaming white marble, but his wife reminded him that - as people here did not use money - it must be something else. A passer-by in military uniform kindly informed them that this was the Council House, and that the Hotel - if that was what they were looking for - was in the street to the south, Gate-side, look for a tall building of glass and steel, can't miss it.

They paraded down South Street admiring the shops. These were mainly two-storey and brick-built, between them some of an antique design with white plaster and exposed black beams. Upper floors had windows with curtains and must be living quarters. Each shop had an awning with the peculiar ability of casting no shadow, and these stretched along the street on both sides in an array of colour. Below, the shops varied in tidiness. Each was small, and displayed its wares either neatly behind a window or roughly in boxes piled up on the stones of the pavement. Fruits, vegetables, fish, frogs, wheat and bread, beer-bottles; the diet of these Alpine people lacked one thing - proper meat. To Rosemary this was a disappointment.

The people on the street, however, were no disappointment, for they were beyond civil. Whether they stood singly or casually chatting in a group, each would give a nod of acknowledgement as the Vicar and his wife passed. One - a young woman bearing pails of water on a yoke across her shoulders - delivered a curtsey, the like of which the Vicar had seen only in costume dramas.

312

Altogether, there was something old-fashioned about this place. The men - those few not in the camouflage outfits and boots of a military sort - wore black suits with tails, brass buttons and pinstripe trousers. Oddly, many wore sandals with black socks, which Rosemary declared to be an affront to Style. Occasionally, though, men in rough leathers strode up the street without a sideways glance, one with the look of a Red Indian, in the tie-dye shirt and flared trousers of a Flower Child from the 1960's. The women - those not in camouflage outfits - tended to the longer dress with flowery patterns, no hats, but their hair bound up in all manner of elaborate patterns. From the corner of his eye the Vicar glimpsed Rosemary fiddling with her own hair as if inspired. The children were dressed roughly in what looked like hand-me-downs from their elders, though one or two sported the knickerbockers and caps of street urchins from the days of Sherlock Holmes.

Among this antiquity the Hotel stood out, half-way along the street, a tower of glass segmented into lozenges by steel struts. The whole edifice stuck up from the street like an icy pinnacle into the sky, though at its base a wooden shop-front better suited the style of the street. Its door was open, and the Vicar and Rosemary made their way across the street towards it.

39 - The Navigator Test

Ordinal returned. He pushed through the throng of the Recruitment and Training Centre with a gleam in his eyes. Excited though he was, he shook out the creases of his spinach-green suit, lowered himself into his seat at the table with a delicate languor, rubbed a hand over his head and allowed his profile to be admired by all who sat there.

He turned to Anna. "The navigator test," he said.

"Ordinal!" Anna exclaimed, suddenly alarmed. "You can't be serious. You expect Lily to take the navigator test?"

"I do. It's her way out of that building. And your husband's."

"But… it's too early… too dangerous. Mysul wouldn't let me take that test."

"That, Anna," said Ordinal, gently patting Anna's hand, "is because your talent lies elsewhere. Just remember the struggle you've had using any sort of key. Without Mysul's help you'd be upside-down in the middle of a pond every time. I hope you don't mind me saying that."

"It's true."

"Well then. Lily has the ability. I admit she is untrained, but all her life she has been a level one navigator. She was born to the role. But level one is not good enough for your daughter. It's a nightmare, being in two places at once, enough to drive anyone mad. No wonder she has fits or 'turns' or whatever she calls them. Just imagine, if we can get her to level two she can take herself anywhere. Up and down channels, the most distant galaxies, even to other seas when she knows what she's doing. She's already done it, with Mysul's help, just as you have. At level two, she can do it herself, no questions asked. It's time for her to reach level two. She has to take the navigator test."

"I don't like the idea."

"Like it or not, it's the best plan. I have discussed it with Mysul. But first, we are agreed, are we not, that she is actually there?"

"You should know, Ordinal."

"We know she went in. We know that is the location of her keys. We know she hasn't come out. It's a fair assumption she's there, even though we can't see her."

"And why is that?"

"Lily and your husband are in the middle of an Omnium, dear Anna, and so it appears that they are not in this universe at all."

Ordinal confirmed that the grangels had wrapped an Omnium around Malbury Hall. They had copied the original Omnium at the Lodge, possibly through treachery, which Ordinal was investigating. Shells of some plastic material coated the walls, ceilings and floors of the Hall, reflections of the spheres of the original Omnium, its universes. The result was that objects, people, everything inside that building was simply not there, but in a little universe of its own. All that anyone could see from outside was a facsimile of how the Hall appeared some time before - empty. It was a good trick, and Ordinal admired their ingenuity, suspecting that their Saida had something to do with it. She was quite clever, not in the Servator's league, but capable. And why should she do this? To hide something.

"To hide Lily and my husband?"

"Or something else. Perhaps something more sinister. We shall find out. Meanwhile, in the Tower's record I see that they are both alive, if not in peak condition. But we can't get to them." Ordinal raised an eyebrow. Nothing inside that building was reachable. In its little universes there now sat - stood, lay or whatever else they were doing - anything that the grangels were trying to hide. They had copied the Omnium and were using it as a shield. Not a very good shield.

There was something the grangels had not understood. The Omnium and its copies were linked. Under normal circumstances, a change made in a copy would not affect the original, but a change in the original Omnium, at the Lodge, would affect all its copies.

"The original Omnium," Ordinal went on, "is under our control. In theory, all we have to do is turn our Omnium off, and that turns off the grangel copy, and everything in that building will re-appear just like that. Pfft!"

"So let's do it!"

"Not so easy," said Ordinal with a frown. "It's easy enough to change its pipework. Unlock the Omnium and fiddle about. But its spheres… The original Omnium doesn't respond to verbal commands, and it takes an age to reconfigure its spheres. There are all sorts of inter-sea messages to send. We don't have the time. Besides, the Omnium controls the security of the Lodge, and channels through the sea, even some into the primary globe. It's not possible to reconfigure those spheres without interfering with the Omnium's functions. The Housekeeper and Cardinal would have a fit."

"So we're stuck."

"No! The grangels have made an error. It makes me smile." Ordinal clapped his hands. "Typical grangel stupidity. Ingenious, but stupid, because they did not take into account the navigator test."

The navigator test was a special case. Ordinal had to admit that they did not conduct the test often, and he could remember only two navigators who had succeeded - one being the Navigator himself, and the other a navigator who got herself lost in a sea without Time.

But, in their current predicament, there was one detail of the navigator test which mattered. The test required a copy of the Omnium to be made, and that copy - and only that copy - had the power of changing its original at the Lodge. If the spheres of that copy were turned off, that would turn off spheres of the original Omnium, and in turn that would turn off spheres in any other copies, including the replica made by the grangels.

It was the Cardinal's responsibility to prepare the test. His first task was to make a copy of the Omnium. This he would take to Mount Cardinal, where he would expand it to a huge size, big enough for a person to get lost in, perfectly filling the caverns under that mountain. Then, Cardinal and Ordinal would fill it with interesting navigational challenges. The candidate had to navigate through the spheres of this Omnium, through those caverns in the mountain, to find a safe route out. Yes, there were trials and tribulations on the way, and Ordinal wouldn't fancy it himself.

"But this is the clever part..." Ordinal rubbed his head and grinned. "In the navigator test, every time the candidate enters a sphere of the Omnium copy, that same sphere in the original Omnium is turned off. Why? Because that's how, in the Lodge, we keep track of how the candidate is doing. Do you see where I am heading with this?"

Anna frowned, but said, "So... every time Lily moves from one sphere to another, from one cavern of the mountain to another, she turns off a sphere in the original Omnium..."

"And because the grangels' Omnium is linked to the original, it will turn off that sphere in their Omnium too! One by one, the shells covering the rooms of that Hall will vanish. Pfft! Your daughter, your husband, whatever else is in that place, will be visible again, and reachable. What an error by the grangels! I love it."

"But how does she get to the Gate, to start the test? She doesn't even know how to use a key."

Ordinal sniffed, looked up at the rafters then down. "She has Navigator's key," he said. "And its last start location was the Safe Gate. Tell her to shake the key, then tap it four times and pause. That will take her back to where the key was last used."

"But she's only level one. In two places at once. She can't get here and stay long enough."

"Mysul will over-ride that. The navigator test is a special case. Lily will get to the Safe Gate, and the navigator test will start at that point. It's a backwards route, but she will manage it, I'm sure. Are we agreed?"

"It might take hours."

"Not at all. I can fiddle that. What shall we say in glober minutes? Twenty?"

"But what will happen to Lily while she goes through the test?"

"She will be asleep. The grangels will not be able to wake her."

"Then so it must be. If she survives…"

"Anna, you should have more confidence in her." Ordinal laid his hand on Anna's. "Lily is a special child," he said. "I shall arrange the test with Cardinal. Remember, when you next communicate with her, tell her about the test, and tell her to tap the key four times then pause."

Ordinal rose from his seat. "Work to do," he said. "Trust her. Just think what will happen when Lily becomes a level two navigator. It's her destiny. Trust her." With a flap of his spinach-green suit he pushed his way out through the throng and into the Square, where he disappeared around a corner.

40 - The Hotel

The Vicar and Rosemary entered the hotel, to find a room of polished wooden panels and a desk, behind which a small plump man with spectacles was asleep in an armchair, behind him a poster advertising a wrestling contest. On his desk lay a folded card, on which was written, 'Humbert, Proprietor'.

"Hello? Mister Humbert?" the Vicar enquired.

"What? Who's there? Form up! March!" Humbert gripped both arms of his armchair and looked around wildly. Then with a tissue he wiped his forehead and adjusted his spectacles. "Hello," he said. "Are you here for the party?"

"Ummm ... no," the Vicar replied.

"Just as well. It isn't here, and it's finished anyway. It was down the street, in Cardinal's house. You are globers aren't you? Globers often arrive in Cardinal's house and very confusing it is I'm sure. Are you lost?"

"No, Mister Humbert. We are guests, and have been advised to visit your delightful hotel."

"Guests! Crikey. And at the front door too. Normally you globers arrive in a room. Do you want a room? They all have views of the Tower. From the look of you I'd say - primary globe. I visited there once, with the Ordinal. It was filthy. We don't have dirt here. Everything washes itself, eventually."

Rosemary butted in with, "No washing! I am sure that would be stupendous, Mister Humbert, but no. We are not looking for a room, but for... guidance."

"What about?"

The Vicar cleared his throat. "We are unsure, Mister Humbert, whether we should stay or leave your... whatever this is. And if we leave, how we might do that..."

"Were you called?"

"I have a vocation. Is that what you mean?"

"I mean, called by Mysul. Recalled. Are you Roamers?"

Rosemary cheerfully added, "We do like the odd ramble of a Sunday."

"Not Roamers then. You should leave. If you were Roamers you'd have to stay. They're all about to be recalled. I have it on the highest authority."

"Why should we leave?" the Vicar enquired.

"Because, my dear sir," said Humbert, rising from his chair and thumping a fist on his desk, "we are at war! You are better off out of it. Get one of the Five to take you home. No, they're too busy. Anna. Do you know Anna?"

"It was she who sent us your way," the Vicar said.

"Oh. Well she can do it, if someone gives her a key. Go talk to her."

This was all very confusing. There was no sign of War, no aeroplanes in the sky, no booming cannon. Yes, there were military men and women on the streets and in the Recruitment and Training Centre, and there were dark, boiling clouds over the distant mountains, but otherwise all was quiet. The Vicar noticed how quiet, for there were no vehicles to make noise, no dogs to bark, nor cats to screech, no radios, no ticking clocks. There had been a subtle hum as they passed the Council House, as if there were machinery inside, and the people in the Recruitment and Training Centre had been raucous, but apart from that - quiet.

"But hang on a moment," Humbert went on. "You might be useful. I have something to show you." He opened a drawer of his desk and

320

pulled out a stack of leaflets, which he spread out. They were colourful, glossy pamphlets of the kind one might find in a tourist information bureau. "I'd like your opinion," he said. "Is the language correct? Would globers understand this? I ask, because this is what we are going to dish out to the Roamers when they arrive. The Ordinal got them printed at the Art Shop. I don't doubt his judgement, but you are the target audience. I'd like your opinion."

The Vicar picked up one leaflet, and Rosemary picked up another. Each had on it the picture of the cathedral which they had glimpsed from the Square. The Vicar's had a title of '*The Gate - an Introduction*'. Rosemary's was '*Visiting the Tower*'.

'The Gate - an Introduction

Welcome to the Gate, our new residents!

We understand that you might be confused. Where am I? How did I get here? It is not every day that you are transported to a place like this. Let me try to answer your questions.

Who am I?

My name is The Ordinal. I administer your Universe. We call that a 'sea'. It is my job to ensure that your Universe runs smoothly, and I live at the Gate, as do you, now. It is my job to ensure that you settle in, have everything you need, and behave yourselves.'

"What!" The Vicar exclaimed. "It says here that the Ordinal administers the entire Universe! Is he mad?"

"Why say that?" Humbert replied. "Don't you think he's up to it?"

"Well, I don't know ..."

"I can assure you that the Ordinal has the full support of the Grand Council - which consists of the Five and whoever else happens to be in the Council House at the time. They don't always listen to him, but that's democracy for you. He also has numerous staff beavering away on the more mundane tasks - surveillance, for example, or how to handle the collision of galaxies, redirection of gravitational waves, and the repair of black holes. It's a full-time job."

"I don't doubt it."

'How did I get here?

You were recalled. Each of you is a special person, and you have been summoned by Mysul (see below). This place is what we call the Gate, and it is the gateway to other universes, other seas. You might think that the Gate is a huge place but in fact it is tiny, as small as a pea. But its influence is universal, and so in a way it is as big as your Universe. This is a special place, for special people. Your Laws of Physics do not always apply. In other leaflets we will make that more clear.

You have undergone a process which we of the Gate call 'conversion'. Now, you are considerably smaller than a pea. But don't worry. You are still yourself, perhaps even more so. If for some reason you return to your world you will remember this place only as a dream.

You might hear yourself called a 'glober'. That is not an insult, just a term to describe those who have been summoned to the Gate from their own world, their globe. There are seven globes with Life, mostly human, but don't be surprised if you see little stones move of their own accord, and do try not to step on spiders.

On arrival at the Gate you will be issued with a uniform. It is compulsory to wear it at all times.

When you have become acquainted with your living quarters (built for you by residents of the Town) you will be allowed to wander freely. You should find this a pleasant environment. To find out more about it, read the leaflet *'Getting around in the Gate'*. Meanwhile, don't go further than the blue mountain, which we call Mount Cardinal. Beyond that the path becomes extremely dangerous. You might even meet Mercenaries, who randomly might give you a priceless gift or bop you on the head, or perhaps both.

Why?

We are at War. It is not a war you will have heard about. We are facing a primeval force, an enemy of terrifying power which will destroy you, your family, your friends, even your Universe, unless you join us in stopping it. You have had no choice in coming here, but we expect you to do your utmost to counter this threat to everything and everyone you know.

Our enemy is a Great Power, created by the Presence (see the leaflet, *Great Powers*) as the embodiment of Hate, a fearful creature who set out from its home sea on a campaign of mindless but monstrously effective destruction. We call it the Grey Angel. And we call the monsters it commands 'grangels'. Our enemy is now your enemy.

Who is in charge?

The Five, the Constable and the Clerk of Council.

As the Ordinal I am one of the Five. Together we crossed into this sea at its beginning, when it became the marvellous Universe you see today. These are the Five:

Mysul. First of the Five and a Great Power. She designed this sea, so if you have any complaints you can take them up with her. She is usually busy. I will not describe her, because she takes many forms, but if you come across an old lady in a white robe be respectful.

The Ordinal. That is myself, and as the Head of Public Administration I administer this sea. My favourite colour is green, and I too am always busy, but you may find me in the Recruitment and Training Centre (see the leaflet, *Landmarks of the Gate*).

The Cardinal. Does his best to predict the future of the sea, all very mathematical. He likes to present himself as a fashion icon of the near past. Don't ask him why.

The Servator. She keeps the record of this sea in the Great Tower (see the leaflet, *Visiting the Tower*). That record is our most precious possession, and the Servator ensures its accuracy in case we need to roll back or move on. By roll back I mean, go back to the beginning and have another go. If you come across a young woman in a white robe with a hood, black hair and piercing eyes, do not try a joke on her. Not known for a sense of humour.

The Navigator. Currently this post is vacant. He or she is responsible for maintenance of the channels which supply the Tower, for the design of routes between one universe and another, and for the overview of our military strategy. See the leaflet *Our Military Strategy* for details.

Foremost among our other officers are:

The Constable. An excellent military tactician, stuffed to the gills with knowledge of battles of the past. Heads up the Town guards and is in overall command of the army. Look out for a yellow uniform and magnificent whiskers.

The Clerk of Council. An outstanding legal mind, responsible for the wellbeing of the Town and its residents. Also holds tremendous lunches in the Council chamber (See the leaflet, *Food and Drink at the Gate*). Detectable by his golden chain and air of authority.

This is only an Introduction, but the first of many leaflets which I hope you will read. They will help you to settle in, and prepare you for the challenge which lies ahead. Until we meet in person, keep your eyes and ears open and don't forget to breathe.

You are special. Remember that.'

"What do you think?" Humbert asked.

The Vicar put a hand to his head. "The language is colourful, colloquial I suppose. Perhaps something more formal would be better," he said. "But the content is… incredible."

"Is that good?" said Humbert.

"I don't know… Rosemary, what do you think?"

Rosemary was studying the other leaflet. "It's totally mind-boggling," she replied. "I think I'm getting a headache. Just listen to this…"

324

'Visiting the Tower

Wherever you stand in the Town, you will see the Great Tower standing on its hill. It is the high square edifice with the tall grey spire, on the edge of the forest (see the leaflet, *Landmarks of the Gate*).

What is special about the Tower? Everything. Everything is stored inside it, the memory of everything which has existed since the beginning of this sea. The Five (see the leaflet, *The Gate - an Introduction*) brought it with them from their previous sea and used it to populate this one. It was a long, tedious job. Ever had the feeling that you have been somewhere when you know you haven't? That's because you HAVE been there before, in that previous sea.

Anything and anyone who has ever had a memory or a dream has contributed to what is in the Tower. (I gather the first to do that - except for the Five - was some creature called Poodle. All it did was go around in circles, which must have been terribly dull. No doubt it bored itself to death).

The Tower is fed by channels through which memory passes. Those channels are in the control of our Servator. Other channels belong to our Navigator, but as that post temporarily is vacant it is a task which I, the Ordinal, have taken on. You will not see these channels. They are visible only to the Five. What you might see, however, if you are allowed to visit the Tower (this is a privilege granted only by one of the Five), is - anyone, and anything that has ever happened. Our Servator is the expert. Ask her if you want to know how it's done. It is all to do with capture, coding and storage.

Some examples:

How did you come to be? At least through the first meeting of your grandparents. What happened? Did they meet in a bar? Become the barman (or barmaid) and watch them get on with it, whatever it was.

Your favourite poet or other author. Become literally the fly on the wall and watch him or her pen those famous lines. To be or not to be, and so on. Marvellous. (I don't quite grasp the meaning of those words but I am assured they are terrific).

Your favourite historical person. The Sermon on the Mount is very popular. Sadly, you cannot be Jesus, or a multitude of other enlightened souls. Jesus and others are not stored as a person in the Tower, because they required no administration and passed immediately through to the Presence. But, you might become some lowly seller of ice-creams or whatever, and watch.

(Most people of the kind globers call Religious are no trouble. Some, however, are violent, corrupt, liars and in other ways indecent, and those - like other criminals - we oblige to re-live their crimes and punishment over and over again. Our Servator takes a particular pleasure in that.)

The Presence. As I have mentioned it I might as well say what it is. It is everything and everywhere. Wherever anything is, there it is, present. There is no escape from it, so it is just as well that it is usually kind. If you are a religious person, you might call it God. Good things, even the bad things, God. Even the Grey Angel, God. Even you, God. Not one hundred per cent of God. That would be madness. Just a tiny bit of it, at the moment considerably smaller than a pea.

I am sometimes asked whether this place is Heaven. And we are angels. No. We do not flap around with wings and annoy people. Heaven, you say? Golly Moses, yes it is. Oh bum. Did I say that? No I didn't. Someone else did. Heaven? Yes. If Heaven is where you go when you die, yes it is. Everything is stored in the Tower, including you.

Nothing is lost. Remember that.'

Rosemary dropped the leaflet onto Humbert's desk and sighed. "It won't do," she said. "It is too personified. I suggest you need an editor. I would be happy to oblige but sadly my diary is full."

"That bad, eh?" Humbert said. "I feared as much. The trouble with the Ordinal is that he writes as he speaks, and he has a terrible habit of forgetting who he is."

"I don't believe a word of it," said the Vicar. "But I do understand it."

"You do? Well, that's a miracle. Not sure I do," said Humbert. "I leave that sort of thing to Mysul. She knows best. Do you want a room?"

"In my Father's house are many mansions," said the Vicar with a glance at his wife. "No, Mister Humbert. Thank you for the offer, but I am afraid we should be moving on."

"Your loss," said Humbert, slumping back into his seat. "I have the feeling you won't be staying long."

41 - A Minister

Twine sometimes found it difficult to operate in two worlds at once. Nowadays he was hardly ever in the office, but no-one complained. Even projection was tiring, so tiring that he had taken to driving a Service car between London and Malbury, to and fro, as if he were just another glober. But what wore him down most of all was the constant stream of demands by Saida, not least one which she delivered one morning.

"A body," Saida said. "We need a host. For the Minister. I can't work with the bits and pieces we've found so far. I have been scraping away in that basement for days and it won't do. Get me a body."

Twine could not argue. If Saida wanted something, then Twine must get it for her. That was the order of the Lord Commander. He knew only that the Minister, God's Minister, was a weapon. It was a weapon which would be decisive in the war at the Crossway. He had no idea what kind of weapon it was. This was Saida's business.

She had transferred the fragments of this weapon to a room on the top floor of Malbury Hall, hidden from prying eyes by her replica of the Roamers' Omnium. She had done this, so she said, because this was the prime site, the very place where the Minister, uncountable years before, had fallen. In the basement of that Hall, in the well which led deep down into the hill, she had discovered many small fragments which dutifully she scraped away and stored in a vase which she took upstairs. Twine had not been in that room. Others had, he knew, for he had seen them materialise on the gallery outside it - women, the black-clad nuns of Saida's monastery which he had briefly visited. But to him the room was locked.

Now she wanted a body. That body had to be alive and human, though it did not matter what sex it was. All it needed was a working brain in its head, so that it could communicate and

328

understand commands. The rest - health, size and shape, intelligence - mattered not at all. As Saida said, "When I've finished with it, it will be self-correcting, and all it will know will be the power of God."

At first, Twine thought of the girl's father, languishing below in the Hall. That's a body, and on the premises. But he might be useful. The Lord Commander had plans for the girl, and nothing would be so persuasive as the torture of her father in front of her. Instead, he decided he should go looking for missing persons, or if they weren't missing then they soon would be.

People go missing all the time. Twine gave it some thought. At night he walked along London's Strand to examine the tramps lying in their doorways. No good. Tramps in London belong to some sort of community and when one goes missing questions are asked.

The body which Twine chose to go missing belonged to a man who accosted him in the car park at the back of his apartment block. It was late at night, and as Twine bent forward to unlock his car a hand grasped his arm. "You got a quid, mister?" came a voice from behind.

There was menace in that voice. Twine turned, his arm still gripped by what he thought to be a young man, but could not see clearly in the near-darkness. "No," Twine replied.

"Twenty quid then." The man's other arm swept around Twine's shoulders. Twine felt a knife at his throat.

This was straight out of the one-on-one combat manual. Inhale, one arm up, grip the wrist, elbow in the ribs, exhale, turn and whip around. Knee in the groin and a haymaker. The man's head jerked back and he fell back against the next car, smashed his head on a wing mirror and collapsed in an untidy tangle of limbs.

A body. Not much of a body. Thin, and it did not have much by way of clothes, more like rags. He checked the body's pulse. Alive, spark out.

Twine looked around. No-one, which was why he had become a target in the first place. No-one saw him wrap his tie around the man's mouth, lift him, tie his wrists with his own bootlaces, open the boot of the car, tie the man's ankles with the tow-rope, and tip him into it.

*

Twine saw him again only once. Saida was proud and showed him off.

This was a padded cell with a white-foam coating from floor to ceiling. At the corners, the green of the interior shell poked through. The young man sat strapped in a chair, just as two floors below the Roamer girl was strapped to her chair in the basement. But this, this was a madman. He sat, head lolling, a grey gag over his mouth, lank black hair spilling forward, in a white straitjacket tethered to the floor with chains.

"That," said Twine," is the Minister?"

"Needs work," Saida replied. "But already you can see what it can do."

She waved a hand at the walls. The white foam had been gouged by fire, melted in dark brown vertical streaks. "That's why we keep it gagged," she said.

42 - The Last Train

How Anna wanted to take away her daughter's pain, and her fear! How she wished it was she who was trapped there in the dark, helpless, and that her daughter was where she should be, in the sun, at school, growing, happy and safe!

On the floor of the Recruitment and Training Centre Anna made out the outline of her daughter, slumped and exhausted, a grey shadow hunched with knees drawn up. But however positive Anna tried to be, she had to admit that she could not get to her, that there was no way in.

"But there is a way out, Lily," she said. "It is something we call the 'navigator test'."

"A test? Oh no," said Lily. "Is it Maths?"

"No. Listen. There are two levels of navigator, and you are level one, a beginner. I think you know that."

"Yes Mum."

"When you pass the navigator test you will get to level two. That means you're not in two places at once any more, and you can move your whole self from one place to another, with a key. So you'll be able to get yourself out, to somewhere safe."

"But how do I do that, Mum? How do I take the test?"

"First you have to get yourself to the Safe Gate. Have you heard of that?"

"Yes, Mum. I rode Navigator to the Safe Gate."

"You did what?"

"Rode Navigator. The horse that talks. He died, though. Mysul was very sad."

"Oh my baby, you have been busy."

"But I don't want to be busy, Mum. I can't tell you how horrible it's been. Those monsters, having to hold them, having to… I can't say."

"That's over, baby. Our guards have captured the part of the forest that the grangels used for that. There won't be any more monsters."

"I wondered why that stopped. What do I do at the Safe Gate?"

"Find a route to the town. It won't be easy, my darling, but I can't tell you any more about it. You will have to be brave, and keep your wits about you. Promise me you will do that."

"I promise."

"Good. When you pass the test you will have a good chance of getting out. And please try to find Dad too."

"Dad's here?"

"Yes, so Ordinal tells me. We don't see him anywhere else, so he must be there, somewhere. He must have gone looking for you."

"Oh, Dad. No, it's so awful here."

"I know, baby. And that's why we have to get you out, and your father. You will need Navigator's key, and choose a time when the grangels have left you alone. Can you do that?"

"Yes Mum. They're not so interested in me now the monsters have stopped. I can do it at night-time."

"Good. This is what you have to do. If you do it correctly, you will land at the Safe Gate. Then the test will begin. Are you ready?"

"Yes Mum. Tell me."

"When the time comes, get out Navigator's key. Give it a shake. Then do this. Tap it four times quickly, then pause. Can you remember that?"

"Shake. Tap four times and pause. I can remember that, Mum."

"Good. Now back to sleep. Tonight, try it. Remember, be brave, and find a route to the town. Good luck, my darling."

*

Lily could tell when it was night by the time on the soundless TV. She squirmed to get comfortable, but that was difficult. Her hands were free, but she could not loosen the plastic ties around her legs which bit into her skin. Saida came in with cereal in a bowl, so they wanted to keep her alive, but the cereal was horrible, tasteless. She drank some water, then Saida left. She could just hear her and Twine from beyond the plastic shell of the basement. They were arguing. She longed for them to go and leave her alone.

Finally, it was quiet again. There was no Saida, no Twine, no Lord Commander. She was alone in the nearly dark with the grinning puppets which twitched in their cases as if to say Hey, I'm a monster too so Let Me Out so I can Eat You.

It was time. She recited to herself, "Shake. Tap four times and pause."

Before leaving her Dad's shop, with the policewoman waiting, she had tied up her hair bunches, each side into a small bun, leaving tails of blonde hair free. Now, with both hands she began to unravel the right-hand bunch.

Her fingers searched inside it and closed on the coin, Navigator's key hidden in her hair.

Now it lay in the palm of her right hand, the gold coin with its silver star. The room was so dark she could barely see. She had to be so

333

careful. One false tap and she had no idea how to correct her mistake.

She shook the key. Three pinpoints of light appeared on it, two white and one strawberry red. She took a deep breath, then tapped it four times, quickly.

Nothing happened. But then the first light turned green. Then the second. And then the third.

*

Lily was free, on her knees and alone on a hillside.

It was like a fine day in early spring. There was no sun, but a cloudless blue sky. She stood, dropped Navigator's key into the inside pocket of her bomber jacket and took stock.

A breeze blew along the crest of the hillside - rather, of half that crest because behind her was nothing, sheer dark. As the purple of the gate oozed away, Lily Moss dared to poke a finger into the blackness but was met by a solid but invisible wall which blunted her finger-nail.

She could go sideways or downhill. Sideways looked pointless, barren ground on both sides between rocks and bushes stretching away into the far distance. Downhill in the valley, though, by a stream which chuckled over rocks and pebbles, lay something more interesting - an ancient railway line. And far away, beyond the crest of the valley's other side she made out the very tip of a grey spire, the Tower's spire. The town must lie ahead.

She needed a bath and a change of clothes, but reckoned she would get neither, not that it mattered, because the air was sweet, and flapping the arms of her bomber jacket filled her all over with an aroma of roses which was nearly as good as a bath. Without a mirror, though, she could not make a neat job of her hair's untidy bunches, so she unravelled them and let her hair hang down her back.

On the opposite hillside Mysul had appeared from a cloud, but there was no cloud now, no welcoming party. She cupped her hands to her mouth and yelled out, "Hellooo! Hellooo!" No response, only the echo of her voice around the valley. She stamped her boots in the dust and set off downhill, picking her way through rocks and bushes, gorse, and thistles. At the bottom, the valley rose steep on both sides, and the stream was narrow enough to hop ever.

As she approached the railway track, its rails rusty, broken and sticking up like the heads of snakes, the valley grew dark. Night fell in an instant and a yellow moon shot up into a starless black sky. A bell rang, as sonorous as the peal of a church bell, and echoes from the rocks filled her ears. Alarmed, she stepped back to the stream.

Along the valley, the rails of the track began to move, to uncurl. Their rust dropped from them in blotches onto the pebbles of the ballast, and with a rustling and a series of thuds and clicks the sleepers dropped down into line and the rails straightened over them, moonlight glinting along their surfaces. The bell pealed again.

From the far end of the valley came a rumble, then a clattering, then the woof-woof puffing of an engine, a steam engine. A chill breeze swept down from the hillside. Around her, in the shadows of the valley, figures rose from the dust - men, women and children in a crowd, all came up head-first with arms outstretched. Startled, Lily stepped so far back she was almost in the stream. They did not look at her. They did not look at each other. They made no sound. These were human figures, but of the past, white- and brown-faced, clad in rags and the tatters of blue military uniforms and caps, long and voluminous dresses, leather jerkins and cowboy hats, all of them with blank eyes looking only at the track. The rails hummed, and from the distance came the train, its steam in great white clouds billowing up towards the moon.

The train stopped by the crowd, steaming and hissing. Lily had never seen such an engine. It was a creature of iron and silver, with a half-crinoline of iron at its front over the rails, a huge upside-down black cone of a funnel, a long boiler, two small and two large silver wheels and a cab. In that cab stood a man in a black uniform and cap. Behind the engine were three carriages, brown with dirty cream tops. Through the windows and open doors Lily made out paintings on the walls inside, old paintings, portraits of women dressed like the women of the crowd.

The man in the cab yelled, "Last train! All aboard! Calling at Long Sleep, Neerdo Well and Terrr-mee-nuss. Last Train! All aboard!"

Towards the open doors of the carriages the crowd rushed, but without jostling for each figure passed through its neighbour, as they clambered into the carriages and took their seats. Lily was frozen to the spot.

Last train, Mistress!" the man in the cab yelled, but Lily was not moving. Wherever it was heading, this was not her train. She shook her head. The man in the cab faced front, and the train moved away in clouds of steam, rattling, hissing, then picking up speed, until the red light at its rear vanished behind an outcrop of rock. Immediately the rails began to curl, and as the sky lightened Lily could see they were again rusty, and again it was like a fine day in early spring.

She suspected danger either way along the rails, so the only way was forward, and up. This was hard going, and she puffed her way upwards around boulders, through patches of gorse, with the crest of the hillside ahead. There, she hoped the town would be in sight, and there would be food, breakfast at least. She had no money but she had stayed at the hotel before without paying.

At the top, though, there was only the view of a forest, stretching thick and wild ahead and on either side for miles. Through it ran a narrow rutted track, towards a mountain far away in a blue haze with clouds around its peak. The track lay directly ahead. She jumped with a thump onto its dusty ground. Tall trees flanked a path that wound between them and curved away into a mass of greenery. Lily picked herself up, wiped the dust from the arms of her jacket, took a deep breath and strode, chin up and looking around, into the forest.

She rounded a corner under the canopy of trees and came upon a blackberry bush, metres high and all-but covering the path. Here was food of a sort, and Lily stretched out a hand and from its prickles picked off a berry.

"Ouch!" The sound came from deep within the bush. Two eyes as wide as dinner-plates blinked open between its branches. "Excuse meehhh," said the bush. "Are you kindly?"

It was the voice of Ordinal, but reedy as if squeezed through an old-fashioned telephone. Why Ordinal should be hiding in a bush with big eyes Lily could not imagine. "I do hope so, sir," she said.

"Then kindly leave my berries alone. They are for the birds."

"But there are no birds."

"What? Oh bum."

Immediately a black crow flapped out from behind the bush and strutted around on the path. "Waark!" it cried and put its head on one side.

"You can have a berry if you ask nicely," said the bush.

"Please may I have a berry?"

"Don't ask me. Ask nicely."

Lily bent down, peered at the crow and said, "Please Mister Nicely, may I have a berry?" The crow waggled its beak, leapt onto a branch of the bush and pecked off a cluster of berries which fell onto the path. Lily picked them up, wiped away the dust, and tried one. It was delicious, sweet, at the same time refreshing. "But why are you hiding in a bush?" she said.

"I am not hiding, kindly. I am a public bush, in perfect condition. A magnificent example of Public Administration. This path, on the other hand, is very dangerous and I wouldn't go down it if you paid me."

"Why not?"

"Because… it is full of traps and nastiness. In fact, it is so dangerous that it is usually chosen as a test for navigators. Did I say that? No I didn't. Someone else did, not me."

"But does it lead to the town?"

"They all do. But one mistake can be fatal. This is a path with no backward step. Try it, and you'll see."

Lily tried a step backward and came up against something invisible but solid.

"Told you so," said the bush. "Usually people head the other way, but you're going inwards. That's very dangerous, in terms of Public Administration. Can't have just anybody heading inwards, dear me no. They might be mercenaries."

"Mercenaries?"

"Remember to feed the mercenaries," said the bush and it closed its eyes. It was just a bush, hogging the path. "Waark!" cried the crow, and it flapped away into the undergrowth.

It did not look like a dangerous path. There were ruts you could twist an ankle in, but it was otherwise flat, and on either side the trees were so tall and their trunks so thin that there was a view over the undergrowth. If anything nasty approached she would see it above the tangle of grasses and bushes and the odd tree-stump. Lily swiftly picked bunches of blackberries from the bush, which no longer complained, and stuffed them into a pocket of her bomber jacket. They would probably turn to mush, but might make a lunch if she found nothing else. She side-stepped the bush and walked carefully on.

From the edge of the path, for protection she picked up a long and solid stick, a straight metre-long branch with a silvery bark. There was nothing special about it. It did have some shape, though, just thin enough for her to grasp it, smooth, and with ends that were cut square, as if someone at some time had tried to make a staff from it; but they had left it half-finished.

As she walked, from somewhere ahead she heard a tinkling sound, like a glockenspiel. It was the tune of a nursery rhyme. Here the trees grew more thickly, their leafy branches hung lower and the bushes grew up to them. It was like walking through a tube of green, until a circle of blue sky appeared through the overhanging branches, and with that came the sound of rushing water, splashing. Now the tune had words.

Play mobile play mobile

The wolf's at your gate

Play mobile play mobile

It's nearly too late

Play mobile play mobile

She'll eat up your shoe

Play mobile play mobile

And then. She'll. Eat. YOU.

They were the voices of children, but no sign of them. Their voices filled the air, and there were giggles and laughs, and the sounds of feet dashing about, but no sign of whose voices or feet they were. The tune and the words went on, over and over, until Lily came to the bank of a river, where the voices and the tune stopped.

43 - The Game of Nouns

This was a canyon. Upstream, a waterfall gushed in a sheet of foam under a rainbow. Downstream, the river splashed between banks of trees over dark and slippery boulders. Ahead lay a rusty iron bridge, though the track over it was wooden, squares of dark panels. At the side of the track sat a figure facing the waterfall with an expression of distaste. It was a statue of sandy stone, a Pharaoh like those Lily had seen in pictures of Egypt, with his head-dress and beard, sitting squarely on a throne, and it was tall, heavy for so rickety a bridge. She took a step forward.

Suddenly Lily heard a rattling and scraping from below, and figures leapt up from under the bridge, one at the far end, another to her immediate left. They were stick-thin and dressed in black, with hoods over their heads and red sashes at their waists. Each carried a long wooden pole with a sword strapped to its end, which dropped over the rails of the bridge with a clang.

Lily tried to step back but could not, nor could she step forward. The pole lay across and in front of her, waist-high. She looked at the figure on her left but could not see its face. It stood there, silent but breathing heavily.

From the trees at the other end of the bridge another figure emerged. It was made of tubes of brightly coloured plastic, jiggling like a puppet, and its head was a Halloween pumpkin which grinned with pointed teeth. This image, though, faded as the figure walked onto the bridge and up to the pole at the other end, part by part taking on a human form, a tall girl in a camouflage uniform, long blonde hair.

"Martha!" Lily yelled, but the figure stood in silence, hands on hips, glowering. Lily called again, but in reply she heard a very different voice.

"Loser dies. No shouters. No sapping. Any piece wins. Play!"

340

Again it was a voice like the Ordinal's but deeper, and it came from the statue. At this cue, the black figures raised their poles. Martha stepped forward. At her feet the wooden panels of the bridge's track took on a darker colour, then black. At Lily's feet, the panels turned to a line of blood-red. Beyond them, outlined in black, stretched a pattern of grey panels eight long by six wide, the style of game-board she had seen in India, for the Game of Nouns.

On both sides of Martha, small black globes rose from the surface of the track, each waving a claw. Lily recognised them, the creatures which Saida had called spikers. They crowded around Martha's feet, claws clacking. By her own feet Lily felt other figures rise, and she looked down. They were human in miniature, male and female interspersed, brightly coloured plaster models, and with a gasp Lily recognised them - models of her father and her mother.

"Bottle!" Martha shouted.

The Game of Nouns. Lily had not played it. She had seen it, understood it only partly, and she had seen Martha win, but now she was playing for her life. Death by spiker, death by the swords of the black figures, death by drowning, death lay on all sides. She was not going to play this game, and tried to step to the bridge's rail but she was trapped on the blood-red line, no escape.

She laid her stick by her feet and with a sigh of resignation whispered, "Three, forward three," then called out, "Castle!" From Martha's crowd of spikers, one on the far left bounced forward onto the first square and rotated, waving its claw. A figure of Lily's mother moved onto the third square of the third file.

"Tree!" cried Martha. Lily tried to remember how Michael had played this game, but she was not going to risk herself on that board. She whispered, "Five, forward two," and cried, "Meat!" Martha herself stepped three squares forward on the fourth file. A figure of Lily's mother moved onto the second square of the fifth file.

"Lampshade!"

341

Lily whispered, "Six, forward left one", and called out, "Cricket!" A spiker hopped onto the second square of Martha's second file. A figure of Lily's father moved onto the first square of the fifth file.

"Wall!"

Lily whispered "One, forward right one," and called out, "Star!"

Martha had made a mistake. That was unlike her. Not that she showed it, because she stood in the middle of the board, still glowering, though the spikers at her back began to rotate in an agitated manner.

Lily coughed to clear her throat. "Castles have walls," she called out, "and how about ten green bottles hanging on a wall."

"Agreed," the statue boomed. On Martha's side, nothing moved. A figure of Lily's father moved onto the first square of the second file.

"Dress!"

Lily whispered "Two, forward right two," and called out, "Wheel!" A spiker rotated onto the second square of Martha's fifth file. A figure of Lily's mother moved onto the second square of the third file.

"Crow!"

Lily whispered "Two, right forward two," and called out, "Matchbox!" A spiker bounced onto the first square of Martha's sixth file. The figure of Lily's mother moved to the fourth square of the fourth file. Martha was going for a long slant, but if she did, she herself would be lost. Martha herself now had to move. It came into Lily's mind that this was a tactic of battle - force enemies to do something they would rather not.

"Music!"

Lily whispered "Three, forward three," and called out, "Brigadier!" Martha moved one square to the right, to the third square of the fifth file. Lily's forces were now moving up the board, and this move was a killer, driving into the space Martha had left in the middle of

342

the board. The figure of her father moved from the third square of the third file to the sixth. At the far end of the bridge, the black figure began to turn his pole.

"Table!"

Lily whispered "Three, forward three," and called out, "Wolf!"

Martha's spiker moved to the square where her father's figure had stood, but that was already gone, onto the black line at the end where it proudly squashed a spiker which exploded in a fountain of black slime. Any piece wins.

Lily had won.

The black figures advanced on the figure of Martha, brandishing their poles. As the slice of the first sword hit her shoulder the jiggling puppet returned. No longer Martha, the plastic tubes of its body were shattered with blow after blow from the swords, and the pumpkin head severed and kicked into the river. Whirling around, the black figures sliced at the spikers, which collapsed like trodden grapes into a purple mush that sank between the panels of the bridge and into the waters below. The plaster models of her mother and father vanished in puffs of smoke.

The black figures advanced on Lily, but put up their poles. "Do you have food for us?" said one.

"For food, we will give you a power," said the other.

"We are hungry," said both, and each extended a hand.

Breathing heavily, Lily tried to return to her senses. The effort of the game, the concentration it required, had exhausted her and she needed food herself. In her pocket were blackberries. She pulled out those which had not melted and placed a berry in the hand of each of the black figures. Then she gulped down two berries herself.

"Thank you, Mistress," said one, and he pulled back his hood. He was an old man, white-haired, brown-faced and with an oriental cast to his face. Greedily he chewed on the berry then extended his hand for another. His companion likewise removed his hood, and was the twin of the other, not least in asking for more. Lily gave them both another berry.

"In return," said the first, "we ask you to remember what you have seen. The way to deal with a spiker is to stand well away and slice it."

"The way to deal with a white rider," said the other, "is to remove its head, by any means."

"The way to deal with a hoverfly," said the first, "is to cut its wings."

"Your strategy was adequate," said the other, "but your enemy was foolish, and in future you should look to your wings. They are good for attack as well as to defend. Look to your wings, young wolf."

"We shall meet again," said the first. "But now, we give you this. In memory of us." He rummaged in his sash and pulled out a curved knife, white but with a brown handle wrapped in a strip of leather. "From the claw of the great white wolf," he said. "She died not at the hands of a hunter, nor in battle, but only of age. This is the sharpest blade in the Gate. It will cut off a man's head with a single stroke. From one wolf to another." He handed the knife to Lily, who held it gently in the palm of her hand and nodded.

"War is no game, Mistress," said the second. "And we do not understand why you are summoned to it. You are young, and small. Your enemy cannot be defeated, and even we mercenaries might turn away. But, you have great powers at your back. Listen to them. Now we bless you, and hope that you will survive your journey."

They stood aside. Lily mumbled her thanks, picked up her stick and walked forward onto the further bank. She turned to wave, but the mercenaries had gone. Only the statue stood on the bridge, staring at the waterfall with a smile.

*

344

On through the trees she tramped, as the ground on either side grew more rocky, the forest thinner, and the path took an upward turn. Except for the patter of her boots in the dust, there was quiet. The air was still. Somewhere beyond the mountain the war was real, and she was walking towards it. The Tower, the town, the Grey Angel, what she had seen in dreams lay on the other side. Here, all that was real was the forest, the dust of the path, and the knife she held in her pocket with Navigator's key. Anyone with any sense would turn and run, but she did not want to take a backward step. They called her a wolf. With the knife in her hand she could slash at the face of the Grey Angel till it burst. The hoverflies were annoying mosquitoes whose wings had to be cut. The corpses were meat. The spikers, gravy.

She was hungry. The blackberries were gone, and the red berries on the bushes looked poisonous. Every so often she glimpsed the crow hopping in and out of the bushes, keeping its eye on her. Otherwise, there was no life in the forest. But as the path rose and began to twist and turn, until it became more of a climb than a walk, she became aware of a throbbing in the ground, the pulse of a distant motor.

What story had they told her friends, to explain why she was not at school? How was Swan? And her new friends, Theo and little Chun, was it Friday? Should she be at the Lodge? Was she followed?

She looked around quickly, but nothing leapt from a rock, nothing poked its head out from the cracks in the mountain which now loomed above her, great slabs of blue stone that reared upward into a swirl of frothy cloud. There were cruel monsters in that other world, and they came from here, cruel monsters who would torture a little girl, who looked human but were devils, and what could she do with one little knife? How she wished she knew more about keys, for all she remembered was to tap it four times and pause. If it worked at all, that would take her back to the House Over-There or to the Safe Gate, which would be useless, for she knew that her route lay ahead, and there was no turning back.

Now above the tree-tops, she rounded a hairpin bend in the path and came to a platform of sandy rock, under a ledge dripping water from its bushes. She let some fall in her hand, and sniffed. She drank a handful. Refreshed, she paced forward to where the path stopped, ahead of her a sheer drop onto boulders, but to her left a fissure in the rock, the mouth of a cave. Here the throb of a motor was louder, and air brushed over her face and tossed the leaves of the bushes. The air was warm, stale with an odour of socks. Somewhere in there, in the dark, something was pumping out stale air, for ventilation.

The only way forward was into the mountain. Slowly, holding her stick before her, she took a step into the dark.

44 - The Art of a Master

Inside the mountain, light came from thousands of tiny bugs which marched in rows along white seams in the walls leaving a trail of luminous slime, first on the walls of the breezy tunnel down which Lily trod, and then in the cavern.

The mountain was hollow. The cavern at its centre was immense, hundreds of metres high and wide, its floor dusty and strewn with fragments of blue stone. Iridescent watery shapes, oblongs, cubes, cavorted through it, each sparkling in the dim light, each bearing a long string of multi-coloured numbers, letters and squiggles which Lily guessed were mathematical but to her meant nothing. Some shapes carried pictures, which bent with the bending of the shapes, brightly coloured forests, monkeys, sky-scrapers and seas, pillars of sand, all writhing in the air and even passing through her, intangible and soundless.

As she took a step from the tunnel's mouth, a hissing grew around her and she stepped aside, looking for snakes. But with that sound everything in the cavern, the myriad shapes, pictures, letters and numbers, drew together into a column of glass that reached high up into the cavern's roof.

From above came a cry, "Join me!" Lily looked up. "Who are you?" she cried. "You'll see!" came the reply. "How?" she yelled. "Knock on the door!" At the bottom of the glass column a doorway appeared, an iron-studded door in a frame of wood. Lily paced over to the door and knocked. "Knock harder! Try again!" came the cry. She knocked harder, so hard that she felt a splinter in her knuckles. "Come in!"

She walked into a classroom of the Lodge. It was Cardinal's room. She looked back, and there at the end of a tube of rock was the cavern. She looked ahead, and saw Cardinal standing before his blackboard, still in his tie-dye shirt and flares, as the door squeaked shut behind her.

"Ah, Lily Moss," said Cardinal. "Doing well, I see."

"I don't know, sir," she replied. "It's all very odd."

"Is it? Oh dear. We try to make everything familiar. Perhaps we have included too much of someone else's expectations. Do I look normal?"

"I suppose you do sir. But it wasn't normal to get here from there."

"Oh, my mountain. It's where I predict. That's what I do." He flipped a golden coin from his hand and caught it in his teeth, then let it drop back into his hand. "Probabilities are my speciality. I rate them from zero to 1. It was a point-six probability that you would get here, but that is now a certainty."

"Yes it is, sir. I suppose."

"You rightly ignored the train. If you'd hopped on that you would have gone to the Tower, and that would be the end of you. Garbage collection, our Servator calls it, which shows little respect for the wandering souls that train picks up. And then you had your experience on the bridge. Did the mercenaries give you anything?"

"They did, sir. A knife, made from the claw of a wolf."

Cardinal laughed. "Ha! That Ordinal, he ruins my calculations every day. I had it as point-eight that knife would not turn up for a thousand of your years. Take a seat. Oh, I don't have one. But I do have this…" With a wave of his hand there appeared in the air the sculpture from Navigation class, the network of spheres and pipes all in a translucent egg, the Omnium. "Remember that?" he said and raised an eyebrow.

"Yes I do sir."

"This is only a copy, but no less beautiful. Do you remember it? Every connection between every part? I reflect on it continually. It is the art of a master, whom I suppose you would call God." He

348

studied the sculpture. "The art of a master," he repeated. "All bound up in this perfect shape. Hold it in your mind. You are going to need it, young wolf."

"I am?"

"Because when you step out of here - and you see now that there is a close connection between the Lodge and the Gate. What do you call the Gate?"

"Roamers Cross."

"I like that name. Inaccurate, but I suppose it's familiar to you. Anyhow, when you step out of here, you will find yourself at one end of that shape, and you will have to find your way out. Usually this is the first step of a navigator's test. But you - you are doing the whole thing backwards, so we will have to make it extra hard. I rate it as a point-nine probability that you will not reach the town, because there is too much in your way."

"We will see about that, sir." Lily blinked, capturing the image of the Omnium in her mind.

"Bravo! You're turning into quite the little warrior. But be careful. If you fail, you will die in the middle of a heap of rock, and then it's off to the Tower with you. That would be sad, but you're only one more human being after all. And don't try using any keys. They're frozen, on my order. Are you ready?"

Lily forced the view of the Omnium into her memory. "Yes sir," she replied.

"Then I shall revise my prediction to a point-eight. Off you go. Look for a cave on the right."

*

The mouth of the cave was round, leading down into a tunnel of black stone lit by the bugs that left white shiny streaks over the walls. Lily poked her stick at the cobwebs, which wrapped around it, and she scraped them off on a rock. Tiny spiders scurried away into dark corners. Cautiously she stepped forward then followed a path of dust downwards, her breathing and the patter of her feet echoing from the walls that curved close to her head, in the air a smell like seaweed.

Ahead, a watery green light grew brighter as she descended, until she arrived at a sharp right-turn, and a spherical cavern whose surface was entirely green, with algae that hung down, and fronds of fern over a curving floor. This was a sea, she knew - a representation of it - the sea which was her Universe, Sphere Six. In the cavern's walls three round port-holes and another in its ceiling were covered by round wooden lids, bolted down. On her immediate left a port-hole was open. From what Lily remembered of Navigation class and the Omnium, that port-hole would lead to Sphere Seven, a safe route. Grasping at the wall she climbed up to the mouth of the port-hole.

Beyond lay a tunnel of opaque and featureless green plastic lit evenly along its length. Into the tunnel she stepped, and walked over the curve of its floor towards its other end, a darker green port-hole.

*

It happened in the blink of an eye. At one moment Riley Moss lay on the mat above a floor of waxy plastic, the impenetrable shell that trapped him in the ballroom of the Hall. It was night, and moonlight through the windows was a sickly green. Then with a bump he and his mat landed on the boards of the floor. The moonlight was white. The shell had gone. He stood. All was quiet. There was no barrier between him and the windows. As quietly as the Vicar's boots would allow Riley stepped over the floor.

The frame of the casement window was rotten, its wood falling apart in his fingers, flakes of white paint falling to the floor. The catch was stuck but it was a matter of a moment, quietly, to pull it up and away from the rotten wood. Gently he levered the half-window up, until there was a gap large enough to slide through.

How sweet the night air was, moist but clean.

He was out.

45 - The Lodge falls

Hearing a patter of feet outside her door, which appeared to come from Ablutions, the Housekeeper of the Lodge jumped down from her high chair and landed on the stones of the floor with a thud. Classes were underway. Students were supposed to hold in whatever was inside them until end of class, except in the direst emergency. She adjusted her woolly hat, stepped to her door, opened it, and strode into the hall, to see only the legs of a boy who hared up the staircase as if pursued by devils.

Something was not correct. She knew that some of the students - particularly Robert and Klaus - were of a nervous disposition, which is probably why their parents were glad to see the back of them; and she hoped that the too-frequent calls to Ablutions were due to the sensitivity of their bladders rather than some failure in the food which she provided. It was always difficult to ferry supplies for the Lodge through its barrier. Everything and everyone who came through that barrier had to undergo checks and transformations which - though instantaneous - sometimes had unwanted effects. Nothing in the Lodge's menu, for example, ever contained spinach, and even the milk occasionally was off when it arrived.

Beside her the Omnium hissed gently on its stand. This was the something which was not correct. The fifteen spheres and their translucent shell were in place, but something had changed in the pipework which bound the spheres together. The Housekeeper could not make out what had happened, but something was out of place.

This demanded a call to one of the Five. Ordinal was in the town, and busy. Only Cardinal would respond, for as usual he was doing nothing underneath his mountain. The Housekeeper returned to her cell, and pressed a button underneath her desk.

In seconds, Cardinal appeared. "An emergency?" he said.

"I don't know," the Housekeeper replied. "There's something wrong with the Omnium."

She and the Cardinal returned to the hall. The Cardinal peered at the Omnium. "I think," he said, "a pipe has moved, down there. Sphere Six is turned off, and that is correct. We are in the middle of a navigator test after all. But there, between spheres Six and Five, there has been a fractional movement of the pipe, and it has gone red."

"That's it!" cried the Housekeeper. "That's what's wrong. It should be white, and it's red."

"Do you have the key?"

The Housekeeper's eyes widened. It had been so long since she had used it. "I… am sure I do…" she said, and stomped back to her cell, returning in a few moments to find Cardinal still peering at the mischievous red pipe. "The key… has gone!" she said.

"Gone?"

"Yes." The Housekeeper was a stranger to Shame, and did not like the feeling of it.

"Then it may be unlocked," Cardinal said, and he laid a hand on the outer shell, which did not budge. "No, it's locked. I hope you realise, Housekeeper, that the security of the Lodge depends on the Omnium, and it seems to me that for once you have let yourself down. Not to mention the rest of us."

The Housekeeper looked down, as do those climbing the scaffold of a guillotine.

"This is exceptionally dangerous," Cardinal went on. "I will have to call the Ordinal. The point of access to the Lodge has moved. And our barrier is down."

*

In his office, atop the platform by his observation window, the Clerk banged another nail in the ceiling and stepped back. He needed a carpenter for this. Above his head, planks wobbled and could at any moment crash to the floor taking their lights with them. His difficulty was - all the carpenters were in the Tower making essential repairs. He could see why. The Grey One had launched a monstrous crowd of shellflies at the Tower, and they swarmed by the thousand from the clouds and down through the trees, bubbles of light directed by their inhuman occupants, massed in lines that swept around like the hands of a clock, at each pass clipping the Tower's spire.

Mysul and an aerial battalion were fully occupied, rising above the maelstrom, white robes flapping, skybolts flashing from their staves onto their enemy's spies. As the Clerk watched, a dark shape came to rest on the sill of one of the Tower's mullioned windows. Inside its shell, the twist of black smoke formed into a toad, with talons, with which it broke its shell and clawed at the wooden slats of the window in fury. Splinters flew from the toad's talons as it struck again at the window, but with a flash filling the screen a skybolt struck and the toad blew apart, returning to smoke which drifted up the Tower's wall and vanished.

"I really, really need a carpenter," the Clerk mumbled, and banged in another nail.

*

At that moment, behind fences of barbed wire where signs declared 'Danger of Death' and 'MoD Property Keep Out', a line of container trucks waited. The site was high up in England's South Downs, a disused Ministry of Defence establishment, overgrown, weeds filling the gaps in its concrete tracks, wind whistling through lines of rusty Nissen huts. It was late evening but still warm after a hot day, and none of the trucks showed a light.

A spy satellite or anyone on the distant road who passed this barren location would see nothing suspicious. In the cab of the lead truck sat a man in a dark-grey suit, bald and grey-faced, beside the driver, a younger man, blonde-haired and with eyes intently peering ahead. It should also not be surprising that the trucks behind were driven by women, all in a body-hugging black uniform.

Nor was it suspicious that - ahead of the lead truck - a mist appeared, turning to a thin line of fog. So high up, as the evening cooled, a sudden fog hereabouts would be natural.

What was unusual was that as the trucks, one by one, drove forward into the slim bank of fog, not one of them appeared on its other side.

*

Truck after truck disgorged its contents onto the drive which led to the Lodge. Hoverflies rose in the air and dispersed in waves of buzzing wings and fire-tubes which dangled, straightened and fired into the building, smashing its sculptures, breaking its windows and walls, bringing down its cornices and its roof.

On either side of the drive cockroach-like insects formed up in circles, and into their bodies the corpses of white riders sprang and were absorbed, waiting while at the front armoured troops of the Black Army advanced. They came on swiftly in a solid square, lines of heavily armoured giants. Where there were railings, they crushed and trod over them.

In a show of defiance, the mechanicals - led by the Housekeeper - drew back their bows and let loose volley after volley of arrows up into the air in a swarm of black pins which descended upon the advancing enemy, but bounced off armour into the fields around the Lodge. Behind them, the Lodge was on fire, from the blasts of skybolts delivered in a constant stream by featureless black drones which circled high above. But nothing could withstand the Black Army, and the mechanicals ran.

Everyone ran. The Housekeeper swiftly gathered her flock and followed Cardinal through the hall and up to his classroom on what remained of the first floor, where the students had gathered in a frenzy of alarm. They crowded around Cardinal's blackboard. In it a circle of yellow vapour swirled.

"Carefully now," Cardinal said, as beyond his window the battlements of the Lodge crashed down into the gardens. "One by one, as quickly as you can."

One by one the students passed head-first through Cardinal's blackboard, followed by what remained of the mechanicals, the Housekeeper at the rear. Only Robert and Klaus held back.

With a flick of Cardinal's fingers, the Omnium appeared from the hall, and hovered in front of the blackboard. The Omnium was large, and though gravity-free it would fit only awkwardly into the hole in the blackboard. Cardinal pushed at it. He turned it. He stepped through the blackboard, extended an arm and began to pull it. "Klaus!" he said, "Push it! Now!" But Klaus still held back, and pushed Robert forward. With a pull and now a push the Omnium slipped through the hole. Robert struggled to get through the hole after it, and he wriggled as the folds of his fat squeezed against the sides of the dwindling gap.

"Klaus! Quickly!" Cardinal yelled.

Whether it was through fear or shock, Klaus stood stock-still against the far wall.

"Klaus, now!" cried Cardinal.

Heavy boots trod on the stairs below. Cardinal's last view of the Lodge was of Klaus turning to face the doorway, behind him a bald man in a dark-grey suit and two giants in black armour.

Klaus and the man in the grey suit smiled at each other.

*

Cardinal's channel between the Lodge and his mountain was short, but the passages which led off it were confusing to anyone but him.

Gravity now affected the Omnium, and as he pulled it along the rock-cut corridor students and mechanicals emerged from the passages, all confused, all with expressions of alarm, and followed.

They arrived in Cardinal's chamber in the heart of his mountain. With a wave of his hand Cardinal dispelled the mathematical shapes which had filled the chamber, and had made most of the arrivals duck or throw themselves flat into the dust of the floor. Behind him a swirl of yellow smoke dwindled to nothing. Cardinal addressed the Housekeeper as she picked herself up from the dust. "Get yourself into the town," he said, "and your mechanicals. It is a point-nine probability we will need them all."

The Housekeeper nodded, and through the throng of students the mechanicals glided towards her. They held hands in a circle. The Housekeeper lowered her head, and she and the mechanicals faded away, leaving the students and Cardinal in the dim light of the chamber.

"You have all just passed through a channel, without the comfort of going to sleep," Cardinal said, looking around at the students. "Does anyone feel ill?"

Robert put up a hand. "I do," he said. "I feel sick. And hungry."

"Unusual combination. But you are lucky to be alive," Cardinal said. "My problem is how to get you out. You're not mechanicals. You're physical creatures, from the globe. From here, I can't carry you out. And you won't want to go back through the channel. It won't take them long to find that their end of the channel is open, and then they will be upon us. There are many passages inside this mountain which they might take. I estimate at point-nine that we are safe here for only a few moments."

"Where is Klaus?" Martha asked.

The students peered around.

"He didn't make it," said Robert. "He's always slow."

The silence in the chamber was disturbed only by the hissing of the Omnium. Students looked at each other with grim faces. Robert seemed the least concerned, but in the eyes of the others was sadness, and fear at the thought of what might have happened to one of them at the hands of the Black Army.

"From what I just saw," Cardinal said, "Klaus will not be joining us. Klaus has joined our enemy."

"Traitor!" little Chun hissed.

"It seems so," said Cardinal, nodding. "A great disappointment."

"I knew it," said Robert. "I was keeping an eye on him all the time. I knew it."

"There is no going back," said Cardinal with a new urgency. "There are two routes out of here - one into the forest, where you will get lost, and the other towards the town. That is where you will go. But it's unlikely you will survive. I predict at point-seven that without help none of you will make it."

Martha put up a hand. "So what can we do?" she said.

Cardinal steepled his hands under his chin and rested two forefingers on his lips. His eyes drifted upward then from side to side. "You won't like it," he said.

"Excuse me, sir," Martha went on. "But if it saves our lives…"

Cardinal put his head on one side. "It might," he said. "That depends on Lily Moss."

Martha jerked back her head. "Lily Moss?" she said. "That little girl who's only just arrived? What does she know?"

"It's not what she knows, Martha," Cardinal said. "It's what she is."

"I knew it!" piped up little Chun. "She's special."

"Mysul's her sponsor," said Theo.

"I don't like her," Robert said. "She's too thin. In Singapore we had a word for girls like her - hockey-stick."

Cardinal pursed his lips, but said, "So who will go first? Who thinks Lily Moss can get you out of here?"

Three hands shot up, those of Chun and Theo, and that of a taller boy. As he did so, Martha glared at him, for it was Michael.

46 - A Gathering of Wolves

Lily began to think this would be easy. If the route involved no choices, and she needed only to balance on curved floors without spraining an ankle, it would take no time at all.

Then she saw the wolf.

In the port-hole at the tunnel's end, the black-tipped brush of a grey tail wagged up and down then disappeared. Then a snout poked out, and a light-grey muzzle, and the wolf's head, a darker grey with slanting yellow eyes. Its body followed, and it sat on its haunches in the middle of the tunnel's mouth, head tilted, with a curious smile. The wolf was small, a puppy, but there were sharp teeth behind that smile.

Lily stopped. She took a deep breath. It was only a sort of dog. She took the wolf's-claw knife from the pocket of her bomber jacket, and walked on, holding her stick in front of her. The wolf backed off, lowering its head but curling its body so that its yellow eyes still looked directly at her. As she reached the end of the tunnel, the wolf looked away, whimpered and darted off into the undergrowth.

There was no telling what else was in here. Again this was a green chamber, but of darker rock and with a breeze that rippled with an animal stink over tall bushes and long grass. Light came faintly from the ceiling and a hissing of air from its port-hole. She clambered down into the mass of bushes and parted the grasses with her stick. The port-holes were open, and she had to choose.

It was more a feeling than a thought. She had to get to the centre. The exit must lie below, at the mountain's base, for - since she had left the cavern - everything tended downwards. But she remembered from the Omnium that the sea below was unsafe. The safe route to the centre, to Sphere One, was over a path to the right.

She skirted the edge of the cavern and set off up a curving path to the right. Behind her she heard rustling in the undergrowth. She turned and held out her stick but saw only waving grass. The port-hole had a rim of black stone, but led to a tunnel again of opaque green plastic. She climbed into it and walked on.

Half-way along, she heard steps behind her. She turned and there sat the wolf, blinking. "Shoo!" she yelled, and waved her stick, but it looked at her as if she were an idiot. She walked on, with the patter of the wolf's claws behind her, to the mouth of the tunnel.

*

Riley Moss slipped through the window, as quietly as he could. He stood in moonlight in a bramble bush, which was a nuisance, but better that than trapped. He could run, but no. Lily was here, and she would be somewhere below, was his guess, in a basement room, the basement which was hidden, secret.

Something was turning these shells off. Someone somewhere was on his side. Anna.

Gently he levered himself out of the bush, crouched, and wormed his way around the side of the Hall.

There was a way in, somewhere.

*

Lily looked out over an entire town which lay at the centre of this maze, in a spherical cavern larger and very different. Brick buildings, with pavements and cobbled streets in the canyons between them, and chimneys which belched out wreaths of smoke, smaller houses around the walls with pitched roofs and windows stained black; these were the back-streets of an old industrial port, all beneath a white sky, all with an odour of coal fires and drains. Lily wrinkled her nose. Port-holes were everywhere, all open. Some buildings rose up to them, some with flat roofs offered platforms to get into them around the walls. The most direct route lay straight ahead, through this mini-town to the next sea, and then down.

"Oh!" she cried, as she felt something rub against a leg of her jeans. It was the wolf, and it curled around her leg, looking up at her and blinking. No biting, no growling, it rubbed its grey head against her leg and looked up as if gazing with love at someone who would feed it. "I don't have any food," she said.

Immediately the wolf jumped down from the port-hole and scampered away into a shadowy canyon between buildings with a yellow sign of 'Peabody'. Lily stepped down onto a cobbled street infested with weeds and set off in the direction that she took to be ahead, between the Peabody buildings. There was a crackling of fires and a ticking of clocks, and in the distance the blast of a foghorn. Water dripped onto her head from broken gutters as she paced along an alley which smelled of fish.

Windows and doors were boarded-up. She was alone in an abandoned town, except for the wolf. It came bounding in from a side-street with what looked like a thick rope between its jaws, and it squatted in front of her. Sausages, with blackened skins. She was so hungry she could eat them all, but with a soothing word to the wolf she tucked her stick under one arm, and with a stroke of her knife sliced one sausage from the string. The wolf looked happy, for its yellow eyes went wide and with the other sausages in its jaws it purred like a cat, rose up, and bounded away. Munching on the sausage, Lily walked on and saw the wolf playing with the sausages in a side alley, jerking them up, smashing them against a brick wall, then gulping down the rest of the string.

She came to a crossroads. In every street there was a mist, which rolled down from the roofs and brought with it a bad-egg smell. Four brown-brick buildings stood on the corners, so tall their tops must reach the ceiling of the cavern, their galleries of black-framed windows shut, but their wooden doors at ground level open. Lily stepped around the shell of a dried-up concrete fountain and headed onwards over the cobbles, all sound muffled by the descending mist, until she heard from far away a howl, the howl of the wolf.

She paused, and looked behind. Too late, she saw in the corner of her eye a flash of white from an open door.

A white body, feet thumping, arms outstretched, naked, man or woman she could not tell, threw itself at her, and knocked her through a doorway. Her stick fell from her hand as she landed on her back in a cloud of dust, above her the empty shell of a brick building.

Before she could recover it was on her, a bald white head with red eyes that stared, folds of white fat, arms like hard rubber that gripped her waist, pulled her up and then down, a body lying on her, flat on the floor, the face inches from her own, mindless, savage, the face of a living corpse. It rolled its red eyes. It opened its mouth, sharp teeth behind sulphurous red lips. It raised its head, ready to bury those teeth in Lily's neck.

But its head jerked back, with a squeak of surprise. Over its shoulder Lily saw the head of the wolf, its fangs deep into the creature's neck. The white body reared back, arms flailing.

Lily's right arm was free. She slashed her knife across the monster's throat. A torrent of white slime spouted from its neck over the floor by Lily's head. She slashed again, and the head came away from the spine, dropped, and rolled into a corner trailing slime. On top of her the body twitched and she pushed it off with a squeal of disgust.

Standing up and breathing hard, Lily saw the wolf nuzzling at the creature's limbs. Brushing dust from her jacket, she took a step away from this nightmare, bent down and retrieved her stick.

If she had been looking where she was going she might have noticed the swirl of dust behind her. Instantly she was gripped by something which froze her body and carried her upwards, up past boarded-up windows, brick walls and black beams, up and further up, faster through hissing air, up through a black hole in a white ceiling, and dropped her like a sack of rubbish on a rocky island in the middle of a blue sea.

*

Riley Moss took care to crouch below the windows as he passed. Around one corner of the Hall he searched for a way in, then along the back. The French windows were a challenge. He had to lie flat on a plinth of concrete and squirm over to them, where he jammed himself against the wooden panel under the glass of the door, raised an arm and tried the door-handle. The glass door opened a fraction but stopped. He closed the door with a click. Blocked.

He was about to squirm away when he felt vibrations from the door. Footsteps, which stopped inside the French windows. Someone was looking out. Over the garden the moon shed a pale light, and a breeze wafted through the long grass. Moss lay buried in shadow under the door. He lay still. Only when the footsteps carried on and then down the stairs to the kitchen did he dare to squirm further over the plinth to the path. At the next corner he stood and looked up. The drainpipes were too weak to carry him. Around the next side, he approached the window of the basement kitchen.

There was light in it, faint but enough to steer him away behind the outhouses, through brambles and nettles, then back onto the path towards the front of the house. He was not going to cross the front, for that was asking for trouble, so he retreated back along the path, behind the outhouses and into the jungle of the garden, where he stood in a tree's shadow and looked up at the house. There must be a way in. Lily was there. Somewhere, Lily was there.

*

Lily dusted herself off. She was bruised but clear-headed and glad to be alive, in paradise.

The sky of the cavern was a cloudless blue, palm trees waving in a gentle breeze over ripples of a dark sea that washed onto the sand of the beach. Behind her, rocks reared up in a pile like a miniature volcano, and behind them on the horizon shone a red sun. It was warm, and tropical flowers in bunches sprung up between the rocks, with a perfume in the air which reminded Lily of how her Dad smelled after a shave. But that was no sun. It revolved like a wheel with a black rim, tongues of flame shooting from it. Lily had seen no port-hole like it, and it was not one she would choose.

She looked around for other exits. She had been pulled off-course, and in this expanse of water where was the route down? She calculated that she must navigate away from the red sun, but as she scanned the horizon she saw nothing but dark water, merging into the sky at some impossible distance.

As she looked over the sea she heard a scrabbling in the rocks behind, and she turned. High up against the skyline, silhouetted against the red sun, the head of an animal poked out from behind a rock. It was a wolf, a full-grown animal which emerged, stretched, raised its head and sniffed the air. It looked down at her. Picking its way cautiously between the bushes, but keeping its eyes on Lily, the wolf came down and leapt onto the sand. It was a male and the size of a small donkey, a wide-chested grey body with a lighter snout and under-belly.

Its ears pricked up. At first it stood quietly, but menace grew in its yellow eyes, as it wrinkled its snout and bared its fangs in the grimace of a predator. Lily held out her stick and cried, "Shoo!" but it did not shoo. It sniffed. Its head shifted from side to side and its claws bit into the sand. She stepped back, with the foam of the sea washing over her feet.

A howl came from the rock-pile and the wolf raised its head. Another wolf surfaced at the skyline. Lily guessed this was a female, for it was smaller, its limbs more elegant, and it made its way down through the rocks with a more precise step until it trotted out onto the sand to meet the male. They nuzzled, and swung around play-fighting for a moment, then sat back on their haunches and scratched. They looked at each other. They looked at Lily, and rose up, heads forward, eyes narrowed. Lily stepped further back, till ripples covered the ankles of her boots. She held out her stick, but the wolves parted, the male swinging to the right, the female to the left, and slowly each paced forward over the sand, red tongues hanging out between white fangs, drawing closer. Lily pulled out her knife and the wolves paused, but on they came until both were close and ready to spring.

A howl and yapping noises came from the rock-pile. The wolves turned and looked up. As if floating on the crest of a fountain a third wolf, the puppy, shot up in the air then fell back between the rocks with a scrabbling and a yelp. The female wolf ran across the sand and leapt back into the rocks, while the male took his eyes off Lily, sat on the sand and nibbled his tail.

Down came the female, and behind her the puppy. It bounded across the sand and ignoring its elders dashed into the foam where it began to rub itself around Lily's legs. Lily stepped further back and felt the wash of the sea on her boots, but the puppy looked up, blinked and had only love in its eyes.

The other wolves approached, heads down but this time with a swish of their tails, and they dashed past her into the water, the puppy setting off after them. Lily turned. The three wolves scampered over the sea with the barest splash. Lily stepped forward into the sea. Under the ripples the sand was firm and shelved steeply ahead, but when by rights they should be swimming the wolves danced over the surface of the sea.

Lily dared to take a step forward, so that her legs should now be a foot deep in water, but the ripples rose no higher than her ankles. She stood on some solid but transparent floor. Ahead, the wolves were dancing, merrily splashing around in a circle. Still with a firm grip on her stick, Lily paced forward over the sea's surface, until she stood close but at a safe distance. She saw what they were dancing around, and with their frenetic splashes enlarging, a whirlpool.

Into a meters-wide dark hole the water was pouring, funnelled down in a torrent of sparkling foam which hissed and every so often sent up plumes of white spray. Around it the wolves danced, leaping, snorting, and chasing, until the male stopped, calmly walked towards the hole, and leapt into it. After him went the puppy and then the female, leaving Lily alone on the sea's surface.

They had guided her to a port-hole which led down. There was no telling whether she could survive the drop, or whether something waited for her down there which it would be beyond her power to overcome. Her chances were low, as Cardinal had warned. With a series of deep breaths she stepped forward, till her feet were on a circle of rock underwater, ahead of her the revolving torrent. She stepped into darkness.

*

This was not falling, more like a descent in an elevator so rapid it brought her insides up to her throat and made her breathless. Walls of rock flashed past, water splashing around them. In seconds she passed from dark to light, green light, the light of another sea of tropical foliage and brown swamps through which she almost fell into another downward tube where her speed increased, and then into a muddy yellow light where she landed with a splash in a pool of chocolate.

It was a bomb crater. White bones stuck up from footprints in the mud which stretched up to a rim of dark earth. The smell was of a farmyard, under a yellow sky where trails of flame and vapour shot overhead with the roar and then the crash of a meteor. At first she thought she was alone, until a head popped up above the rim, the head of the wolf puppy, its head on one side as if to say Why don't you play with me?

Lily climbed up the bank of the crater, slowly, slipping. At the top, her view was of a brown field stretching into the distance, carpeted with flattened stalks of hay around muddy puddles. There was a creaking and a clunk, as wooden lids fastened over port-holes in the side walls and behind her in the crater, except for one, ahead and far away. As there had been at the beginning of this maze, there was only one way out.

The adult wolves lay flat in the field, asleep. Their puppy bounded up to Lily, wrapped itself around her legs then scampered down into the field where it began to gnaw at the hay. Lily slid down and as her boots landed on the soft earth of the field she heard a howl from behind the crater.

The wolves jumped up, sniffed the air and wagged their tails. Around the crater a pack of wolves, eight of them, trotted into the field. They were of all sizes but the same grey breed, and in meeting the other wolves they set off a mad bout of sniffing, tail-wagging, rolling, jumping and play-fighting, with the puppy dashing about and nipping at its seniors' legs. From the other side came a further pack of wolves, who joined in with such energy that Lily could not make out one wolf from another in the maelstrom of grey furry bodies. They took no notice of Lily, who stood in the field, perplexed.

Soon, though, the madness subsided. The first male, largest by far, detached himself from the pack, and head down trotted towards Lily, but when he was very close he turned. He jumped back, his hind quarters bulging into Lily's legs with such power that in a second she toppled over him and found herself astride his back, legs lifted from the field. With her stick she prodded at the ground to keep her balance but when the wolf began to move forward and she felt herself tipping into the mud she grasped the wiry fur at the back of its neck.

The wolf set off at speed, with Lily clinging to it, legs dangling and her stick tucked under one arm. "Whoah!" she cried, but the wolf sped on regardless, leaping through tufts of grass, on either side the thud, the splashing and the raucous gasps of other wolves.

After some moments of this chase Lily felt bold enough to lift her head to see that her wolf and the others were speeding towards the open port-hole in the distance, in front of it a mound of earth. She dared to sit up. Though the ride was bumpy, though she lurched from side to side, though hay-stalks slashed at her face, it began to be enjoyable, even exhilarating, with the massive body of the wolf beneath her, its muscles pumping, her hair streaming back, and on either side the other wolves trailing behind. They were a pack, and astride the male it came to her that she - and he - were its leaders.

She twisted the fur of her wolf's neck and he swerved to the left. Behind, the other wolves followed. She twisted it to the right and the pack swerved right. She dared to take one hand from the wolf's neck and held up her stick, jamming her knees into the wolf's ribs. Immediately her wolf and the others came to a halt, so sudden that

368

Lily was jolted forward and nearly ended up in a puddle. She recovered her balance and pointed the stick forward.

Howling, the wolves lurched off again, directly ahead. This was hunting, this was a cavalry charge, and at the end of it there would be a feast, of flesh, of blood, but only if they worked together and the pack followed. She held out her stick horizontally to the left and the wolves on the left all came up into a line, breathing hard. She switched her stick to her right hand and the wolves on the right all came up into line. Now all the wolves were dashing forward in a single line abreast. She pointed her stick behind her to the right and the wolves on that side fell back into a trailing line. She did that on the left side with the same effect. Now she and her wolf were the tip of an arrow-head aimed at the mound of earth ahead. Even the puppy was there, at the end of the right-hand line, vigorously striving to keep up.

She extended her arm to the left and thrust out her stick, vertically. The wolves to the left moved out as one to the left. She pulled her stick back and they came back into line. She tried the same manoeuvre to the right and the wolves on the right moved together out further to the right, and then back as she brought the stick back to her chest.

Leaning forward, Lily dared even to take her hand from the wolf's neck. She steered with her knees. She cried out, not with words but a howl, of delight, of power, as the pack thundered on across the field like a grey arrow under the yellow sky.

That sky was changing. Its trails of fire and vapour came lower by degrees. With the fizz of an angry wasp a stone on fire whizzed past Lily's ear. She lowered her stick and the wolves halted in two lines trailing behind her. They sniffed, they splashed paws into the mud, their blood was up and they were eager to dash forward, mouths gaping, snouts pointing at the mound of earth ahead.

A trail of vapour shot from beyond that mound and another fiery stone whizzed past her as she ducked. Something beyond the mound was targeting her. She pointed her stick down and forward. The pack advanced, slowly, until they were a few dozen metres from the mound, when a fusillade of red-hot stones shot across the mound's grassy top towards Lily's head. Lily fell from her wolf into the mud to avoid them and they fizzed away into the distance, landing with a splash behind her, but the wolves carried on until Lily waggled her stick downwards and they came to a halt at the base of the mound. Lily squirmed over the soggy ground to meet them. Whatever was beyond this mound of muddy earth could not see her now, neither could she see it. A rain of stones shot up, and fell just behind the pack, steaming in the mud.

With the wolves pawing at the ground behind her, Lily squirmed up the mound. First she saw the rim of an open port-hole in the yellow wall, with a tube of opaque green plastic leading to yet another sea.

Then, in the split-second in which she dared to lift her head above the grass, there was horror.

Insects with human faces. Creatures of her nightmare. Back down the mound she slid, gasping, as another volley of flaming stones shot high in the air, landing with a roar only just behind the pack.

She knew them now, insects grown to monstrous size, metres long, with the appearance of a cockroach, feelers waving over the shine of their black shells as they rose on thin jointed legs, flexed their jaws and clawed at the air. Between their jaws a gaping hole flamed and smoked, the mouth from which the stones, the cannon-shot, must have come. There were five or six of them. Lily could not be sure.

But the horror came not from the insects, terrifying though they were, but from what lay inside them; for these insect-machines were guided by human corpses, naked, the very same breed as the creature which had thrown itself at her in the town of the central sea. Their lower halves protected by the insects' shells, each lay flat along its host's back with arms buried in the insect body, its head up, hairless, its face fixed in a grimace, red eyes staring ahead.

What was their strength? The savage curling jaws, and the shots that came from their mouths. What was their weakness? The legs of these creatures were weak, and the backs and heads of the riders were exposed. She could not do this alone. The pack had to overcome them to reach the next and last sea. Lily fetched the knife from her pocket and clutched it in her left hand.

She paused. She breathed. She remembered what the mercenaries had said to her. She looked at the wolves. They looked at her. This was her battalion of wolves, her people. She turned, and drew a deep breath. Standing in the lee of the mound, she held up her stick vertically. She howled, and thrust her stick to the right. Immediately, the lead male and the wolves to the right dashed around the right-hand flank of the mound.

Such a tumult of growling, snapping, howling and explosions of vapour resulted that Lily could hope only that the insects had turned, open to attack from the rear. Switching hands, she raised her stick vertically and thrust it to the left. The other wolves dashed around the left-hand flank of the mound. Lily crouched and approached the grass of the top. The insects had turned. They faced her right wing. Their cannon-shot was useless, for now this was a battle at close quarters and any shot would pass above the heads of the wolves; but the cruel jaws and the sheer weight of the insects would have been weapons in themselves had not the wolves been so agile, darting between the insects, snapping at their legs, crunching, and leaping onto the backs of the riders.

Around came her left wing, attacking from the rear. They leapt onto the backs of the insects, burying their fangs into the riders, clinging to the white flesh and overbalancing them, toppling them over. Lily dashed down the mound into the fray. A crippled insect came down. She slashed at its rider's neck and its white head rolled off into the mud. Flaming stones shot up uselessly from the insect's mouth and landed behind her on the mound. Then another and another, cutting, slashing, bodies of insects crumpling, their riders spilling into the mud and decapitated by Lily or by a wolf.

Within minutes, bodies of insects lay twitching on the earth. The carcasses of white riders lay headless, wolves gnawing at them, tearing, feasting on their flesh. Lily squatted on the ground. She inspected her troops. All were safe. Even the puppy was busy gnawing at the arm of a rider. She watched as her wolves stalked from carcass to carcass, sniffing, each wolf different, but each one of her pack. She looked at her knife, and at her hand, both drenched in a white slime, which she wiped off on the grass of the mound, and slid the knife back into her jacket's pocket.

Suddenly she was tired. This was no place for her, with horror on every side. She had strength which she had not expected, but it was wearing off, and the exhilaration of the moment had passed. She lay back on the mound and tried to calm her breathing.

This must be the lowest level of the maze. Ahead through the porthole lay the third sea. In there must lie an exit, at the mountain's base. At every step the route became more difficult, but none of her wolves must suffer, especially the puppy, which scampered up the mound and licked at her ear. That was disgusting. The little tongue which moments before had before been sucking on a corpse was now slobbering over one side of her head. She sat up, and wiped her ear with a sleeve of her jacket.

As she did so, she saw the carapace of an insect fall apart on the ground.

She had an idea. She would armour her wolves. Slowly she trod through the carnage, the puppy at her heels. From the mud she picked up the remains of the carapace. It had fallen into two parts, and she picked up the smaller. Jet-black and as shiny as mirror, it had the feel of metal. She tried it on the puppy's back. Too big. The puppy looked up in wonder, turned, and gnawed at the new toy, or tried to, for its fangs failed to make the slightest scratch in it. It shook itself and the would-be armour fell off. No string, Lily had only her belt or boot-laces to tie it on, and those she was not giving up.

The larger fragment, though, might fit her. It was about the size of her torso, and it curved into two hooks which might fit over her shoulders. She picked it up and tried it on. It slipped off. Then she tried it over her back. That was better, for the hooks held it in place, and its base fitted at her waist. She had armour at her back, just like a cockroach. It was a pity she could not do the same for her wolves, but something was better than nothing.

It was time to move on. She raised her stick and howled. The wolves looked up. She strode forward and tilted her stick forward, kicking aside the dismembered carcasses of insects and riders.

With no obvious regret at leaving their dinner, the wolves fell into line behind her, the first male at the front. Together they climbed a muddy bank to the port-hole, and then into the green tube, the wolves' paws clacking on the bare plastic. Ahead, a yellow light filtered through the trunks of trees.

As she approached the tube's end Lily saw that they were entering a wood, of tall trees with thin trunks but a canopy of branches overhead. She stepped out onto a carpet of dead leaves, sensing no danger.

47 - The Black Army

At first it was an easy path. Lily shuffled over a carpet of leaves with the wolves spread out on either side, snuffling around tree-trunks and leaving their scent, but soon the path took an upward turn to the crest of a hill. Overhead, the tree canopy was thick and green, but the sky was a dull yellow and ahead clouds of smoke rose in the damp-smelling air.

As she reached the crest she lowered her stick, and the wolves halted in their tracks, sniffing. Below, the tree-line ended abruptly as the hill led down to a dusty plain, scarred by ravines and ditches, and on that plain a sight which struck her first with wonder but then with a fearful hopelessness.

Across the plain spread a black army, a seething mass of dark bodies in squares which shifted from side to side, floating metres above the ground and passing over each other in a slow and sinister rhythm.

High above hovered giant mosquitoes, dozens of them, such as she had ferried into the House Over-There. Lily narrowed her eyes. In squares at the rear rippled carpets of bulbous and shiny black heads squashed together, trailing tentacles and stingers as if they were jellyfish but with saucer-eyes. Around them jostled insects of a terrifying size, cockroaches, feelers waving, and hoppers made for jumping for they had powerful backwards-jointed legs, scaly spines and heads which were all feelers and claws; but none could jump because each was intertwined with its neighbour, woven into line upon line of black scales and snapping heads.

From the tubes which hung down from the mosquitoes came flashes of light that struck at the hoppers, which lurched away and took the rest of their square with them. Like the lasers of a stadium light-show the mosquitoes' beams flickered at all angles over the mass of black, and whatever they hit they scalded. Only the jellyfish escaped the attention of these insect shepherds. Even the cockroaches received an occasional misdirected blast, but to no effect. When by some mischance a light-flash missed its target, a plume of black smoke erupted from the ground, rising to join the clouds which swirled overhead. And there was more, in the clouds. Hard to see but slowly moving, black airships circled, box-shaped and featureless, as if up there watchful eyes inspected the parade.

At first sight, the front squares were less sinister, because their components appeared to be human. Each square was a grid, racks of giants in black armour from head to toe, as stiff as metal. Intermittently one would wave a lance and utter a guttural cry. Lily could hear them from here. As if they were toys they were strapped to thick metal rods attached to their backs, which clicked alternately from side to side taking a line of giants with them. From this distance they might be more amusing than dangerous, the figures of a table-football game, but each of those figures was a heavyweight, as Lily could see from the dust which rose from their boots and from their gouging of the earth in a slow, mechanical rhythm which was hypnotic and far from human.

There could be no way through, and no way back. In the far distance a triangle of daylight drew her eye. It must be the way out, the end. But silhouetted against it a figure stood on a sloping mound. Human, hard to make out, probably a man, tiny at this distance. Friend or foe, there was no telling.

One mosquito detached itself from the parade. It rose above the others, its tube dangling, and headed at speed directly towards the hill-top and Lily. She gestured with her stick for the wolves to fall back into two lines behind her. On came the mosquito until it hovered at the edge of the tree-line, then began to flit from side to side, frustrated, with a buzzing like wasps trapped in a jar. It lifted its tube and fired through the branches. The light-beam hit the ground metres in front of Lily, into a pile of leaves which smouldered but were too damp to catch fire. The mosquito fired again, and this time only scorched the bark of a tree in front of her. Its movements became frantic. Lily watched with her fear mounting and took shelter sideways behind a tree, peering out as the mosquito rose and fell, searching for an angle, until in desperation it launched itself into the tree canopy, smashing through its branches, landing on the path with a crash and a shower of leaves, and stood, pulsing.

It was a giant but it had a weakness. She had known that since she rode these beasts into the House Over-There. Its fire-tube hung down. It could not fire sideways or ahead, and its legs were thin - but there was a sting under its fire-tube which could be deadly. Slowly its head shifted from side to side and its wings fluttered. It took a step forward, until its body was level with the tree where Lily hid. It could see her wolves, in two lines stretching back into the trees. It took another step forward. Lily pulled the knife from her jacket pocket.

She leapt, onto the mosquito's back. She rode it as she had ridden them before, and as it bucked beneath her she hacked at the wing-joints. The knife sliced them as through the tenderest plant-stem. Unbalanced, the mosquito toppled to one side as its wings fell onto the path.

With a final slash, Lily severed the beast's head as she tumbled into the leaves. The head rolled along the path, and from its now-uplifted tube came a last blast of burning light which struck at a tree beside the path. Down came the tree, its branches flailing.

As Lily picked herself up from the debris of the path, a branch struck her as it and then she fell.

*

"Mum? I've been hit."

"Oh God."

"Can you see me?"

"You're lying down. Your head, it's bleeding. Wait."

Anna froze in her seat in the Recruitment and Training Centre.

"Is there a problem?" said the Vicar.

Lily lay unmoving on the boards of a floor. She saw only chair-legs and the under-side of a wooden table. "Mum," she said, "am I dead?"

"No, baby," Anna replied. "If you were, you would be in the Tower and we couldn't speak. What hit you?"

"A tree. A branch fell on me."

"You're fading. You must be waking up."

"Yes. It hurts. I suppose that's a good thing. But I'm stuck, Mum. Can't go on. There's too much in the way."

"Whatever it is, go around it, or above or below. You're the navigator."

"Yes Mum."

*

Riley Moss studied the rear of the Hall in moonlight. There must be a way in, a back door, a tradesman's entrance. All old houses have a tradesman's entrance. To the right, the outhouses and the path were clear. Nothing there. To the left, brambles and a stunted tree shadowed the building's corner, a mass of foliage through which he and Lily had forced a path on their first evening at the Hall.

Moss edged through the shadows of the trees until he stood within a few metres of the building's corner. In the moonlight, the foliage around it looked thick and prickly. He crouched, and wriggled through wet grass until his head ran into a bramble branch that scratched his scalp. Stifling a groan, he peered into the foliage but saw nothing. He stretched out an arm. The earth was soft and wet, but his fingers closed on a hard edge. He ran his fingers along it. It felt like a step.

He snapped off low-lying twigs of bramble, which lacerated his fingers with scratches he could feel but not see. He slid forward. It

377

was a step, which led to another. Wedged under the bramble bush, Moss levered himself up. Brambles tugged at his back, then snapped or swished away. With one hand on the trunk of the stunted tree he pulled himself around, and felt his feet on the step. Trampling the foliage as quietly as he could he stepped down, into a branch which slashed at his throat, and he swallowed hard to stop himself from crying out.

Ahead, part of the wall was lighter than the black stone around it, and it had dark vertical panels. A door.

*

Lily opened her eyes and blinked, looking up at the yellow sky. She propped herself up on one elbow. On the path she was lying with a tree branch at her side and her cockroach armour sticking up from a pile of leaves. Flames licked around the stump of the tree hit by the mosquito's final burst of fire. Her wolves had gathered on the path and looked at her as if unsure whether to comfort or eat her.

The smell of damp earth filled her nostrils and the pain from her head and shoulders came on with a jolt. She lifted a hand to the side of her head and it came back with blood, from a gash over her right ear. It stung and she gasped. But she was lucky. Only one branch of the tree had hit her, with a glancing blow. She tried to stand and failed, but took a deep breath and wobbled to her feet. The carcass of the mosquito twitched on the path. She picked up the cockroach armour and slung it over her back.

So close, but now with an army against her. Valiant though her wolves had been against a handful of the enemy, she could not expect them or herself to take on hundreds of these creatures. She picked up her stick and planted it vertically into the soft earth of the path. At this, the wolves as one lay down, then rolled over on their sides. Some appeared instantly to be asleep, others gnawed at their claws. She turned towards the plain, where the black army manoeuvred. There was no way around. Their squares drifted from

378

side to side, right up to the curving walls of this cavern. There was no way above. The only way was below.

Long and straggly lines of shadow were etched deep into the surface of the plain, ditches and deeper ravines, clefts of whatever rock lay beneath. Some were short, but others stretched into the distance. If one was long enough, and deep enough to provide cover, then there was the route, perilous with the black squares above it, mosquitoes and watchful eyes overhead.

There seemed no alternative, but few ravines reached to her hill. One to the right looked long and deep, but it was far away. Closer, one to the left stretched in a series of zig-zags as far as she could see, but it looked overgrown, strewn with boulders and patches of impenetrable darkness. It would be hard going. She had never been more tired, and her legs trembled. Her head throbbed and she wanted only to sleep, but sleep would not come while there was danger ahead.

Time to move. The wolves leapt to attention when she took her stick from the ground, and then it was a shuffle through the trees until she came to a slope which led down into a gully. The surface was slippery with leaves, and she slid down, her wolves following pell-mell behind her. As she turned towards the plain, the slopes of the gully became a cleft between walls of rock, ten or more metres high, at its base a winding track of sand and pebbles through which trickled a ribbon of water. She led the way, the wolves in line behind her.

Above her towered the vertical grey rock of the ravine. In a daze she clambered over and around boulders, through rotting vegetation, with her feet sinking into a watery ooze along the ravine's floor. She knew that they had to be as silent as spies in the night, and the wolves knew too. Something in the gloom infected even their spirits, and they made hardly any sound as they padded in a line behind her, quietly sniffing and with heads down.

When she came to a corner, she peered around to inspect the second leg of the zig-zag. As she cautiously stepped around the corner she felt a vibration through her feet, rising up from the ooze, a thud repeated, a drum-beat. A deeper shadow descended, and in fear she and the wolves looked up. Slowly a black square passed overhead, tentacles of its jellyfish trailing over and disturbing sand and pebbles which cascaded down the walls in a haze of dust. Lily and her wolves froze as it passed and passed back.

Breathing as softly as she could, Lily walked on. To her right the mouth of a cave opened and she dared to peer inside. In the distance, dimly lit, lay lines of boxes with translucent sides and the shape of coffins. As she watched, from one of the coffins rose the body of a mosquito, which shook itself, unfolded its wings and rose upwards and out of sight. They were breeding, these creatures, here under Cardinal's mountain, and in every passing moment more of them would be above and around her, and in her way.

She walked on, stumbling at the next corner then freezing as pebbles tumbled with tiny splashes into a puddle. No reaction from above, though her heart was pumping wildly. She turned the corner, the wolves behind her with their tails down, slipping over the pebbles. Ahead, a boulder all-but blocked the path. As quietly as she could, Lily manoeuvred her way around it, then looked back to see that the wolves could safely clamber through.

"Lily Moss."

In the shadow of the boulder stood a man. The wolves backed off, eyeing him but with heads and tails down. She heard, "Lily Moss" again, but his lips did not move. She felt his words in her mind.

He was almost a skeleton, dressed in dark-blue rags, with an untidy mop of black hair. Cold and sadness came from him in waves, that depressed Lily's spirit, that would send her to sleep and into the deepest nightmare unless she resisted. She resisted. She lifted her chin and formed in her mind the words, "Who are you?"

"Join us," came the reply. She recognised that voice, from the House Over-There, from the well of the cellar, the guttural growl of a man impossibly old. He took a step forward and the wolves began to whimper. He took a further step and now, in the light, Lily could see a black aura around him, like the outline of a cartoon figure, which twinkled and pulsed.

Suddenly his right arm jerked forward, fingers clawing at the air. In another voice, softer and desperate, he whispered, "Help me. Please. Before it's too late. I am in a coffin. It has a number, on the glass. Go back. Go back to the coffins. My number is ten thousand and eight. No, seven. No, six…"

"I can't go back," said Lily.

"She can't go back." The first voice returned. "Roamer scum. What use is she? None. Be quiet, damn you. In a few thousand beats of God's heart you will be gone and I shall be ready. Lily Moss, do you hear? There is no escape. Save yourself. Join us."

"No."

"No? You say No… to God's Minister? Then be damned. I should bring the Army down on your head here and now, but it is not mine to command. Not yet. Soon." He raised his head. His eyes were dark pools, seemingly without pupils. "I have despatched one navigator and you will be the second. Your time is… close." He nodded, as his figure shrank to a ball of inky black, and vanished.

Where he had stood, the wolves paced around, sniffing. The puppy wolf cocked its leg over the spot and left its scent, which was both uplifting and macabre.

Lily breathed hard. Whatever it was, this Minister, who spoke with two voices as if one were trapped inside the other, it could not hurt her now. Above her head there were hundreds of others who could do that. It was a ghost, an illusion, something planted down here to guard the passage, to frighten off, but it would not work. She frowned and tried to release her tension quietly. With a determined jab of her stick into the sandy ground she turned and walked on.

*

Riley Moss ran a hand over the door. Rotten, flakes of wood fell off through his fingers. Gently he pushed at it, but it did not move. He felt further down and there was a lock. This could be a door which led nowhere, or it might be blocked by a plastic shell. He snapped off a straight twig and pushed it into the lock. It passed through, more than six inches, no shell there.

He had to break it open. What lay inside? Somewhere, Twine with a pistol, and probably others. It would be insane to make such a racket. Lily might be somewhere else. But he would never know unless he broke down that door. Into his mind came echoes of years before, Army basic training. Be alert. Stay low. Use what's lying around. Move fast. The element of surprise.

Moss leaned back, and kicked with a grunt and all his strength at the lock of the door. The wood around it burst into splinters. Suddenly he was back in Belfast, breaking down the back door of a pub where an IRA bomber was telling stories to his pals. He kicked again, and the wood of half the door splintered. A feeble flickering light shone through. He crouched. Something was in the way, a stack of wooden boxes. He kicked at them and they fell with a clatter onto a floor.

He pulled himself through. She was here. Slumped in a chair with her back turned to him, Lily was here. Small basement room, crammed with junk, a television, an open door. Puppets in glass cases, could break the glass and probably sever an artery. A mad place and she was here alone. He crouched and edged forward. Behind her chair he peered around. She was breathing. His eyes swept the room. His ears - footsteps, running.

Swiftly he took up a position by the wall to the left of the door, a metal bucket at his feet. He crouched under the television. Empty though it was, that bucket smelt rank. The footsteps stopped, outside. Through the open door poked the barrel of a pistol, at the level of Moss's head.

"Moss. Show yourself." It was Twine. From above Moss's head the light of the television played over his daughter's face. "Moss," Twine snarled, "Game over. Show yourself or I kill her now."

Moss swept the bucket in an arc upwards at the pistol, and beyond, at the hand that held it and the face behind the gun. A shot into the ceiling and plaster rained down. The pistol fell to the floor. Moss lunged at Twine waist-high and threw him back onto the stone of the cellar floor where his head hit the floor with a crack. Twine lay still.

More footsteps, and through the doorway of Capstick's cinema Moss saw Saida, her face ghastly pale. She held a hand to her mouth, and vanished on the spot as if switched off.

Now the only sound was that of water gushing in the rife below the cellar floor, and of Twine's laboured breathing. Moss dashed back to Lily, who grunted as if emerging from a deep sleep. Her arms were free but her legs were strapped to the legs of the chair with plastic ties.

Moss swung the bucket into the case of the sailor puppet, smashing its glass into fragments on the floor, as the puppet twitched and grinned at him. Carefully he picked up a dagger-length fragment of glass. He crouched at his daughter's feet. Looking up, he saw a gash over her right ear, bleeding. Not deep, a flesh wound with the beginnings of a bruise. The glass dagger was sharp. The ties fell apart at the merest touch of it. Gently he took hold of Lily and lifted her from the chair.

*

The end was close.

Daylight filtered into the ravine, and its floor began to lead upward. As Lily trudged on, she saw more of the mound of earth that rose at the exit, and then the human figure at its top. But it was not alive. It was a statue, the statue of a grey man, his right arm raised and the index finger of his hand pointing up. It was the Lord Commander, Chatham the goblin, surveying the plain where his troops manoeuvred. Statue though he was, the fear of him made her break into a run at the side of the mound, pointing her stick forward, her wolves passing her in their eagerness to get out. She ran, they ran, but as the triangle of daylight loomed ahead of her, suddenly she felt a blast at her back that knocked her to the ground. She looked over her shoulder. From behind, a mosquito fired another blast of burning light, which struck the cockroach armour on Lily's back and glanced off into the mound, making a black and smoking hole.

It was as if strong arms had picked her up, for she felt herself flying towards the triangle of daylight. Another blast came but missed. Daylight was metres away. She swerved to left and right but no further blasts came. She threw herself at the light, rolling and tumbling over the ground.

She was out.

Lily blinked, and rose from the dusty platform of rock on the mountain-side. Relief came to her in a series of shudders which made her breathless. Ahead, a path ran down the mountain between trees and green fields. She looked around. Her wolves sat on their haunches in a circle around her, patiently waiting.

The puppy wolf trotted forward and licked Lily's hand. It looked up with yellow eyes, but in a second those eyes were brown. The puppy began to grow, rising on two legs, its tail shrinking. As its fur vanished the flesh of its body grew and Lily made out the pattern of a camouflage uniform. The head took on human features - black hair, and the broad, smiling face of little Chun, from the Lodge.

Around the circle the same transformation occurred. From the body of the first female wolf Martha emerged. From the first male wolf, which she had ridden in the cavalry charge, came Michael. The others followed, until Lily was surrounded by the students of the Lodge, her wolves.

Little Chun stepped back. "Our Navigator," she said, and bowed her head.

*

Riley Moss held Lily in his arms as he pushed himself backwards out through the broken door and through the bramble bush, towards the moonlight.

"Chun," Lily mumbled.

Moss thought of the quickest way back to safety, the main road. Maybe flag down a car. At least it was public. He would have to carry her. But he kept to the shadows, creeping around the forecourt's edge as Lily began to wriggle in his arms. He avoided the gate but stepped over a broken-down stone wall into the undergrowth at the side of the avenue of whispering trees.

"Dad," Lily said. "You can put me down."

He let her slip from his arms, and she stood, wobbled, fell against him then breathed deeply and opened her eyes. "Dad," she said. "Oh Dad."

"Steady, my darling," Moss said. "No time for that now. We have to get moving. Can you walk?"

"Yes."

"Then let's go. Try to be quiet."

They walked at the edge of the avenue between the trees. On through the shadows, with moonlight flecking the tops of poplars and pines, they stepped carefully to avoid snapping twigs by the side of the rutted track which led to the main road.

Ahead, Lily saw a light beyond a bank of bushes. Friend or foe? They paused, but the light vanished. There were rustlings in the undergrowth as the track turned down the hillside, the main road not in sight.

In a flash, a dark-haired figure in a purple sari appeared on the track some yards ahead of them, her back towards them. She held a lantern whose light spilled along the track. Lily grasped her father's arm. "Saida," she whispered. "A grangel."

"I know. How the Hell did she get there?"

"She can get anywhere."

Saida turned, saw them, and vanished.

The next second, the flash of light came from behind. Moss turned, but too slowly. With a swing of her arm Saida brought her lantern crashing down on the side of his skull, knocking him to the ground, where he groaned and in horror Lily saw his eyes close. Saida stretched out her thin arm, in her hand a kitchen knife. "Come with me, Lily Moss," she said. "I have a new place for you. A safe place."

Lily stepped back. The lantern's light was yellow and from below picked out the creases in the old woman's skin. Lily fumbled in her pocket and pulled out the wolf's claw knife. "One more step," she said, "and I cut you open."

"A Roamer knife?" Saida smiled. "What a prize. You can do what you like, darling. I'm not really here." Saida vanished and re-appeared some paces away. "See?" she said. "But I'm as solid as you darling when I need to be. Do you like climbing trees? I can climb trees." She vanished, and re-appeared sitting on a branch above Lily's head.

Lily reached again into her pocket, and brought out Navigator's key. "What's this?" hissed Saida from above. "Another Roamer toy? Looks like a jewel. I love jewels. You may have noticed…"

Lily dropped it. The key slipped through her fingers into a nest of leaves. The angle of Saida's light changed and Lily knew she must have jumped down. "Give me that," grunted Saida, striding forward.

But in the light from Saida's lantern Lily saw the key. She bent down and retrieved it. Quickly, she tapped the key four times then grasped her father's arm. One key-light turned green, and then the second. The pause was long enough for Saida to bare her teeth and thrust her face within inches of Lily's own. The third key-light turned green. As Saida's face melted into a mist of rainbows, Lily Moss was no longer in two places at once.

She chose Roamer's Cross.

48 - Two Mothers

Lily expected to land at the base of the mountain, where she had left her wolves, the students of the Lodge. But as she spiralled towards Roamers Cross, grasping her father's arm, she felt a tug at her other arm. In a whirl of pin-point white lights which flashed around them she was pulled off course, not in a vicious way, not as if it were Saida trying to cling to her, but in a kindly way, gentle but firm.

At first the place where she landed seemed to be entirely blue, but then she realised she was on all fours, her hands sinking into the plushness of a blue carpet. At her side, her father groaned, lifted his head and said, "What hit me?" He struggled to his feet.

"A lantern," Lily replied. "Saida." Lily stood, wobbled and blinked at her father.

"Much more of this and my head will drop off. Where are we?" said her Dad. Lily rolled her eyes and shrugged. She turned, and saw Mysul.

The chamber of the Gate's Council spread around them, its stone walls perforated by arching windows which gave out over the town and the distant Tower. From the back of the chamber semi-circular tiers of wooden seats, in the style of an ancient Greek theatre, led down to the circle of carpet where a long table stood under a navy-blue drapery with a pattern of fifteen globes in a circle.

At the table stood Mysul. "I wanted to be here, at this moment," she said.

This was not the immortal Mysul of the Council and the Court, the grim mistress of Roamers Cross, but the Meizel of Swivelhurst School, an old lady in a beige twin-set, and a double string of white pearls. Her hair was grey and tied-back into an elaborate bun, her eyes twinkled, violet-blue. Her skin as tight as parchment seemed to emit a pale and gentle light.

From behind her stepped a woman. "Anna!" Riley Moss exclaimed, and he took a pace forward.

But Lily was faster. She ran to her, threw her arms around her mother's waist and looked up into the face she had seen only in photographs and in dreams. "Mum!" she said as tears welled up, "Mum." Her hands flattened against her mother's back as if to test that she was real.

"My baby," said Anna. "You have been so brave." They clung together, Anna running her fingers through Lily's hair and both sobbed. Lily turned her head and flattened her face under her mother's chest. "My little darling," Anna said. "Who would have thought you could survive all that?"

"Is it over now, Mum?"

"No, my love. But what we have to do, we will do together."

"Yes, together," said Lily, looking up. Her mother was real, alive. The warmth she had been denied for most of her life was in her arms. Suddenly she was a baby again.

With a glance and a nod towards the old lady, Riley Moss came up to them, lifted Lily, held her up, and with their heads on a level put an arm around both of them. They stood with heads down and together, each with a stream of tears. Moss choked back his sobs and let Lily down, where she clasped an arm around both of her parents' waists.

"Mother," said Anna.

"Yes you are, Mum. My Mum," said Lily.

Anna looked down with a smile. "Mother," she repeated. "Join us."

As Lily turned her head, Mysul came forward and laid a hand on Lily's shoulder.

"This is my mother," Anna said. "Your grandmother, Lily."

"Lily Moss," Mysul said. "My grand-daughter. My only grand-child."

49 - Welcome to the Gate

Just as Riley Moss had told Lily that her mother was 'lost', so had Anna been vague, saying that her parents had 'passed over'. Passed over to where? Here, wherever this was. Heaven? Not the Heaven Riley had imagined. He had not sprouted wings. No-one had thrust a harp in his hands. He looked at his hands. Same old hands. Hell? Not hot enough.

His head swam with it, even more when the old lady lifted her arms and began to fade, into a mist which grew around her, spread across the chamber, star-like points of light glittering within it. Her voice came to his mind with one word - "Love." The mist cleared and she was gone.

Riley was dumbstruck. Up to now he had witnessed strange events - the journeys with Anna, the mystery of the House Over-There, and Saida's peculiar ability to appear from thin air - but old ladies do not turn into mist and vanish. With a hand to his head he said, "Who? What was that?"

Neither Anna nor Lily seemed to think it odd. "Mysul," said Anna.

"I knew it all along," Lily said. "I just knew. My Granny. I just knew."

"Your grandmother is a Great Power, Lily," Anna replied. "I don't think she'd like to be called Granny."

"But how…?" Moss said.

"Welcome to the Gate, Riley my love," said Anna. "You are going to find it all very strange. But I should explain something to Lily…" she went on, looking down. "You know I love you, Lily, and always have, and I love your father and always will, even though we were apart for so long. But do you love us, Lily? Really?"

"Of course I do, Mum. That's silly."

"You are attached to us, Lily," Anna said. "That's natural. Even though we were apart, you always knew I was there for you, and your father was right there with you. Lucky man." Anna's smile at Riley reflected his, and she may have guessed that, inside, he felt a warmth that at the same time comforted and set off a tingle throughout his entire body. "But Love," Anna went on. "That's not the same. If you love someone, there's nothing you wouldn't do for them. You might even die for them. That love, comes from Mysul. It is what guides her, and us, the love that makes sacrifices, that unites, that does not divide, that grows and is never ashamed of itself. Feel that love once, Lily, and you have it forever."

"I do love you, Mum. And Dad. I used to kiss your photograph, every night."

"Sweet baby," said Anna with a smile. "But imagine something even more. Mysul's love is for everything - the stars, space, us, everything. Love, even for the Grey Angel."

"No!"

"Yes. Even what we think is wicked, evil, even to that she gives her love. This is how it has always been, in this sea and everywhere she has travelled, taking her love with her. Pain comes with it. And even Mysul can get annoyed, can feel pain. She will fight to protect her Love. Sometimes she can even get quite cross!" Riley could see Anna's laugh make Lily tremble. "And love does not always triumph," Anna went on, "but it does not die. It cannot die. Mysul cannot die. We appear to die, but because we know her love, and are loved, we are as immortal as Mysul. Nothing is lost."

"Nothing is lost," Lily repeated.

"Soon," said Anna, "Mysul will show you what her love means, what it does. Then you will know. She herself is the best example. In this universe she made the love between its parts, and that includes the love between souls, our souls, each one different. As an example she took a husband... the Ordinal."

391

"Ordinal is… my grandfather?"

"Her partner, your grandfather, and her eyes and ears in our world. She created him, so he has every reason to be thankful."

Lily smiled.

"Mysul also had a child," Anna went on, "because that is another, special love. I am that child. And then you came along, all by Mysul's design. Mysul chose your father carefully…"

"She did? Why me? I thought you did," Riley said.

"Of course I did, silly. But do you remember your mother's mother?"

"I do. Welsh. She was a strange one. A wise woman. Loved her to bits."

"A witch. Mysul's daughter and the grandson of a witch, in love," Anna said. "The right parents for Mysul's new Navigator, Lily Andreyevna Moss."

Lily swallowed hard and eagerly said, "Have I passed the test?"

"You have," Anna replied. "You have done that, and more. But there is even more to do, and quickly. Mysul will help you." A veil of sadness fell over her face. "But hold this moment in your memory. These are dangerous times, and each of us will have a duty. Those duties will be different. Riley, you will have to stay in the town. Find your feet. Is that the correct phrase?"

Riley nodded.

"I must re-join my battalion," Anna went on. "Lily, you will re-join your friends. They are waiting for you. It will be as if you had never left them."

"So we can't be together?" said Lily.

"We are together. Here. And nothing is lost," Anna replied.

Lily nodded. "If you say so, Mum," she said. "But let's not say goodbye."

"No, we won't," said Anna. "But for a short time, we have to go our separate ways. Mysul will carry us."

As his wife and daughter in turn went the way of Mysul, fading, slipping from his grasp, each with a smile, Riley Moss smiled back but was overcome by a fear of abandonment in this place of unknown powers and danger. He had tried to be strong, but inside him was a coil of sadness, of dread, though it was a kindly light which shone through the windows of the chamber, and from outside came the voices of people, normal people. Breathing out a sigh, he forced himself to turn, and he stepped slowly out of the chamber and into the light of the street.

*

"We're here. Finally," said Theo in a tone of wonder, as he surveyed the landscape of Roamers Cross. "Mysul, the Council, the Tower, everything we heard about at the Lodge. Can only see a bit of a wall, but I know it's all there, behind that hill."

"And the war," said Michael at his side.

"Why are you here?" said Lily, from behind them on the platform at the mountain's exit. "Has something happened at the Lodge?"

Theo and Michael turned to face her. "Destroyed," said Michael. "Cardinal got us out, and he put us into that maze where you found us, or rather we found you."

"Destroyed?" Lily said, picking up her cockroach armour. "That lovely place?"

Michael nodded. "Grangels. The mechanicals put up a fight," he said. "But they're not made for it. It was over all too quickly."

"We couldn't have got out of the maze without you, Lily," said little Chun.

"And I couldn't have got out without you," Lily replied. She smiled, but then frowned. "We're not all here, are we?" she said. "Who's missing?"

"Klaus," said fat Robert from one side. "In Singapore, we had a word for people like him. Slime."

"He's a traitor, Lily," Chun explained. "He opened up the Lodge and the grangels poured in. Their Lord Commander and everything. I've not seen monsters like that, not till we came here. Huge men in black armour, and the insects… we were so scared. He's a traitor. There's no mistake."

Lily sighed. "Then we had better get going," she said. "We will be needed. This way, wolves," she said, and pointed her stick down the path.

Lily led the way downhill. At her side, little Chun said, "Did you see me take a pee in that forest? Ewwww, wasn't that disgusting? And who was that horrible man, near the end?"

"The Minister, God's Minister he called himself," Lily replied.

From behind, Theo grunted. "They have no shame, these freaks," he said. "Using the word God like that. For a freaking monster."

The descent was gradual on a dusty path between fields and coppices, under the light of a sunless but bright sky. They skirted the hill and turned a corner.

There, below, lay the town. Immediately it was a surprise for Lily to see how small the town was, more a village. The landmarks she remembered from her dreams were there - the town Square which had four streets leading from it in a cross, which is why she had always thought of it as Roamers Cross; two tall buildings on the square; the red-tiled roofs of smaller houses; little shops with striped awnings that overhung the streets; and beside them taller buildings, some oblong with flat roofs, one that reared up in a pinnacle of steel and glass.

What she had not realised - because never before had she seen the town from above - was that it stood on a high platform of rock, whose black crags and grassy escarpments rose from flat fields and hedgerows, behind it the forest and the Great Tower on its green hill, and further on a range of mountains, where plumes of dark smoke drifted as if from a forest fire. From crevices in its rock, paths beneath the town led down to the fields, and on the path which led up in a curve towards them there was an extraordinary sight.

"It's a pack of mechanicals," said Martha. "I've never seen so many. This must be where they're from."

Emerging from under the town, a line of people began to walk up the path. More emerged, until it was a crowd, swarming over the path, and in the centre strode a long line of women in smocks and woolly hats, each of them blowing on brass instruments, all to the beat of a bass drum banged by a man in a yellow uniform with a red sash. "I didn't know mechanicals were musical," said little Chun. Each of the women played her own tune but to the same beat. The result was, as Chun described it, "Like killing a pig slowly."

"That's the Constable!" Martha cried, and it was, banging with gusto on his bass drum with the occasional twirl of his splendid moustaches. At the head of the crowd, a small plump man waddled uphill wearing a pillbox hat and a green robe, around his neck a heavy gold chain, the Clerk.

He puffed and panted, and after some minutes arrived in front of Lily and the students of the Lodge, then stepped forward and raised a hand. The band stopped playing. "As Clerk of the Council," he cried, his voice booming along the path, "I welcome the arrival at our Gate of a new battalion, to which Mysul has given the name of Wolves. I give a special welcome to its leader and navigator, Lily Moss, who has undergone severe trials to get here, including torture, yes torture, at the hands of our enemy's Lord Commander." Gasps came from the crowd, and from behind Lily. "Oh, and several others I don't know," he went on. He stepped forward. "You're looking a little peaky, dear," he whispered to Lily. "That's a nasty gash on your head. You want to get that seen to." He turned, and waved his arms. "Now back!" he cried. "Business to do et cetera. Lead the way, Constable!" With that, the entire crowd turned and made their way down, the band striking up with an appalling blare of horns.

Lily and those she would now call friends remained. "Wozzu tortured, Lily?" Sidney whispered, fingering his spectacles. "Poked with spears and stuff?"

"He burned me in the knees," Lily replied. "I got scars but they're healing."

"Look!" Michael cried. "In the sky!"

Above the town, two figures rose into the sky, at first like birds but as they turned and made their way towards Lily's group their human form became clear. "They're flying!" Theo gasped. "Oh my gosh, can we all do that?"

"Try it," Lily said, and Theo hopped up and down, but with no result. "Guess there must be something special about them," he said.

Together, each arriving with a balletic landfall, came Cardinal and Anna. Anna smiled but stepped aside as Cardinal came forward. "If I may have a word," he said. "First, my congratulations," he said to Lily. "You performed more effectively than I predicted." Lily bowed her head. Cardinal went on, "No doubt it was a shock to come up against a half-dozen of our enemy's creatures, terrible, savage beasts. They were only some of our captives, but you and your wolves dealt with them very effectively."

"A half-dozen, sir?" said Lily with a frown. "But there were hundreds."

"Say again. Hundreds?"

"In the last cavern... sea... hundreds, a black army, insects and white riders, and the mosquitoes..."

"Hoverflies. And hundreds of others, you say."

"Maybe thousands. And the Minister. He called himself God's Minister."

Cardinal turned to Anna. "They were not mine," he said. "I will investigate." He turned back to Lily. "You have done even more than we thought. And what is that on your back?"

"The shell of a cockroach, sir. It saved my life. A hoverfly hit me but its light-beam bounced off. Knocked me over but that was all."

"May I borrow it?"

"Yes sir," Lily said, and she slipped the armour from her back and handed it to Cardinal. "Thank you," he said. "This could make a difference. I will have to re-calculate. Excuse me." The students watched open-mouthed as his body became transparent and - just as Navigator had - expanded to a huge size then drifted away on the breeze.

"You can fly, Mum!" said Lily.

"I am in an aerial battalion. But you can't, sorry. You have to stay on the ground, for now."

"That's unfair."

"Unless Mysul thinks otherwise. She wants to see you. I know she has something to tell you."

"In the town?"

"Yes."

"OK," said Lily. "Wolves!" She waved her stick forward. "To the town! And no peeing in the trees!"

"Ewww," said little Chun.

50 - Before the Storm

In the Square outside the Council House, Riley Moss came upon a scene of intense activity. Over the cobbles men and women dashed by, pulling handcarts loaded with building materials - blocks of concrete, steel girders, sacks of sand, pickaxes and ladders - all with cries of encouragement from children watching from the walls. At the centre of the maelstrom, waving his arms, stood a bald man in a green suit. Sidling through the stream of traffic, Moss approached him and said, "Excuse me..."

"What?" The man directed a cart down a side-street, then another towards the rear of a building whose sign read, 'Recruitment and Training Centre'.

"Is there somewhere I might be useful?" Moss said. There was something familiar about this man but Moss could not quite place him.

The man briefly looked Moss up and down, then shouted at a passing cart, "Under not over! West wall!"

"Have we met before?" Moss asked.

"Southsea," the man replied, and furiously waving at a child trying to cross the traffic shouted, "Stay back, idiot!"

"Eh?" Riley said.

"We met in Southsea. Mister Moss, if I recall. You came to repair the heating. That's when I gave your daughter one of our keys."

Riley blinked. "Silas Bolney?" he said.

"It's the name I used. Hey you! Let the girders through! Steel before concrete! Bonehead!"

Moss leaned forward. "I am supposed to have killed you, Mister Bolney," he said. "The Police arrested me on a charge of murder. Who did it?"

The man lowered his arms and for a few moments let the chaos take care of itself. "Unlucky. It was a spiker," he said. "Oh, no doubt you have only just arrived. You will find accommodation under the town in due course. That is what we are building, for all our new arrivals. Now hop off. Work to do... and by the way, here I am known as Ordinal. Now kindly get out of the way."

Moss threaded his way through the traffic to the door of the Recruitment and Training Centre, and peered in. A group of men and women in camouflage uniforms hovered inside the door, examining what looked like a shell of black metal, passing it from hand to hand. "Is this really hers?" a woman said. "Look, you can see where the hoverfly hit her, that little dent, right there..." said another, before - with a chorus of "Oh... so brave!", and "Our Navigator!" - they looked up and cried, "Here she is!"

"Dad!" Lily flung herself at her father's back and grabbed him by the sweater. Riley Moss staggered forward from the onslaught, turned and clasped her to him. The talk around him, the praise, had made her sound ten feet tall but here she was, a Saxon elf, small but cuddly, and still with a livid red gash above her right ear.

"Lily," said Riley Moss. "Does it still hurt?" He held her head in his hands and looked into her eyes.

"It's OK, Dad," she replied. "Just a scratch."

"Sure?"

"Sure as eggs, Captain. But I have to go. I'm wanted in the Council House. I don't know what it's about."

"You'd better go then, my darling. Come back safe."

*

399

Outside, the members of her Wolves battalion were standing along the walls, gawping at the traffic and the buildings. Lily dashed by. "Is that the way to the Council House?" she asked a passer-by, and was directed to its portico of columns. Inside, she recognised the corridors of her dreams, streams of carpet leading to offices from which came clacking and a continuous hum, and then up a staircase to the Council chamber.

There was an ominous quiet in the chamber, its air still and heavy as before a thunderstorm but with a fragrance of lavender. Lily felt her feet sink into the blue carpet. At the table sat Mysul in a jet-black robe. "Come, child," she said. "Sit with me." She turned in her seat as Lily approached and waved a hand at the seat next to her. Sliding her stick under the table, Lily sat in the most proper manner she could imagine.

"Lily," Mysul said, softly and directly to Lily's mind. "You have come far, child. But now you must go further. And quickly. Out there…" she said, waving a hand at a window, "our enemy has its forces on both sides of us. It is preparing its final assault. I doubt that we can resist."

"Can't we just drop an atom bomb on them?"

"Child!" The old lady's eyes twinkled and she let out what was nearly a laugh. "No," she said. "That would rip this sea apart. Our resources are limited, our weapons are limited. That is not my rule. It is the rule of the Presence. This sea is mine, but its Gate is bound by limits set by the Presence, which is in all things and everywhere at once, and a power far greater than me or the Grey Angel. Nothing must affect the greater plan of the Presence. Do you understand?"

Lily did not, but nodded.

"To defend ourselves," Mysul went on, "we have only basic weapons - gravity, light, fire. Our only explosive weapon is the mine, and its power is limited. You will think our weapons old-fashioned - swords, knives, sticks, rocks and stones. We have bows, but their arrows will pierce only the weakest armour. Our most powerful weapon is one invented by our Servator. I wish we had more of them. In the town they call it the 'Mysul staff'. I have one here."

Mysul bent down and from under the table she drew out a long tube of shiny white metal, with a black button set on one side at its tip. She held it upright. It towered over Lily's head. "The power of lightning," Mysul said. "The skybolts, the bolts of lightning which sparkle from a staff like this are a brave sight, devastating in the right hands. I have ordered one to be made for you, child."

Mysul seemed to expect a response, but Lily was squirming with discomfort and on the edge of fear. This talk of weapons and lightning, and of a staff which would be hers and so she would be expected to use it, made her take a deep breath and blow it out as she looked down at the carpet and said nothing.

"Why do I tell you this?" Mysul said. "War, weapons, a Mysul staff of your own? If our Navigator were here, he would tell you. He would say that it is a task of the Navigator to direct our defence, to move our resources from one position to another. With what we have, we have been successful so far. But we may be reaching our end, and already it may be too late, unless we introduce new assets, new thinking, a new Navigator. You."

"Me... Mysul?"

"Some will say you are only a foolish child. Ignore them. Listen. You inherited the key of the Navigator. Now you shall inherit the role. The Navigator has many tasks and can perform them with powers which only I grant. You shall be one of the Five. You will take a seat at Court and at Council. There are five seats, and one shall be yours. You shall be my right hand."

Mysul raised her right arm. From her hand grew a globe of glass which expanded without sound into a watery cloud which surrounded Lily, Mysul and everything in the chamber. Underwater, the shape of Mysul drifted, shifting and reforming like molten glass while in the cloud stars and constellations twinkled and between them flashed jagged lines of orange light. Comets sped past as the cloud slowly revolved.

Her mouth open with surprise, Lily heard Mysul's voice. "You will navigate to any location in this Universe without harm. With my love and with the power I grant, you will be at one with your destination. You shall know the channels, their names and numbers. You shall make channels and open gates. Their keys shall be yours." With a twirl of Mysul's hand, the cloud, the stars and the comets shrank back into the globe of glass and vanished.

Lily felt herself wiped clean, by shock, by something in her head which had woken up and was glowing behind her eyes with a light that stretched down to her toes, which curled with tension inside her boots. "But why...?" she whispered. "Why me?"

"You have trusted me with your life, child," came the reply. "I shall trust you with mine. But to become the Navigator I must make a change in you. That change, with your agreement, I will make now and here."

Lily sat with her back straight. "Yes I am... ready, Mysul," she said.

"Then, we begin."

*

At first, when Mysul laid a hand on Lily's head, nothing happened. But when she took it away, everything happened.

Lily Moss stood alone in a bubble of black glass. She did not breathe, but it was enough to be aware, and gradually she became aware of the light. It grew from the base of the bubble, a curtain of white diamonds twinkling against the black, and they spread around her and over her head, so many that their light overpowered the darkness. They were constellations, galaxies that revolved, stars. Their dark backdrop split into drifting oceans of blue, red and green which stretched away to infinity. Some stars were only circles of black with a white rim, and from them filaments of an orange light glowed through the oceans in a universal grid. She saw in all directions at once. No longer did she have two eyes which stared only ahead; she felt and was aware of everything on all sides, though there were no longer sides, only the roundness of everything and the veins that coursed within it. Those veins, those filaments had names, and numbers.

She was drawn towards a point where the filaments gathered. At first they were like the veins of an eye, but orange, and where they met was only a tiny hole in an ocean of blue. She edged closer. And closer. Something was there, a speck of dust. Into it the filaments pulsed. It was a world. She surfed a filament into it, other filaments splashing around her, in them sparks of white light, until she stood in blue sky with the town of Roamers Cross brightly lit below. The filaments pulsed into the Great Tower above the forest, channels of light she could not have seen without the eyes of a Navigator. She looked inside the mountains, and saw the enemy, waiting. She saw the Gate, and the Grey Angel, red waves of hate pulsing around it. She saw, but she felt more. She felt pity, for the paths she saw would lead to war, to bloodshed and death, and she felt anger that it must be so. She felt love, even for the enemy.

"There," said Mysul.

Lily was awake and blinked. "I have been where I should not, and seen what I should not."

Mysul smiled. "Did you feel my love?" she said.

"Yes, I did."

Mysul nodded, gravely. "Soon you will understand more," she said. "What is within you will surface. For you, this is a beginning. For others, the end is near. I am recalling them, all of them, to defend the Gate. I cannot tell how many will survive. If any."

"Roamers?" Lily said.

"From your world and others. All of them. It is a throw of the dice. But you, you are the Navigator."

51 - Councils of War

The Five sat alone in the Council chamber wearing robes of black and with heads bared, behind them the blue tapestry of the fifteen seas. Outside, the town was quiet. The frenzied activity of preparing for its defence had subsided into an eerie stillness, as if over its inhabitants there hung a shroud of anticipation which was not quite fear but a resignation that worse was to come.

"Ordinal," Mysul said. "Tell me of the town."

"Preparations to house our new recruits are all-but complete. I suggest that the order is given for their recall."

"I so order it," Mysul said. "And the Gate?"

Lily Moss spoke up. "We defend the hills and forest with our first-line battalions. Sapper platoons have been busy. My own battalion of Wolves has operated across the plain undetected. Through our Servator I have taken advice from military commanders of my world. Though the Constable is more experienced, I hope I can do justice to what they have taught me."

"I am sure you will," Mysul said. "The Tower?"

The Cardinal coughed and flipped his golden coin. "One aerial battalion and three ground-based," he said. "And in the town, so far, only a few guard platoons under the direction of one commander. We need those new recruits immediately. We will have to train them by injection. There is no time for them to acquire any sort of experience."

"Not enough," the Servator said.

Mysul leaned back. "That depends on how we deal with the Minister. Servator, your calculation."

The Servator twitched her robe and said, "The Minister. At every beat of the Angel's heart it grows stronger. In terms familiar to our Navigator, I calculate that it will be fully operational in three and one-third hours from now. That calculation is based upon the rate of the heart-beat of all Great Powers."

"And Cardinal," said Mysul. "Your prediction."

The Cardinal drew a deep breath and replied, "If the globers arrive in good time, I estimate our success at point-six, provided that the Minister is destroyed. But if the Minister becomes fully operational, I estimate our success at point-two. Only you, Mysul, can match it, and that will distract you from the defence of the town and the Tower."

The issue, which the Cardinal and the Ordinal explored, was that much had changed since Lily set out on her navigator test. She herself, unknowing, had witnessed one change - the transfer of the enemy's Vault, its hatchery and the point of its images' projection, from beyond the Gate and into the base of Mount Cardinal. It was there, in the last cavern, that Lily had seen the birth of hoverflies from their lines of dusty coffins. Such a place, equipped with incubators and the mechanism for projection, would by now have around it a ring of steel, the most savage of the Angel's creatures, all the more determined because it was their offspring they were protecting.

"That came at a price," the Ordinal said. "It took much of the Angel's power to steal a sea channel and direct it through the Gate into the mountain. No wonder it delays, while it recovers its strength. Eventually the Presence will react and Grangel will pay the price, but not in time to help us."

Meanwhile the power of the Minister had grown with every beat of the Angel's heart. When Lily encountered his spectre the Minister was not fully formed, still with the soul of a human body within him. But now, he had made himself unreachable, deep under Mount Cardinal, within a shell of the Angel's power which embraced the base of the mountain and those cohorts of the Black Army which

Lily had seen manoeuvring, now reinforced through a back channel from the Lodge.

The mountain's base was a black hole in Mysul's universe. This was an insult to a Great Power, and Mysul banged the table in fury, her eyes ablaze. Could this be slowed down? What was the name of the human creature whose body the Minister inhabited? No-one knew.

"Perhaps," said Lily Moss, "the back channel has a back channel?"

Mysul raised an eyebrow. "Investigate, and be quick," she said. "Take your staff. You know how to use it. Now, to your posts. Time is against us."

*

Anyone who happened to train a telescope into the clouds over the village of Swivelhurst, on a normally quiet Thursday night, might have spotted something which was not at all normal - a blonde-haired girl who hovered in mid-air high up, just under the cloud layer, wearing a long black robe, a white staff in one hand, as she looked down on what once was her home.

It was so small, the village of Swivelhurst. Through the street-lights she picked out its railway station, then the High Street where her Dad's shop would be closed. Perhaps Percy Bee had been released and was looking after it, and the warehouse up Hedge Lane behind the station. Down there a square of darkness must be the playing-field of the school, and the chain of lights at its side the path where people walked their dogs and headed for the pub. Down there lived the Ormerod family, Swan, Nathalie, all in their beds and unaware that their futures depended on a plain by a forest, a mountain, a tower, and a town to which many of them - those who were Roamers - would soon be recalled.

How many would vanish from down there and find themselves an impossible distance away, at Roamers Cross? Any from her school? Miss Chesterton was probably one. Maybe Nathalie, maybe Swan.

What would they think when they were handed a weapon and told to fight something which came from their nightmares?

It had been the matter of a moment for Lily Moss to navigate back to her world. Moments now were all she had. The clock was ticking. She blinked, took a deep breath and swept through the clouds at high speed to the east, towards the channel which first she had entered in Cardinal's bus, the channel to the Lodge.

Entry to that channel was her first obstacle. She saw it below, drifting along the main road to the east, a filament of orange light, jagged, twisting and turning, reaching up through the clouds. Its key was the Omnium, which Cardinal had summoned from his mountain to the Council House, where Lily had reset and opened the channel. She waited until the road was clear, then down she hurtled to the road's surface and under the glare of the highway lights she shot forward into the tube of the filament's end, was surrounded by familiar cloud, for a second felt herself numb, and shot through and out, over the track of stone which once had led to the Lodge.

The scene was of utter devastation. Of the buildings of the Lodge barely one stone was left on top of another, and everywhere were black and smoking ruins, all inside a bowl of hills and blue sky which gave an artificially colourful backdrop to a sad sight. Cardinal's bus, on fire, lay on its side, seats spilling out over the gravel of what had been the forecourt. Heads, arms and legs of the statues at the front gate lay in a pile of broken debris.

Among them lay a body not disjointed, all of a piece, a skeleton.

Lily swooped over it. Stripped of flesh and bleached white, it was the skeleton of a young man, lying spread-eagled on the debris with one arm extended and a broken finger pointing to the sky. The skull lolled to one side, its jawbone fixed in a grimace. The skeleton wore the tatters of a Lodge uniform, a camouflage uniform stained by dirt and fire. Only one student of the Lodge failed to reach the mountain under Cardinal's guidance.

Klaus, the traitor. Justice.

Lily narrowed her eyes. Somewhere was the second channel, from the Lodge to the Gate, and her next obstacle, if it had been closed. This was not one of Lily's channels, which she could see criss-crossing in a grid of orange through the ground and sky, each with its name and number, each linking the Gate with Mysul's universe. This channel was Cardinal's, held open by Klaus to let the Black Army through. It was a minor channel, hard to spot in the mass of channels so close to the Gate; but in the grid of orange slim filaments of blue blinked. These were the channels between the Lodge and the Gate used by the Five. They blinked, for they were closed. Except for one.

A filament of blue light stretched up to the sky from somewhere on the other side of the Lodge's ruins. Lily swooped forward and looked down. The blackboard of Cardinal's room lay in the rubble, swathed in an oily smoke from books and papers on fire. Slowly she descended. Her feet should have landed on the blackboard's surface, but they passed through. The channel was open.

That was the second obstacle, but the third was the most dangerous. There was no telling what awaited her at the channel's end. She noted the channel's name and its number. She noted its position, between four orange channels which twisted skywards like the strands of a rope. At the other end could be nothing, or the Black Army, or the Minister itself, but she had prepared Navigator's key for an instant return to the town Square. She might fail, if the channel ended outside the sphere of the Minister's protection, gaining nothing. She had to be inside it, where the Minister lay waiting.

With her free hand she pulled the wolf's-claw knife from a fold of her robe, and she dropped down through the oily smoke, through the blackboard, and into a rock-cut passageway.

It was empty and dark. Only her staff lit the way ahead. Cobwebs dangled from its low roof, and wooden doors were set into it, all but one closed. She peered through. A sandy floor led downward and cautiously she went through, holding her staff before her. The tunnel turned and there was light beyond, from a yellow sky.

She emerged on a platform of rock overlooking the statue of the Lord Commander on his mound of earth, though now the Black Army was not arranged in squares but in lines, all facing the triangle, the way out behind the statue. Quickly she doused the light of her staff and crouched down. Hoverflies circled ahead, and above them black drones, watchful eyes.

She was inside. Somewhere below, the Minister lay in the Vault under the plain, its power growing with every beat of the Angel's heart. She had to work quickly. First, she had to detach the far end of the Lodge's channel. She pictured its name and number, reached out and grasped it. From her hand a faint blue light stretched behind, along the passageway to the channel's end. She gripped the channel and pictured its colour, yellow for this cavern's sky. She exchanged its start and end. Then, the channel's start had to be cast outside, beyond the Minister's sphere of protection. She did this as if she had done it before, which she had not, but as Navigator had known before her so did she know how to root the channel's beginning, as Mysul directed, on the hillside between the town and Mount Cardinal.

She checked her handiwork. From the platform beneath her feet stretched the jagged wire of a channel, across the space of the cavern and out through the triangle of light behind the Lord Commander's statue. She had made a way in.

Her work done, Lily tapped Navigator's key which hung around her neck, and in a flash she arrived in the Square, where she stood before the columns of the Council chamber in sudden confusion.

Light from the Recruitment and Training Centre fell on the cobbles. That light should not be there. Stars were in the sky, and a moon. For the first time in her experience of this town, it was night.

*

The Council of War was held on the ridge between light and dark, at the Crossway which the Roamers called the Gate.

The Lord God could not pass through the Gate until the sea was ready to receive him. He could stand at the Gate, with the powers of three conquered seas behind him, and make himself visible, but he would go no further until he was assured by his commanders that the tide of battle had turned in his favour. It was for that reason he had created his commanders, or adopted them from conquered seas. It was for that reason that he had deployed the instrument of projection, as he had before, so that the images of those commanders - and those appointed to them - should be transferred to act where God Himself would not.

At a mountain's peak, atop a cliff of scorched and blackened rock where dark vapours swirled as from a volcano's slopes, the commanders of God's army stood in order of rank, the Lord Commander at their head with his servant Twine at his side, kneeling. All wore battle-dress, the armour of the Lord Commander standing out for its grey sheen against the black of the others.

God stood above them, his immense body silhouetted against the swirling purple and yellow vapours of the Gate, above him only the darkness of infinite night.

None could doubt his majesty. His armour was a glistening grey, his helmet the head of a black bull. Through the vapour-clouds his eyes flashed red. From each shoulder, wings outspread like grey curtains gathered to the claws of his gauntlets. In his right hand, God held a silver staff which he raised and lowered in a slow rhythm, at every beat making a thud that carried through the ground as if from his heart. His power could be felt. It was electric, magnetic, hypnotic and inescapable.

The Lord Commander waited. God looked down upon him.

God's thought was clear, directly into the minds of the Lord Commander and the others; and there could be no argument, only action in accordance with God's Will. How different was he from the Presence, who haunts the Greater Sea, sleeps, and acts only when there is some catastrophic disturbance in his web, or some rebellion by the Great Powers, of which God Himself had been one? How misguided was it to use the term 'God' for the Presence, rather than for God Himself who was here, visible, and immortal?

Now, one Great Power was ranged against another. God Himself and the Mysul of these Roamers. There could be only one outcome - exile of Mysul, destruction of her sea, and of the Tower where its memory was preserved. What was the point of that Tower and its channels? God Himself knew all that needed to be known. All logic, everything could be deduced by and through him.

Into the mind of the Lord Commander came the question, "You are ready to summon those I sent into this sea?" The Lord Commander's answer was, "My Lord God, we are ready. Those who remain in the globes shall be those we have identified for further service. Disruption, division, doubt and despair. Those are their watchwords."

"Your God is content. You shall kneel."

As he knelt, into the mind of the Lord Commander came the words, "Tell me of my Minister".

"The Minister waits, my Lord God," the Lord Commander replied. "Within three thousand beats, he will be ready."

"It has been too long," came the thought, "that I have been without my Minister. The Minister shall take command of the Third Wing. Commander of the Third Wing, return to the dust from which I gave you form."

From the staff of God shot a bolt of light that parted the vapour-clouds. It struck a commander, who stood transfixed for a moment, then became a pattern of multi-coloured pixels which fell to the ground.

Into the Lord Commander's mind came a question, "We have them from both sides?" The Lord Commander replied, "Yes, my Lord God. At your command we shall execute."

God raised his left arm, glittering silver through the vapour-clouds. He gripped one horn of his bull-helmet, raised the helmet from his head and held it under his arm.

God showed his face.

It was the face of a pale young man, sharp-featured with black pupil-less eyes, and those eyes flickered in their study of his commanders with the amusement of one inspecting a parade of puppets, as a mane of yellow hair drifted in the vapours and settled behind his shoulders. The beauty of God struck deep into the heart of the Lord Commander, as it had before.

God spoke. His lips twisted apart and from the monstrous vacancy between his jaws with a flash of fire came one word, which boomed with an explosive force across the mountain.

"Execute."

52 - The Rapture

Across the world, people lost their memories. It happened swiftly. Thousand upon thousand, at one moment they walked in their fields or sat in their homes, offices and schools with a light in their eyes, but in seconds that light dimmed, leaving them blank, forgetting how and why they had got where they were, how they might leave, and whose house is this?

It was a terrifying vacancy, an instant dementia which closed down systems of thought and feeling, leaving its victims in a few short moments in a state of confusion but then of paralysis which was at first mental, then physical, then terminal. This was a pandemic of... something; but its targets included so many medical, academic and research staff that few remained who could shed light on how this could be happening - a virus, an allergy, something in the water, something from Space.

Then people began to disappear. This was not a matter of the occasionally missing person, but a full-blown exodus. Those who believed religiously in a 'rapture' in which the holy would be transported to Heaven, were convinced that their time had come. They would be saved, from a world suddenly overcome by a Great Plague of oblivion.

At first only a few hundred vanished. They did so at any time, at any place, in the full light of day or safely in their beds at night. Crossing a road, a man would not reach the other side. He was no longer there. A bus would crash into a shop-front when its driver vanished from behind the wheel. In a supermarket, the woman behind a till would offer up the customer's change, which dropped to the floor as her hand - and the rest of her with it - disappeared. The manner of their vanishing suggested that rapture was an unpleasant experience. For a split-second some other image of them would appear, and it was loathsome. "Insects," was the most common term, "huge flailing-about black insects".

Across the world this was something which governments found impossible to manage, but they tried, with emergency legislation whose purpose was not made clear to the public, with news blackouts, and generally with denial. It took the calling-in of a great many favours to keep this quiet but also agreement among affected Heads of State that what was needed was calm, while this event was investigated.

Some of it, though, was all too visible. A newscaster vanished live on screen. In the chambers of national parliaments members would stand to speak, and disappear in mid-sentence. Most seriously affected were the media, major corporations and institutions of government. One of the largest businesses in Africa and Asia - G-Range by name - disappeared overnight. Its premises stood empty, its trucks without drivers. Even if they had been allowed to do so, the media would have found it difficult to report on these catastrophic events, for their own staff had died or disappeared, forcing an immediate succession of media-company mergers which left them and their public even more confused.

That was the first wave of the exodus. Within five days it stopped, and when there was time to think, a feature of this so-called 'rapture' stood out. There was doubt about the identities of the people concerned. Birth certificates were missing or obviously faked. In families where one member might give information about another, they all vanished.

Within days it started again, but this was different. It was larger - in one day affecting over two hundred thousand people - and now there were no insects, but a silvery cocoon would form in a second around the target, who would freeze and shrink to a pinpoint of light which shot skywards into infinity. This was more like the rapture that the religious had expected. Many who knew of it - and still that was only by word-of-mouth - were ecstatic with a divine pleasure, and would stand at their windows, hands uplifted, praying to be taken. This stage was quickly over, and in the aftermath it was clear that its character had been unlike its predecessor. It affected all types and orders of people - even some primates and other animals. 'The Rapture of Noah' it came to be called.

414

They left behind a world not in crisis - for most of the world remained ignorant of this event, and the sum total of the disappeared was less than three hundred thousand - but in a state of puzzlement. There had been no invasion by Monsters from Space, no Martian fighting machines had landed, no alien warships had hovered over the world's cities and dumped fire and brimstone on the heads of unsuspecting citizens.

A Great Plague had begun and a chunk of the world's population had - without a word - disappeared. Where did they go? Are they dead? No-one knew.

53 - Chaos in the Chamber

In the chamber of the Grand Council the noise was tremendous, people dashed hither and thither with papers, which they dropped; there was a general flapping of hands, standing up then sitting down, shouting, and through this mayhem mechanicals wandered knitting as they went, trailing balls of wool which unravelled and tripped the unwary.

Beyond the screen of wood panels which separated the main- from the ante-chamber lay the source of much of the noise, from animals, cats screeching, dogs howling, donkeys braying. In the main chamber sat the Clerk and the Constable. They gazed at the throng as if watching someone else's drama, waiting for a lull in the commotion. The Recorder, slouching in an armchair at the edge of the chamber, was asleep.

It took a sudden and determined blast of his trumpet by the Constable to bring some order into this chaos. He stood and yelled out, "Stop! Stop, stop!"

Heads turned towards the lower table. Bottoms sank onto seats. Wool was speedily re-balled. The noise from the ante-chamber, however, was not diminished, and it was about the noise that the first speaker - Humbert, the Hotel's proprietor - spoke. "Where do we put them?" he asked. "We've not had animals like this before. And there are birds, great big gangling things that peck and leave their droppings over everything. Where do we put them?" He sat down, to a smattering of applause.

The Clerk rose and smoothed down his robe. Leaning forward he said, "We were prepared to receive many thousand individuals of the human sort, or of species now under translation. All of these are undergoing induction and re-training, and are housed in the underground facility constructed for that purpose. But..." he said, glancing around, "it came as a surprise to the Council that other creatures are involved. As a public nuisance, I shall direct our guards to remove them to the fields and let them loose. They will be as confusing to our enemy as they are to us. Do we need to vote? No? Then so be it. Guards, clear the ante-chamber!"

A line of soldiers in yellow-and-green uniforms, filed out through a side door at the back. There followed a banging, thumping, the clacking of hooves and animal cries, whistles and barks, until the noise subsided as the animals were led down to the street.

"What is next on the agenda?" The Clerk sat.

The Constable whispered, "Appointment of a Navigator."

"Oh yes," said the Clerk, and he stood. "Are they ready?" he whispered to the Constable, who nodded. "Then blow your trumpet again, man. This is good news for a change. Oh, and you'd better get up. We need all the seats now."

The Constable rose and blew mightily on his trumpet. The Recorder leapt from his armchair. The sonorous blast was enough to quieten the audience, who sat back in anticipation. "Be upstanding!" cried the Constable. "For the Court!"

He moved aside, leaving the five seats at the Council table empty, as - at the side of the blue drapery which hung behind that table - Anna and Riley Moss emerged and took up their position by a far wall, holding hands.

In all five seats at the Council table grew clouds of white light, which flashed away to reveal five figures in jet-black robes, hoods covering their faces. Together they pulled back their hoods, to reveal Mysul at the centre; to the right the Cardinal, to the far right the Servator, to the far left the Ordinal; and at Mysul's right hand, Lily Moss.

The applause was deafening. There were cries, laughter. There was jumping on seats and the throwing of woolly hats in the air. At the side, Anna grasped Riley's hand tightly and drew his arm across her chest.

Mysul raised a hand, and the audience quietly resumed their seats. "We have a Navigator," she said, in a voice which was soft but carried easily around the chamber. There were sporadic outbursts of clapping. "She who was known as Lily Moss," Mysul went on, "now in all formal circumstances shall be known as the Navigator. She has the duties and the powers of the Five which I have granted to her. Once more the Council is complete."

Loud cheers filled the chamber, stopping only when Mysul raised a hand and said, "Clerk, you may continue with our agenda."

The Clerk stepped forward and made a deep bow. From a sheet of paper he read, "Item Three. Report by the Constable." He stepped aside as the Constable pushed past.

His chest swelling, medals jingling, the Constable struck a dramatic pose and declared, "Our situation is deeply perilous." He looked around. Faces which had been joyous were now grim and fearful. "The primary globe is under attack by some insidious device which steals the life of those we are sworn to defend - those families, those children - removes their history, their intelligence, reduces them to mere shells of themselves, and finally - as if each of them were stung by a spiker - kills them. It is a plague. And we know who is responsible, do we not?" The word 'grangel' was spat out on all sides.

"Yes," the Constable said, peering forward. "And that is trouble enough. But there is trouble to come. Our enemy, the Grey Angel, has established channels into the base of Mount Cardinal, into which have passed a great many of its forces." He began to pace back and forth. "Consequently, we are now threatened on two sides, from the Gate and from Mount Cardinal. There is no doubt that the current pause of its operations is no more than that, and that a grave and potentially final assault will soon be in progress."

Mysul turned to the Cardinal. "Tell the Council about these channels," she said.

Cardinal nodded. "Two," he replied. "One stolen from the Presence, a sea-to-sea channel which the Grey Angel cannot hold open for long. The second, is a channel between the Lodge and the Gate. When the Lodge was destroyed…"

At this the crowd erupted with shouts of "No!" and "How?" Mysul held up a hand. "The Lodge is destroyed. By treachery. We will deal with the consequences. Cardinal, continue."

Cardinal sighed. "On the advice of the Ordinal, I closed that channel, but had to re-open it to allow the evacuation of the students. It was held open, by treachery. There is evidence now that both channels have been used to transfer elements of our enemy's so-called Black Army into Mount Cardinal, the first from beyond the Gate, the second from the Lodge."

At the words 'Black Army' there were gasps from the audience. A camouflage-clad young man rose from his seat. "We've faced them before and thrown them back," he cried, "and we can do it again!" He resumed his seat, to much applause.

Mysul raised a hand. "Constable," she said, "what are the implications of this?"

The Constable turned to face Mysul, and bowed. "Your Eminences," he said. "We are obliged to divide our resources. And although we are tempted to address the suffering of the primary globe, we must look to our own defences first, for without us that globe - and the others - shall become no more than charnel houses floating in a sea of dust. Not only must we have a sufficient presence at the Gate, now we must defend this place and the Tower against a direct assault from Mount Cardinal. Yes, we have acquired new resources, the many thousands who have joined us from the sea, but their training has only begun. Even so, I suggest that some may serve in Munitions and as town guards. We will, however, require aerial support, and that will deplete our resources at the Gate."

"So be it," Mysul said.

"I must insist," said the Servator, "that priority is given to the Tower. Grangel spies have already damaged its fabric, and it requires aerial support to deal with them."

"That support," Mysul said, "shall continue. And that will have to do for now."

"I suggest, Eminences," the Constable said, "that we discuss contingency plans, should the worst happen."

At this, groans rippled through the audience. Never before had such a suggestion been made. The guards had always dealt with intruders and there had never before been a need for contingency.

"Should the worst happen," Mysul said, "we have a simple choice, to roll back or to leave. Cardinal, your thoughts…"

Cardinal flipped a gold coin. "That decision, should be made by the Five. At the last moment. Can we vote on that?"

"So be it," Mysul said. "Let me hear Aye for those who agree with the Cardinal. Now." Shouts of 'Aye' filled the chamber. "It is agreed that the Five will make that decision," she said. "To leave, we require a destination. Navigator, your thoughts… "

Lily Moss looked up. "Mysul," she said. "I have discussed this matter with the Cardinal. The nearest in the Omnium is the seventh sea. It is a safe route, and so obvious that the Angel may not expect us to choose it. The sea is empty and can easily be filled from the Tower. I am working on the course now."

"Continue with that work," Mysul said. "Do you have thoughts about the first globe?"

Cardinal leaned forward. "We have one in mind, Mysul," he said, "but we do not wish to influence your design adversely. If - as in this sea - it is in the primary globe where Life begins, then we suggest that it should be protected by a chain of material-rich but unpopulated globes. We suggest that the number of globes should be at least seven."

"We will see about that," Mysul said. "Servator," she said, "are you ready to package the Tower?"

"Mysul," the Servator replied, "its packaging can be immediate, but I cannot hold its weight for long beyond this sea."

"So be it," Mysul said. "Then it is just as well that we would leave for an empty sea. Our business is concluded. We can only wait."

*

In the town square, Lily - now returned to a camouflage outfit - stood hugging her mother and Dad. "You were wonderful, baby," said Anna. "One of the Five. Such an honour."

Riley nodded and said, "We were so proud, to see all those people clapping, for you. I cried."

"Oh you didn't, Dad!" Lily exclaimed and she blushed furiously.

"Not that I understand much about it," Riley said. "It's all a dream."

"I wish it were," Anna said. "But Riley dear, you should leave. You are not one of us. You are a normal human being and I love you for that. You can get back to the world. I can take you."

"I'm not leaving you. I am not losing you again. Take the Vicar and his wife. Everything I love is here."

"All you'll be offered is to be a town guard. A staff is not much use against a Black Army veteran."

"A stick was good enough for Lily, and it will be good enough for me."

Anna sighed. "Well I had better take the Vicar back anyway."

"Not so fast. He and I have a date with Ordinal to visit the Tower. That might be interesting."

54 - On the Morning

Paper of The Ordinal (3)

Report to the Grand Council

Intercepted and translated by Silas, Ordinal

*

It is my privilege to address you, at this critical moment.

I am a soldier in the army of our Lord God, and my rank is that of Lord Commander. All others are subordinate to me.

On the morning of a battle which shall be decisive, and in which the person of the Lord Commander himself will be at risk, it is customary that he will commit his thoughts to some kind of writing, for the guidance of others.

This is the morning of just such a battle. In accordance with God's Will I am dictating these words to my secretary, Saida. I am a plain speaker. However, I shall permit Saida to embellish the text with refinements of her own.

It is morning. With what remains of her power, Mysul has introduced day, night and their transitions, complete with a sun and moon. I welcome that. I am reminded of the mornings of the glober world to which I was despatched by our Lord God. There was always an uplift of the spirit when the sun rose, even though I did not sleep.

I suspect that Mysul has it in mind to make the environment familiar to those she is recalling from the glober worlds, or perhaps she wishes only to introduce a little drama, a little variety into this, her

422

last moment. Either way, it is futile. Mysul's sea is strange and over-complicated. I can assure you that - when this war is won - we shall replace her worthless experiments with the simplicity of dust. Then once more we shall be alone with our Lord God and we shall worship Him.

At this moment we are seated on a hillside overlooking the great plain of the Crossway, where in a short time the battle will begin. I have an impression of twilight, which comes from the haze of camp-fires and from dust where divisions of our Black Army are manoeuvring below. Across the plain we see the Roamers bustling about in the trees, busily preparing their defence, for all the good that will do them.

The result is inevitable. There is a tide in these grand events, and it flows with us. Through me I feel the beat of God's heart. My armour trembles with it. We shall wipe the Roamers from the face of this universe. Great Power though she is, Mysul shall flee, to take her nonsense elsewhere. What she leaves behind we shall destroy, for it is blasphemous and worthless.

Of those who inhabit the cosmos of Mysul, evolved through a bewildering array of experiments, some have intelligence, some even believe themselves Mysul-like, but they are only the cargo of evolution, with one exception - the Roamers. I see them now, across the plain, scurrying about in dark places like the vermin they are, enemies of the Lord God. For too long the war between us has been a stalemate. I concede that there is a discipline behind them, but never before have they faced what they face now. Annihilation.

One of the Roamers we shall allow to survive, and I have issued an order to that effect. That is, their Navigator. We shall need her to unlock whatever secret places Mysul has abandoned. I have long wanted to own a Navigator, for we have no-one with that ability.

But now, I believe that we are ready. We have sufficient munitions, and the Black Army is reinforced and unstoppable. We also have an element of surprise. God's Minister, our most powerful weapon, will join us from a direction for which the Roamers are not prepared. My concern is only that the Roamers also will have reinforcements. How many, I cannot be sure. This is an unknown. I prefer not to deal with unknowns, but I am confident that their reinforcements shall be overcome, as shall the others.

It is customary for the Lord Commander to appear on the battlefield in person, not through the instrument of projection. I follow that custom, as does my servant Twine. My army sees me in the flesh, mortal as are so many of them. My aspect is human, for that was the pinnacle of evolution in the second sea where I was born. Much of my army is not human, and some remains projected, but whatever our aspect and circumstances we are all partners in a contract of service to our Lord God, and in that contract I shall not expose my Army to dangers which I would not myself face.

What follows shall be the inevitable conclusion of this war, which I may witness, or I may not. Whatever the outcome for me, I am entrusting this account to Saida, and she shall place it in the hands of our Lord God.

For now, I close with what for so long has been the rallying cry of my Army - Bring on the day.

This is the day.

55 - The Tower

"This is what we protect, with our lives," Ordinal said. "You said you wanted to see it, and here it is."

They stood together on a hill of close-cut grass, around them trees of the forest which bent inwards and shed their leaves in a circle around. Above the Vicar and his wife, Riley Moss and Ordinal loomed the Great Tower. The Vicar declared it Magnificent and put his hands together in an attitude of prayer. "I detect a Norman influence," he enthused. "Note the round arches. Eleventh century, splendid buttresses. It's tall, isn't it? Why are the windows all boarded up?"

"To keep the rats out," Ordinal replied.

"Very wise," said the Vicar.

They entered through a windowless metal door, into a chamber of stone far larger than the base of the Tower had suggested. Ranks of waist-high bronze tubes stretched into the shadows, and around them drifted glassy shapes, some human, some animal, some in groups but more often singly, looking as if made of water, slowly moving, melting and re-forming until they passed over the tubes, where they were projected upwards in a silken stream. The ceiling was transparent, and above it a myriad tiny lights twinkled in what looked like a mass of boiling water, as if peering upwards into a kettle, but sky-blue. Whispers filled the air, interspersed with music, very faint - a flute here, a harp there, with the occasional thrum of an orchestra which phased in the manner of a radio searching for distant stations.

In the centre of the chamber a dark-haired woman in a gold-hemmed white robe stood with her arms folded.

"Ordinal, you have brought globers," she said. "Here?"

"May I introduce," said Ordinal to the others, "our Servator. This is her domain."

"Why have you done this, Ordinal?" she went on. "I hope it's not for some trivial purpose. Who are these globers anyway?"

"May I introduce," Ordinal said, "Mister Moss, father of Lily." Riley Moss bowed.

"Ah. That makes a sort of sense," said the Servator, delicately inclining her head.

"And the Vicar of - where was it? - somewhere, and Rosemary his wife," Ordinal went on. "I hope that the Vicar may act as my backup at some point. I am allowing him a view of my papers."

"Backup?" the Servator said. "Now you're speaking my language. Well, if you must, come in. I don't have much time for a demonstration." Her visitors edged forward, uncertain of what a demonstration might involve.

"I'm sure," Ordinal said, "that our guests would be happy to observe the Servator's choice."

"Male or female for the two men?" said the Servator. "I suggest female. It will give them both a new and useful experience. And perhaps male for the lady. Ditto."

"Whatever our Servator suggests," Ordinal said.

"What century?" she said. "Five before now, I think. Females, let's see, and a man... " She waved a hand over three of the bronze tubes. "What part of the globe are you from?"

"The United Kingdom," said the Vicar.

"Let's go for England," said the Servator. "Blood everywhere. Heads chopped off. Loved it."

Instantly, the Vicar, Rosemary and Riley Moss felt themselves rise, through the ceiling and into the shimmering mass of blue water and twinkling lights. Three of those lights attached themselves to them,

426

and then there was a feeling of falling, and an aroma of manure. Around them in a square, head-height walls of rough stone enclosed a field of grass bordered by rose bushes and dwarf oak trees.

"You appear to be a woman, Vicar," said Riley Moss.

"So do you," the Vicar replied. "But I am not in control of this body. We are certainly chattering, and I can hear it, but it's not chatter coming from me."

"I am the King of... not quite sure," said Rosemary.

The chatter was indistinct, muffled and phasing, but the view was clear. They stood in a garden. From the Vicar's point of view, Riley Moss was a woman of about twenty-five years, with her hair in a snood, a broad face, wide eyes, a narrow waist, and a dress that spread in a brown triangle across the grass. To Riley Moss, the Vicar was a younger woman, her black hair bound up in a curious construction which looked like the gable of a house, with a serious pale face, narrow eyes, and a dress which was red and richly embroidered in yellow. To both of them, Rosemary appeared as a young and handsome man with a flat yellow hat, a dark-red uniform, breeches and pointed shoes, and a stomach that was prominent.

"I can hardly breathe," said Riley Moss. "It's the corset."

"What torture women put themselves through," the Vicar said.

"Who do you think we are anyway?"

"I have no idea. Ladies of the Court possibly. This is a very nice garden."

"I am the King of England, and other places," said Rosemary.

"Whoah," said Riley Moss. "I'm being tugged."

In a second, the three of them arrived back in the base room of the Tower.

"The Boleyn sisters and Henry the Eighth," the Servator said. "Love following them. Terrible tragedy. I think I will give the King more of a hard time."

"Astonishing," said the Vicar. "Their lives. Are stored," and he pointed a finger upward. "There?" he said.

"Consciousness and data," Servator replied. "Everything is connected. Nothing is lost. We don't store grangels of course, only the results of what they do."

"Oh yes," Moss said. "Like Saida…"

Servator stepped forward with a new fire in her eyes. "Saida?" she said. "You have met that devil?"

Moss coughed into his hand. "Ummm… yes," he said. "It was not a pleasure."

"Pleasure!" Servator exclaimed. "The only pleasure I'd get from meeting that thief is to stomp on her head with the pointiest of my large collection of shoes. Pleasure, indeed…"

As she spoke, from outside came the howl of a hooter, followed by the booming of a drum, like a heart-beat, loud and insistent.

"Out, Ordinal," said the Servator, glancing around. "And you three. All of this has to be packaged. This is it. We are under attack."

428

56 - Prepare for Battle

On my return from the town of the Roamers I, the Vicar of Malbury, lost my memory of these events. Only when a box - wooden with a lid of some reflective metal - arrived on my desk, seemingly from nowhere, did memory stir in me again. It contained a sheaf of papers, hand-written in a style strangely old-fashioned. The first of those papers was this simple introduction:

My dear Vicar

I hope that you and your wife are well, and have suffered no ill effects from our process of conversion. In this box I enclose as promised certain papers which you might find enlightening and from which you might deduce the conclusion of the events to which you and your wife were briefly exposed.

It may be that you remember nothing of this. But remember, two things. What was it you saw in the basement of the Great Hall of Malbury? You did see it. You remember now. What caused the explosion in your own home, your Rectory? A faulty gas fire? No. You remember now.

I hope you will not be disappointed in us.

The Ordinal

If it were not for those papers - and a souvenir portrait of the Great Tower of the Roamers which I scavenged from their hotel - then the whole thing would indeed have seemed to be only a dream. But those papers and that portrait woke up memories, for - as the Roamers would say - 'Nothing is lost'.

Moreover, a second set of papers appeared on my desk one Monday morning, in a similar box. What follows, is my reconstruction of what occurred after my departure, based upon both sets of papers.

I have no doubt that my accuracy shall be tested.

*

Paths up into the town from the fields were blocked-off with broken rocks and whatever furniture was heavy enough to be an obstacle. Guards were stationed along walls and in a solid phalanx in the town Square. Shops were shut, as were the doors of all buildings. Between them and in the Square scuttled residents, their children and mechanicals, alarm on their faces, not knowing whether to go in or out, looking for shelter from what they did not yet know. In the fields, battalions of Roamer troops were arranged in squares between the town and Mount Cardinal and uphill to the Tower. Overhead an aerial battalion circled, the white robes of its members glowing in the light of morning.

"We have done what we can," said the Ordinal, looking out towards Mount Cardinal over a chest-high wall. "Never before has there been an assault on the town."

The Cardinal nodded, but said, "We must respect Mysul's decision. Our Navigator has given her a way in, through the Minister's protection, but she will use it only at the last moment. Otherwise the Minister will move, and at least we know where it is now."

Below them, the Vicar and his wife stood under the awning of a shop, Riley Moss at their side.

"You have to get yourself away, Vicar," said Riley Moss. "This is no place for you."

"I am beginning to think you are right, Mister Moss," the Vicar said. "But I am not sure how."

"Ordinal is up on the wall there, behind the Council House. He can help you out, I'm sure."

"Yes, a good plan. God be with you, Mister Moss."

"And with you, Vicar. And Mrs Ellis."

The Vicar and Rosemary trudged along the street, then into a side-street beside the Council House and to the town wall, where they ascended a series of stone steps, to find Ordinal and the Cardinal gloomily contemplating the hillside. "Excuse me, gentlemen," the Vicar said, "but I am not sure that we belong here."

"No, you do not," said the Ordinal, turning. "Cardinal, can you oblige?"

"I can," the Cardinal replied. "Anything, to distract me from this for a few moments."

"Wait," the Ordinal went on. "I made a promise to you, sir. Papers. You might find them enlightening. However things go, I shall get them to you. Look for a box on your desk. If we succeed then perhaps you might learn more. If we fail, then my papers will be little comfort, for the Angel will be upon you at the time of its choosing. Now, it is better that you return." The Vicar nodded.

"Take my hands, sir and lady," said Cardinal. "I believe you know how disconcerting this can be, but the effects wear off quickly."

Together, the Cardinal and the Vicar and his wife vanished.

*

Atop a mountain overlooking the plain and the distant Roamer-infested forest, the Lord Commander surveyed the field of battle. He held a lance bearing a black flag, the tip of the lance pointing down. Beside him stood God's Minister, projected from the Vault. Behind him stood his servant Twine, and Saida who was nervously rubbing the rings on the fingers of one hand.

The Lord Commander had summoned his full battle-dress, his grey armour polished, the visor of his helmet closed but his dark eyes visible through its lenses, the grid of an amplifier over his lips, and he stood with legs apart in the attitude of a warrior. The Minister

431

remained in dark-blue rags, a skeletal beggar with an expression of deepest gloom. Twine wore a suit of black chain-mail, in his hand a crossbow. Beneath them, on folding chairs arranged over a shelf of rock, sat the divisional commanders and fire support, each armoured, each with the long-distance lenses of their helmets fully open, each holding in their gauntlets a console, a black screen which displayed the plan of battle.

"You are the strategy," the Minister said. "I am the power. Where are you placing me?"

"Where you are already. In their rear," the Lord Commander replied. "I shall drive the Centre, here. How close are you to full power?"

"God's breath fills me," the Minister replied. "I shall be ready within a thousand beats of His heart."

On the plain below, three divisions of God's forces prepared for battle. On either wing, white riders drove their insect chariots forward and back in what looked like circles of ever-moving maggots. In the centre, squares of the Black Army shifted from side to side, shepherded by many hundred hoverflies, whose rays flashed white through the dust. Above them swarmed shellflies, eggs of light guided by their ghostly inhuman occupants, a spiker slung below each. Even higher, where clouds from below had gathered into a grey haze, featureless oblongs of black metal, drones, drifted like leaves on a stream.

"There will be no need for subtlety," the Lord Commander said. "They have new resources, but untrained. We shall simply roll over them. I myself have abandoned my image and stand here in the flesh of my mortal body, so confident am I of our success on the ground. And with our drones, our hoverflies, and with you, Minister, we shall also have control of the sky."

"I am only the channel of God's power," the Minister said, "but I am a power which these vermin have not seen before. And will see only once."

"Ah," said the Lord Commander, "we are observed."

432

On the highest hill of the forest stood the Constable and Lily Moss, her battalion of Wolves behind her in a line. Little Chun was proudly carrying the stick which Lily had given her. The Constable was scanning the mountains and the plain below with binoculars. "Typical plan of battle," he said. "Brute force. No imagination whatsoever. Obviously the fellow is no student of Thucydides."

Below, men and women in uniforms of dark grey were filtering back into the trees. "The sappers are back," said the Constable. "They did a good job. The plain looks completely flat."

"Now," Lily said, "we must appear stronger than we are. And after the first skirmish, that is when we must appear weaker than we are."

The Constable smiled. "I approve of your strategy," he said. "And you have the power of Mysul with you now. I see you have a Mysul staff. Have you tried it?"

"I have. I hit more often than I miss."

"Good, Navigator, we may need that. Our aerial battalions may need your support."

This was the Mysul staff which Lily had taken with her on her journey back into the mountain. But now her robe was white, from shoulders to ankles, with a golden hem, a robe the same as her mother's, in the aerial battalion which was circling in the sky behind the hill.

She turned. "Wolves!" she cried. "Each of you take a platoon down there, to the centre. Keep moving. Spread out. Make noise. Make fire. Be bigger than you are. Keep looking up here. If I raise my staff straight up, and fire directly upwards, then I want you back here. Go!" Her wolves spread out and ran downhill.

As she watched them go she saw, pacing through the trees of the hill's other side, two black figures each with a long pole to which a sword was strapped, the Mercenaries. They approached, and the

Constable gave them a disapproving stare. "You are who?" he said. "The lady knows who we are," came the reply.

"I do," said Lily. "You are welcome, sirs. May I place you in our wings?"

"So you have learned the value of wings," said one. "May we lead?"

"That won't do," the Constable said. "We have perfectly good wing commanders already, thank you."

"Constable," Lily said. "These are not ordinary men. We can learn from their experience." She turned to the Mercenaries. "I am happy for you to support our wing commanders," she said, "and I now give that order. At my command you shall ensure that the left wing appears weak and falls back behind the hill. I hope that is understood."

"It is, my Lady," said the other. "We will await the command."

"Now, Constable," Lily went on. "I must inspect the defence of the town. When the enemy advances, you shall give the alarm."

"I shall, Navigator," he said, turning back to survey the plain with his binoculars.

In the manner of the Five, Lily breathed in and stretched herself to a size so great that her consciousness lay in the sky, then with love she directed herself back to the sky above the town.

*

"They strengthen their centre," said the Lord Commander. "Or appear to. This means nothing. Twine, summon the commander of the Second Wing."

In moments there stood before the Lord Commander his subordinate in black armour, humanoid but for the feelers which dangled beneath his visor. "Commander," said his Lord, "Let us be clear about your first manoeuvre. At my signal you will begin your advance on the

434

left. This is a diversion, to distract the enemy from the centre. Your direction is towards the ravine to the left of the highest hill of the forest."

The Commander of the Second Wing bowed and grunted, "As you command."

*

Above the town, Lily joined the members of an aerial battalion. She floated at their centre while they circled around, men and women in robes of white with yellow backpacks, all clutching their staves and with grimly determined expressions. "Remember," she said, "their drones and hoverflies can fire only downward. You must get above by whatever means to bring them down." One replied, "We understand, Navigator. They are quick to rise. We will have to be quicker."

"How many of you hold aerial mines?"

"All of us, Navigator. According to your order, through the Ordinal. He put many of our new arrivals in the Munitions section and they have worked quickly."

"And well, we hope. Good. When the signal is given you must be quick. Much depends on your speed and agility."

Grim-faced, each of them nodded.

Lily flew down over the town. It was a toy village, and like a toy it looked fragile. Somewhere down there was her father. She paused in mid-air, but could not make him out among the milling-about bodies, the carts, the thrown-together defences at the town's gates. As the Constable had advised, battalions of Roamer troops were positioned in squares on the path from the mountain and in the fields leading to the Tower. Few of them held Mysul staves - most were no better than sticks - and the archers had little room to move. Against this enemy, their weapons were all-but useless. They could only buy time until the Roamers of the plain could join them.

435

Already it seemed to Lily that the town would be sacrificed to defend the Tower, and how could her Dad be saved? She wanted to fly further down, find him, take him to the plain where he and her mother could be together, but there was no time.

With a tear in her eye she turned and flew back across the hills to the plain.

57 - The Advance

Lily Moss stood atop the highest hill of the forest, overlooking the plain where the Black Army manoeuvred and the hillside where her own troops busied themselves in the trees. At her side, the Constable - feet planted apart and head held high - twirled his moustaches and uttered a series of impatient grunts. A line of flares lay at his feet, their cases red, green and white. These were Lily's means of communication with her battalions, but now she was one of the Five she did not need to sleep or dream, but only to think of her mother to communicate with her and the others.

"Mum, where is Dad?"

"With the town guards, my darling, by the Square. Your father has no training for our sort of battle."

"I hope we all stay safe."

"Nowhere is safe. We can only do our best. Where are you?"

"Back at the Gate, Mum. Remember, the first wave will stay low until the Constable's signal. Then it must rise high and fast. At the second signal, the second wave must rise and follow my command."

"We will. Mysul is with us in the first wave, then she will return to the town and dispose of the Minister."

"Granny!"

"Don't be cheeky. She can be Granny when this is over."

"They're coming. The shellflies and drones are on the move."

"We are ready."

*

High above the plain of the Gate, a swarm of shellflies, so many thousands that they formed a wide cloud of jostling light-bubbles, white against the black of the mountain behind, began to spread forward. They came on quickly, each with the ball of a spiker slung below. Above them, the drones which before had drifted aimlessly now formed into black lines abreast and drove on through the clouds.

From across the plain came the beat of a drum, booming across the plain from the black mountain beyond. With the ground thumping beneath her, what Lily saw now on the plain and in the sky were only shapes, impersonal blocks of power which jostled for position. All that she could see of the Gate was a dark cloud of vapour, but she knew that the Grey Angel stood there, and this was the beating of his heart.

The Constable fired a white flare, which hung smoking and glowing above the hill. Immediately from behind the hill rose the first wave of Lily's aerial battalion. They rose high and fast, dozens of them as angels in the sky, each with a staff, their white robes flapping, their hair streaming back as they flew forward and distributed themselves in the sky above the forest. Mysul herself led the wave, searching the sky, a staff in each hand.

In the clouds the drones halted, and from them came a web of red beams which swept in a pitiless arc across the forest hill. Whatever a beam touched, burst into a plume of flame. There was chaos below among Lily's battalions. Trees and people were ablaze.

Her aerial battalion flew forward, higher, and dispersed, detaching their backpacks which fell onto the drones where they split into streams of yellow fire. Drones wobbled, crashed into each other and began to fall from the sky, landing on the plain in clouds of dust and mangled black girders. Cheers came from below on the hill, but other drones came on, spreading their fire closer to Lily's hill, ever closer, until the aerial battalion dropped onto them, wildly firing blasts of lightning from their staves, as the drones fell and crashed into the trees. The few that remained swept back through the clouds towards the black mountain.

But the shellflies came on, spreading to the width of the hill. Those at the front began to drop spikers into the trees. The aerial battalion let fly with blasts of skybolts. Where they hit, a shellfly would fold into itself and melt away, but still their spikers fell, down into the forest. In and out of the shellfly swarm the aerial battalion darted, firing at will. Mysul twirled, rose, fell and rose again, skybolts pouring from her staves like electric rain. Shellflies and their spikers imploded in mid-air. In minutes, no shellfly was left, but their cargo lay between the trees below, in the undergrowth.

The horror of a spiker came clear to Lily when she saw one leap from a bush onto a sapper. It engulfed his head, smothering, its claw jammed into his neck, its black body now growing transparent, veins pulsing, as he fell, the spiker with him. Another member of the platoon slashed at the spiker and burst it, but too late. This happened across the hill. Lily feared for her wolves, but none of the dead were hers, as far as she could see. There was no telling how many spikers remained in the bushes, and no time to deal with them, for on her right, in the distance, a circle of black began to advance.

"He advances his wing," the Constable said. "I suspect a diversionary move. We should counter. I suggest we move a battalion to the right wing."

"No," Lily said. "Counter that with the first wave of our aerial battalion. They are already visible. By moving them we suggest there are no more. This is the time to appear weaker."

"At your command," the Constable said. He fired a green flare, to the right, which the first wave of the aerial battalion followed, until it stood high above a clump of trees in a ravine on the right wing.

At that moment the tempo of the Grey Angel's heart-beat doubled. Lily felt it through her feet. "That can't be!" she cried in alarm.

"It is very annoying," the Constable said.

"No!" Lily cried. "The Minister will be ready earlier than we thought! Mysul!"

Mysul twirled, lifted her staves, and flew away towards the town.

Lily would have followed, but before her eyes the plain had erupted into columns of dust. Half-way across, the enemy's left wing was under fire, from long-distance skybolts and now from below, from the Roamer mines. Plumes of earth, dust in tornado clouds, exploded from beneath their white riders and insect chariots. Into the craters left by the mines they fell, where they set off more mines across their front. Where they could see through the dust-cloud, the white riders directed their beasts around the craters, and their spindly legs set off even more mines, which demolished the front of the wing, leaving it a writhing mass of twisted white bodies and insect parts. The wing halted, uncertain of safe paths through the carnage.

"Let us hope," said Lily, "that our enemy believes they are the only mines we have."

The Constable grinned, but turned back, narrowed his eyes and said, "Here it comes. They advance."

As the heart-beat of the Grey Angel grew louder, the enemy's right wing moved forward, and in the centre of the plain the squares of the Black Army with it. Hoverflies circled above, their laser-rays darting from square to square, keeping them in line. But they were not alone. Behind the Black Army a man strode through the dust, carrying a lance with a black flag held aloft.

"Who the devil is that?" the Constable said.

"He calls himself the Lord Commander."

"The devil he does."

"The devil he is."

The Lord Commander halted, but the white riders of his right wing came on, as did the Black Army, its grids of black humanoid figures ahead of him clicking robotically back and forth. He planted his lance in the ground.

"Constable," said Lily. "Signal the left wing to fall back."

The Constable set off a red flare to his left. Immediately Lily's battalions fell back through the burning trees. She saw one of the Mercenaries among them. They ran through bushes on fire, ignoring spikers, who burned alongside the bodies of her battalions' troops in the bushes and on the ground. On the other side of the hill they halted, the Mercenary at their head, brandishing his sword-staff.

"Constable," said Lily, "signal to the second aerial battalion to rise."

"We can only hope," the Constable said, "that our enemy falls into the trap."

*

In the town square, Riley Moss stood in line with a platoon of guards. He had been issued with a camouflage uniform which hung off him like a sack. In front of them, over the cobbles of the square, paced a dumpy little fellow, similarly clad but with glasses, Humbert from the Hotel. "Eyes front!" the little man cried, in that hectoring tone often found from little men in charge of bigger. "Arms up!" Riley was about to lift his arms, but noticed that on either side the guards were simply holding their sticks forward. That is all they were, sticks, batons, useful only when facing an unarmed enemy.

"To the right," yelled Humbert, "quick march!"

The line of guards set off through an alley to the town wall. Above them, the Ordinal and the Cardinal stood gazing towards Mount Cardinal. The guards lined up against the wall, on their left a tunnel which led to a path down to the fields. It was full of junk, building stones, furniture, piled up to its roof, a fragile defence. Riley estimated that he could push it down with his baton alone.

*

The heart-beat of the Grey Angel had reached the town. Above the guards, the Ordinal sighed, "If only we had sappers."

441

"Couldn't spare them," the Cardinal said. "It has always been a point-nine probability that we would not need them here."

"I just have the feeling that we will."

"It is a point-nine probability now, Ordinal, that your feeling is correct."

Into the dark triangle at the base of Mount Cardinal, where the path down toward the town began, a man walked, hunched, seemingly hesitant. At this distance he appeared insignificant, a small dark figure in what looked like rags. He stepped forward and raised a hand. On either side of him, figures marched out into the light, black armoured figures which would be men if it were not for the mechanical, clockwork manner in which they strode down the path. Above them, from the triangle poured a stream of black drones and hoverflies, which rose quickly into the sky, wings beating furiously, fire-tubes hanging down.

"Look!" cried the Ordinal. "Mysul is in the sky! Oh may your aim be sure, my love!"

Above the sky-bound carpet of drones and hoverflies, Mysul and an aerial battalion circled. Before the enemy had time to rise, Mysul and her legion swooped. Their backpacks fell on drones, flipping them from the sky, and on all sides they blasted at the hoverflies, which tumbled in a rain of broken limbs. But these were not Mysul's target. Leaving her battalion to the task, she swooped lower, and with both staves she blasted tongues of fire at the man standing before the dark triangle.

"What is she doing?" said the Cardinal.

"Do you recognise that creature?" said the Ordinal.

"There is something familiar…"

"Remember, when we came across…"

"The Minister!"

442

Before Mysul's skybolts could hit, the Minister vanished, and re-appeared a few metres to one side. More sky-bolts came, and again he moved.

"An image," the Cardinal said.

The Minister spread his arms and from each hand issued a bolt of red fire which Mysul swerved to avoid. She swooped lower, her white robe trailing behind her as she grazed the heads of the oncoming Black Army and launched herself directly at the Minister, firing with both staves. Then in a flash she disappeared.

Caught off-guard the Minister staggered back, but even from the town his shout was heard, "Forty-one beats, Mysul! Forty!"

*

It was the gravest insult that her enemy, another Great Power, should plant within her domain a mechanism to grow and protect its creatures, a Vault. As Mysul stood on the platform of rock where Lily had tethered her channel, in the cavern where her Navigator had met the Black Army for the first time, the violet-blue of her eyes turned to a deep red of fury. She saw its creatures below, hoverflies issuing from a spout to the side of a ravine, Black Army guards at the Vault's entrance, squadrons in lines waiting to head out towards her town. She swooped from the platform, down towards the entrance of the Vault. Scattering fire to left and right, she burst through the line of Black Army guards, and into the wasps' nest of her enemy's Vault, where she hovered for the moment unchallenged.

The cavern stretched into shadows ahead. Many thousands of transparent coffins lay in long dusty lines. As she watched, hoverflies ascended, and she despatched them with blasts from her staves. But she was looking for something more. She flew on, scattering fire to light her path.

With a low ceiling and yellow dust over the rock of its walls, a further cavern opened, at its centre a statue of white marble from which jagged flashes of electric light crackled and struck at the

443

coffins around it. The statue was of the Grey Angel, the interloper. It was the heart of the Vault, and the projection point. With a single blast she smashed it to fragments which spiralled through the dust. Around, many hundreds of coffins lit up. Their lids opened. Creatures within them began to move. Mysul swooped over them, searching. She could not tell which of these abominations was the Lord Commander and which the Minister. Searching was pointless. She twirled in mid-air and aimed low. "This," she cried, "is for Lily." Her skybolts smashed into the coffins, destroying their occupants. Arms and legs were raised in a last protest. Heads, wings, evaporated. With a final blast of all-encompassing fire, Mysul swooped away and out of the Vault, out from under the mountain, and rose back into the sky.

What she had not noticed in her fury was that the coffins closest to the projection point were empty. And on the lid of one was etched a number - zero.

*

"They just vanished!" the Constable cried.

On the plain of the Gate entire lines of white riders and insects had disappeared. The Lord Commander, though, still stood in mid-plain, his head turning this way and that, and the Black Army marched on, close now to the forest. Already, the rods which bound the robotic soldiers of its front squares were falling away, to release them into the trees, and hoverflies were breaking away from their task of shepherding the others.

"Over-confidence," said Lily. "Constable, signal to the right wing to advance, and for the second aerial battalion to support the first. We must get behind. It is time to drive them."

The Constable sent off a flurry of flares. In a moment, high in the sky the second aerial battalion rose with Anna at its head. They flew to the right where they joined the others in rising high above the plain. Beneath them, with a Mercenary at their head, Roamer

444

battalions swarmed from the trees, formed into phalanxes and advanced, steadily, purposefully, then more quickly as they approached what was left of their enemy's left wing. Men and women, young and old, all lowered their staves and from them a wall of fire raked across the white riders and their insect chariots, which broke apart and burned into a plume of black smoke which Lily could smell even from the hill, a stink of the foulest decay. Above them, skybolts rained down as the aerial battalion swooped over the hoverflies and burned them apart. The Roamers fell upon the carcasses of the enemy, stripped off the cockroach armour, held it up as shields and reformed their phalanxes, which now were behind the Lord Commander and moving to Lily's left.

The Black Army and the enemy's right wing began to turn leftward, where her wing had retreated, away from the onslaught and away from the Lord Commander. "Ahead!" came his shout. "Forward!"

Now it was the shepherds that were shepherded. Above the hoverflies, the aerial battalion swooped and drove them to Lily's left. The enemy's right wing, and then the Black Army followed. "No! Forward!" the Lord Commander shouted.

As the Black Army came to the tree-line, the trap was sprung. Mines exploded along the plain, sending out great plumes of dust, rock, and body parts. The ground beneath the white riders, insects, and then the Black Army itself crumbled and fell away.

"Constable," Lily said. "Signal to our left wing to advance."

"At your command. We have them now."

In a blaze of fury, the Lord Commander turned and from his claws beams of light poured onto the phalanxes behind him. There were casualties. People fell, but for the most part his rays glanced harmlessly off the Roamer shields and burned into the dust of the plain.

To Lily's left, her battalions led by a Mercenary charged out of the trees and fell upon the scattered remnants of the enemy, which were struggling in the craters and pits left by the mines. The insects, the hoppers, the white riders were easy prey. The Roamers stripped off

445

the armour which they held above their heads as shields against the rays of the hoverflies. But not for long, for around circled the aerial battalions who again poured fire upon the hoverflies, which tumbled from the sky, the survivors retreating in a furious cloud back towards the black mountain. Some of the humanoids of the Black Army escaped into the trees, where they were cut down by the battalions of Lily's centre or leapt upon by their own spikers.

Others, now detached from the rods which had held them in lines, and no longer with hoverflies to guide them, milled around between the plain and the forest, humanoids, insects, a seething mass of unconnected fury, as likely to turn upon itself as upon others.

The Lord Commander whirled around. Something had left him. In the carnage around him the grey armour of his body flashed and his head gyrated as if it had become an independent being and insane. But from behind him came the beat of the Grey Angel's heart.

*

Men of giant size in armour, with swords, lances, axes, and great guttural shouts; they rushed down towards the town in a river of black, down from Mount Cardinal, above them hoverflies which had escaped the assault of the aerial battalion. They had no order, they were berserkers, but the impetus of driving downhill carried them through and over the first squares of the Roamers which were slaughtered on the hillside. Then the weakness of the aerial battalion became obvious. They would not, could not fire over the town. All of them, even Mysul herself, had to fly lower and fire sideways, and even then with limited success.

Worse was to come. By the exit from the mountain, from inside a circle of Black Army guards stepped the man in rags. In seconds his body swelled into a grey curtain which spread up and over the mountain, thrusting out triangles in the sky where at each apex his head appeared, grown to a monstrous size, snarling, red-eyed, black lips wide and white fangs exposed. From under those heads the talons of black claws clutched at the sky. One head, its hair writhing

446

like a nest of snakes, shot forward until it hovered metres away from the Ordinal and the Cardinal on the town wall, who stepped back, aghast. "Miserable vermin," it said. "See how war is fought."

The head swept back, as from each of the claws under each of the heads came shafts of light, white light with an inner streak of black, which struck at the walls of the town, vaporising wherever they touched.

"Shaker rays," the Cardinal groaned. "Forbidden, forbidden." As the shaker rays swept towards them, the Ordinal and the Cardinal exchanged glances and disappeared.

Mysul swooped. She held herself in mid-air between the mountain and the town, with the heads of the Minister snarling before her.

At each head she let loose a volley of skybolts, and for a moment each jerked back but returned with a grimace and greater fury, the beams of shaker rays filling the sky. To and fro, to and fro, with skybolts and shaker rays, above the hillside Mysul and the Minister, the channel of her enemy's power, slashed at each other in a renewal of their stalemate. Neither could die, each could only press forward in search of a moment of weakness, one minor misjudgement or act of folly.

*

Lined up at the wall, the town guards heard them coming. The enemy arrived in a blaze of rays from above, from hoverflies which flew at will across the town, fire-tubes dangling and burning all below. One hit the Council House, and flames leapt up before them as its masonry tumbled into the street. Within seconds there were loud cries from the tunnel, and the crack of wood splintering under axes. "Guards!" yelled Humbert, "Form up! Two ranks! First rank with staves forward! Second with staves up!"

As soon as the enemy broke through the barrier in the tunnel, it was obvious that the guards could not withstand a frontal assault. "Retreat!" Humbert yelled, "To the Square!"

To Riley Moss, this was even more ludicrous, suicidal. As Humbert dashed away, and the rest of the guards behind him, Riley Moss scuttled behind a fallen block of masonry. He saw the stream of armoured men turning towards the Square, clumping over the cobbles in their heavy boots, no sign of their eyes, hidden behind black visors with a grey flash. The stream of them went on, and on, but at its rear the pace was less furious. Some of them took a position at the mouth of the tunnel as sentries. One walked under the wall towards him. He was a foot taller than Riley and a foot wider, though that might have been the armour. He may not even have been a man, for the armour concealed all within it. Dealing with troops like these, fully armed, when defenders had only sticks and stones from fallen buildings, was a nonsense. It was better to fight a guerrilla war, abandon the town, camp in the forest, anywhere but here.

On came the soldier of the Black Army, swinging his axe. Fight or flight? Riley had no choice. In seconds he would be detected. To flee would be to get an axe in the spine. As the soldier passed, Riley stuck out his staff between the man's legs, and he tripped, landing face-front on the cobbles with a clang of metal. Riley wrenched the axe from the man's hand, and struck at his head. Trailing a red slime the helmet came away and rolled over the cobbles, but it was empty. These soldiers were armour, living armour, no less powerful for that, but armour which could die.

Now with the axe in his hand, Riley hid behind the block of masonry. Another soldier rushed forward with a clumping of boots. Riley crouched, and as the soldier appeared struck upwards between the man's legs. The soldier doubled up, as Riley moved aside and with a single stroke chopped away his helmet.

What Riley did not know - for he could not have seen - was that the Black Army had quickly slaughtered the guards left in the Square, and had turned towards the Council House. A dozen of its soldiers had formed a platoon to clear the wall. They came from behind. Riley heard, and turned. Slowly they advanced. Slowly the giants approached, swinging axes and swords.

Riley held up his axe. Slowly they surrounded him, but quickly struck. In a rain of blows from axes and swords, from men who had no faces, Riley Moss fell. There was pain, acute and total, but it passed. As his eyes closed for the last time Riley Moss saw before him a tall man with a chalk-white face, wearing a black suit, who held out his hand.

He sat by the window of a train. Beside him sat the man in a black suit. "You can call me John," he said, staring ahead.

It was an ancient train, a steam engine. In the wood-panelled compartment Riley sat opposite a mother and her small boy, she in a long dress of blue and a flowery hat, he in a leather jerkin and knickerbockers.

The train stopped in a valley by a crowd of people who rushed forward, holding out their arms, leaving behind a small blonde-haired girl who stood by a stream. There was something familiar about her, and Riley gave her a wave as the train pulled away.

"Where are we going?" he said.

"To the Tower. We are nearly there."

"I hope that little girl will be OK."

"There is nothing you can do for her now."

58 - The Lord Commander

Lily felt a tug in her chest and then a sudden panic as if a hand were squeezing her heart. "Oh," she murmured. "Something... someone... has changed."

"Yes," the Constable replied. "Look."

Mid-plain the Lord Commander was kneeling, the flag of his lance fluttering in the wind from the carnage around him. He rose, as across the plain boomed the heart-beat of the Grey Angel, and he turned with his lance stretched forward. Behind him, down from the mountain came a line of dark humanoid figures, pressing through bushes and grass until they stood on the plain. They came tentatively forward, all in the armour of the Black Army except for their leader, a small man in chainmail, in his hands a crossbow.

"Constable," Lily said with a frown, "Signal to the right wing to withdraw."

But too late. Just as the Constable fired off his flare, the Lord Commander spread his arms wide, and from his lance poured a new light, a white light but pale, in which waves of black pulsed.

"Shaker rays," the Constable said. "With a gamma carrier. Forbidden by the Presence at every Gate. Could tear the whole sea apart. This is desperation."

The Roamers of Lily's right wing felt it first. As the rays of the Lord Commander's lance fell on them, the shields fell from their hands and all, unprotected, men and women, a Mercenary among them, were struck by an instant and overpowering heat, swayed, and trembled as the fabric of their being fell apart. In seconds they burst into clouds of white smoke which drifted away across the plain.

Lily made the signal for her wolves to gather, raising her staff upright and firing into the sky. In moments they joined her, carrying knives, sticks, and swords they had gathered from the wreckage below, but some were missing.

"Robert?" she said.

"Caught by a spiker," said little Chun with her head down. "Killed. We were too late to save him."

"Marco? Sidney?"

"Burned," Martha replied. "They stood together, and they were hit by the same blast. From a hoverfly, or a drone, we can't be sure."

Lily drew a deep breath and blew it out. "Wolves," she said. "Our target is their Lord Commander. Are you ready to advance?"

In the line before her were only nods, with a "Yes!" from little Chun.

"Suicide," the Constable said. "You have no defence against the shaker ray. Only Mysul could withstand it."

"Constable," said Lily. "I know his weakness. It is... me. He needs a navigator. He told me that himself. He will not kill me. He had the opportunity, but he did not do it. Now, I will distract him and stand in his way, and you will signal to our aerial battalion to attack him from above. Do you understand?"

"You will put yourself and your battalion in harm's way. Are you sure, Navigator?"

"I am sure."

"At your command." The Constable sent a green flare up and directly ahead.

Re-formed, the aerial battalion with Anna at its head swooped over the field of battle. "Wolves!" Lily cried. "Wherever you came from, we are going one way. Forward, and together! Let no-one say you were not brave. Now is our time, and nothing is lost." She held her staff pointing down at the plain. "Forward! For Mysul and for me! Forward!"

Her stride downhill turned to a run as she felt her wolves around her, her hair streaming behind, her staff ahead, the branches whipping at her, and her feet flying over rocks, bushes, bodies, black earth and then the dust of the plain. Firing from her staff she cleared a path through the heaving chaos of what was left of the Black Army as her wolves followed, with the figure of the Lord Commander, Chatham the torturer, ahead.

"Down!" she cried and pointed her staff into the dust. Her wolves fell to the ground and crawled forward into the shelter of a low ridge of dusty rock. Lily flew up, above the Lord Commander, and fired a bolt at him from her staff. It missed, and sent a plume of smoke up from the plain.

The Lord Commander lowered his lance. "Navigator!" he yelled. "Stand aside!"

But in those few seconds in mid-air Lily had opened up a gap beneath her. The Lord Commander crouched, and directed his fire across the plain.

The ridge of rock was no defence from the black-in-white rays. As the Lord Commander's fire raked along the ridge it exploded into fragments, and behind it, one by one as she turned her head, Lily saw the wolves of her battalion hit, and burst into smoke which drifted upward, slowly.

For each small cloud she had a face and a name. For each she felt the stab of a knife in her heart. For each she felt the weight of guilt, for leading them here.

Little Chun, her friend.

Theo, who gave his hand to her when she climbed on the bus to the Lodge.

Martha the almost-woman and Michael the almost-man. And the others. Drifting as smoke across the plain, the Black Army in chaos behind. Gone.

452

The rage of battle grew in Lily's eyes. But from above came a blast of fire, from Anna and the aerial battalion. The Lord Commander was hit, struck by the skybolts, and his body jerked with the pressure of it, sending his shaker rays off at all angles, one scraping by Lily's head. He yelled, "Then die! Die!" and he tumbled back into the dust, his lance beneath him, his helmet rolling away through the dust.

Lily was on him in a second, and stood over him, the wolf's-claw knife in her hand. "Who is the inferior animal?" she gasped. "Who is the predator now?"

The eyes of Chatham the torturer swivelled in their sockets out of control. His neck was broken and his grey head lolled to one side, his tongue protruding between black lips. "Na... vi..." he mouthed as his body trembled and jerked beneath her. From above, a skybolt flashed into his face, melting the grey flesh and leaving only the bone of a skull.

"Na... vi..." chattered the skull with a hollow voice from below its throat, "Na... vi..." Lily ended the horror with a slash of her knife up between the joints of his armour into the Lord Commander's heart.

In a fountain of red Chatham's body went limp, then trembled in the dust, the rays of his lance feebly but remorselessly eating away at his remains.

59 - Town and Plain

Above Mount Cardinal the battle between Mysul and the Minister raged.

Her skybolts rent the grey curtain of the Minister's body, which sealed over in seconds as he poured his rays of black-in-white at her, and she deflected them with her staves, turning them back on their source, obliterating the head which had delivered them.

But the heads re-grew, snarling, until Mysul enveloped herself, the Minister and the mountain in a boiling white fog which spread down the hillside, covering the bodies of the slaughtered Roamer squares.

Through that fog shone the flash of skybolts and black shaker rays, as the entire mountain trembled and those left in the town and on the Tower's hill felt the shock of battle through the ground.

*

'Your master is overthrown."

The voice of the Second Wing's commander was factual and robotic. He stood a metre taller than Twine, in the armour of the Black Army, a grey flash on his helmet. Into the dust he threw the screen with its plan of battle. 'Now it is to me that our Lord God speaks," he said. 'Servant, your master requires a last service. Revenge. We wait for God's Minister to deliver our victory. Take no backward step, or you are dust."

One by one the commanders discarded their screens, and formed into a line behind the commander of the Second Wing. Together they turned and began their march back to the black mountain, leaving Twine alone in the swirling dust of the plain. Ahead, four hundred metres away, he saw the ridiculous little girl in her white robe, at her feet the body of his master. That such a power should be overthrown by a girl he should have killed when she was a baby, was a disgrace, a blasphemy. A commander such as he... if he wanted a Navigator, a key-holder, it was his right to have her. To fail, to die at the hands of that child and her mother - impossibly wrong.

Hatred boiled within him. The scar in the palm of his hand was jet black. He fixed a bolt into his crossbow, crouched, and lay flat on the dust of the plain, holding the crossbow before him. He was out of range. Quickly he squirmed forward in the cover of bodies of insects and white riders and of dunes of dust thrown up by the Roamer mines.

A hundred metres away he raised his head, dust in his hair, the ground hot through his chainmail. The mother had landed by the girl's side. They were embracing, in their white robes. It was a horror, to see the body of his master at their feet while these worthless creatures celebrated victory, a hollow victory, a moment of triumph which he would cut short.

*

It was as Lily had predicted. The town had to be sacrificed to save the Tower. Pleas from her Servator filled Mysul's ears. 'They are close! Too close!"

The Minister was weakening. All heads but one had disappeared and the curtain of his body was shrinking, down through the white fog. Soon he would again be no more than a man, but the forces he had let loose had stormed through the town and onto the paths which led up to the Great Tower. Before them, Roamer squares were drawn up with weapons which would prove futile. Above, a solitary aerial battalion of Roamers was fighting fiercely against an overwhelming force of drones and hoverflies. The few that remained of the town's men, women and children were streaming out into the fields where they were picked off group by group by blasts from above. Some made it to the forest where they were leapt upon by spikers from their nests in the undergrowth. Only one platoon of guards escaped, running across the fields towards the mountain, sheltering in the trees of the path until they vanished into the foliage at the mountain's side.

Mysul abandoned the Minister in the fog, turned and swooped away across the town towards the Tower. She ordered her troops of the plain to cross back over the hills, but as she gave that order a wide stream of black-in-white fire coursed beneath her and enveloped the town and the hills to the plain - the last, unhindered blast of the Minister's power.

She found herself flying through a swirling pillar of black smoke, and debris which shot up in a fountain from a town which no longer existed. It lay beneath her, a blackened crater lower than the fields from which it had risen, empty of life.

*

'Riley!" Anna cried.

With horror Lily saw behind the hill a spiralling tornado of black cloud rising into the blue sky, slowly at this distance, but she knew what had happened. She struggled to speak. "It's Dad... isn't it?"

Anna lifted her head and gazed at the cloud. 'Yes," she said.

Lily felt her mother's breath quicken. She felt the shock enter her also, and a rush of tears to her eyes. She looked up. Her mother held her chin up, but tears in a delta scarred her white cheek and gathered to her lips. "The town..." Anna whispered, 'is gone. Your father... has fallen. Nothing is lost." As if to convince herself she repeated, 'Nothing is lost."

'Dad? Oh Dad. No." Lily's eyes closed, squeezing her tears as she began to choke, then to sob, drowning, and she fell to her knees.

Anna put her hands on her daughter's head. "Nothing is lost," she said.

For some moments Lily clung to her mother's knees in shock, the white robe spread around her, spotted with dust and the grime of battle. She opened her eyes. Little things imprinted on her memory - a scar in the dust, a small blue and unfeeling stone, the leather strap of her mother's sandals.

"Who knows what other sacrifices we have to make," Anna said, "to save the Tower. We have paid such a price. And now..."

But at that moment, as Anna reached down to comfort her daughter, an arrow shot across the plain from beyond a dust-dune. There was a thud. Lily felt her mother jerk back and she looked up. An arrow with black feathers had pierced Anna's robe and stood out from her chest, planted in her heart. Anna began to fall backward. Lily clutched at her mother's legs, willing her upright, but with her violet-blue eyes wide with surprise Anna fell in a cloud of white dust. Lily crouched at her side, her own heart bursting with fear, and breaking.

"Oh," Anna whispered. "My love." She winced, and for a moment her body trembled. "I... see the sky. I... am. We are together. Nothing... is..."

But Anna's eyes had closed. She lay still, in the dust, her blonde hair spread out as if she were asleep, the arrow standing up from her heart, the blood of her life seeping into the white of her robe.

It was such a small arrow, a thin shaft of golden metal with black feathers. Her mother could not breathe, was not breathing. Her father had died, fallen in the town. As Lily crouched in the dust she felt rise within her an overpowering grief, pressing her down at her mother's side. She must die too. They must be together. It was unbearable to be apart. Only instinct told her to survive, that there was on the way towards her own heart another arrow, a shaft of golden metal with black feathers.

As if Time itself had slowed Lily looked up, saw the arrow in the air and threw herself down so that it spun above her head into the ground behind. Whatever it was, it was slow. It took time to reload, too much time.

457

Lily stood, her white robe billowing back, her staff showing forward. Possessed by anger she fired, and fired again, her bolts raking across the dunes in a line of exploding dust. A body rolled sideways, in black chainmail, a head with hair the colour of dust, a small body which crouched, searching for shelter. Finding none, the man stood and he edged forward, his crossbow at the ready. She saw his face. Twine. He fired, lower this time, but the arrow was slow through the swirling dust and Lily destroyed it in mid-air. Twine came on. "Scum!" he yelled. "Scum! Let yourself die! Let yourself die!"

Lily levelled her staff and with teeth clenched she fired. With a single blast she blew apart his chainmail and opened his chest in a shower of blood which pitted the dust as he fell backwards. The crossbow spun from his hands. Twine thrust an elbow into the ground, trying to rise, but his jaw slackened as blood foamed from his lips. His eyes flickered as he fell back and lay spread-eagled in the dust. His limbs shook, then he lay still.

With a new anger, Lily rose from the ground, and turned in mid-air towards what remained of the Black Army. She fired senselessly across the ridge where her wolves had fallen, into the heaving mass of black-armoured bodies and insect chariots, already turning upon each other in a maelstrom of unguided fury. Channels of her fire cut into them, through them. None could hurt her now, for she could not be hurt more. It was the freedom of revenge and the blue of her eyes turned to scarlet red.

"Stop!" It was the voice of Mysul.

From beyond the hill, Mysul flew above the trees towards her, a staff in each hand. She halted in mid-air. "These are creatures of the Presence," she said. "We do not take revenge without thought." She looked down on her Anna, her child. Slowly she descended, not with tears, but with head bowed and arms outstretched. Though there was a torrent of sound around them from the death-throes of what had been the Black Army of the plain, Mysul and Lily stood over Anna's body in a sphere of quiet. Mysul knelt at her daughter's side, and then the tears came, as she stroked Anna's white cheek and said, "Anna. So beautiful. Created of my love. Your spark is in

458

me. We shall never be apart." Gently and breathing deeply she slowly withdrew the arrow, and threw it metres away into the dust. Lily fell to her knees. "Mum…" she sobbed and fell forward over her mother's body.

"Come," said Mysul gently. "There must be a farewell. Until another time. Come. Stand, Lily. We cannot stay."

Her face awash with tears and dust Lily stood, unsteadily. From behind, the heart-beat of the Grey Angel thundered across the plain. She turned. Descending from the Gate, down the slopes of the mountain came lines of black-armoured soldiers, lances upturned with scarlet flags which flapped through eddies of dust. They shouted as they marched, struggling to keep up with the man who strode ahead of them.

His grey armour glistened and in one hand he held a silver staff, under his other arm the head of a bull. As he approached, he looked to be no more than a young man, sharp-featured with blonde hair which spread back over his shoulders, but with every step he grew taller and strode more quickly over the ground, through paths of fire on either side which consumed all they touched, so that he seemed to advance on golden clouds of dust.

As he drew nearer she saw his eyes, glowing red like coals of fire and fixed on her. He grew taller, taller, through the smoke and dust, the immortal Grey Angel.

Black wings unfurled from his back as he looked down on them with the pitiless unblinking stare of an automaton, a Titan, Death himself advancing. He raised his staff to the sky.

"Come," said Mysul, and she cradled Anna in her arms. "We must say farewell."

*

On one side of the grave in the churchyard of Malbury, the Vicar stood with a Bible in his hand. By him stood Riley Moss, wearing

459

the patterned sweater of his field trips. Behind him under a tree stood John, the black-haired boy and now a man, white-faced. It was a frozen scene. Nothing and no-one moved. No eye blinked. No bird sang. There was no breeze to ripple the trees or the undergrowth, no music from the church, no sound of life. A sun was in the sky. The grave was already filled, a hump of brown earth over it, and a stone marked the grave of Anna Moss. But no date of birth nor of death.

To be so close to her father but so far was the deepest cut of grief for Lily Moss. He stood, but he was not there. He did not move, not even the flicker of an eyelid. None of the three on that side of the grave appeared to breathe. To know that her mother lay there was the final dart of ice in her heart. There would be revenge but not yet. She could not take revenge. She was not even allowed to cry. She was the Brigadier with mucky boots who could not cry when her Dad and her Mum died.

Lily stood between the Ordinal and Mysul, who handed her a blue orchid. Lily stepped forward and laid it on the earth.

Together all three turned away. As she turned, Lily saw John, under the tree, move. He bowed but with his white face uplifted. He swept an arm sideways, then lowered his head.

"The Tower and the Omnium are safe," said Mysul. "Our Servator stands at the Navigator's gate. We shall join her."

60 - Indian Valley

The forest was aflame. Soon it would be dust. Against a blue sky the ruin of the Tower stood like a broken, blackened tooth. Fire rolled down, bursting with a roar around the skeletons of trees, smoke billowing from undergrowth which crackled and dissolved into a tide of flame which overcame the silhouettes of the last guards one by one. Flashing across the blue sky, hoverflies of the enemy rose and fell through the boiling clouds in a dance of triumph. The Grey Angel was long gone. It had raised its head across the horizon, bared its teeth and turned its back. All defences were over-run. It was over.

On the other side of the last valley, above a stream and the twisted rails of the ancient track and a stream which soon would cease to exist, five figures stood facing the inevitable end. The heat and the light of it was on their faces. The smell of desolation, of melted earth and sulphur rose through the ground. Two men, two women and a girl, all in white robes spotted with ash and seared by the wind, they had with them only what they had saved in their last act of sacrifice, the memory of their Universe, their sea, in themselves.

Mysul lifted her head. Her grey hair streamed back as she jabbed her two staves into the ground and said, "Ordinal, you were with me at the beginning. Is this the end?"

"Mysul, my soul," Ordinal said, hunched over his staff. "It cannot be otherwise. The Council left the choice to us, should this moment come. To roll back or move on."

"I see no reason to roll back. Cardinal, you agree?"

The Cardinal nodded and ran a brown hand through his mass of dark hair. "My soul," he said. "The Grey Angel anticipates that we roll back. The probability is point-eight that it waits at the beginning to use our powers against us, and to remove all form from this sea. If

461

we choose to transfer, the probability is point-nine that the opportunity will arise to undo what it has done here. Reason demands that we move on."

"So be it," Mysul said. "Servator, is the Tower ready?"

The Servator, her pale face almost hidden by a veil, raised a hand. She paused, the light of the advancing flames flickering over her stone-white robe. "My soul," she whispered, "our Navigator holds the Omnium in herself. I hold the dimension of Time, and the Tower's memory. This I can bear, but only through the first flicker of a new sea."

The Ordinal said, "But what of the Minister?"

"Weak," Mysul replied. "We shall not make that mistake again." She turned to Lily Moss and looked down. "Child," she said, "this is a moment of great sadness, but also of opportunity, and hope. The war you have witnessed is never-ending, but in seas of change there is a tide. We leave for a new shore, where the tide shall turn." She lifted her head, and turned for a last look at the fires behind them. "All that remains, Navigator, is for you to set the course. You have prepared the key?"

"My soul, I have," the child replied.

"In what order shall we enter the gate?"

Lily drew a deep breath. "I shall lead with our Servator to my right," she said. "I ask that she holds my hand, for without the dimension of Time I shall be lost. Behind by one pace and one pace to the right, three shall enter shoulder to shoulder. This gives us our trajectory beyond the gate. Otherwise, there shall be no form. We would never meet again."

"So be it," Mysul said, uprooting one staff and leaving the other as if a token of their return. "Follow."

Flames were already licking across the stream on fallen branches and wisps of undergrowth. The five figures turned their backs and through the rocks and bushes picked their way uphill, robes billowing in blasts of burning air that swept down the valley. On a ridge of grass and bracken they halted, ahead of them only a starless night. "Ordinal," Mysul commanded, "summon the gate."

The Ordinal held up his staff, which glowed blue against the black sky. Around them a mist gathered into the hemisphere of a sparkling blue wall, curving behind them and to each side. At the edge, between light and dark, a block of basalt rose from the ground, a metre-high cube of glistening black stone veined with white. "Forward, Navigator," Mysul said.

The child stepped forward until her feet touched the stone. From inside her robe she took a golden coin. The Servator joined her and extended a hand. As their hands touched and then clasped together, into Lily's mind came a voice. "We are here," it said. "All of us." It was the voice of little Chun.

"My soul," said Lily, breathing hard, "are we in position?"

The three behind looked at her and at each other. There was no telling whether this would be the last time. Mysul paused. She looked forward, and to left and right. "We are, Navigator," she said. "You may open the gate."

Gently the child lowered her golden coin onto the stone, which slipped down without sound into the ground as the coin rose back between her fingers. Ahead of her a sphere of cloud rose and grew from the edge of the darkness, and through that a path over the dark, a dusty track, unrolled towards an archway, vapours of white and purple hissing and swirling within it.

On either side of the track figures grew from inside the cloud. They wandered, and watched. It became a crowd not of ghosts but of memories, welcome memories, and they smiled at her. On each side of the track they stood, nodded, talked and laughed, being themselves - little Chun and the others, the Clerk, the Constable, mechanicals, her father hand-in-hand with her mother, Anna.

Lily choked back her tears. With her head up, she said, "With me, pace for pace. My soul, at your command."

Mysul lifted her staff. "Together," she said. "To a new sea, and a new Tower." She paused, then, "Now."

Pace for pace the Five traversed the path through the cloud into the archway. As they entered and the vapours swallowed them, each dissolved into a mist of rainbows. As if squeezed by an invisible hand, the blue wall, the path, the cloud and the archway trembled, shrank, coalesced, and were sucked into a pinpoint of white light which flashed across the black sky, and vanished.

###

About the Author

Jon Cole

Academic, Musician, IT & Information Specialist, Writer

*

Website: http://www.rekindle.co.uk

Facebook: https://www.facebook.com/jon.cole.733

Twitter: https://twitter.com/joncolegm

LinkedIn: https://www.linkedin.com/in/joncole733

###

Printed in Great Britain
by Amazon